# SONS OF HEAVEN

Wilmot was filled with unreasoned anger at himself. Tomorrow there would be pressure on all hydrant hoses to blast intruders off. Tomorrow there'd be barbed wire on the other ladders to the bridge. Tomorrow, it would be a floating fortress. Tomorrow, tomorrow . . .

He turned to Manos who had joined him on the wing. 'Give the order to repel boarders,' he demanded. 'And issue an SOS signal immediately.'

The Greek appeared to be in a trance. 'L-let's see what they want, my friend. S-see what they want . . .'

'Give the order, Captain,' Wilmot repeated. 'Or I will.'

Manos shook his head.

Wilmot snatched the bullhorn from its cradle and raised it to his lips. 'CREW – REPEL BOARDERS BY ALL MEANS POSSIBLE! NOW! BEFORE IT'S TOO LATE! NOW, DAMMIT!'

*Also by Terence Strong*

Whisper Who Dares*
The Fifth Hostage*
Conflict of Lions*
Dragonplague*
That Last Mountain*
This Angry Land*
Stalking Horse*
The Tick Tock Man
White Viper
Rogue Element
•*available from Coronet*

*About the author*

Terence Strong, the author of eleven bestselling
thrillers, is renowned for his detailed and authoritative
research. A freelance journalist and writer, he has a
keen interest in international and political and military affairs, and special forces in particular.

You are welcome to visit the Terence Strong Web Page at:
http://www.totalweb.co.uk/tangledweb/authors/tstrong.html

For Princess

Behind this fiction
lies the terrible truth.
This book is dedicated
to all those held hostage,
for whatever reason,
around the world.
They are not forgotten.

# THE SONS OF HEAVEN

The legend of the 'Old Man of the Mountains' was brought back to Europe from Persia by Marco Polo and by the Crusaders.

Al-Hasan ibn-al-Sabbah was a strange religious and terror leader attributed with having magical powers, who turned fine young men into his fanatical followers by allowing them to experience Paradise.

Under the influence of drugs they would reputedly be taken to a secret walled and perfumed garden, where wine and honey flowed, to be intoxicated by love and music.

In the cold light of day they would be told that they were Allah's chosen and had been privileged to a glimpse of the Paradise that was to come.

They were truly 'the sons of heaven'.

Believed by their foes to be high on drugs, Sabbah's *hash hashins* (from which the word *assassins* derives) terrorised the Middle East without fear, destroying their leader's religious and political enemies. Amongst their murder victims were Conrad of Montferrat and Count Raymond of Tripoli. They also attempted to kill Saladin and Prince Edward of England.

Even today, in the twentieth century, the legend of SABBAH – the Old Man of the Mountains – lives on . . .

# AUTHOR'S NOTE

The legend of Al-Hasan ibn-al-Sabbah, or the 'Old Man of the Mountains', has been as distorted over the centuries as the stories of King Arthur, Robin Hood and Dick Turpin.

In the near-inaccessible high pass of the Alamut Valley in Iran, all that is left of the supposed castle are a few low walls of crumbling brick and mortar. And it is highly unlikely that the sheer-sided valley could ever have been turned into the perfumed garden with pavilions and palaces to which Marco Polo referred with such chilling romance.

Yet Sabbah has entered into the folklore of various terror groups in the Middle East today, and he is revered as the shining example to which modern terrorists should aspire.

*Sons of Heaven* is based on the continuation of that fable – a composite of actual terror organisations and splinter groups that insidiously permeate the Middle East. Partly Abu Nidal, partly Husain Mussawi, partly an inner faction of the Iranian *Hezbollah* Party of God – as reported in *The Independent* when an eyewitness Amal hostage in Lebanon confirmed on his release that even *Hezbollah* and Iranian Revolutionary Guards were afraid of the 'special guards' of the secret closed section where he was held.

I am particularly indebted to one of Britain's leading hostage negotiators for his advice and patient explanations, and to other police and special forces experts who helped in piecing together a realistic chain of events to unfold in this story, but who prefer to be unnamed.

9

Also it is only right to apologise to those good people who were unwittingly drawn into my necessary deception to gain entry into the Sultanate of Oman, where writers of political thrillers are not welcome. Only they may know who they are, and I hope I will be forgiven when they have read the result.

Over the years many expatriate British officers have served in Oman, several in capacities similar to that of the character of Major Harry. To avoid any speculation or embarrassment to individuals, I can state categorically that he is entirely a figment of my imagination – to the extent that I have given him a 'department' which, to the best of my knowledge, does not even exist. Similarly Shaykh Zufar and his Ministry are entirely my own invention.

Finally a special thanks to Captain Hugh Wiltshire of Quest Holdings Ltd. For he is the real-life inventor of the incredible sea-skimming Jet Raider, and kindly allowed me to bestow that honour on the fictional 'China' Clay.

Like so many things, the existence of that craft just goes to prove that fact really can be stranger than fiction.

TERENCE STRONG
LONDON 1989

*My thanks go to the many people who have contributed so much to my research and the final resulting story:*

*IN LONDON: To Lucy and her charming Iranian friends whom I shall just call 'Older' and 'Famous'. To ship's master Captain Eric Long who helped invent* Clarion Call, *and swimmer-canoeist John who taught me several ways to hijack it. To Leslie and to Ivan who left no doors unopened. And, as so often before, to my trusted Arabist friend John Carter, author of* Tribes In Oman.

*IN PARIS: To journalist David Paskov, my mentor in all things French, whom I persuaded, most enjoyably, to climb off the wagon; security expert Christian; publisher James Taylor for his insight into Paris life; Alan Gillings and Beatrice, and to my delightful agent Boris Hoffman* who is working hard to sell the French edition of this tale!

IN OMAN: To Kevin for his immense help. He was in at the beginning and will no doubt be there to the end. To the indescribable Mark Mallett, editor of Oman Today and compulsive wadi-basher, and our good companions. Not forgetting the hospitality and curry of Roger, nor the calm patience of Tim Edwards who introduced me to the horrors and delights of diving in the deep.

# PROLOGUE

There were four of them.

Dark spectres creeping furtively between the cathedral columns of the copse, careful to avoid the dappled pools of silver that penetrated the overhead canopy of leaves from the waning moon.

They were nervous and alert, heads stiffly raised like animals sniffing for the scent of danger carried on the wind.

Through the ghostly green viewer of the nightsight, Captain Robert D'Arcy was able to identify three of them before they reached the perimeter of the stump-scattered clearing.

It wasn't difficult, despite the blackened hands and faces. D'Arcy knew the men well, intimately almost. They made up the local PIRA 'active service unit'. A farmer, a baker and, appropriately enough, a life insurance salesman.

That was O'Neill, their leader, and a particularly unpleasant specimen who had repeatedly evaded conviction. Always insufficient evidence and a cast-iron alibi. He would strut the village streets with the smugness of a cat who knew it still had several of its lives left. Arrogant, proficient, and exceptionally vicious.

Typically, D'Arcy noted, he carried an Armalite AR18. O'Neill favoured the cheap and very nasty 'Widowmaker', and was frequently heard to boast how he had contributed to its chilling reputation.

D'Arcy watched as the man settled down to wait, to be certain. Patient. Always professional. That was how he had survived so long.

The Provo's head turned slightly, scanning the clearing. Then a jerking motion as his eye caught the movement high up on the road embankment. A torn piece of blue plastic from a fertiliser bag flapped irritatingly from the barbed wire fence.

The 'distractor' had been deliberately placed by the Special Air Service team. Its purpose was to lure the eye away from the cunningly concealed observation-post just a few metres away. The position had been dug in the dead of night two weeks earlier, tunnelled into the embankment overlooking the clearing. When completed, the foxhole had been roofed with a roll of chicken wire, over which the turfs had been expertly relaid.

That damp and cramped space was to be home for as long as it took the Provos to revisit their arms cache. For two weeks the four-man Sabre team – Villiers, Rix, and the 'unholy alliance' of Monk and Pope – had endured the monotony of self-heating canned rations and the indignities of defecating and burying the results in the confined space. Although worse to suffer, each man would swear, was the incessant call of a pair of nearby wood pigeons which drove them to the very edge of insanity.

Always two on stag while two slept, their only link with the outside world was via the Clansman radio.

A welcome break to the monotony would be the daily passing of the postman, whistling as he cycled down the lane beyond the barbed wire. And the dairy van that came to collect milk churns from the surrounding farms. All such comings and goings were religiously timed and entered in the log.

Two months earlier, at the Regiment's characterless brickbuilt Stirling Lines barracks outside the county town of Hereford, D'Arcy had been summoned unexpectedly to the office of Major Johnny Fraser. The quietly spoken Scot was commander of the Counter-Revolutionary Warfare Wing of the SAS, which specialised in antiterrorist training techniques.

"Ah, Rob," Fraser greeted, "I believe you've met this

14

old friend of ours, Brigadier General Roquelaure. General – Captain Rob D'Arcy, my 2IC . . ."

D'Arcy's face broke into an impromptu grin as Roquelaure rose to shake hands. The Frenchman was shorter than he remembered. Or else it was an illusion created by the added inches around the waist which filled the immaculate grey silk suit.

"Hello, Pierre, what a lovely surprise! *Ça va?*" The Frenchman's handshake was as firm and dry as ever, and his pale blue eyes twinkled amid the laughlines in the broad face. But even the ingrained tan, earned during years serving in French colonies around the world, could not disguise a certain gauntness in his features.

"*Je suis fatigué, mon ami, très fatigué –*" Roquelaure turned to Major Fraser. "Forgive me, Johnny, how rude you must think us both."

The CRW chief waved the apology aside with a short laugh. "No problem, Pierre, even I could follow that."

"You're still with the *Ministère de la Défense?*" D'Arcy asked.

Roquelaure nodded. His role, D'Arcy knew, was that of liaison between the Secret Service – the DGSE – and the *Group d'Intervention de la Gendarmerie Nationale.* It was the French equivalent of the SAS antiterrorist group and both units regularly exchanged ideas as well as training facilities. "*Oui,* for my sins and my grey hair, I am with the *Ministère* still."

D'Arcy frowned. "Then I can guess why you're here."

"The Paris bombings," Fraser confirmed grimly.

Roquelaure raised his hands in a very Gallic expression of despair. "I have never known the city in such a state of near panic, *mon ami.* Such carnage and human misery. Bombs in the Champs Elysées, and the Préfecture of Police near Notre Dame, and the rue de Rennes. No one wants to use the Métro or even our cafés any more. The streets are deserted. There has been nothing like it since the Algerian business. For once our politicians are even agreeing that we need help, and have swallowed their pride."

15

D'Arcy smiled tersely. Whilst British and French special forces happily co-operated, politicians on both sides of the Channel perpetuated the history that the countries were each other's oldest enemy. As Roquelaure had once told D'Arcy: "The trouble is our people are too alike in their approach to nationalism. You British think you are the best, while we French *know* we are. *Mon Dieu*!"

"We're exploring areas of co-operation," Fraser admitted cautiously. "But I've called you in on a matter of what the general can do for us. Would you like to explain, Pierre?"

The Frenchman nodded, opened a pack of Gitanes and lit one. The pungent, bitter aroma instantly filled the room. "This campaign in Paris, Rober', we believe it is to gain the release of the Lebanese terrorist Georges Abdallah. He is serving a four-year sentence, and we have just moved him to a new prison to prevent an attempted jailbreak. We believe his brothers may be behind these outrages. But this gang, whoever they are, have powerful help from a Lebanese Shi'ite faction calling itself the *Pessarane Behesht*."

D'Arcy shook his head. "Don't think I know them."

Roquelaure grimaced. "Unfortunately, I think you will in time. Translated it means – er, you say – sons or children of paradise. Or heaven, if you prefer. It doesn't translate exactly, but the meaning is clear. They are religious fanatics associated with the Iranian Party of God – or *Hezbollah*, and run by a leader who calls himself Sabbah."

"Sabbah," D'Arcy repeated softly. "That rings some bells."

Fraser consulted the computer print-out on his desk. "The name first began cropping up in the mid-seventies, Rob, in connection with the Palestine Liberation Organisation. It's an adopted cover name, we gather, derived from some eleventh-century assassin in Persia – which gives a clue to the man's background. A Shi'ite Lebanese with Iranian ancestry. But little is known beyond that. Conflicting descriptions and always confused reports as to his whereabouts. Very mysterious, and very professional."

"He's no longer with the PLO?" D'Arcy asked.

Fraser shook his head. "In the late seventies Sabbah became disillusioned with Arafat's softly-softly approach and virtually went freelance – like Abu Nidal some years before. He moved with a group of followers to Libya. There he acted on his own and Gadaffi's behalf for several years. Political assassination, bombings in Europe, and two aircraft hijacks." Fraser looked up from the print-out. "But it was during the downfall of the Shah and the Islamic Revolution in '79 that he really moved into the big league. I think the general has greater detail on more recent events."

Roquelaure stubbed out his cigarette. "Unfortunately, Rober', I do not need to consult notes. The facts are ingrained in my heart. You see Sabbah was involved with training young Iranians for the '79 uprising in camps in Libya, Lebanon and Syria. By the time Khomeini took over, Sabbah had found his – er, roots – I think you say. A cause and a divine mission. He still maintained his links with Libya, but drew closer to Iran. Indeed it was he who brought the alliance between the two countries closer together in their campaigns of state-sponsored terrorism.

"In March '82 there was a meeting in Teheran of Shi'ite revolutionary movements from all over the Arab and Western worlds. A major campaign was established and one hundred million dollars immediately allocated to support worldwide terrorism in the name of Islam. It was organised by the Iranian Foreign Ministry's Department for the Export of Revolution. And one of its chief exponents was . . ."

D'Arcy saw it coming. "Sabbah," he murmured.

A silence fell between the three men; the air in the small room seemed suddenly chill.

"The rest is history," Roquelaure said wearily, lighting another Gitane. "Sabbah formed a sort of inner caucus of the *Hezbollah*, although their actions took place under a confusion of names. Even the PLO use the name of

17

*fedayeen* after the original Sabbah's 'men of sacrifice'. Nevertheless, he had been so successful by '84, that he was given permission to expand his Sons of Heaven, creating suicide squads to attack his Arab enemies – and, I regret, France."

D'Arcy raised an eyebrow. "Why France in particular? You once played host to Khomeini."

A wan smile crossed Roquelaure's tired face. "And since the Islamic Revolution we have given sanctuary to his enemies. And, thanks to Sabbah and his *Pessarane Behesht*, we have paid the price, believe me. So penetrating his organisation has been one of our prime objectives, as you can imagine."

D'Arcy leaned against the wall, his arms folded. "With what success?"

For a moment the general's gloomy expression lifted slightly. "After many failures we managed to get one of our agents – whom I shall call 'Tashakkur' – into a Sabbah cell operating out of Tunisia. It is he who gave us the information that I have just passed on to Major Fraser."

D'Arcy's eyes moved across to the CRW chief who now had a TOP SECRET file open amid the pile of print-outs. "This agent, Tashakkur, reports that the *Pessarane Behesht* have developed links with PIRA, along with *Action Directe* in France, and West German terrorists associated with the former Bader-Meinhoff gang. It's the usual story of scratching each other's backs. According to Tashakkur, Sabbah is acting for Libya and Iran to smuggle arms to Eire. Vast quantities, some of it very sophisticated – valued at some sixty million pounds sterling – will be smuggled in over the next couple of years. PIRA will get a large part of the consignment, while the rest will be distributed to *Pessarane Behesht* and other Iranian terrorist networks throughout Europe."

D'Arcy let out a low whistle. "Using Ireland as the usual back door to Europe? Thank God your chap's been able to give us some warning."

An apprehensive silence followed as Fraser and Roque-laure traded glances.

Fraser said quietly: "Not quite, Rob. The first shipment has already landed."

For D'Arcy, the next few days were filled with frantic activity as he established a special unit within the SAS's own 'Kremlin' intelligence department. Ongoing liaison was opened with Roquelaure and the French intelligence community, UK Customs & Excise, the RUC and Irish Special Branch.

At the end of the initial period, all the pointers were that the information from the agent Tashakkur had been correct. Sifting through the usual glut of rumour and speculation from Republican neighbourhoods resulted in no actual evidence or proof. It was clear, however, that something big had happened. A consistent thread running through the gossip in the drinking clubs was that the arms had been concealed in elaborate preprepared bunkers throughout Eire, ready for when they would be needed.

If quantities of weapons had already been distributed to Sabbah's *Pessarane Behesht,* or other Iranian terror networks in Europe, there was no word.

Unfortunately Tashakkur was in deep cover. There was no way to communicate with him, let alone request additional information. Roquelaure would give away no more than that his agent could now be anywhere in Ulster or the Republic of Ireland.

When the break they'd been hoping for finally came, it was from an entirely different source. The information was received via a dead-letter drop from a long-established and trusted Army Intelligence informer in Armagh.

Once decoded it warned that quantities of weapons were due to be smuggled over the border, some of which were highly sophisticated and would require demonstration and instruction before deployment. For this reason a 'foreign team' would cross the border to link up with O'Neill's active service unit.

There was no mention of Iranians, the *Pessarane Behesht*, or Sabbah. But the implication of the 'foreign team' was obvious.

Immediately D'Arcy pushed the button, and his carefully prepared contingency plan was under way. Within hours the full might of the British security apparatus had homed in on O'Neill's village. Informers were discreetly contacted, sometimes during house searches or under the pretext of arrest. Observation-posts were set up and telephones tapped. Elaborate eavesdropping and remote-controlled surveillance devices were positioned at the known homes and meeting places of O'Neill's gang.

Before the first week was out, a clear picture was emerging. A small quantity of arms had already crossed the border and had been hidden in a cache. The approximate location was identified. There the weapons would be left until O'Neill's unit was sure that the heat was off. Then they would be joined by 'foreign gentlemen', who would demonstrate how to use the weapons.

"Those foreign gentlemen will almost certainly be members of Sabbah's *Pessarane Behesht*," Roy Bliss told D'Arcy.

Bliss was a scruffy individual in his early thirties. His badly pressed suit and unkempt ginger hair belied the fact that he worked for the Secret Intelligence Service and was responsible for liaison with his French counterparts in the DGSE. Despite his seedy appearance, D'Arcy knew him as an efficient field officer with a sharp, sardonic sense of humour.

Bliss lit his umpteenth cigarette of the meeting, cupping the flame with nicotine-stained fingers. "Sabbah's blokes are bloody dangerous and unpredictable, as you've no doubt gathered. So we don't want any mistakes. Your job, pal, is just to watch and learn. No heroics. If their operation is as big as we think it is, there's no point in pulling in small fry. Or chopping just one tentacle off an octopus.

"Besides which the Foreign Office is adamant that they don't want any dead Iranians turning up on British turf, terrorist or not. If you hadn't noticed, the FCO is up to its usual trick of putting Britain last. They've had a policy of quietly helping the Khomeini régime ever since it came to power. For convenience they play along with the charade that British hostages in Beirut aren't held on orders from Iran. We even let the little sods have an arms-purchasing office in London. And, along with half the Western world, we supply them arms, ammo and explosives to keep 'em sweet in Teheran. Apparently we still want influence there when all the trouble dies down." Bliss inhaled deeply in disgust on his cigarette. For him it was quite a speech. "So no corpses, pal, right? The FCO doesn't want anything to upset our relationship with the mullahs. Or with our French allies for that matter; they've got troubles enough of their own."

D'Arcy said quietly: "I hear what you're saying, Roy. Rest easy, there'll be no problem."

That night for the first time D'Arcy had moved into the covert observation-post to join the four-man Sabre team assigned to watch over the arms cache. As he squeezed into the cramped position his nostrils filled with the all-pervading stench of damp peat which nevertheless failed to hide the smell of unwashed bodies completely.

"I'm going in to take a closer look," D'Arcy announced. "Establish exactly what's involved."

Villiers, a rangy veteran sergeant of the old school, grinned widely, showing the gap where his front teeth had once been. "We can do that for you, boss."

D'Arcy shook his head, understanding the other man's mild sense of resentment. "Not this one. There's a complicated history. I want to see it for myself."

Villiers wasn't happy, and neither were the other three. But then D'Arcy wasn't a man to argue with. He was always willing to discuss things, but once he said no that was it.

"Bloody officers are all the same once you scratch the surface," muttered Rix, a stocky corporal from Yorkshire, as they watched D'Arcy begin his leopard crawl down the slope towards the cache.

"Not the boss," Villiers disagreed. "He's all right. Came up through the ranks before he joined the Family."

Rix wasn't convinced. "With a name like his?"

"Frog ancestry, he can't help that. He's all right, you'll see when you've been with us a while longer. You won't find a man or officer with a bad word to say about him."

A retort began to form in Rix's mind, but was stillborn as he realised he'd already lost track of D'Arcy's path of descent. He shifted the image-intensifier, scanning slowly. Nothing. And the only cover was grass no more than eighteen inches long. He was good, was D'Arcy, he had to give him that.

Villiers chuckled, his grin white in the earthy gloom. "You're looking in the wrong place, mate. The boss is already there." He pressed the send-button on his PRC 349. "Okay, boss, still all clear. Safe to proceed. Over."

Below them a soft shadow detached itself from a gorse bush and slid smoothly towards the lichen-covered tree-stump that marked the location of the cache.

There was no telltale glint from the heavy black-bladed survival knife as D'Arcy prised away the thick trapdoor of moss.

Up in the OP a thought occurred to Villiers. " 'Course, you never know what motive the boss might have for going hi'self."

Rix's eyes darted sideways at his companion. "Such as?"

The sergeant shrugged and squinted into the viewer. "Such as setting up an 'own goal'," he suggested cheerfully. It was the sort of approach to terrorism that appealed to him. "There's been a few recently."

"I bloody hope not," Rix replied. "We could all end up on a bloody civilian murder rap. Besides, it's bloody counterproductive."

"Who says?"

"The experts, the psych-ops blokes," Rix retorted in a whisper. "It's been the official line since Aden."

"Official line," Villiers sneered. "Well, I don't think it's counterproductive. The boss don't think it is either. We only talked about it last week. As he said, it's proven fact that at least ninety-five per cent of Provos who blow themselves up never do it again." He grinned malevolently.

"He'd never get clearance."

"Perhaps he ain't bothered. So an explosives cache goes up and some Provo gets blown to teensy-weensy pieces. Who's to say what caused it? Unstable stuff, gelly."

"The Micks know what they're doing nowadays. Caches don't blow up by themselves."

Villiers smiled. "Then there's been a lot of thick Provos storing explosives lately."

"It's not policy," Rix insisted.

"If it was, they wouldn't tell the likes of you and me. Just brief the man who had to do it. We've all heard the rumours. Anyway, if that's what the boss is doing, I'm all for it. Orders or not."

Rix shook his head. "You're a thug, Pete."

"Yeah."

D'Arcy had returned to the OP with a full list of the contents stowed in the black plastic dustbin buried beneath the mossbed of the clearing. But the find was disappointing. The cache had not been booby-trapped, which indicated a low-grade store. The contents confirmed it; it was not what everyone had been expecting, hoping for.

He reported just four Kalashnikov AK47 assault rifles, several hundred rounds of ammunition, and a greaseproof package which probably contained some type of explosive. There was no sign of the rumoured RPG-7 anti-tank launchers, nor the SAM-7 missiles for use against helicopters.

Perhaps after all Tashakkur had been wrong. Or perhaps it was the local Army Intelligence informer who had misinterpreted what was going to happen. Disappointment and apprehension dampened the spirits of D'Arcy's operational headquarters and the OP team who remained cocooned in their muddy underground tomb. Still watching, still waiting.

Nothing happened for another three days of mind-numbing boredom. Then at dusk two sets of footsteps were picked up by one of the seismic ground-sensors buried on the approaches to the clearing. A pretty local girl and her boyfriend passed through the copse, chatting and laughing intimately. They crossed the clearing but didn't stop.

In all probability innocent, the couple could just as easily have been checking that the cache remained undisturbed. The shutter on the camera with the powerful telephoto lens flickered rapidly in the OP. Routinely the suspects' presence was radioed to D'Arcy for the Royal Ulster Constabulary or Army Intelligence to check them out.

The girl, it transpired, was O'Neill's niece.

Anticipation at the covert OP and at D'Arcy's headquarters rose steeply. Justifiably as it turned out.

The following night the figure of a man, dressed from head to toe in black, slipped out of the copse and approached the cache. He carried a collapsible entrenching tool which he used to dig down to the sunken dustbin. With his back to the OP, it was not possible for the SAS team to see what he was doing.

D'Arcy had already been called from his bed by the time the man was closing up the cache again, apparently leaving it intact and without removing any of its contents.

Villiers radioed for instructions. Intervene? Negative, D'Arcy replied. Roy Bliss's warnings were still fresh in his mind.

In fact he could scarcely risk mounting a surveillance operation in case the stranger became aware that he was under observation.

To D'Arcy's chagrin the stranger in black had to be allowed to melt away into the darkness. After studying photographs taken through the nightsight, D'Arcy agreed with Villiers that the man was not a known member of O'Neill's local Provo unit.

But, whatever his true identity, it was clear that the man

had been checking to establish that the weapons were still in position. That, in turn, suggested that something was imminent. Perhaps, after all, Tashakkur's information had been correct.

That night, D'Arcy decided he would rejoin Villiers and his team at the OP.

D'Arcy was jolted from his recollections by a movement down at the edge of the clearing.

O'Neill had decided it was safe. The movement had been a beckoning hand motion.

A second figure crawled up to his side. The newcomer was slightly built, wearing dark jeans and a military-style anorak. Although a knitted balaclava masked his face, it was obvious he was asking a question. O'Neill shook his head and pointed to the treestump in the clearing.

D'Arcy heard the faint metallic click beside him as Villiers took more photographs through the nightsight.

Shrugging, the newcomer began to crawl across the carpet of moss, alone. Every few yards he would stop, cock his head to one side, and listen. Satisfied that he could hear nothing, he continued. Several times he repeated the process until he reached the treestump.

Villiers' coarse whisper grated in D'Arcy's ear. "O'Neill's pulling back, boss. Him and his two cronies are pulling back."

Irritably D'Arcy waved the sergeant to silence.

The SAS captain was aware of his heart pounding as he watched the newcomer lift the trapdoor of moss and extract the black dustbin lid. Then the man reached down and carefully, one at a time, removed the four Kalashnikovs. Again he peered inside, and lifted out several cardboard boxes of ammunition.

"Boss," Villiers hissed. "O'Neill's almost out of sensor range."

D'Arcy ignored the remark, instead mentally reminding the stranger not to forget the greaseproof pack of explosive.

25

Again the figure glanced around, listening to the rustle of the treetops. Once more he reached inside.

The sheer brilliance of the flash caught D'Arcy by surprise. Magnified through the nightsight, it blinded him instantly. He was equally unprepared for the ferocious power of the blast which contemptuously tore apart the body of the man at the cache, and sent shockwaves of displaced air pulsing over the hide.

D'Arcy fell back, gasping, his eardrums throbbing with pain.

He did not, could not, hear Villiers utter his astonished profanity.

"And you say you had no idea it was rigged?"

D'Arcy held Major Johnny Fraser's penetrating gaze. "I inspected it three days earlier. I suspected the lid might be wired, but it wasn't. And inside there was no sign of a booby-trap that I could see."

The atmosphere in the small office was tense and claustrophobic. D'Arcy felt like a man on trial and, despite his commanding officer's usual relaxed manner, he had a suspicion that he was exactly that.

Roy Bliss's brooding presence behind him confirmed his worst fears. The man had been sitting on the hardback chair, his very inclusion at this debrief as silently intrusive as a schools inspector in a classroom. Listening, observing, saying nothing, missing nothing. Ensuring that he would have the right answers to give his masters.

For the first time he spoke. "May I ask a question, Major?"

Fraser glanced at D'Arcy, who nodded his agreement. The sooner he knew what was on the SIS field officer's mind the better he'd like it.

Bliss said: "You were the only person to go to that cache in the entire period of the observation? Is that what you're saying, D'Arcy?"

The formal use of his surname, he knew, was deliberate. A distancing of old friendship. "Apart from the unidentified stranger the night before the explosion, yes. I was the only one."

Bliss sniffed and lit an untipped cigarette. "And it's not possible that some third party could have got to it unobserved? Maybe one night when a mist came down?"

"No way."

The SIS man smiled crookedly. "And what about your own chaps? I suppose there's no chance that one of them could have decided to take a private initiative?"

"No, sir. They're all trained professionals who've served for many years."

Bliss studied his cigarette end closely. "What about Villiers? He's a bit of a cowboy, isn't he?"

Major Fraser shifted awkwardly behind his desk. "I'm afraid, Mr Bliss, that comment is *decidedly* out of order."

While D'Arcy welcomed the support from his chief, the intervention had no effect on Bliss; in fact the reverse. The ruddy colour of the man's cheeks deepened. "Out of order, Major? This whole business is *decidedly* out of order. I must remind you that Villiers has a somewhat chequered history. How many weeks did he spend in the glasshouse at Catterick?"

It was D'Arcy's turn to feel resentment. "That was years ago – long before he even joined the Regiment. A young roughneck from the Glasgow back streets."

Bliss's cold grey eyes narrowed. "Leopards and spots," he murmured. "Leopards and spots."

"The captain's right," Fraser added. "He'd never have been admitted – let alone have been allowed to stay in the Regiment – unless we were completely satisfied with both his behaviour and psychological make-up."

"I understand," Bliss said softly, "that Villiers generally approves of setting up what we term 'own goals'?"

"He approved of the *idea*," D'Arcy agreed. "He's seen too much of the Provos' barbarity and cowardice, their intimidation of the innocent. He's seen too many killers walk free from the courts with smiles on their faces. Yes, he approved in principle, but that was just his private view. Villiers does what he's told."

Bliss wasn't to be deterred. He was like a dog with a bone and wouldn't be shaken. "And I gather you share that view, Captain?"

D'Arcy was taken aback. "Well, I'm not opposed to it – like half the Regiment. In certain situations."

The crooked smile returned to Bliss's face. "I'm glad you have the good grace to admit it. On more than one occasion you have been overheard approving the concept."

"A soldier cannot be prevented from holding a private opinion," Fraser reminded. "Provided it isn't made in public, nor affects his actions in the line of duty." Momentarily his eyes met D'Arcy's. Clearly he was as concerned as his friend with the line and tone of the SIS man's questioning.

Bliss rose to his feet and brushed spilt ash from his crumpled brown suit. "So if neither you nor Villiers – nor any of the other three at the OP – had a hand in this 'own goal', how do *you* explain that you failed to see the wiring?"

D'Arcy shrugged; he'd pondered the same question countless times himself. "The only rational explanation is that some sort of pressure-plate was used. Or a mercury tilt-switch. Arranged to detonate as the packet of explosive at the bottom was lifted."

Fraser nodded uncertainly. "That's feasible. Tell me, Mr Bliss, do the lab reports shed any light on what was used?"

The SIS man leaned with his back against the door, arms folded across his chest. "The explosion was so strong that any detonation device evaporated. But I must tell you that the explosive was PE4 as used by the British Army. Plastic-coated packaging fragments have been found."

D'Arcy swallowed hard. The implication was as clear as it was deadly to his defence. "The Provos have used stolen explosive before."

Bliss appeared not to hear as he stubbed out his cigarette

in the ashtray on Fraser's desk. "You realise what you are saying, D'Arcy? If a cache is booby-trapped it is normally to prevent it from falling into the hands of the security forces. The lid would have been wired in such a way that the Provos could disarm it themselves and retrieve their weapons. But a pressure-plate or tilt-switch couldn't be defused by anyone. It would have been solely to catch an RUC or Army patrol. It might explain why you didn't see it, but certainly not why the Provos set it off themselves."

D'Arcy sighed. This was going round in circles. "Some internal feud?" he suggested. "Do we know the identity of the victim yet? I'm damn sure it wasn't one of O'Neill's men."

Bliss raised a quizzical eyebrow. "You haven't heard? It was an Algerian student from Dublin."

"What?"

"He had come over from Teheran on an Iranian passport. One of several hundred youngsters who study there. His code name with French Intelligence was Tashakkur. That's Farsi for Good Luck. It looks like his ran out."

D'Arcy was stunned.

"So you see, Captain, we've been landed with a difficult diplomatic incident. Exactly what we were at pains to avoid. Your men were on the scene immediately afterwards, and we are faced with explaining a dead Iranian student scooped into a bodybag on one hand. And on the other, how do we explain to the French DGSE that one of our overzealous SAS soldiers has blown up one of their top undercover agents?"

"Just a minute!" D'Arcy protested, springing to his feet.

"No, Captain, *you* wait!" Bliss retorted. "In view of your pronounced approval of this type of waste disposal method, I've had the Criminal Investigation Branch inspect your quarters and your equipment. Amongst it is a considerable quantity of unauthorised explosive, ammunition, detonators and fuse wire."

D'Arcy was astounded. "Everyone squirrels odds and ends . . ."

"Enough!" Fraser snapped, standing behind his desk. "Forgive me, Mr Bliss, but you had permission to sit in on this debrief. Not to turn it into a witch-hunt." His eyes were steel. "Correct me if I'm wrong, but no legal proceedings are being considered?"

"That's down to the Crown Prosecution Service," Bliss replied matter-of-factly.

"On what evidence?" D'Arcy demanded.

Bliss shuffled uneasily, and fumbled in his pocket for his cigarettes. He looked straight at D'Arcy. "No, pal, you're right. There's no evidence to prosecute. Couldn't be really, could there?" He smiled thinly. "But what we've found is enough to convince those who matter. I've got it in the neck over this. More important, my boss at Century House has too. A high-flying young Turk who made his name over the Shalayez defection a few years back. He's looking for a scapegoat to appease the Foreign Office. Unfortunately for you, pal, he doesn't have to look too far."

"What are you trying to say?" D'Arcy asked darkly.

Bliss drew deeply on his cigarette before replying slowly. "I'm not *trying* to say anything, Captain, I *am* saying it. Look, we've always worked well together. Christ, most SIS officers and the men from the Regiment we work with are damn near blood brothers. There's no room for acrimony. So I'm warning you as a friend."

D'Arcy frowned. "Warning?"

"I know my boss. The evidence against you may be a bit circumstantial – but it's enough. Even if the entire Regiment give you their support, and I'm sure they will, it won't count for tuppence when my boss tells the MOD and the Foreign Office he knows who was responsible. In his position he doesn't need evidence, pal. Just a nod and a wink in the right places."

D'Arcy wasn't at all sure he welcomed Bliss's friendly words of advice. "But you, Roy – *my* blood brother – are quite prepared to make a detrimental report in the first place? Ignoring my protest of innocence?"

Bliss said smoothly: "Your statements will be noted. I'm just doing my job. It's in the hands of the Criminal Investigation Branch now."

Those bastards, D'Arcy thought savagely, they were far more ruthless and insensitive than any civilian equivalent. If anyone could make an innocent visit to grandma seem like attempted murder for an inheritance, they could. Expert stitchers-up.

Suddenly Bliss decided he'd said enough. He stubbed out his second cigarette and announced: "I need to be going. No doubt you've much to discuss." He nodded farewell to Major Fraser, then turned to D'Arcy. He didn't offer his hand. "Sorry, pal."

As the door shut D'Arcy felt relief.

"Evil little creep," Fraser growled from behind his desk.

D'Arcy shook his head. "No, Johnny, Bliss is okay really. As he said, he's just doing his job. How the hell is he supposed to know if I'm telling the truth?"

Fraser steepled his fingers on the desk before him and studied D'Arcy carefully. He'd known the man who stood in front of him for more years than he cared to recall. They'd long ago become friendly rivals as two of the few officers who returned to the Regiment regularly for additional tours of duty which had frequently coincided.

Already second-in-command of 22 SAS, Fraser was hotly tipped to become the Regiment's colonel within the next five years. D'Arcy was due to push a desk in Whitehall for three years, after which he was equally expected – according to rumours in the Mess – to fill Fraser's shoes as 2IC, heading up the antiterrorist CRW Wing. Two professional competitors and great personal friends. Two high-flyers who were more than likely to become full brigadiers and generals in the fullness of time . . .

And if one high-flyer should accidentally fall, Fraser thought angrily.

"Pardon?" D'Arcy didn't catch the muttered words.

"Did you do it, Rob?" The edge to the soft Edinburgh brogue was as hard as steel.

D'Arcy felt his hackles rise. "Do you have to ask?"

"I am asking you."

"I didn't do it, Johnny. And you don't have to ask."

Fraser nodded. "I didn't think you did. Neither does the Old Man." He took a deep breath. "But Bliss is right about his boss. I've come across him. Bloke called Lavender. And if you want to know about him, just ask Sarn't Major Hunt. He had the misfortune of working with him when old Mike Ash failed to beat the clock.

"The Old Man is under pressure to have you 'Returned to Unit'. He doesn't like it any more than I do. But, apart from the FCO, SIS and now the MOD screaming for blood, there's the bad press coverage in the tabloids. Typically they're speculating that an SAS team on surveillance set up an 'own goal' as though it were gospel. The Opposition is even demanding an inquiry."

D'Arcy watched his friend closely, scarcely believing the words being spoken. Any moment now he had to awaken and find himself in the cold sweat aftermath of a nightmare.

"The colonel wants you in his office tomorrow morning at 0900 hours," Fraser added. Then, carefully: "Don't be surprised if you find your majority waiting for you."

D'Arcy's eyes narrowed like a cat's. In these circumstances the rank of major at this stage in the game had all the hallmarks of a farewell gift. The only card the CO had left to play.

Fraser read the expression on his colleague's face. "Advice from another friend, Rob, have your resignation with you tomorrow. Take the initiative and go on your own terms. What do you think?"

The SAS captain didn't reply immediately. He was trembling with the suppressed rage and anguish of the helpless.

He looked down at Fraser. "I think, Johnny, that either the Provos or this Iranian terrorist Sabbah discovered the identity of Tashakkur in their cell and set him up to blow himself to smithereens. That's why they started evacuating while he was still at the cache. And that's why they'd stowed only four obsolete Kalashnikovs. I think they didn't even know my men were there." His chest heaved with indignation. "What do *you* think?"

The silence that followed hung bitterly in the air between them.

Quietly Fraser said: "I think that's very likely."

D'Arcy said: "The CO will have my resignation at 0900 tomorrow. From the Regiment – and from the Army."

Before Fraser could reply, D'Arcy had turned on his heel and left. As the door shut his military career ended.

# TWO YEARS LATER

# 1

The desiccated coast of the Sultanate of Oman passed off the portside of the 15,000 tonne freighter *Clarion Call*.

A dipping sun bled its light over the jagged teeth of the cliffs and spilled out across the approaches to the Gulf. The ruddy irradiation appeared to becalm the agitated blue water of the day, transforming the sparkling sapphires to a deep and tranquil ruby glow.

Even the sultry offshore breeze, Tom Wilmot noticed, had ebbed away. Now the evening air was almost still, heavy with the musky smell of the land.

He moved to the rail and watched the distant shore.

For some the call-to-return came from Africa, for others it was the Far East. But for Wilmot it would always be Arabia. The nomads of the desert, their customs and their colourful, sometimes savage history. The days of the camel trains, harems, rival sheikhdoms, desert forts, the ivory smugglers and the slavers. Small wonder it had fired the imagination of storytellers through the ages. Days of unremitting heat in a harsh, baking landscape. Perfumed nights when the sensuous secrets of the veil would be revealed.

Wilmot smiled to himself. Most of that had gone today, of course. Many Arab capitals had taken on a skyline like New York's and the nomads had exchanged their camels for four-wheel drives. The city populations travelled from air-conditioned homes to air-conditioned offices in air-conditioned cars. It was almost possible to exist without suffering the hammer heat of the sun. But, Wilmot knew, for all the new roads, hospitals, schools and clinics that now criss-crossed the interior, lifestyles had changed little. To an Arabist like Wilmot it was the true consolation.

He watched a fishing dhow, trailed by gulls, weave its course across their bow. Unmoved by the might and power of the modern freighter.

The echoing boom of the foghorn blasted from the bridge like the wrath of God, shattering the stillness as its warning reverberated across the water.

It shook Wilmot from his thoughts and forcefully reminded him of just how illusory was this twilight calm. For the great *Clarion Call* was steaming towards the most dangerous waters in the world, the Arabian Gulf. Through the tight gap of the Strait of Hormuz and into the long, narrow waters flanked by Saudi Arabia and the small Arab states to the south and, spanning the entire northern coast, the Islamic Republic of Iran.

An unhappy, isolated land, it had been locked in war now for eight years with its neighbour Iraq.

At the head of the Gulf, where the historic Tigris and Euphrates rivers met, their two armies had slogged at each other like two prizefighters to the cost of thousands of innocent lives. In all that time no quarter had been given, and none taken.

The war had long ago spilled into the Gulf itself. Aircraft from both sides had attacked shipping destined for its enemy or allies. It had reached such a pitch that the Royal Navy's long-standing Armilla Patrol had been joined by the awesome power of the American fleet.

Mines had become the latest menace, lurking like sharks to bite holes in the hulls of passing merchantmen. And maybe worse, Wilmot considered, the dreaded Boghammars. Fast Swedish-built gunboats, manned by fanatical Revolutionary Guards and armed with heavy machine guns and grenade-launchers. Without warning they would appear from the sea haze, a swarm of deadly killer bees capable of terrorising towering tankers and freighters with a thousand explosive pinpricks. The Boghammars had a firepower out of all proportion to their size and had caused the death or maiming of many innocent seamen.

It was to minimise the damage from any such dangers that Tom Wilmot was aboard. He had excellent qualifications for a 'sea-marshal', the official title given to the job he had been hired to do by InterCon Asset Protection.

IAP was a private security firm which had sprung to international recognition in under two years. Its boss Robert D'Arcy, an ex-SAS officer, had contacted Wilmot while he was kicking his heels after leaving the Royal Marines Special Boat Service. Already discovering that civilian life as a not very convincing insurance salesman could be mind-numbingly boring, he had leapt at D'Arcy's unexpected offer. His wife Pauline was none too happy at the thought of her husband sailing into the most dangerous waters on earth. But she was finally persuaded that it would actually be safer and far better paid than their former service life. Besides, with a baby on the way, they needed all the money they could get.

For Wilmot it was a welcome opportunity to work with D'Arcy, a man he'd only met once before on a joint SAS–SBS training course, but whose reputation was almost legendary amongst special forces. Not an easy achievement in the world of cynical professionals who had seen and done it all themselves.

It also meant the chance for Wilmot to return to various Arab states where he'd served at different times during his service with the SBS. In fact the skipper had promised that on the return leg they would call in at Mina Qaboos in Oman for a few days. There he planned to look up a few old friends still serving with the Sultan's armed forces.

But first *Clarion Call* was bound for the camp of the Arabs' enemy, Bandar Abbas in Iran, to deliver the cargo of agricultural machinery from Brazil. At least their destination meant they should be in no danger from the Revolutionary Guards and their Boghammars. Not, at least, if the Iranians' internal communications were reliable, although on that score Wilmot had his reservations.

An air attack by Iraqi jets too, was only the remotest

possibility so far south, although mines were another matter altogether. Those bastards could be *anywhere*!

But, whatever danger lay in store, it was a good day's steaming away yet, on the far side of the Strait. Meanwhile he had been tirelessly drilling the lethargic multinational crew in fire-fighting and damage-control techniques to prevent panic and to keep the ship under way at all costs should the worst occur.

Wilmot glanced at his watch. If he didn't go over the final plans with the captain now, the opportunity would be lost before they reached the danger zone.

He walked back alongside the fore cargo holds towards the three-tier superstructure at the stern. From there it was a short, hard climb up the inner stairwell to the level below the bridge. There he found Dimitrios Mános in his sea cabin, already indulging in his first medicinal Pernod of the evening.

"Ah, Wilmot, greetings my friend!" the Greek growled good-humouredly.

His giant frame was sprawled awkwardly on the cramped bunk bed that had clearly been designed for men of more diminutive stature by the Japanese shipbuilders. Likewise the soiled white shirt was hardly able to contain the powerful barrel chest with its heavy gold medallion that glinted amid the tangle of greying hair at the open collar.

"Evening, Dimitrios, I thought we might go over the defence plans in readiness for tomorrow."

The Greek's dark eyes looked pained beneath the heavy beetle brows. "Always my friend you are on the go. You never relax. You train and rehearse my crew, you give me plans and revisions of plans until my mind pops. And now, with the sun over your English yardarm, I just need to have a little quiet thinking time to myself . . . And here you are again!"

Wilmot grinned. He'd learned to like Mános on the long voyage from Brazil. With his wild hair and beard – once lush black but now threaded with silver – he would have looked more at home on a buccaneer's square-rigger than on the bridge of a modern freighter. Wilmot enjoyed parrying the Greek's gently mocking provocation which suggested that all these complex precautions were unnecessary.

"We can talk over a bottle of Pernod, Dimitrios, no problem."

A gold tooth twinkled amid the rough beard as the captain laughed. "Ah, you have found the weak spot in my defences, my friend."

Wilmot smiled as he sat on the edge of the bunk. "That's what I'm trained to do."

Mános slopped Pernod into a second tumbler. "Such talent! Such waste! I tell you we have nothing to fear from the Iranians – they pay for this cargo." He handed the drink to Wilmot. "You should worry about some American jet-jockey from a carrier, high on coke or hash. Already today you see that Yankee frigate and its high-handed manner. What are you *Clarion Call*? Where are you bound? What is your cargo?" Mános belched lightly. "Who the hell does he think he is, eh? And then at night we get buzzed by their secret helicopter that sees in the dark, knowing any time they blow us out the water if they please!"

"That's their Force 160," Wilmost consoled. "Looking for Iranian mine-layers."

"I don't care what they are, they make me nervous!"

Wilmot laughed. "I worry about everyone, Dimitrios, not least you. You'll need to be fresh and alert tomorrow."

Mános glowered momentarily. His fondness of alcohol showed in the moist dark eyes that reminded Wilmot of prunes simmering in their own juice. "Have you ever seen me drunk, Wilmot?" he challenged.

"I can never tell with you whether you're drunk or sober. You're always the same."

Mános considered Wilmot's honest observation for a second before suddenly roaring with laughter. "There, there, my friend, you worry enough for both of us."

"That's what I'm paid for." The Greek's constant

amusement at his professional caution was beginning to irk. "That's why I want to be absolutely certain that we are agreed on everything, including our route."

"Our route?" Mános echoed, reluctantly trying to concentrate his mind.

"For a start we should give Khor Fakkan a wide berth." This was the last popular anchorage in the United Arab Emirates before the Strait. "The less contact we have with other shipping the better. Likewise our course should avoid Didamar Light at Musandam where the British convoys form up."

Mános shrugged. "You do not even trust your own Royal Navy?"

"I just don't want any accidents, no intelligence picked up from monitoring radio exchanges. That way the only serious risk will be from mines – although that's unlikely outside the Gulf. And when we near Bandar Abbas I don't trust the Iranian Guards and their Boghammars to find out who we are before they start shooting."

Mános nodded sagely. "Sure, sure, they are wild cards, you are right. You never know who they take orders from. Even if they have orders." He leaned forward conspiratorially, his breath thick with liquorice. "Two friends I lose in the Gulf. Good men. Many times we share the Pernod back home. One has his head blown off in a grenade attack. Another, a tanker skipper, he is last seen running down the companionway, screaming with his clothes and hair on fire. It takes him two days to die."

Wilmot was suddenly aware of the smallness of the cabin, and the urgent hum of the air-conditioning.

Mános placed his tumbler firmly on the bunkside cabinet. A statement of self-discipline. "I joke sometimes with you, my friend. But I tell you, nowadays these are the devil's waters. I have run the risk three times a year for the past five years. This trip will be safe, but next time – who knows? I have enough." He sat up suddenly. "Right, tell me your plans."

Wilmot felt relief that at last he was being taken

seriously. He consulted his notebook. "From first light we should maintain radio silence. We'll use our speed to keep any passing ships out of visual range.

"We should keep our radar range scale on two thousand metres fixed alarm – that'll also pick up any helicopters in the vicinity.

"Our radio officer should listen in to Channel 12 for general warnings and 105 for aircraft approach warnings at ninety miles out."

"And our protection?"

"All precautions are virtually complete," Wilmot confirmed. "As you know we've fitted Kevlar composite armour sheet around the bridge and bridge decking. That'll give protection from shrapnel. Acetate window protection is complete. All Formica partitions and tables that can splinter have been backed with plywood. All the deck fire-lines have been protected by armour plates.

"I've now completed installation of the new electronic decoy system –" He paused, knowing that should please Mános. Few skippers trusted the mechanical six-foot bow decoys of right-angled steel that were wound out, looking like a ship's figurehead designed by Picasso. He felt mildly cheated when the Greek acknowledged with an unenthusiastic nod. "The crew have virtually finished fitting the RAM radar-absorbancy pads to all the angled surfaces on the superstructure. We'll make a hard target for a missile to lock on to."

"And the crew are fully drilled?"

"Yes, we've got emergency procedures as good as we're likely to get them, and fire-fighting teams will be on standby in relays from dawn tomorrow until we dock at Bandar Abbas," Wilmot replied. What he really meant was that the crew were so red hot at abandoning ship, in the case of a real attack the problem of fire-fighting would be academic.

"You seem to think of everything, my friend."

Wilmot closed his notebook with a snap and a grim smile. "I wish I could be so sure, Dimitrios. It is always the *un*expected you have to expect. We cannot afford complacency."

Mános chuckled throatily at the other man's seriousness, then, glancing at his watch, climbed to his feet. He put his arm round Wilmot's shoulder. "And all this protection is not really for us, eh, my friend? It is all because the insurers at Lloyd's charge lower premiums. What a wicked world we live in. Come, we go to the bridge, yes?"

Wilmot followed up the aft stairwell. On his way along the short passage to the wheelhouse, Mános peered into the radio room and called out to the operator: "Hey, Jayant, radio silence as from now, right? No more signals to your million relatives in Bombay or wherever it is."

The shirt-sleeved Indian spun round in his swivel chair, looking most offended. "Please, skipper, always you say that, and always you know I do no such thing." His head shook rapidly from side to side in protest.

Mános grinned broadly. "If you say so, Jayant."

"But, skipper, I am now due to make routine signal to head office . . ."

"No signal," Mános growled. "Let them stew. I don't trust those blabbermouths in Monaco. They will know soon enough when we reach Bandar Abbas."

"But it is three days now –" Jayant protested.

"Do you give the orders on this ship now, my friend?" Mános's smile was full of menace.

Jayant was no fighter. His family back home depended on his regular pay cheque and he was painfully aware of it.

'What was that about?" Wilmot asked.

Mános shrugged. "There's been some problem with the radio."

"No signals for three days? I should have been informed."

The captain shrugged. "It's all right now. There's no problem. Jayant has it fixed."

Only the Filipino first mate, Canillo, was in the wheelhouse with the Korean general rating who manned the autohelm.

"All correct, skipper," Canillo reported as the ship's master squeezed through the bulkhead. The deck officer was a quiet, courteous young man who had been blessed with a virtually permanent smile.

Mános ordered him to reduce speed to Slow Ahead before following Wilmot out onto the starboard bridge wing. The sun had finally disappeared behind the Omani coastline, leaving the inky smudge of the *jebel* cliffs outlined against a tangerine-streaked sky. Twilight was fading fast.

"Tell me, Tom Wilmot, what do you see?" Mános asked huskily.

"Sea and sky," Wilmot answered, sharing what he assumed was the captain's sense of awe. "A very stunning sea and sky at that."

The weatherbeaten skin around Mános's eyes crinkled as he scoured the horizon. "Sure, sea and sky. Sea and sky. And that is all I see every day for the past thirty years. Every day. And not always so beautiful."

"You sound like a man who has had enough."

"Yes, my friend," the Greek sighed, "I have enough. Sea and sky – and death in the Gulf. I do not need this. It will be my last voyage, this one."

Wilmot could understand that. "So you're retiring?"

"Sure, I retire. I have a little deal going. I make a few drachmas so I can live in comfort with my good wife in my old age, eh? She will like that – she hardly sees me for thirty years." He laughed and placed his big hairy hands on the rail. "Soon she'll wish I was back at sea again."

Just as Wilmot was about to reply, Canillo's shout of warning came from the wheelhouse: "HEY, SKIPPER! SMALL CRAFT APPROACHING DEAD AHEAD!"

Both men turned. At the autohelm the Filipino first mate had binoculars to his eyes.

Wilmot followed the direction of his gaze as the warning call of the foghorn boomed. At first he couldn't make them out. They were low and dark in the water, hidden by each sluggish wave that passed. It was the fluorescent wake, churned by powerful outboards, that first gave away their position.

Momentarily his heart stopped. Christ, not Boghammars!

He immediately chided himself. That was impossible. Iran was still two hundred and fifty miles away, a good day's steaming at ten knots. Besides, these looked like heavy-duty black rubber inflatables. They were travelling fast, side by side, slamming into one wave crest after another as they closed.

Where the hell had they come from? Were they a boarding party from a US warship? The Americans tended to be heavy-handed with their policing methods in the Gulf. No, surely there'd have been a radio challenge first.

Then Mános echoed his second thought. "I expect it is an Omani patrol." He didn't sound unduly perturbed.

Wilmot didn't reply, his mind was racing. The Omanis used patrol boats, usually skippered by expatriate British officers. This wasn't their style. There was something menacing about them, particularly the dogged way they kept to their head-on collision course.

Then he remembered the radar blip that had been on their screen ever since the Red Sea, the ship having been on the same course behind them ever since *Clarion Call* had departed from the Gulf of Aquaba. The previous night it had overhauled them for the first time, suggesting by its latent speed that it wasn't the light freighter he had assumed it to be. By dawn it had disappeared off their radar screen somewhere ahead.

It was a crazy thought really. What could a Jordanian ship possibly want with *Clarion Call*? But Wilmot couldn't shake the thought from his mind. Somehow he was certain that the mystery ship was the origin of the two black raiders. Already they were little more than seven hundred metres away. It was pure good fortune that they had been spotted at all.

The foghorn boomed again, and Mános was suddenly galvanised into action. In three brisk strides he was in the wheelhouse.

"What are we making?" he demanded of Canillo.

"Seven knots, skipper," the Filipino replied anxiously.

Mános grunted. "Reverse engine," he ordered.

Canillo reached for the controls.

"I don't like it," Wilmot breathed.

Mános's eyes were fixed on the Gemini inflatables. "You want I run them down?"

The great monster began to shudder, its rivets shaking, as the variable-pitch propeller of the 17,000 horsepower Burmeister & Wain diesel was thrown into reverse. It took time to stop a 15,000 tonner, like a deadweight on the Cresta run.

An expression of deep concern clouded the Filipino's face as he anticipated the order that didn't come. At last he could wait no longer. "Skipper, sir, I take avoiding action?"

Mános shook his head slowly. "They've been warned, hold her steady."

Then Wilmot saw it. Knew how they had got so close without being picked up on radar. A special forces technique he'd used many times himself. Waiting submerged with deflated dinghies and a high-pressure air bottle. Target in sight. Hit the button. Two attack craft from nowhere before the target ship's crew knew what hit them . . .

Ahead the two Geminis suddenly parted company, their snub bows splashing angrily like enraged dolphins as they split to the left and right of *Clarion Call*'s looming bows. For a moment Wilmot thought Mános had successfully called their bluff. Then he saw the buoyant line stretching out between the racing craft.

Christ, he'd been a fool! They were going for the classic 'washing-line' hook-up – a standard SBS method of submarine rendezvous. He of all people should have seen it coming.

47

He yelled at **Mános**. "It's a boarding party! Full speed for God's sake!"

Mános was rooted to the spot, seemingly paralysed.

The Filipino gawped, uncertain what to do. The helmsman shifted his balance nervously.

Wilmot pushed Canillo aside, reaching for the control panel and rang Full Ahead.

The captain suddenly came alive. "How dare you . . . !"

Wilmot ignored him and depressed the alarm klaxon to call the crew to action stations. The deckplates shuddered as the diesel struggled to regain power.

But even as the urgent bark of the klaxon filled his ears, he knew it was too late. If only they had maintained speed, *Clarion Call*'s bows might have sliced the line between the inflatables. Or at least turned what was about to happen next into a disaster for their attackers. But, instead of smashing the bodies of the boarding party against the ship's side, the slow speed enabled the manoeuvre to go with clockwork military precision.

The line struck just above the ship's dreadnought chin housing. It acted as a pivot, allowing the Geminis to pass each side of the towering black hull. Wilmot raced back out to the bridge wing. He was just in time to witness the starboard inflatable being drawn alongside amidships. Simultaneously the grappling irons swung over the ship's rail and the black-clad raiders began their ascent.

Bewildered crewmen gathered at their action stations, glanced in alarm at the steel spiders coming over the side, at each other, and then up to the bridge for some kind of instruction.

Wilmot was filled with unreasoned anger at himself. Tomorrow there would be pressure on all hydrant hoses to blast intruders off. Tomorrow there'd be barbed wire on the other ladders to the bridge. Tomorrow it would be a floating fortress. Tomorrow, tomorrow . . .

He turned to Mános who had joined him on the wing. "Give the order to repel boarders," he demanded. "And issue an SOS signal immediately."

The Greek appeared to be in a trance. "L-let's see what they want, my friend. S-see what they want . . ."

"Give the order, Captain," Wilmot repeated. "Or I will."

Mános shook his head.

Wilmot snatched the bullhorn from its cradle and raised it to his lips. "CREW – REPEL BOARDERS BY ALL MEANS POSSIBLE! NOW! BEFORE IT'S TOO LATE! NOW, DAMMIT!"

But the startled multinational crew had no stomach for a fight. Even though some had armed themselves with crowbars, shovels and kitchen knives, not one took a step towards the ship's side. They stared, motionless, as the first black-clad commando appeared at the rail, his wet suit dripping with spray and his M16 assault rifle held level. A companion joined him, leapfrogging over the side. He advanced towards the crew, motioning with his rifle. If there was a hero amongst them, he quickly changed his mind. Wilmot watched resignedly as the assortment of improvised weaponry clattered to the deck and arms were raised.

More commandos were over the side now, speeding towards the stairwell that led to the bridge.

Wilmot turned to Mános. "Quickly, get the gun from your cabin!"

The captain's thick lips curled in disdain. "You want to get us all killed, my friend? You forget I retire after this voyage."

There was no time to argue. Roughly Wilmot pushed Mános aside and sprinted into the wheelhouse. If only he could keep the intruders from the bridge for a few minutes while he organised an SOS signal to be sent. He would use his own 9 mm Browning which was in his cabin.

"Canillo," he snapped at the Filipino. "Get Jayant to send a signal. SOS. Pronto!"

The man's mouth dropped. "Jayant's not here. The radio room is locked."

"What?" He couldn't believe it. Everything was in there.

HF and VHF radios, telex and the satcom suite. "On whose orders?"

"The skipper's."

"Never mind!" Wilmot dived through the short passage and took the stairwell three steps at a time to the deck below. He shouldered his way through the door to his cabin and heaved out the holdall from beneath his bunk. Damn and blast Mános, he cursed, as he fumbled for the automatic and checked its magazine. Damn Mános and his bloody retirement plans!

He turned to find the Greek barring his way. "Wilmot, my friend, do not be foolish. This is no use."

"Just get the radio room open, Dimitrios, and send a bloody signal!"

Mános didn't move. Beyond exasperation, Wilmot pushed the big man aside. He checked down the stairwell to the main deck. He could see no one, but heard the hard breathing and running footsteps. Getting louder. Maybe there was still time for him to break into the radio room himself?

Still swearing beneath his breath he launched himself back up the stairwell to the wheelhouse. Instantly he froze. The Filipino first mate and the helmsman stood rigidly to attention, faces pale, hands raised.

In the hatchway to the bridge wing stood the commando, crouched over the M16. Damn, the bastard had used the outer ladder! Wilmot took in the rubber suit, the ammo packs on his belt, the black balaclava and the drooping moustache. Seaspray dripped on the deck to form a puddle.

Wilmot's finger tightened on the trigger of the Browning as the two men faced each other, both a split second from death.

Then the harsh rasp of the cocking handle came from the stairwell behind him.

"No, my friend! Don't get yourself killed for this."

Wilmot froze, his eyes not moving from the commando. Slowly, his mouth suddenly dry, Wilmot lowered his automatic and let it fall noisily to the deck.

Raising his hands, he turned slightly until he could see Mános standing with the weapon pointed at the base of his spine.

Wilmot's eyes narrowed. "You fucking Judas," he breathed.

# 2

Morning sun angled low over the mixed Docklands development of old warehouses and new luxury apartments, setting alight the turbid green waters of Flax Wharf.

From beneath the sheet Chantal Roquelaure peered out into the bright and airy bedroom level of the converted building. With shafts of dusty light streaming through the lofty windows, it was all too much. Momentarily she regretted her choice of such pale yellows and greys for the décor, and shut her eyes again tight.

The rhythmic clank of steel drifted up from the lower open-plan living level, and she could hear the hard rasp of his breathing as he worked the multigym.

She hadn't been aware of D'Arcy leaving the bed. He possessed, she had discovered, the ability to move with remarkable stealth and agility for someone of such a powerful build. No, she had sensed his absence rather than felt it. It was like that between them now.

It would be only minutes after seven, she was certain of that, dimly aware of his footsteps as he returned to the bedroom level. Seconds later she heard the shower running.

Yes, it was seven. Opening her eyes again, she lifted her head until she could see the shower cubicle, his tall shape outlined in the frosted glass.

Still he maintained a near-military personal régime, even though he'd been out of the Army for nearly two years. Up on the stroke of six – with or without an alarm – and a glass of orange juice before a three-mile run around the old unloading docks of Flax Wharf. He would return to a brisk twenty-minute work-out on the Nautilus. When he had showered he would bring her a light breakfast in bed on the few days every month that she was able to snatch from her busy schedule in Paris. As demand for her services as an interior designer grew by the day, she found herself aching for the opportunity to make the Channel hop to Docklands Airport. Even if it was only to spend just a few hours with him.

The hiss of the steam shower was replaced by the drilling of the cold water and moments later D'Arcy emerged, a towel around his waist. Without looking in her direction he moved behind the bathroom partition.

She kicked the sheet aside, and padded naked across the polished teak floor. He was lathering soap around his determined jawline, jutting his chin at the mirror. The deep blue eyes didn't notice her reflection as his fingers pulled the skin taut across his cheekbone for the blade. She noted with approval the strong nose, very slightly hooked as she imagined an Ancient Roman might have looked. And the very black, thick hair which was still damp, plastered in a curled comma against his forehead. And that scar that sliced across his right cheek, almost all the way from his ear to the corner of his thin, rather cruel mouth. It cut a pale streak across the weathered tan of his skin. When he was angered she had seen that it could suddenly pulse with colour.

He saw her then, and felt her hand playfully squeeze his buttocks through the towel.

"Hello, kitten." His voice was hoarse with the faintest hint of a Scots accent. The crooked smile rakishly transformed the severely chiselled lips. "I didn't think we'd see you yet. You were awake half the night."

She kissed his neck and ran her finger lightly down his spine. "Yes, *chéri*, and it is worth every precious moment," she said, softly rolling her 'r's and elongating the vowels in the Parisian manner that he always found so bewitching.

"And you're not tired?"

"No," she lied, resting her head on his shoulder while he continued shaving. "You breathe new life and fire into me always."

He grinned at her reflection in the mirror, and she thought about their lovemaking the night before. How tender he was at times, yet on other occasions he could be almost brutal. As though he were trying to bury some sense of anger deep inside of her. Yet it was then that she found herself responding most strongly to him, matching his ruthless passion with her own. Deep scratch marks down his back had earned her the 'Kitten' nickname. Perhaps he should have called her 'Tiger'; last night she'd drawn blood.

"I think maybe you come back to bed?" she suggested.

He rinsed his face and towelled it dry. "A tempting offer, sweetheart, but today's hectic. Chasing the dollar – or should I say the franc. There's a party coming over to talk about security for the new diamond mines opening up in Guinea." He took a pair of boxer shorts from the wardrobe and pulled them on. "Why don't you join us for lunch? A pretty face might clinch the deal."

"That is very sexist, Mr D'Arcy," she laughed. "I sometimes think you are just using me."

He reached forward and kissed the tip of her nose. "Ah, but it works. Every time you come to a business lunch we win the contract."

"And I do not even get my breakfast in bed today?"

He selected a petrol blue Anderson & Sheppard suit from the wardrobe together with a silk Coles shirt. It brought a smile to her face to recall how hopeless he'd been with fashion when she first knew him. Totally at a loss unless he was in his beloved DPM camouflage or a ribbed military sweater. Civilian clothes were instinctively chosen to be subdued and inconspicuous for undercover operations. She was pleased now that, usually, her natural designer's sense of fashion was beginning to rub off. But it remained an uphill struggle.

"Dave's due in at any moment," he explained. "We're trying to squeeze in a breakfast ops review before the diamond people turn up at nine thirty."

"So, you neglect me. Take me for granted, I think, Mr D'Arcy."

He looked across to where she sat, naked, on the bed. A petite twenty-eight-year-old, with the long-legged elegance of a gazelle and the most stunning wide green eyes which always appeared to be laughing. Impudent humour was something she exuded even when, as now, those full lips were pouting in mock anger. Even first thing in the morning when her straight fair hair was a tangled muddle.

"Go and put some clothes on," he said. "You're distracting me."

"Good."

He laughed and, still buttoning his shirtsleeves, clattered down the open steps to the living quarters and the kitchen area.

As he plugged in the coffee percolator and began slicing a loaf for toast, he thought again just how lucky he had been to meet her.

That had been not long after he had left the British Army, nearly two years before. His resignation and its acceptance had happened with a speed that left him winded. Anxious to be rid of their embarrassment, the Ministry of Defence had moved with almost indecent haste to oil the wheels of bureaucracy that dumped him unceremoniously on the unfamiliar pavements of Civvy Street. With just two suitcases containing all his worldly goods, and his 'majority' which, under any other circumstances, would have been his most treasured possession.

"Take it, Robert," the colonel had said at the fateful early morning meeting. "Accept it in the spirit with which it is awarded. For loyal service to the Regiment and your friends here. It's not an empty gesture, you have earned it. In this situation it is necessary to bring it forward a little, that's all. They might not like it at the Ministry or the Foreign Office – they will see it as the Regiment's signal of disapproval of their actions. Accept it, Robert. They can't take it away from you."

He had rented a flat in an unfashionable area of South London, just months ahead of the property developers, and begun his search for a new career.

A rash of private security companies had sprung up during the previous decade, mostly run by ex-SAS officers, many of whom he knew. He was assured by friends that any one of them would welcome a man of his talents and exemplary record. He had begun the endless round of interviews in buoyant mood, putting the past firmly behind him. But, despite encouraging noises made at a succession of meetings, nothing positive was offered. As Christmas approached, his patience and his money were running low. And when he heard that other SAS officers of lesser experience had since been offered jobs with the same companies he had seen, his suspicions were aroused.

His exasperation was not eased by a patronising, weasel-faced resettlement officer who was intent on his finding a job in banking or insurance. He was adamant that D'Arcy should steer clear of security work, and had developed near apoplexy when D'Arcy had jokingly suggested that he might become a mercenary.

That joke, however, was becoming increasingly less funny with the onset of the bitter December weather.

The message from General de Brigade Pierre Roquelaure had come out of the blue on a morning when D'Arcy's spirits had plummeted to new depths. He was now certain that there was a conspiracy to have him blacklisted. Short of cash, and missing the companionship of the only friends he had known for years, he had called in at the Special Forces Club behind Harrods. At lunchtime he rang Roquelaure's château which was situated on the northern outskirts of Paris.

The general was in ebullient mood. "My dear Rober'! At last I find you." He had sounded genuinely pleased. "I only recently hear what has become of you since that terrible business in Ireland. I am so sorry because I feel partly to blame. My superiors they are very angry at the loss of our agent Tashakkur. They do not understand what it is like in the field – or rather, more truthfully, they put politics and self-interest first. True Frenchmen! Appease the political masters with someone else's head on a plate." He chuckled dryly. "A sacrifice to the gods who pay their salary. I did not know it was your head they serve."

"It happens," D'Arcy replied cautiously, unsure as to where all this was leading.

Roquelaure grunted down the line. "You take it well, Rober'. Practice with your SAS 'embuggerance factor', I suppose. Well look, I have something I should like to talk over with you. Tell me, you are doing anything over Christmas? With family, or going abroad perhaps?"

"I've nothing planned."

"Do you know I have a chalet in the Savoy Alps, just outside La Clusaz? Excellent for skiing, downhill and cross-country – like you do in the Army, yes?"

D'Arcy was still uncertain. "Sounds delightful."

"If you are at a loose end, go whenever you like. My daughter Chantal is there, and I'm sure she'll welcome the company." He hesitated, searching for the right words. "She has a little personal unhappiness at the moment – I am sure your presence will cheer her up. I'll join you around the 20th. Just get a flight to Geneva –" He paused again, this time sensing D'Arcy's unease. "– Rober', I understand your coffers may be a little, er, stretched. I promise your expenses will be covered and it will be well worth the trip."

And so it turned out to be.

His first surprise had been meeting Chantal.

Even in fashionable loose-fitting slacks and a cashmere sweater she exuded that elusive Continental *chic* as she pored over her interior designs on the large dining table, her close-up spectacles pushed up on her forehead like aviator's goggles. D'Arcy was immediately stirred by the sight of her and those large, inquiring green eyes. Her manner was light and friendly but, on reflection, she had been far more subdued and introspective than the girl who was later to become his lover.

Outside the chalet the first of the winter snow was starting to fall.

At the time romance had been the last thing on his mind. Besides which she was his friend's daughter, even if she was not quite young enough to be his own. There were still ten years between their ages.

While he awaited the arrival of Roquelaure, he had spent his days on the high pass of Les Confins, trying to recapture the Nordic skiing technique of his Army days. It had never been one of his more accomplished skills, and now the knack seemed to elude him completely. One day, her latest commission completed, Chantal had promised to join him on the *loipe* in the afternoon.

He had waited at the rendezvous and hadn't actually recognised her as she approached. He had been idly watching a girl in her twenties as she skated easily up the slope towards him. With blonde hair tied casually in a ponytail, the flair and easy grace of her movements had filled him with admiration. She was a million times more practised than he would ever be.

Her eyes sparkled with mischief and the sun played on her hair as, to his surprise, she deftly swung across in front of him.

"Mr D'Arcy! I think you do not recognise me!" she challenged, feigning hurt. "Do I make so *little* impression?" Then she noticed his boots. "*Mon Dieu*! How do you ski in those?"

D'Arcy grinned. "With difficulty. Army issue, I'm afraid. Haven't used them for years, now I can hardly remember how . . ."

She pulled a face. "You come with me. I am very good." She winked to show that she was only joking. "Follow me."

He knew then that she loved the snow and the mountain air, as she lifted her knees in the easiest and most graceful skating turn he had ever seen.

"See," she laughed. "Soon it all comes back."

And from that moment he was in love with her as he had never been in love before.

Their relationship was not an immediate thing, but blossomed swiftly and steadily from the first seeds of their chemistry together. He learned that she had recently heard that her fiancé, a French diplomat, had died at the hands of terrorists in Beirut. Roquelaure may have hoped that D'Arcy would raise his daughter's spirits, but as far as D'Arcy was concerned it was Chantal who lifted his.

It began over that first Christmas break when Roquelaure arrived to explain how he was interested in setting up an international security company, and wanted D'Arcy to run it.

The Frenchman saw the possibility of fast and substantial profits for the right sort of operation: with his contacts and D'Arcy's expertise, he believed that they couldn't fail. He saw a lean, efficient and open – if discreet – company that would attract the big money available from governments, insurance companies, and respectable international corporations.

In particular, he was convinced that the French authorities would welcome the concept of a British-fronted security company to look after their interests. Such services would be especially welcomed in politically sensitive areas of the world – provided that Roquelaure was on the board. In that way the French would not be easily open to criticism, being one step removed from operations.

Normally cautious of foreigners, the French found in D'Arcy a man they could trust. Not only had he been partly brought up and educated in France, he was well-known and respected as a result of his SAS liaison work with the French military and security services.

Roquelaure dismissed any possible problems resulting from the Tashakkur incident.

As pragmatic as ever, the same men who had demanded D'Arcy's head over the arms cache explosion, were quick to recognise a talent they could now exploit to their own advantage.

And so InterCon Asset Protection had been born over cognac by the huge chalet fireplace in La Clusaz with a blizzard raging outside.

In the months that followed Roquelaure's drive and enthusiasm had matched D'Arcy's own. The Frenchman had access to the ample funds necessary to lease the main London office and D'Arcy's new home 'over the shop'. Which was just as well because the elaborate security system and high technology office equipment would have been far beyond D'Arcy's personal means. Computers and word processors were installed together with all the telex facilities and communications suite necessary for efficient worldwide operations.

The French subsidiary was run from Roquelaure's own office in his château, the grounds of which provided ample space for firing ranges and equipment demonstrations, as well as uninhibited staff training.

Hardly had the paint dried in the spacious Docklands nerve centre than the telephone rang. It was Roquelaure with their first job. The president of a former French colony in Africa wanted a bodyguard protection team and a review of his personal security. It was the first of a flood of assignments to arrive during the early months. In fact it was such a torrent that it threatened to swamp the infant IAP.

Virtually all came on recommendation from Roquelaure or his cronies in the French security services and government circles. D'Arcy didn't inquire how many backhanders were being paid, but it became clear after the first accounting period that they were quite substantial. Nevertheless handsome profits remained to reinvest in the burgeoning business.

By the end of its first chaotic year IAP had installed antiterrorist security systems for several embassies and the private residencies of businessmen, including the provision of several VIP protection teams. Advice on arms purchases had been given to several Third World governments with training backup provided for police and antiterrorist units.

Twice the company was called in to negotiate ransom demands from the kidnappers of wealthy industrialists. The outcome on both occasions was successful in terms of lives saved and intitial demands dramatically reduced.

By the second year IAP's chronic manpower shortage had largely been overcome and the entire operation more efficiently organised. While various overseas training programmes continued, including the provision of security staff for diamond and gold mining companies, more diverse and interesting assignments materialised as IAP earned the trust and respect of its clients.

An assortment of undercover intelligence operations were mounted in Djibouti, French Guiana, Senegal, Beirut, Zaire, Chad, the Pacific Island of New Caledonia and many others. Most involved intelligence gathering against political insurgents, terrorists or drug smugglers. The company's golden rule was that, whenever appropriate, IAP's presence should have the approval of that country's government. If ever an assignment appeared dubious, unofficial sanction was sought from either the British or French governments. So far, D'Arcy was thankful to recount, those interests had not yet conflicted.

As the pungent aroma of fresh coffee permeated the living quarters, D'Arcy considered their biggest current problem. That was the recruitment of 'sea-marshals' to advise on shipping protection, especially in the Gulf. Demand for experienced personnel far outstripped supply, and competition for recruitment was fierce with rival UK companies. Their efforts to organise a separate Marine Protection Division looked like being an ongoing uphill struggle . . .

The sudden hoot of a car horn outside heralded the arrival of Dave Forbes.

D'Arcy checked at the window, then pressed the admittance switch to open the automatic gates below that led into the old warehouse loading yard that now served as the company car park.

Chantal joined him in the kitchen, swaddled in a white terry towelling robe. "I'll finish getting the breakfast, Rober'," she offered with a smile. "You start your meeting and I will bring it down."

Thanking her with a quick kiss he descended the stairs to the first floor which housed half-a-dozen partitioned executive offices and interview rooms, an open-plan secretarial area, and the ops room.

It was here that Dave Forbes ruled supreme, enthroned behind a vast Neville Johnson desk, and a guard-of-honour formed by computer VDUs on one flank and a bank of telephones on the other.

Before him stretched the conference table, each place marked by a fresh writing pad and neatly sharpened pencil.

A soft beige leather settee and coffee table were set aside for more informal conversations, whilst behind security drapes the entire far wall was covered by a giant map of the world. Various coloured pins marked the deployment of IAP personnel. Above the map was a succession of clock faces denoting the time of day at major capital cities in the different time zones.

'A glorified travel agent's' was how D'Arcy had unkindly described Forbes's grandiose design. Typically unmoved, the veteran ex-SAS sergeant had replied gruffly: "Well you asked for the most sodding efficient and modern nerve centre, boss, and that's what you've got." Then with a typically evil grin, he'd added: "And you've got my resignation, too, if you don't like it."

And that was even before he'd been officially hired. Chantal had rushed to Forbes's defence, and had won a friend for life. D'Arcy could hardly disagree with one of France's most highly regarded young interior designers.

The head-hunting of Dave Forbes was the best move he'd yet made, although he'd never admit it to the man's face. Forbes had been poached from a rival security company at a time when the infant IAP was in chaos.

Work had been flooding in at such a pace that it threatened to swamp the overstretched staff and put the entire operation in jeopardy. This had resulted in a neglect of paperwork by those more used to working at the sharp end. And while no assignment was badly handled, stupid mistakes and oversights did occur.

"It's a question of accidents looking for somewhere to happen," had been Forbes's initial reaction of horror.

Almost from the moment he stepped through the door, peace and order began to settle over the disorganised mayhem. Within the week he had in turn poached his ex-PA from his previous firm.

'Brandy' Slade was a stunning American in her late twenties who was nicknamed after the colour of her hair. But the slim good looks and humorous approach belied a ruthless business efficiency and cunning that would have been welcomed by the chairman of any multinational. From a US military family background, she recognised the importance of paperwork, but also the necessity to streamline it for the executive staff who were essentially men of action. It never ceased to amaze D'Arcy to watch hardbitten veterans fall over themselves to comply with her wishes. Brandy Slade was enough to make the most overgrown of men weep in their beer. Yet she did it all with a laugh and a smile, and they loved her to a man. At last, even invoices were going out on time.

"Morning, boss," Forbes greeted, swinging awkwardly through the security door. The remaining stump of the leg he had lost on his last mission for 22 SAS was causing him increasing discomfort as he grew older.

D'Arcy sat on the edge of the desk. "Thanks for coming in so early, Dave."

Forbes grunted and dumped himself in his swivelling leather throne. "Beat the bloody sparrows up this morning. Hope there's a brew on."

"Chantal's doing the business."

Forbes grinned lasciviously and ran a finger over his heavy Zappa moustache. "She's over? Worth getting up after all. Migrating birds from Paris – it must be summer."

D'Arcy laughed. "Hardly migrating, Dave. She's only here for three days – as usual."

For a moment the operations manager's eyes became serious. "You want to ring that little bird, boss, if you don't mind me saying. Before she flies away. It's a big wicked world out there."

"Mind your own business. Talking of which, let's get this review meeting on the road."

Forbes smiled sweetly to show he didn't appreciate the rebuke, and punched up the VDU display nearest him. "On the general front, boss, our biggest problem remains recruitment to this new Maritime Protection Section. It's all very well to call it a Division, but the truth is we've got five bods on the payroll. Our rivals are queueing up outside the SBS and Royal Marines and throwing money at every bloke who leaves. Since the Gulf War's hotted up it's got very silly."

D'Arcy grimaced; they were in danger of losing at least two unfulfilled contracts. "Any ideas?"

"I've been talking to an old chum from the *Hubert Group* of the French Marine Commandos about recruiting some of their ex-combat swimmers." He warmed to his subject. "It strikes me, boss, that if Nadirpur Shipping is handled right, we could sell them a French-speaking 'sea-marshal' team on a regular basis."

"How's Tom Wilmot getting on with them?" D'Arcy asked. "What's he on, *Clarion Call*?"

Forbes raised his eyebrows. "That's a good point; I wish we knew. I was onto their shipping office in Monaco last night, and again they hadn't received a signal. That's four days, the last time just after *Clarion Call* left Djibouti."

"Do they seem concerned?"

"Not at all, but I am. They're very relaxed and French about it. But I'm disappointed with Tom Wilmot; I thought he was a good man."

"Tom's not the skipper," D'Arcy pointed out. "Radio

silence isn't necessarily his idea. Could just be a breakdown."

Forbes shook his head. "Not *Clarion Call*. She's up to her funnel in satcoms, radio, telex, the lot."

"What's on her manifest?"

The operations manager swung round to face a second VDU and punched some keys. "Agricultural equipment from Brazil."

D'Arcy grunted. "Possible, but bloody unlikely."

"That's why I'm not too happy about the silence." Forbes grimaced. "Mind you, if anything had happened I expect Nadirpur's office in Djibouti would have heard something."

D'Arcy nodded. "Okay, I'll phone Nadirpur in Paris later today. It's probably just a breakdown in communications from his Monaco office. As you've said before, they're a slack bunch down there. Bound to be with no chief breathing down their necks."

"*Bonjour*, Davey!" Chantal entered carrying a tray loaded with orange juice, coffee and wholemeal toast. She was still in her dressing gown.

Forbes's grin nearly split his face in half. "What a sight for sore eyes! And how's my favourite mademoiselle?" He rose in his throne to receive the welter of kisses she lavished on him.

D'Arcy knew it was a deliberate ploy to provoke him; Chantal often teased him about his jealous streak. Only Forbes could get away with such outrageous flirtation in front of him.

"I hope you realise, Chantal," D'Arcy scolded, "that I shan't get a stroke of work out of him all day now."

At that moment the trimphone warbled and Forbes picked up the handset. "IAP – oh, right. Hang on." He turned to Chantal who was pouring the coffee. "Call for you. It's still on night-line."

She shrugged. "I hope it's not business. I say only for important things. You put it through to Brandy's office, yes?"

"Sure, baby." His eyes followed the rolling motion of her hips as she sauntered towards one of the adjoining offices while he patched through the call.

D'Arcy lit a small cigar, his first of the day. "So if we pull off this diamond mine contract today, we can cope?"

"I reckon so." Forbes stabbed a finger at the screen. "I thought I'd pull Johnson's team off the Chad training course. They've more experience and they're due for a break. I'll allocate them to the diamond mines, and put a new team into Chad. Break 'em in gently."

"And isn't Buster due back soon?"

"Yeah, his mob are due in today." Again he poked the keyboard. "1200 hours at Heathrow, coming in from the Pacific. Two weeks leave." He grinned.

In unison they quoted Brandy's ubiquitous catchphrase. "After the paperwork!"

As they laughed together, Chantal reentered from the side office. Instantly D'Arcy knew something was wrong: her face was ashen.

"What is it, kitten? Trouble?"

She appeared not to hear immediately, her mind pre-occupied. "Oh, I am sorry, Rober'. There – there is a problem on my last designs. I have to get back to Paris."

"Right away?"

She smiled stiffly. "I am afraid yes."

"It's serious?"

Shrugging, she said: "It is hard to say. I must get ready now."

D'Arcy hid his disappointment. "Dave will organise your tickets." He thought the green eyes looked moist. "Chantal, you're crying?"

Her laugh was brittle, almost angry. "No, I do not cry. Just the smoke from your awful cigar. I go now."

Fifteen minutes later she had her overnight bag packed and was ready to catch the radio cab that pulled up outside.

She kissed D'Arcy quickly on the mouth. "*Chéri*, this may take some time. Maybe it will be a while before I see you again. I will ring. I love you." Another kiss and she was gone.

D'Arcy resumed his review with Forbes but found his mind curiously distracted. It wasn't just that Chantal had left so suddenly. There had been a strange look in her eyes when she'd said farewell. It wasn't an expression that he recognised and yet he thought he knew her so well. He was left with a nagging feeling of unease.

Eventually he drew the meeting to a premature close; at least they had covered the most important topics.

Forbes looked at his watch. "I could have spent another hour in bed."

It was eight thirty and an hour before the diamond mine delegation was due.

The front door intercom buzzed sharply. It was too early for Brandy. Maybe Chantal had forgotten something and returned.

Forbes pushed the intercom button. "IAP. Can I help?"

"*Roy Bliss here.*" It sounded as though he had a cold.

"Who?"

"*Roy Bliss. From the Firm.*"

D'Arcy checked his surprise, and switched on the video set that transmitted from the outside security camera. There was no mistaking the fuzzy image of the man in the dishevelled raincoat who was talking uncomfortably into the intercom. A cigarette butt was squeezed between two nicotined fingers. "It's him all right."

"Century House?"

"Apparently. Presumably he's still with them."

"You don't look too pleased. Perhaps he's bringing some business."

D'Arcy's smile was tight and bitter. "Well, it won't be a social call, but then it's hardly likely to be a contract either."

"*Hello, can you hear me?*" Bliss squeaked irritably. "*I'd like to see Major D'Arcy.*"

D'Arcy nodded.

Forbes said: 'Okay, Mr Bliss, I'll come and let you in."

He switched off the intercom and stood up. "You sure you want to see this guy?"

"No, but I'd better. We used to be on good terms until that business of my resignation from the Regiment."

"Oh, that." Forbes clearly knew all about it, but had never asked questions. "That explains a lot."

Minutes later Bliss was shown into the operations room. The man was much the same as D'Arcy remembered him. The ginger hair was more salt than pepper and thinning noticeably, and the alcohol veins in his florid cheeks more pronounced. His eyes were still as hard and grey as slate. The worn brown suit beneath the grubby mackintosh could have been the same one he'd been wearing when they last met.

"Hello, Rob." He kept his hands in his pockets, his only acknowledgement a slight inclination of the head. His eyes were wary, unsure of the welcome he would receive. A wan smile came to the thin lips. "You're looking fit."

D'Arcy eyed him suspiciously. "You look pretty much the same."

Bliss shrugged, and the smile deepened a fraction. At least D'Arcy hadn't bitten his head off. "Nothing much changes, Rob, you know. Life grinds on." He looked around, taking in the mass of high technology equipment, the modern, luxurious and efficient-looking furnishings. D'Arcy could almost hear the pounds sign ringing up in his mind. "Looks like you're doing all right for yourself. Could do with some of this kit down at Century."

"I'm making a living," D'Arcy replied flatly. "No thanks to you."

"Ah." Bliss's smile had trouble staying in place. "Sorry about all that, pal. Just doing what I was told, you know how it is. I put up a good case in your defence, believe me."

"Thanks." Coldly.

"My chief wouldn't have any of it though. Still, it looks like the Regiment got the last laugh, eh?"

"Meaning?"

"*Major* D'Arcy." The smile began to falter under the strain. "Sounds good. Suits you. Befitting."

D'Arcy sighed. "This is Civvy Street, Mr Bliss. And I think by being blacklisted by your people could be taken as the last laugh, don't you?"

Bliss waved at his surroundings. "*This* is blacklisting? Wouldn't mind someone blacklisting me."

D'Arcy's patience was wearing thin. "What do you want, Bliss?"

The man sensed that the small talk was not going to achieve anything. His smile melted and he looked more natural without the strain of trying to maintain it. "A word, pal. A private word." His eyes darted in the direction of Forbes who was now busying himself at his desk.

"Dave and I don't have secrets, Mr Bliss."

"Roy." The smile bubbled up again before he could stop it. "Call me Roy. And I really do think this should be between the two of us."

Forbes looked up from his papers. "Why don't you use the small interview room, boss. I'll bring some coffee in."

D'Arcy nodded. "All right, Dave. But Mr Bliss won't be staying long enough for coffee."

He led the way past the conference table to a small partitioned office. It was sparsely furnished with two cream leather easy chairs and a low table.

As D'Arcy shut the door, Bliss reached into his pocket. "Mind if I smoke? Can't seem to give the bastard up."

"Go ahead."

They sat down and D'Arcy waited while the man fumbled with damp matches and decided how to begin. In the end Bliss decided on the direct approach. Abruptly he said: "You've a client, Nadirpur Shipping – Paris and Monaco."

"Is that a question or a statement?"

Bliss drew thirstily on his cigarette, exhaled, then looked down at it with distaste. "A Paris-based operation which actually runs out of Monaco for tax benefits and so forth. The sole owner is a wealthy Iranian. Nader Nadirpur. Fifty years old, effete, and lives on avenue Foch. Fond of cats and collects porcelain."

"I don't discuss my clients."

" 'Course you don't, pal. But I've no such qualms. Your client Nadirpur became part of the *nouveau riche* under the Shah in the seventies. Got out at the start of the Islamic Revolution, settled in Paris and invested his fortunes in freight shipping. Currently owns three ships including *Clarion Call*."

What had started as anger at questions about one of his clients turned instantly to alarm at what was about to be said next. Bliss read the signs. "No, pal, the news isn't good. Your client is running arms into Islamic Iran."

"Agricultural machinery," D'Arcy corrected.

It was Bliss's turn to become angry. He leaned forward, his words coming out in a hissing stream. "Don't piss about with me, pal. If you didn't know it, Brazil is one of the biggest arms suppliers in the Gulf War – to both sides!"

"So what?" D'Arcy retorted. "You name a Western country that isn't supplying at least one side. Both countries are fighting a bloody war, for all the good it might do them, and both obviously need spare parts to keep their forces from grinding to a halt. I'm merely hired by Nadirpur, at the insistence of Lloyd's, to protect his ships in whatever way possible. If the manifest says agricultural machinery parts, it is not up to me or my company to question it."

Bliss drew back under the onslaught. He studied D'Arcy carefully for a moment. "You've changed, pal."

"And whose fault is that?"

The SIS man lit a fresh cigarette off the butt of the first. "Do you remember Sabbah? And the *Pessarane Behesht*?"

The breath caught in D'Arcy's throat. "I could hardly forget."

Quietly Bliss said: "And if I said your client Nadirpur was dealing directly with the *Pessarane Behesht*?"

D'Arcy frowned. "Meaning what exactly?"

Bliss smiled and this time it appeared genuine. "That's

70

what my people would like to know. As you're aware, things are very confused in Iran. It is often impossible to distinguish between the government and the various terrorist organisations it's spawned. In this case it no doubt suits Teheran to do deals for arms unofficially through outfits like the *Pessarane Behesht*. It's not the arms as such that worries us."

"Then what is it you want?"

Bliss said: "We want Sabbah. And we want him dead."

D'Arcy almost choked at the melodramatic statement. "Good for you. Do invite me to the funeral."

"Your client is dealing with the *Pessarane Behesht*. It's an ideal opportunity to find out what's going on. Keep your ear to the ground. Find out Sabbah's location. A place and a date, that's all we need. Then we'll take him out."

"Who is this 'we'?"

"Sabbah's made enemies in just about every Western and Arab country, barring Libya and Syria."

"I'm not interested. Nadirpur is my client and pays my bills."

"And what about your old friends in the Army? Have you forgotten them so soon? It's arms supplied through Libya by the *Pessarane Behesht* that's blowing up young squaddies in Ulster now, pal. That arms shipment we were trying to locate when Tashakkur got topped was only the first. You heard about the *Eksund*. Okay, we stopped that shipment, but there've been plenty of others that we haven't. A great bloody stockpile hidden in bunkers until the time is right. Not to mention supplying other Iranian terrorist cells throughout Europe. Think on that, pal!"

D'Arcy's anger flared. "It *used* to be my job to think about that, remember? 2IC of CRW at Hereford. Now my sole concern is for my clients."

A sudden expression of concern flickered in Bliss's eyes. "I don't think we want to alert Mr Nadirpur to this conversation, Rob."

"Don't you?"

"It would be very unwise . . ." He hesitated, then gestured around the small room. "I mean, it would be such a shame to put all this in jeopardy."

"Is that a threat?"

Bliss blew a near-perfect smoke ring. "Organisations like yours, Rob, do not exist without the tacit approval of the government of the day. If Century House had a mind, they could make life very difficult. And my chief can be very vindictive, as you will recall."

D'Arcy shook his head in disbelief. God, could he really be hearing this? Memories of those nightmare days after he first left the Army crowded in on him.

"Listen, pal, I'll tell you something." Bliss lowered his voice conspiratorially. "My chief isn't too fond of you SAS blokes – too many awkward questions for his liking. So when he learned you'd left with rank of major he was bloody furious. It was as good as the CO signalling to all concerned that he disagreed with my chief. So he put the word out, blocking your chances with any ex-Regiment security outfits. Pure malice."

"So it wasn't my imagination?"

"It wasn't a popular move in the department. I didn't agree with it and neither did anyone else who'd ever worked with you." Bliss stubbed out the remaining shred of his cigarette. "So I let a decent period elapse, then got in contact with Roquelaure. Put him in the picture and suggested the two of you might like to think about working together. At the time there was no future for you in Britain."

D'Arcy was incredulous. "You did that?"

Bliss laughed uneasily. "I do have a decent side to my personality."

"Your chief didn't mind me linking with Roquelaure?"

"He wasn't too chuffed, but there wasn't much he could do. London and Paris have been exchanging love letters in recent years – he wouldn't want to be seen as the one to upset the romance. Roquelaure's a pretty powerful man across the Channel."

"Seems like I owe you an apology."

"Not necessary, pal," Bliss replied with a dismissive wave of his hand. "I only told you, so you don't get the idea everyone in SIS is against you. Don't let it colour your judgement over this request on Nadirpur."

D'Arcy looked at his watch. The diamond mine delegation would be arriving shortly. "Look, I appreciate what you did, Roy, but things have moved on. As I said earlier, my clients' interests must come first. But if anyone's got anything on Nadirpur's connections with the *Pessarane Behesht*, it'll be Roquelaure. I'll mention it to him."

Bliss shook his head vigorously. "This is a British show. Roquelaure is in too deep with the French, and their views on terrorism don't always coincide with ours."

"Roquelaure happens to be my partner, Roy."

The SIS man tapped the side of his nose with a nicotine-stained finger. "A word from the wise, pal, don't always let the right know what your left is doing, especially when you're dealing with the French. Keep a little something in reserve for yourself."

"What are you suggesting?"

Bliss shrugged. "That Roquelaure is using you because it suits him and his government. Step out of line, or rock the boat, and he'll drop you in it from a great height without a second thought. Keep it to yourself, and just find out what you can about Sabbah." He stood up. "And don't say anything to the girl."

The scar on D'Arcy's cheek pulsed. "Are you going to explain that remark?"

"She is Roquelaure's daughter, Rob. Don't be too trusting. Maybe her infatuation with you is genuine, but maybe – just maybe – she's Roquelaure's insurance policy in case you ever step out of line."

"Do you want to walk out now, or leave head first?"

Bliss smiled nervously. "Just a thought to bear in mind. I'll be in touch."

D'Arcy threw open the door. "Don't bother."

"My chief feels he has a score to settle with you, Rob.

Don't go giving him a stick to hit you with. Think it over. I'll see myself out."

For several moments D'Arcy stared blankly at the wall, his anger seething, his mind spinning.

Forbes pushed open the door. "That was some session, boss."

"You heard?"

"I forgot the mike was on and the video rolling. You can see an action replay later."

"When are those diamond people due to leave this afternoon?"

"Around four, I guess."

"I want to be on the next flight out to Paris."

*My name is Philippe Chaumont.*

*I remind myself of this every day because I have not heard my name for three years. For it is three years since my car was stopped one bright, sunny morning as I was driving to my embassy in Beirut.*

*I say three years, but it may be more. It may be less. But I have experienced three long cold seasons in this cellar. Three winters. You wouldn't imagine winters in the Lebanon to be cold, but they are. They are cold in this cellar. Even in summer it is cold in this cellar. In winter it is damp as well. You get to tell the difference. Even when you are blind.*

*I am, to all intents and purposes, blind.*

*There is no window, no light in this place. And whenever a guard comes I am to put on my blindfold.*

*On one occasion my self-appointed barber carelessly pushed the cloth too high. But all I saw was sharp white light. It felt like a screwdriver gouging into my eyeball, yet I imagine it was only the illumination of a lantern. I wonder,* if I am ever freed, if I will ever see again. Will my eyes still work? Muscles waste if you do not use them. Sometimes I think I can feel my eyes, unused, festering and rotting in their sockets.

And I might as well be deaf. There are few sounds to be heard in my cellar. Water gurgles in the old pipes to which I am chained. At night there are scratching sounds. I imagine it to be the noise of rats. Sometimes they rattle the tin bowl on the floor, searching for scraps I have missed. I do not fear them, not even mind them. They are my friends. Sometimes I think that most in the world I should like to be able to see them. Scurrying about, free.

My guards have rarely talked to me since my interrogation. Not one word, except to give abrupt orders like "Sit", or "Stand" or "Come". In the early days I tried to converse with them – to say anything, but they remained silent.

When I first arrived at this building I heard the words "God is great" and "Long live the Pessarane Behesht". I understand Arabic and Farsi quite well, thanks to my language courses as a junior diplomat. I think Pessarane Behesht means "Children of Heaven", or "Sons of Paradise". Is it these people who hold me?

I believe in God.

I never used to believe in God. Now I do. And I know that my captors cannot be of His kingdom. Whichever paradise they come from, it is not His. It is not mine.

My God is love and purity and strength. My God has filled me with His power. Sometimes, as I lie still, half in the realm of sleep, I imagine that my body is hollow, made of glass. And I feel it filling slowly with a glowing golden liquid. Slowly pouring down my limbs, until it swirls around my torso, my chest and fills my head. I feel such joy then. Because I know that nothing can hurt me. Because inside me there is nothing to hurt. No bones, no nerves, no sinew. Neither flesh nor blood. Just golden liquid which cannot be hurt. All that can be done, finally, is for them to smash the hollow glass mould of my body. And if they do that the liquid will escape and I will be free.

*So I no longer feel the pain that I did when they first asked their questions. I suppose that was when I first reached out for God. He answered me and blessed me with the enjoyment of pain, so that every turn of the screw, every searing probe of burning iron brought me closer to ecstasy. Until they left me alone in my dark, silent womb. I was safe there within the Virgin Mary. She protects me here, no one can touch me now.*

*Sometimes I have friends for tea.*

*Father came yesterday. He is such a lovely man. We didn't talk much when I was a child, but since my teens I suppose you could say he has really been my best friend. We laugh and joke together, and put the world to rights. The only sad thing is that as he gets older he is afraid of dying. He lets it slip occasionally. I tell him it is not something to worry about. He will be able to meet my dear mother again.*

*Maybe she'll come to visit next week.*

*Not this week. I like to space out these special treats. Then I can spend a few days looking forward to it, planning, and afterwards recall everything we said.*

*And this week it is Chantal. Tomorrow I expect. She's my fiancée. She doesn't like it here, she finds it upsetting. So I shall go to her. We'll meet in the château rose garden, we both like it there.*

*We'll laugh and kiss, and drink wine from a picnic hamper. But we won't make love. No, that's one thing we mustn't do. That would be foolish, do you see?*

*There's a noise. I can hear the key turn. So I tie up my blindfold.*

*There are two of them. I can smell body odour. They are pulling me to my feet. And, God, they're releasing the padlock.*

*I can hardly stand, there can be no muscles left in my legs. But it doesn't matter because they are carrying me at the elbows, propelling me up the steps. Suddenly my senses are assailed from every direction. The noise is what I hear most, so loud. Everywhere people are talking, traffic sounds* are ringing in my ears. I smell fresh-baked bread and fumes from cars.

And, joy of joys, there is a slight lightening of the darkness within my blindfold, and I can feel the warmth of the sun on my skin.

I put my hands out in front of me, groping as a blind man must. My fingers touch the rough wood, a splinter pierces my flesh. I feel around its shape.

Emotions race through me, excitement and fear, not knowing which should be right.

My tongue speaks as I recognise the shape beneath my hands. "A coffin."

It is time for my glass body to be shattered.

A voice says: "It's the safest way for you to travel. Get in, Philippe Chaumont. You are going home."

My mind is stunned as I climb in. I should be full of fear. But, as I listen to the hammers nailing on the lid, I can think of only one thing.

He called me by name.

My name is Philippe Chaumont.

# 3

The machine gun spat death under the throbbing Persian sun.

Its bullets sang inches above his head so that he was forced to eat dirt as he crawled beneath the criss-cross pattern of barbed wire on the training run, pressing himself against the dusty yellow earth.

Sweat ran from him in rivulets, gathering in his armpits and along his back until his drill shirt stuck to him like a second skin. The salt stung his eyes so he could hardly see, the blue bandanna of the *Pessarane Behesht* failing to staunch the flow of perspiration from his scalp.

Yet Jalal Shamlou was hardly aware of the discomfort. He felt only elation that he would be first across the training run. That by coming first he would shut the fat mouth of the training sergeant. That he would vindicate the faith that Sabbah himself had in him. That he would fulfil his promise to Allah and his mother to become the greatest soldier the Imam's army had ever known.

Jalal Shamlou would avenge the death of his older brother who had been mown down on the swampy banks of the Shatt-al-Arab by Iraqi artillery. He would avenge his father's death at the hands of the Shah's SAVAK secret police. He would avenge the humiliation of his mother whose poverty had forced her to scrub on her hands and knees for the wealthy bourgeoisie.

Euphoria pulsed through his veins as each agonising, twisting movement of the crawl brought him nearer to the end of the run. Every muscle screamed as he forced himself on, digging his elbows into stony ground to haul himself forward, the carbine cradled across his forearms.

Shamlou gradually became aware of heavy, laboured breathing joining his own. A harmony of matching gasps.

He turned his head, cursing in anger and frustration.

Darvish Hamman was gaining on him. The bulk of the man was moving with the easy agility of a lizard. Solid square shoulders powered him effortlessly along. Gaining ground after a slow start. The jaw of the hard, grimed face was determined, the gimlet eyes fixed on the objective.

Renewing his effort Shamlou wriggled on, harder and faster now, becoming careless and lifting his body too high. The machine gun rattled again and he felt the breath of its bullets in his hair. He had reached his limit and he knew it. He could feel the strength seeping from his tortured muscles.

Inexorably Hamman drew level. Shamlou tried to hold him, matching movement for movement. But he did not have the endurance, the sheer willpower of the older man. Dust from the thrusting boots choked him, blurring his vision as Hamman eased ahead. He could feel the grit beneath his eyelids.

Then he could see again. It was the end of the training run, and Shamlou was up and sprinting, clear of the barbed wire and running the gauntlet of thunder flashes on the straight before the finish.

He summoned one last surge of power, tripped and fell over the line, Hamman crossing it just inches ahead of him.

Gulping breath down his parched throat Shamlou rolled onto his back and watched as the rest of the *Pessarane Behesht* cleared the wire and began their final run. He had done it. He had beaten them all. All that was except Hamman. Always Hamman.

"Well done." He felt the rough hand of congratulation on his shoulder. The voice was hardly out of breath.

Shamlou shrugged away the hand, ungraciously. "*Allah*

*akbar*," he murmured, knowing the words would irritate his rival.

For although Hamman had never said, Shamlou knew he hated expressions of spiritual awareness. Knew he hated the mullahs. Knew he hated the Imam and the new order he had created with the Islamic Revolution. Knew he hated him.

Shamlou knew all these things, and could prove none of them. The Sabbah instructor sergeant knew, too, but he was also unable to prove anything. At least he had the consolation of being able to goad and insult Hamman with impunity, the way that sergeants the world over do. Insult his middle-class parentage, insult his background of wealth and privilege, insult the regular forces from which he came, insult his manhood.

But today the shadow of the sergeant was cast over Shamlou.

"You insult Allah. You allow a man old enough to be your father to beat you. Is this how you repay Sabbah's faith in you? I have a good mind to put you in the women's camp; there you might stand a chance." The intimidating bulk of the sergeant stood between him and the sun, gloating over the panting youngster. Enjoying his humiliation, his shame.

"The boy did well." The voice belonged to Hamman.

Of all people, Shamlou did not want his support.

The sergeant turned to Hamman. "Shut your face, *taghouti*. I am not talking to you."

"Leave the boy alone."

The sergeant's rough olive complexion paled with indignation, then a sneer of rotten teeth broke across his face. "Well, well, *taghouti*, what have we here? You seem to have become very fond of this girlish fellow."

He reached down to Shamlou's mop of sweat-slicked hair, grabbed it in his fist and twisted the young man's head until he faced the sun. The skin was smooth, marred only by an immature moustache above the upper lip. The eyes were dark and beautiful with long black lashes. "Yes, I can see what you find so attractive."

"I said, Sergeant, leave the boy alone."

Hamman had drawn himself to his full height. Even then he remained shorter than the overweight sergeant by several inches. Yet to the group of panting young *Pessarane Behesht* who had begun to take an interest in the confrontation, Hamman still made an imposing figure. What he lacked in stature was compensated by the solid set of shoulders, and his calm self-assurance.

The sergeant jutted his face and glared into the other's eyes. Then, when Hamman did not flinch, he pulled slowly back.

"Are you threatening me?" the sergeant demanded, pronouncing each word with care.

"I do not need to threaten you, Sergeant. I am a captain in special forces."

A sneer returned to the other man's face. "In the *Pessarane Behesht* you are nothing."

The group of recruits drew closer, intrigued. No one had ever challenged the sergeant before. Never like this.

Hamman said slowly: "And where have you fought on the front, Sergeant?"

The instructor swallowed hard, pushed out his barrel chest. "I have done my duty to Allah and the Imam, have no fear of that."

Slowly Hamman eased the blue bandanna from his shaven head and dropped it to the ground. "Leave the boy alone, Sergeant. If you are so good yourself, with so much battle experience, then you will race against me down the training run. Without rank. Man to man."

A gasp went up from the gathered knot of onlookers. All eyes turned expectantly on the sergeant.

"This – this is a ridiculous situation." The voice quavered. "And it is gross insubordination –"

Hamman's eyes glittered. "Then why don't you give the boy the praise he is due?"

The eyes of the sergeant tore themselves away from Hamman, and glanced down at Shamlou. "You have done well, boy. Sabbah will be proud of . . ."

The words seemed to stick in his throat. He turned abruptly on his heel and marched away, the crowd silently pulling back to let him pass.

Hamman helped Shamlou to his feet. The young man looked curiously into the older man's eyes, seeking, not understanding.

"We do not choose each other, boy," Hamman said quietly. "But we share a billet. Like it or not we are comrades-in-arms."

Shamlou nodded, confused by his feelings of gratitude and anger that this well-bred *taghouti* should have come to his defence. He turned and walked away, the crowd of his young *Pessarane Behesht* friends closing in to congratulate him for coming second in the training run. For to them he was the victor. Because Hamman was a *taghouti*, and he didn't count.

Hamman watched as the young men shuffled off towards the camp. Wearily he picked up his blue bandanna from the dust. A grim smile flickered at his lips as he stuffed it into the pocket of his fatigues and followed the others at a distance.

From the shadow of the mouth of the umpire's tent three men watched.

One was slightly taller, slightly older than the other two and was bearded. All three wore Polaroid sunglasses that reflected the returning group of *Pessarane Behesht*, and the solitary straggler.

"They are beginning to emerge," the bearded one said. "Our best prospects are starting to show themselves."

"Did you see the way Hamman stood up to the sergeant?" the youngest said.

"The sergeant is a fool," the bearded one replied.

The third man added: "He is denting Shamlou's confidence. That is a shame, for he is doing well. He, out of all of them, would do our will. Sacrifice himself."

"Then we must restore his confidence," the bearded one said. "He has found new support amongst his brothers.

Even Hamman. It is time to let him know that he is amongst the chosen."

"Why did you come to my help back there?"

They were alone now in the rough mud-brick billet. Each lay on a crude canvas cot, thankful for the cool shade.

"Why shouldn't I?"

Shamlou cautiously accepted the hand-rolled cigarette that was offered. "You do not like me."

Hamman almost smiled. "Have I ever said that?"

The young man felt the rasp of the coarse tobacco at the back of his throat. "You have not put it into words."

The evening sun shafted through the deep-set windows and Hamman studied the smoke as it drifted through the golden beam. "I am a professional, boy. A professional of the special forces. I am your comrade-in-arms. One day I may fight alongside you. You don't want to fight alongside a man who hates you."

"You fought for the Shah," Shamlou reminded darkly.

"No, I served Persia under the Shah. Now I serve Persia under the Imam."

Shamlou sat on the edge of the cot and studied his feet. He chose his words with care. "They say you changed allegiance to save yourself. That really you hate the Imam and the Revolution."

"Who says these things?"

"My friends."

"Then you should choose your friends more carefully."

"The sergeant says it, too."

Hamman turned to face the young man. "I doubt that the sergeant has ever seen a shot fired in anger. You have seen more action at the front than he has. As for me, I am a professional. I command Boghammars out of Bandar Abbas and I have a team of combat swimmers. All professionals; for a long time there was not one Revolutionary Guard amongst us. We had all trained with the Americans and the British at the time of the Shah. We are the best.

83

Your precious Imam needs us as much as Persia does itself. If the professionals hadn't been driven out or shot by the revolutionaries, then we would not be losing this war with Iraq now."

"We cannot lose the war," Shamlou retorted. "We fight in the name of Allah and the Imam Khomeini! It will be His victory."

Hamman stiffened. "Next you'll be talking about immortality."

Shamlou leaned forward, trying to reach his new-found friend, to explain things the older man did not understand. "Do you not realise, Darvish, that to die for the Revolution is the greatest thing we can do as mere mortals on this earth? At the hands of our country's enemies and the enemies of Allah. Immortality begins only after our death. What we can expect hereafter depends on how we live our lives now! Do you not see? To die in this war on earth ensures our immortality! Is it not better to die ten times only to come back to life to be killed again and again! In the name of Allah, Darvish! *Allah akbar*!"

Hamman was unmoved. "Save your talk of martyrdom for your young friends, boy. As a professional I can tell you that no war has ever been won by dying for Allah or anyone else. Wars are won by killing your enemies. Let them be the martyrs."

Shamlou pulled back in disgust. "You blaspheme."

"I speak the truth. Look, boy, look." He rolled up the cuff of his fatigue shirt to reveal the tattooed script above his right wrist: *To God and Yourself be True*. "Remember that. I am not a cleric, I can speak only of what I know. I simply do my best to run my life in accordance with the Holy Koran. I try, but I am only human, and sometimes I fail. But I try. No man can do more."

Shamlou shook his head in despair. He recognised that this man was good, wanted to reach him, save him, didn't know how.

The duty cook interrupted them, a big jovial man from Isfahan. He carried two tin mugs of tea. As members of the *Pessarane Behesht*, they received this special privilege.

"Well done, Shamlou." Reluctantly the duty cook turned to Hamman. "And you, too. Everyone talks about you being first today. And how you both put the sergeant in his place."

Shamlou grinned widely, took the mug and watched as the man left.

"There is tomorrow," Hamman said. He eased off his boots and raised his feet onto the cot. "Get some sleep now. Tomorrow will be harder than today."

Still glowing with inner pride, Shamlou swallowed down the tea and fell back on his pillow. Yes, today had been a good day. One of the best since the day he had been selected from the fighting Revolutionary Guards at the front by the mullah with the gold tooth. Chosen for his faith and his proven fearlessness in battle.

He recalled his arrival at the camp near Busheir three months before. Battered single-decker buses had disgorged their load of bewildered recruits. They had been drawn from a mixture of Revolutionary Guards, regular armed forces and *Basijis* peasant volunteer units to attend the camp for the chosen. There had been around a hundred of them, each selected because of acts of bravery, religious dedication or because, like Hamman, they had very special skills.

They had been shown a herd of goats by the sergeant, who had instructed the bemused young fighters to wade in and capture one animal each and fit it with a collar and lead. The scene that followed was hilarious bedlam that produced side-splitting laughter as battle-hardened veterans tried in turns to coax, threaten and chase the jittery beasts who had no mind to co-operate. But the moment of innocent farce was shortly to become an unnerving black comedy.

For the first two weeks of basic retraining each *Pessarane Behesht* recruit was to feed and muck out his charge, groom and milk if necessary. In those dark days of torturous physical training, great bonds of affection were formed between men and beasts. Pet names were given as the dumb goats listened to the endless moans about the training staff and their sadistic ways.

Then, one evening, the men and their goats were called to gather on the drill square where a huge fire of logs burned fitfully in the centre. There the sergeant instructor announced that each man should take his combat knife, slice the throat of his goat and drink a cupful of its still life-warm blood.

Shamlou tossed and twisted on the edge of sleep. Remembered the eerie dancing shadows of the fire that night, the sweat on the faces, the squeal of dying animals. The sickly sweet smell of fresh blood. Chins running with vermilion, the sound of retching and the exultant cries of *Allah akbar*!

The night of the martyrdom of the goats had stained Shamlou's mind and haunted his dreams ever since. The deliberate act of brutalisation had disturbed many of his comrades, too. One had said it was like a scene from Dante's *Inferno*, but Shamlou could only guess what he meant.

Few of the first recruits survived the initial four weeks of training. You never knew when someone was rejected from the course until after it had happened. One night a cot would be empty, the recruit gone. No one knew where; no one dared ask.

The cadres had been separated then into different courses run by instructors from Pakistan, Libya, North Korea, Palestine and South Yemen.

Although from peasant stock, Shamlou had received a good education and was selected for a specialist course. It was entitled 'Kidnap and Hostage Operations against Enemies of Islam' and was run by Shi'ite instructors from Lebanon. The course was exhaustive and exhaustingly complex, beginning with the history and origins of kidnap and finishing with a detailed examination of modern case histories. It covered moves and countermoves in negotiation for ransom or the release of prisoners, kidnap and evasion techniques, attitudes and *modus operandi* of all police forces in Western countries.

Hamman had been on a separate course on both air and sea hijack procedures.

As sleep finally came a confusion of scenes from the past weeks tumbled through Shamlou's troubled dreams. They became more and more disturbed until he found himself wrestling against unseen hands. Cruelly vivid images of the night of the martyrdom of the goats returned. And then he felt as though he had been lifted, transported on ether through time and space itself. Curiously weightless. The cool of evening streamed over his hot, delirious body, caressing his naked skin.

Then, slowly, a sense of peace settled over him. As though he lay in deep, soft cushions of swansdown. The unfamiliar feel of satin was against his flesh.

Although drowsing in a semisoporific state, his senses were heightened to such a pitch that he wondered if he were hallucinating. The sparkling fragrance of frangipani filled his nostrils, but he also detected the musky odour of burning incense. Sounds in his ears were as clear as crystal. Water gurgling and splashing against the gentle background fluttering of a reed flute and the vibrating strings of a lyre. Voices he heard too, whispering and laughing softly.

Torment ebbed away from him. He stretched his body like a cat, enjoying the cool satin on his naked skin, shifted his legs languidly.

Then, in his dream, he heard her voice. It can have been no more than a few paces from him. A soft, full voice that read the words in little more than a whisper. "Sit near my tomb, and bring wine and music – Feeling thy presence, I shall come out of my sepulchre – Rise, softly moving creature, and let me contemplate thy beauty."

He recognised the words of Hafez; he loved poetry like all Persians. Had heard them spoken many times, never before with such sweet meaning.

He didn't want to look, didn't want to see, wanted to

see more than anything in the world, feared what he might see.

His vision was misty, yet the colours were vivid and rich, almost glowing in intensity in the hazy, flickering glow of the brass oil lamps. They were stationed around the white walls of the garden, casting soft shadows amongst the rose bushes and beyond the arched cloisters across the lily pond. Above him stretched the endless sky of aquamarine velvet, clusters of stars hanging like silver grapes. The night air against his naked body was warm and dry.

He was aware of others there, too, but he could not determine who or where. Beneath the pavilion arches stood young attendants, bare-chested and turbaned, looking straight ahead, expressions of serenity on their flawless faces.

Soft female laughter. His eyes wandered across the jade marble floor, scattered with silk Kashan carpets, to a shadowy alcove. Determined the gleam of light contouring the naked shapes. Felt passion, animal and unrestrained, swell in his loins.

"Shamlou."

His eyes moved, lazily, hardly under his control. Saw her, felt the surge of blood within him. Full of awe and wonder.

She sat on the mosaic parapet of the fountain. A gossamer robe cascaded in long flowing lines from her shoulders onto which the raven's wing hair peeped from beneath an ivory silk *hejab*. She held the headdress across her face with her teeth so that only her eyes could be seen. Her eyes watching him. Dark, wide eyes full of provocation and gentle mischief.

Strangely he felt no shame at his nakedness, made no attempt to cover himself. Just watched the woman who had read the poetry, having no control over events in his dream.

Slim, olive-skinned hands closed the book of verse on her lap, placed it to one side. Again she looked at him, then let the *hejab* fall. And he saw for the first time that her skin gleamed with gold oil, individual pigments catching in the lamplight, emphasising the whiteness of her delicate smile.

She stood gracefully, allowing the gossamer robe to flutter from her shoulders, revealing a slender body that had been annointed from head to toe in glittering, perfumed oil. The light caught the smooth sculptured curves of her breasts and played along the rise of her belly and sparkled on the simple gold waist chain.

"Shamlou." That voice again, its timbre stirring his loins. "You are chosen."

The smell of her filled his being, intoxicated him, and he watched with fascination as she took the small porcelain cup by his side and dipped it into the fountain. Smiling, she pressed it to his lips and bade him drink.

It was strangely sweet. Like wine. Was wine, the fountain flowed with wine. It trickled over the edge of the cup at his lips, coursing over his thin youthful body, gathering at the root of his sex.

He shut his eyes then, knew what was to happen, felt that his loins would burst.

It was almost midday when Shamlou awoke. He had slept curled like a foetus, and now stretched awkwardly in his cot. The bright light from outside hurt his eyes as he scanned the room. To his surprise Hamman, too, lay on his cot, snoring lightly.

Why had no one disturbed them? They should have been on a course since dawn. He did not understand it.

He planted his feet on the earthen floor, feeling strangely troubled, yet strangely elated.

The dream. It had been the dream. A dream so vivid, so raw, so beautiful that it had been reality. It took a moment for him to absorb the shock of it. He, Shamlou, had had the dream. The dream of the *Pessarane Behesht*. The dream of the chosen martyrs. A glimpse of paradise.

It had been a rumour amongst the recruits from the moment they had arrived; he didn't know who started it.

Neither the sergeant nor any of the instructors had ever mentioned it. Only Sabbah himself had said to him, in a private conversation: "Shamlou, you have no doubt heard the rumour. The story of the dream of paradise. The dream of the chosen. I do not know how true it is. Some claim it is so, and I cannot disbelieve them. It is an award for their faith in Allah, I think. So I choose them above all others to carry out the will of Islam, because I know they will not fail me."

"I should like to dream that dream, Master," Shamlou had said earnestly.

The bearded one had smiled with gentle understanding. "Then I, too, hope that one day you shall. And if you do, you will know that you have been called."

Joy swept through Shamlou, and he stood from his cot and shook Hamman's sleeping form.

"*Allah akbar*! God is Great. Long live Islam. Death to the Great Satan!"

Hamman opened his eyes, instantly irritable. "Shamlou, what in the name of Allah is going on? Shut it, can't you?"

But Shamlou could not prevent the words bubbling out in an almost incoherent stream of excitement. "I am chosen, Hamman, I have been chosen to do the work of Allah. I have had the dream."

Hamman sat up, shaking his head to clear his brain. "What are you talking about?"

"I have had the dream. The dream of the martyrs."

"What?"

Shamlou could stand the older man's incomprehension no more. He must tell someone who would understand. He pulled out a fresh set of fatigues from the locker, talking as he dressed hurriedly. "It was paradise, I tell you. Music and scented flowers in a garden of indescribable enchantment, Darvish. And a woman so beautiful, so loving . . ." He swooned at the recollection. "The things we did together, I cannot tell you. Even the water of the fountain turned to wine."

Hamman fell back against his pillow in silence. He was deeply disturbed.

When Shamlou left to pass on his good tidings the old soldier stood and stretched, and stared thoughtfully out into the harsh daylight beyond the window.

He had said nothing to young Shamlou. But he, too, had had the dream.

As he lit his first cigarette of the day he looked down at his hands. They were trembling.

A chink of light in the run-out aperture of the anchor chain, high above his head, told Tom Wilmot that dawn had arrived.

That meant that he had been isolated in the chain locker in *Clarion Call*'s bows for between eight and nine hours. It felt like as many years.

The raiders had been smart, he had to give them that. They had been ruthlessly efficient without ever resorting to unnecessary violence. Always professional, always in control. Although, he recalled bitterly, that wasn't difficult when the skipper of the pirated vessel was on your side.

Bloody Dimitrios Mános!

Was this the Greek's bloody retirement pension plan, the deal to which he referred? Some insurance scam no doubt. To allow him to spend the rest of his days getting under his wife's feet while he pickled his brains in Pernod?

Of course, the raiders had identified Wilmot immediately. He was cut out from the herd like some troublesome old bull, and frogmarched the length of the ship to the chain locker. He'd been stripped naked and thrown an old boiler suit to put on. Anything concealed in his clothes would be found as they searched through them at their leisure. Even his shoes had been taken and replaced with plimsoles, minus laces. They'd bound his hands behind his back with plasticuff strips and done the same with his feet.

As his life didn't appear to be under immediate threat he hadn't attempted to abrade the plastic restraints on a sharp metal edge. He knew anyway that the stuff was a damned sight tougher than it looked. No, he would wait to see what happened. Wait for an opportunity. Be a good boy and hope that the raiders began to trust him. Let him out of this goddamm steel prison for a start.

If only he could be reunited with the rest of the crew he'd be in with a chance. Predictably enough they had been marshalled together in the Mess. At any rate that was what Wilmot had predicted might happen if ever *Clarion Call* were boarded. He remembered thrashing out IAP's 'preventive procedures' with D'Arcy and Dave Forbes back in London. At that time the company's Maritime Protection Section comprised, laughably, just him, Tom Wilmot.

Yet stowing a Sarbe emergency radio beacon in the crew's mess had been his recommendation. He just wished to God he'd chosen the bloody chain locker instead.

After the boarding, *Clarion Call* had fast been wound up to full revs and steamed on, apparently without change of course. Wilmot had remained alert to one or two minor variations to the helm until he eventually succumbed to a disturbed sleep in the early hours. He had been woken by the change of engine pitch and a shuddering as the ship began a series of tight manoeuvres. Then the engine was closed down abruptly and a complete and eerie silence fell. Just the creak and strain of a ship at rest and, somewhere below, the lazy slap of water against the hull.

Wilmot assumed that they'd reached their destination with still an hour to go before sunup. He had the distinct impression that everything was running to the raiders' plan.

His recollections were interrupted by the sound of feet on the deckplates outside the locker. He heard the rasp of the hatch latches as they were turned. Sunlight seared into his retinas.

"You, out." The command was quiet, but authoritative. Wilmot noted the Arabic accent, placed it as Jordanian, but wouldn't bet his life on it.

Rough hands lifted him to his feet, released the binding

92

and helped him out onto the deck. Already the sun was baking in its intensity. Through squinted vision he saw that a second raider was standing back, armed, in case an attack was made on his colleague. Again the professionalism. No cowboys these, Wilmot decided. This was a government force. Someone's government. But God knew whose.

They stood back as he stumbled along the deck towards the aft superstructure.

He took his time, using the opportunity to collect his bearings, to check the angle of the sun. *Clarion Call* was in a steep-sided inlet that might have resembled a Norwegian fjord had the towering sentinels of decaying rock not been bleached by the tropical sun. Already the highest points had melted into the heat haze.

The spot had clearly been chosen well. Lines ran ashore, hugging the ship to a narrow shelf of shingle which fell sharply away beneath the clear green water. It was more than sufficient to clear the freighter's draught. He saw raiders on the bridge and others on the shingle shelf, sorting out vast canvas sheets of camouflage material. Already some were in place, draping over the sides. He guessed that within the hour *Clarion Call* would have merged completely with the rocky sides of the inlet. Glancing towards the mouth he saw the broken rim of the *jebel* on the horizon, under a mile away, shutting off the square.

Taking account of their speed, time and angle of the sun he placed the ship's position as somewhere on the southern flank of the vast Musandam peninsula that formed the Strait of Hormuz. But *somewhere* was as close as he could get. There must be a hundred miles or more of inhospitable coastline, a confusion of high-sided bays, inlets and outcrops. Deserted, too, except for the occasional fishing village.

Perhaps a dhow might pass, but nothing more. Even a military patrol boat was unlikely. There was nothing here to protect, nothing worth protecting.

To all intents and purposes *Clarion Call* had vanished off the face of the earth.

By the time they climbed the stairwell, Wilmot had counted eight raiders, including the one who stood guard outside the crew's mess. All, he noticed, had changed from wet suits into black polo sweaters with matching denims and woollen commando skullcaps. No attempt had been made to wipe the camouflage cream from their faces. In the heat the gel had begun to run; it was as good a disguise as any.

Wilmot decided that the man who had fetched him from the chain locker was the most likely looking leader.

"Am I to be allowed to join the others?" he asked.

The black eyes above the trimmed moustache were without emotion. "Get in there."

Wilmot tried again to draw him into conversation. "How long are we to stay here?"

The leader pushed open the hatch. "No talk. Get in."

To reinforce the message he gave Wilmot a shove. Everyone looked up from around the mess table. They'd all been sitting in the fug of tobacco smoke playing cards, shooting craps or reading. No one looked particularly perturbed. Nor, Wilmot noted, particularly pleased to see him.

The only exception, perversely, was Dimitrios Mános.

He heaved his bulk out of the chair at the head of the table. "Hey, welcome, my friend. Come and join me. They allow us some fresh coffee." He turned to one row of sullen crewmen. "Move aside. Let our sea-marshal in. Poor man's been in the solitary all night."

Given the opportunity Wilmot would have chosen to have sat anywhere except next to Mános. Unfortunately, or fortunately, the captain was right next to the bench locker in which Wilmot had hidden the Sarbe emergency beacon. It was too good to miss.

He squeezed past the crew and sandwiched himself between Mános and the Gambian cook called Friday.

"I am sorry they put you up for'ard, my friend," Mános

said. His breath reeked of aniseed. "I say no, but they insist. They know you are once with the British SBS, so they take no chance. But this morning I do the insisting. I say let him join us, he will give no trouble."

"Thanks," Wilmot said without conviction. He leaned back against the cushions and shut his eyes, allowing his left hand to trail over the seat, out of sight beneath the level of the table. "And are you going to tell me what this is all about, Dimitrios?"

The broad shoulders shrugged. "A commercial hijack, my friend. It happens all the time. Today there is more piracy than a hundred years ago."

Beneath the seat, Wilmot's hand located the locker handle. "That's no excuse for you to join in."

"I tell you I need to retire. This offer is too good to turn down, and it is good because no one gets hurt. I am finished with the sea."

"And who are the raiders?"

"I do not ask. Jordanians, I think. I do not want to know."

"Jordanian commandos," Wilmot repeated, half to himself. So he had been right about the mysterious ship that had followed them all the way from the Gulf of Aquaba. His fingers released the catch and fumbled blindly inside.

Mános poured a steaming tin mug of coffee. "It is best not to ask questions. I was approached in Rio by an old friend that I trust. With him is an Arab. Very wealthy, very educated. A businessman, or maybe a diplomat. The deal is simple. I do nothing. There is a lot of money just to do nothing. Half of it is up front, lodged in an account in Athens."

"What happens to the cargo?"

A shrug.

"What is the cargo? What's in the containers?"

Another shrug. "Agricultural machinery parts. You see the manifest."

"And the crew, what happens to them?"

Mános's eyes were moist with alcohol and lack of sleep. "Nothing, we have been hijacked, that's all. We tell the truth."

"Damn!" Wilmot cursed as he upset his coffee, the scalding liquid dashing his leg, the mug disappearing beneath the table. He bent to retrieve it and used the opportunity to reach for the beacon in the locker and pull the pin.

He sat up and placed the mug back on the table. "Listen, Dimitrios, you and your crew will hardly be telling the truth, will you? I suppose they are all in on it?"

Across the table the Filipino first mate Canillo and Jayant, the Indian radio-officer, looked suitably sheepish.

"Don't be smug, my friend," Mános said, suddenly angered. "Most of these poor buggers, they work their lifetime for the pittance that owners like Nadirpur pay. There is no work in their own countries, so the only place they can go is to sea. Every month their pay goes back home for their wives and families to keep alive. Yes, my friend, they are in on this thing."

But Wilmot was only half-listening, instead he was imagining the silent signal pulsing out of the Sarbe beacon. It would be heard over hundreds of miles for up to ten hours.

"I wish I had not done this," Friday the Gambian mumbled disconsolately at Wilmot's side. "It is not right. Criminal. We will be caught."

"Probably," Wilmot said.

Mános leaned towards Friday. "Listen to me, you black bastard, you made your choice like all of us. Now we are shipmates together." His laugh was dry. " – in the same boat."

"Sink or swim together," Wilmot said. "Is that it?"

The Greek eyed him darkly. "And you, are you with us? There is a cut of ten thousand dollars in it for you. All you do is go along with the stories we tell."

Wilmot looked scathing. "I'm a sea-marshal, Dimitrios."

Mános laughed throatily. "You want to retake the ship from the commandos, eh? Maybe with Friday to help you?"

"Are you still tooled up?" Wilmot asked.

"What?"

"Armed. Do you still have that gun?"

The Greek showed his gold tooth in a demonic smile. "You think I will shoot you if you do not go along with us, eh, my friend? No, those hijackers do not take chances, even with someone on their side."

"Then there's no chance I can retake the ship, really, is there?"

"So you are with us?" Mános pressed.

Wilmot hedged good-humouredly. The Sultan of Oman's Air Force was British-trained and extremely efficient; already a pilot could be picking up the beacon signal. "I don't have much choice. It would be my word against all of you."

And, my Judas friend, Wilmot thought, either you or the commandos would make sure I didn't live to tell a different tale.

The bulkhead door burst open. In the hatchway stood the commando leader, his M16 held as though he intended to use it.

"You, Wilmot!" he shouted. "Where is it?"

"Where's what?"

The leader stepped forward and levelled the rifle at Mános. "The distress beacon. You have ten seconds to think about it and I blow out the captain's brains. One, two, three . . ."

"Okay, okay." Wilmot relented, holding up his hand. He reached down to the locker, extracted the beacon and tossed it onto the mess table.

"That was very stupid, my friend," Mános muttered.

"How did you know?" Wilmot asked.

"No questions," the leader snapped, and picked up the beacon.

Wilmot shrugged. Most probably the signal had been

97

picked up by the Jordanian's mysterious mother ship. Anyway, how they knew didn't really matter.

What mattered was that he could be in for a very long wait. And a very short life expectancy.

He wondered what his wife Pauline would make of the sudden disappearance of *Clarion Call*. Hoped she could take it, hoped she would take comfort in the child that she carried.

# 4

Paris was grey and brooding.

D'Arcy's aircraft had nosed cautiously down through the dense, sluggish cloudcover which had kept the lid firmly on the sultry atmosphere of the city for the past week.

Passengers at Charles de Gaulle Airport were hot, uncomfortable and irritable. Carrying just a handgrip, D'Arcy was able to leave them waiting for their luggage and took a taxi direct to the Champs Elysées. Every driver seemed as ill-tempered as the airline passengers he'd left behind, his own complaining that his migraine wouldn't stop until the threatened storm broke.

It was prematurely dark for the early summer evening, and many vehicles already had their lights on. The pavements were overflowing with the crowds, many of them tourists in shorts and summer shirts. He was thankful that the lightweight suit and polo shirt had been on the first hanger to hand. With humidity soaring he was already perspiring.

The anxiety didn't help. He'd been increasingly anxious ever since Roy Bliss's unwelcome visit that morning. Anxious about the veiled threats from Bliss's boss at SIS. Anxious that his client might be mixed up with a terrorist organisation. And anxious that his relationship with Chantal might not be all he thought it had been. Then there was the silence on *Clarion Call* from Nadirpur's shipping line office in Monaco.

For the umpteenth time he checked the rear window.

He scolded himself. He'd become almost paranoid since he'd talked to Bliss. He hadn't phoned Nadirpur in case Century House had a tap on the line. And he had deliberately caught his flight with just minutes to spare.

He paid the cab off on the east side of Etoile in the towering shadow of the Arc de Triomphe and took the pedestrian subway across to the west. He used the long passageways to reassure himself that no one followed, before emerging at the start of avenue Foch.

The 16th *arrondissement* is one of the most exclusive residential districts of Paris and avenue Foch is its crowning glory. A millionaires' row for the aristocracy, film stars and the kings of international business empires.

After a short walk the road widened out into an elegant, sweeping avenue with tree-shaded sliproads on either side. The windows of the five-storey buildings, with ornate wrought-iron balconies, peered down condescendingly at the passers-by, smug in their classic mantles of ivy and flowering creepers. High railings guarded the small courtyard gardens, the gates of which were usually protected by push-button security-code entry locks. The smell of wealth was as strong in the air as the fragrance of flowers from the garden borders.

Nadirpur's residence was halfway along the avenue. D'Arcy punched the intercom button and introduced himself to the disembodied Oriental voice at the other end. After a considerable delay and some confusion, he was told to wait.

Eventually one of the studded oak double doors opened and Nadirpur's Vietnamese manservant trotted down the crumbling stone steps.

The youthful face was inscrutable and unsmiling with a flawless pale bronze complexion. The suit was as unpretentious as it was expensive, carefully cut around a body that had spent a lot of time in a gymnasium.

"Mr Nadirpur invites you to meet him." Stiffly polite.

"Ahn, isn't it? We met once before." D'Arcy's smile was not reciprocated.

"I believe so. Follow me, please."

Inside was in total contrast to the pockmarked exterior. A gleaming chequered-tile floor, satin-sheen walls, a chandelier of dripping crystals and a carved mahogany staircase that was carpeted all the way to Nadirpur's apartment on the fifth floor. D'Arcy was shown into the massive hallway and through one of five adjoining doors into the living room.

Nader Nadirpur stood by the balcony window looking out over the avenue. It provided a much needed patch of light in an otherwise sombre room lit only by two silk-shaded sidelamps. That was not enough to compensate for the oppressive opulence of the dark panelling and heavy antique furniture. Only the gentle green illumination of the large tropical fishtank added serenity and prevented the room from having the atmosphere of a funeral parlour.

A cat was cradled in the arms of Nadirpur's silk Cardin dressing gown. The animal stared at the newcomer with obvious hostility. It was in marked contrast to its owner's shy smile of welcome.

"Mr D'Arcy, what a welcome surprise!"

As he stepped forward the chocolate hackles rose on the cat, its mouth drawn back in a snarl.

D'Arcy looked at it warily. "I'm sorry I couldn't telephone first."

Nadirpur appeared not to hear. Long, manicured fingers smoothed the cat's coat. "Forgive Czarina, Mr D'Arcy. She's terribly spoiled and doesn't take easily to strangers. Russian Blues are very jealous, you know." He turned to his manservant. "Please take Czarina for me, Ahn. Give her some of her favourite grilled kidneys, it may put her in better humour.'

Ahn stepped forward. The cat didn't protest, circling happily between the huge biceps, trusting them not to crush her.

"And I am sure Mr D'Arcy would like a little refreshment. I am afraid I don't keep brandy."

"You have a good memory, Mr Nadirpur. We've only met the once."

The Iranian smiled graciously. His face was unlined, belying his fifty years by at least a decade. "I only drink champagne. Maybe a glass of Krug as an excuse to celebrate?" He laughed daintily. "Or maybe, in your line of business, a Taittinger might be more appropriate – I believe it was a favourite of James Bond."

D'Arcy couldn't resist a smile. "I am only a humble security adviser, Mr Nadirpur. Very routine."

"Then we'll compromise. Bring a bottle of that Bruno Paillard, Ahn. The '79 has a delightful flavour reminiscent of almonds. Yes?"

"Fine," D'Arcy said and waited until Ahn had retreated behind the door with Czarina.

Nadirpur settled himself comfortably opposite D'Arcy on a leather padded chaise longue. "I don't imagine you make a habit of calling on your clients unannounced, however delightful it is to be in your company."

No doubt such perception had contributed to the man's wealth, D'Arcy considered, as he sought the most diplomatic way to accuse his client of dealing with a terrorist organisation. "You're right, of course, Mr Nadirpur, my visit isn't strictly social. It concerns the shipment aboard *Clarion Call*. Supposedly spare parts for agricultural machinery."

Nadirpur smiled blandly. "Quite correct."

"May I ask how you became involved in the deal?"

"A little outside your remit, isn't it, Mr D'Arcy?"

"Not necessarily. Please bear with me."

The Iranian sighed resignedly. "I was approached here in Paris by a member of the commercial section of the Iranian Embassy and asked to arrange shipment from Brazil, that's all. I expect because they trust a fellow countryman – the Iranians have had bad experiences with supplies from abroad. Payment made, but no goods delivered. That sort of thing."

D'Arcy chose his words carefully. "But, if I understand

correctly, you are not a particularly keen supporter of the Khomeini regime?"

The laugh was light. "I most certainly am not, Mr D'Arcy. But then I don't wear my heart on my sleeve. That is bad for business, particularly when Iran is desperate to import so many goods because of the war. Besides, even if I don't support the Islamic Revolution, it is still my country."

"And who supplied these goods?"

"An international trading company. Spidex International Trading. They have an office here in Paris . . ." He hesitated, a frown fracturing the porcelain brow. "But I would think you know that, they were introduced to me by your partner, General Roquelaure."

Thankfully the distraction of the door opening gave D'Arcy the opportunity to hide his surprise as Ahn carried in a silver salver and two tulip crystals filled with Bruno Paillard.

"Most kind, Ahn." Nadirpur touched the man's wrist, a small gesture of thanks. D'Arcy saw the eyes engage, the fond look momentarily brighten the manservant's emotionless face.

As Ahn withdrew, D'Arcy said: "Our company isn't usually concerned with the background to commercial deals, Mr Nadirpur. There'd be no need for General Roquelaure to mention it to us in London." He sipped at the expensive champagne and wished it had been brandy. "And the problem – if it is a problem – is on the customer side. You said the man was from the Iranian Embassy's commercial section?"

"That's what he said and I have no reason to doubt him. A Mr Azadi, I believe."

"Did you know that Mr Azadi may have connections with an Iranian terrorist organisation?"

The ticking of the carriage clock was suddenly magnified in the acute silence that followed.

A small pink tongue darted over Nadirpur's lips. "What exactly do you mean by *terrorist*? That is something that is rather difficult to define in present-day Iran. Do you mean he represents a Lebanese faction like Islamic Jihad or that he is of the *Hezbollah*, the Party of God?" Another shy smile. "*Hezbollah* are zealots, Mr D'Arcy, but no one in Teheran would call them terrorists, even if acts of terrorism have been attributed to them. I suppose Mr Azadi might belong to the *Hezbollah*."

"How about the *Pessarane Behesht*?"

This time the arrow struck home. Nadirpur swallowed hard. "Oh. Excuse me, Mr D'Arcy."

"Obviously you've heard of them."

"Who hasn't? Certainly every Iranian exile knows the name. Several murders of Shah supporters in exile have been attributed to them . . . It is so difficult, you see, to know who in Iran you are dealing with nowadays."

D'Arcy sympathised. "You can't have been expected to know. With state-sponsored terrorism anyone from an ambassador to an embassy chauffeur could be one of them."

"It is a sobering thought."

"Are you aware that the consignment contains weapons, not machinery parts?"

"No, but I am not surprised. I am only the carrier. Iran is fighting a war for its survival. It is entirely within its rights to buy arms legally." He replaced his glass on the table. "Now, you must tell me how you've heard about all this?"

D'Arcy gave a potted version, not mentioning that Bliss had instructed him not to warn his client. "British security contacted my London office. They fear the weapons may be used to arm terrorist cells in Europe, and not just Iranian."

"That is a terrible thought. I must be more careful in future."

D'Arcy shook his head. "There could be a reason why you should be more careful now. For your own personal safety."

"And that is?"

"Until I left London there'd been no signal from *Clarion Call* for four days."

Nadirpur sat upright. "I beg your pardon? I have not been informed of this."

"Should you have been?"

The Iranian shrugged. "Perhaps not. Communication breakdown in ships is not unknown. Either electronic, or more usually human breakdown. Besides, my office in Monaco is not the most efficient. It is what happens when the boss is not breathing down their necks."

"Can you call the office? Check if the ship has already arrived in Bandar Abbas, or if there's any news from Djibouti, the last port of call?"

"Not until tomorrow morning, I'm afraid. But I'm sure there will be a simple explanation –" Concern clouded his eyes "– Mr D'Arcy, do you *seriously* think that I could be in any danger from these people?"

D'Arcy contemplated the glass in his hand, turning it so that the light caught the cut crystal edges. "I'm in the prevention and protection business, so I'd be failing in my duty not to warn you of the possibilities. While you co-operate with them, the Iranian government will no doubt overlook your political leanings – and I've little doubt they'll be aware of them. But if they suspected you of double-crossing them, that could be a different story. I would urge particular caution, at least until *Clarion Call*'s whereabouts are confirmed. If there is still no news in the morning, I recommend that you let me supply a professional bodyguard and review your personal security."

Nadirpur looked pained. "I don't really think that would be necessary. I doubt anything has happened to *Clarion Call*. Not only has it been sailing in calm coastal waters, but it also has one of your sea-marshals on board. Besides, I have Ahn to look after me."

"He really should be armed, you know, just in case."

Another pained expression. "I do not care for firearms, Mr D'Arcy. Ahn is a trained Thai boxer, and is handy with the rice-flail."

"I'm afraid prevention is more important than physical heroics. Is he properly trained in bodyguard duties and evasive driving, for instance?"

Nadirpur shifted uncomfortably. Avoiding a direct answer, he said: "I really do not cherish the idea of some – heavy, I think you call it – moving in. Privacy is important to me." A gentle smile. "And I think Ahn may be more than a little put out by the idea."

D'Arcy rose to his feet; there was no more he could do. "Very well, Mr Nadirpur. We'll speak tomorrow. I'll give you a number where I can be reached in any emergency." He scrawled it quickly on the back of his card. "I hope I haven't alarmed you unnecessarily, but it is better to be safe than sorry."

The Iranian offered a cool, loose handshake. "I promise I will not open the door to any strange men."

Large drops of rain began to fall as D'Arcy stepped out into avenue Foch. Pedestrians scurried for cover. Umbrellas were produced as though by magic as thunder threatened close by.

Taxis vanished as the rain gathered momentum, and he was obliged to take the Métro from Etoile to Concorde station. In the commonplace crush of damp and steaming humanity returning home after a day's work in the city, worries over Nadirpur and *Clarion Call* seemed grossly exaggerated.

On reflection he was sure that it had been his own personal brush with the Sabbah organisation two years earlier that had caused him to overreact. No doubt the morning would find *Clarion Call* in Bandar Abbas and all would be right with the world.

Even Roquelaure's omission to tell him that he'd been involved in setting up the deal with Iran seemed less mysterious as the Métro train cruised beneath the Paris streets. The générale had always had many irons in the fire long before their partnership had been formed.

As he emerged from the station at place de la Concorde,

the rain was hissing down, sluicing the pavements and overflowing the drains. Traffic was at an angry crawl, a dazzling confusion of lights and wet reflections in the premature darkness. He was soaked before he reached Chantal's place off the affluent rue du Faubourg-St-Honoré, the home of a dozen *haute couture* fashion and perfume shops. Her apartment house was an imposing Napoleonic block which presented solid, unwelcoming doors to the street.

Chantal's mouth dropped as she opened her apartment door and registered the sodden, bedraggled figure on the landing. "Rober'! – what are you doing here? You are wet to the skin!"

As she stepped back to allow him in, he thought he detected a slight reluctance in the gesture.

"I'm sorry I didn't phone first . . ." he began defensively.

"Nonsense, *chéri*." She reached up to kiss him, and as he held her to him he was aware of her slender nakedness beneath the ivory silk robe. She pulled back and smiled nervously. "It is a lovely surprise. Come, you must get dry."

She led him into the semicircular hall with its high vaulted ceiling from which a chandelier threw its bright light over the pale lemon and white walls. "I have a guest with me, Rober'. An old friend. He will be leaving shortly."

Before he could respond, she threw open the door. The man sitting on the chintz sofa rose awkwardly to his feet. D'Arcy guessed he was Chantal's age, perhaps a year or two older. Neat black hair, with dark intense eyes set in a handsome sunburnt face. His shirtsleeves were rolled, his tie askew at the open collar of his shirt.

"Rober', this is Jean-Paul. A very old friend of the family," Chantal introduced. "Jean-Paul, this is Rober' D'Arcy, my English friend."

"*Bonsoir, monsieur.*" An offered hand.

D'Arcy saw the two wine goblets on the table; the empty bottle of Haut-Brion.

The words of Roy Bliss rushed in his ears. "*Don't be too trusting. Maybe her infatuation with you is genuine, but maybe – just maybe – she's Roquelaure's insurance policy in case you ever step out of line.*"

D'Arcy said darkly: "I don't want to interrupt your cosy get-together."

Chantal's expression froze. "Er – Rober' – what do you mean?"

He was aware of her hand draping her robe, covering the length of tanned bare calf where it gaped. "Is Jean-Paul the reason you left England in such a hurry?"

Her green eyes blazed at him. "Don't be so stupid." Then she followed his gaze to the wine glasses, suddenly understanding what he was thinking. Angrily she added: "I tell you, Jean-Paul is an old family friend. I know him since we are both children."

"That doesn't make it any better."

"It is not what you are thinking."

The skin pulsed in D'Arcy's scar, but his voice was calm and steady. "Isn't this the time of day Frenchmen meet their mistresses? A quick detour on the way home to their wives?"

"How dare you!" Chantal spat with the look of a wounded animal. "How do you think such a thing!"

His face stung as the room resounded to the sharp slap across his cheek. She stared at him, wide-eyed.

D'Arcy's reaction was instinctive, his arm a rapid blur of movement as the back of his hand whipped out in retaliation. With a gasp Chantal staggered backwards, reaching for the chair back to steady herself. Her robe fell open to the waist, her small jutting breasts exposed, heaving with indignation. But she seemed unaware of it as her green eyes glared back at the man who had struck her.

Gingerly she felt her mouth with her fingertips; they came away with a splattering of blood where she had bitten her own lip.

Jean-Paul was on his feet. "Monsieur! I protest – "

D'Arcy's eyes didn't move from the girl. "Don't even think about it! Chantal will come to no harm. Just pick up your jacket, Jean-Paul, and get out."

"You bastard!" Chantal hissed, her eyes locked on his in a battle of wills.

"I – I will not go –" Jean-Paul began.

D'Arcy was losing patience. Out of the side of his mouth he grated: "For God's sake, man, get out of here. Go now."

Chantal was regaining her composure. She dragged her eyes away from D'Arcy, pulling her robe closed. She swallowed hard, sniffing back her tears, before she said: "It's all right, Jean-Paul. Do as he says, please."

The Frenchman stood his ground.

Another sniff, a nervous pat to put her hair in place, and a meek smile. "Please, Jean-Paul. Thank you, but it is all right now."

Uncertainly Jean-Paul picked up his jacket and moved towards the door. He paused, glowering at D'Arcy's back. "I will phone later. To see that you are all right."

She nodded dumbly, her eyes shut.

Footsteps receded, the front door opened and closed.

Chantal's shoulders dropped with relief and her eyes opened. D'Arcy thought how clear and green and beautiful they were.

She said slowly, accusingly: "What a jealous bastard you are."

D'Arcy hadn't moved. His lips were compressed into a thin line as he awaited some explanation.

She pulled a tight smile. "I need a cigarette." Moving to the sideboard, she picked up a pack of Chesterfields and lit one with trembling hands. She inhaled deeply, savouring the smoke, then turned. "Jean-Paul and I were lovers, it is true. But years ago in our teens. He was the first boy in my life. To him I lost my virginity."

D'Arcy's scar flickered; he said nothing.

"But it is also true that he is an old family friend." She spoke rapidly but with her eyes averted, as though she didn't want to witness his reaction. "We have become great friends. You know, platonic –" A brittle laugh, "good chums, as you English say. We talk of many things, have no secrets from each other. That is why I do not bother to change when he calls. I am just out of the bath. It does not seem to matter."

"Perhaps it should."

She was more relaxed now and looked straight at him. "No, especially tonight it did not matter. Not what he had to tell me. It was why I had to leave you this morning."

D'Arcy's eyes narrowed. "You said it was business."

A tight smile. "Let me pour you a brandy."

"No need."

"I could do with one myself."

She poured two balloons and took them across to him. "Sit down because I need to tell you something." They sat together and she reached out for his hand. "You must understand. Today should be one of the happiest of my life. Yet somehow it is not."

D'Arcy waited.

She moistened her lips with the tip of her tongue. "When we first meet, all that time ago at La Clusaz. You remember that I am sad. My fiancé had died in Beirut."

"I remember you were very quiet. We were strangers."

"I was sad." Her eyes were very close now. Luminous and green. "You never ask much about him."

"Sometimes it's best not."

A shy smile. "Because you are a jealous man?"

"What happened?"

"He was a junior diplomat serving at our embassy in Beirut. He was kidnapped by terrorists." She spoke a little faster, eager to get it off her chest. "We had no word since. It is common practice for diplomats to be tortured for information. Not so civilians, but diplomats have been tortured to death." She looked into his eyes, watching his reaction. "To save my suffering Papa tells me he is dead for sure. And now . . ."

D'Arcy saw her tears begin to well. "This morning, the telephone call. With news he is alive. He is to come home. That is why I meet with Jean-Paul to tell me about Philippe."

"Philippe?"

"His name is Philippe Chaumont."

He awoke early after a disturbed sleep.

Beside him Chantal tossed restlessly, the tangled sheet half off her naked body. Perspiration glittered on her skin in the steely pre-dawn light from the balcony window.

He wouldn't get back to sleep now, he knew that.

Slipping quietly from the bed, he moved into the living room. The light had been left on, forgotten. As though the moment of passion had been frozen in time. Her robe lay discarded on the floor; beside it his own sodden pile of clothes had spread a wet stain of rainwater onto the carpet. There were now two dead bottles of Haut-Brion on the table.

Even in the stale electric light he could visualise the scene like an old, blurred snapshot. Chantal's strange reaction after she had told him about Philippe Chaumont. Her passion had almost been a celebration, an unburdening. He examined the yellow bruises on his biceps, the scratch marks across his chest. She had been almost in delirium, consumed with an animal desire. Her nails had dug into his flesh while he had tasted the blood of her cut lip as they kissed. And as she hurt him, he had hurt her back and she seemed driven to frenzy.

Outside the rain had continued to torrent, the urgent rattling of the shutters interspersed by drumrolls of thunder and forked lightning.

Then, suddenly, it was as though she were making love to another man. He couldn't get the idea out of his head. There, on the deep-piled carpet of the elegant apartment on rue du Faubourg-St-Honoré, she had been making love to a man incarcerated in the slums of Beirut.

From the handgrip he found lying by the door, he pulled

out his lightweight kimono and put in on. It took a few minutes in the kitchen to make the mug of strong chicory coffee to which he added a liberal lacing of brandy.

Returning to the living room he killed the light and the images of the previous night, drew the curtains, and threw open the windows and shutters. Sweet, cool morning air swept in as he settled in a chair by the balcony to watch a new day begin on the Paris street below.

By seven, after more coffee and a cigar, he had still not been able to bring any order to his confusion of thoughts.

One thing was certain. He could not afford to lose her. She had filled an emptiness in his life and he knew that he would be devastated if she left now. It had happened before with other women. He did not want that to happen again; perhaps, he reasoned, it was why he had never asked her to move in with him. Keep a small distance between them. That way you didn't get hurt.

But it was too late for that now. Somehow she'd crept through his defences without him realising. It was probably inevitable. No man could resist such charm, such beauty and good humour. Even her fiercely independent streak appealed to him, excited him, challenged him to tame her. They had come to share so much, and not just in bed. And now all that was threatened.

Chantal had not said how she now felt about Philippe Chaumont, and he felt unable to ask. Mostly he feared the answer he did not want to hear. He deemed it unwise to push the matter while she was clearly still in a state of emotional shock.

He tried to imagine how she might be thinking: the sudden joy that the impossible had happened, that a man had returned from the dead. The sudden rekindling of past memories and passion for the man she had been about to marry. Followed by the utter devastation of the guilt of her own betrayal.

No, D'Arcy decided, it was going to be a difficult time for her. However much he wanted the answer to his unasked question, he was going to have to wait for it.

The decision made, he showered and dressed quickly, then went out to buy a freshly baked *baguette* for breakfast. The air was much clearer after the night's storm and his spirits lifted.

He returned to the sound of Europe Numéro One radio news chattering from the living room and the rushing of the shower.

Chantal emerged, towelling her hair, as he finished slicing and buttering the *baguette*. "Did you sleep well, *chéri*?"

"Fine," D'Arcy lied. "And you?"

She sat at the table with a shrug, the green eyes troubled. "I dream a lot. I cannot remember exactly. It was not very nice." She forced a smile. "And you, Rober', what do you do today?"

"That depends on a phone call." He sampled the doughy texture of the bread. "A ship's overdue with one of my men on board. I'll get a phone call this morning after nine. If it's been located I'll have to get back to London. If not I'll be obliged to stay on in Paris a while."

"That would be nice."

He wasn't sure that it would. "Yes. But under the circumstances I'd prefer to have news of the ship."

"Of course."

"What about you? Business?"

"No, I cannot concentrate until I know about Philippe for sure. Unfortunately these things can take much time. So I think I go to Carita's to have my hair done and a manicure." She laughed lightly. "That does not take too much concentration. Maybe we can meet for lunch?"

"That would be nice."

"The Espace Cardin?" she suggested. "Or maybe the Tsé Yang?"

"I don't mind."

"The Tsé Yang, then. It's on rue Pierre-Premier-de-Serbie. Say one o'clock."

"Fine."

She reached across for his hand, gripping it tightly.

"I want to thank you, Rober', for being so understanding about all of this with Philippe."

A smile hesitated at his lips. "And for hitting you yesterday? I'm sorry I did that."

Her eyes were clear and bright. "I do not love you for being gentle, *chéri*. When you struck me last night I – I felt only that I wanted you. That is *fou*, mad, isn't it? I think our relationship is very special."

"And your relationship with Philippe?" He didn't mean to say it; the words were out before he could stop himself.

He felt her fingers stiffen on his fist. "He is not at all like you. Very kind, very gentle."

D'Arcy's laugh was harsh. "You make me sound like an ogre."

"Don't be silly. I just mean that he is so different from you . . ." Her voice faded as her words rekindled memories.

The trimphone extension warbled urgently from the wall. Chantal reached for it and spoke briefly before handing the receiver to him. "It is for you. A Monsieur Nadirpur. He sounds very agitated."

D'Arcy glanced at his watch. It was only just turned eight.

"Mr D'Arcy, thank God you are in! Something terrible has happened."

"The ship?"

"What? Oh, no, well not directly. Can you come over here right away?"

"No problem. I'll be there as soon as I can." He hung the receiver back on its cradle. "That's one very upset client."

"What is it about?"

"He wouldn't say. Just that I've got to get over there fast."

"It is rush hour. Traffic may not be good."

"I'll take the Métro."

"No, I will take you. It takes just a second to put on my leathers."

114

He grinned. "Am I ready for this?"

A few minutes later Chantal gunned the monstrous Harley Davidson out of the apartment block courtyard, with D'Arcy astride the pillion. It was a hard, fast drive through the congested streets, the girl picking her way expertly through the back streets to avoid the worst of the jams.

It took only fifteen minutes before she was removing her bulbous black space helmet outside the house on avenue Foch.

To D'Arcy's surprise it was Nadirpur who answered the entry phone, and again the man himself who came down to let them in. He looked anxiously left and right along the avenue before hastily fumbling to open the gate.

"This is Chantal, a friend of mine," D'Arcy introduced, but Nadirpur was so distraught he hardly noticed her.

"I am so glad you are here," he kept repeating as he led the way briskly up the staircase.

Everything in the apartment appeared normal until the door of the drawing room was opened. Gone was the atmosphere of sombre calm. It had been shattered along with the glass tank, the debris of which lay scattered on the carpet. Dead fish formed glittering patches of colour against the dark water stain. Some had floundered right across the room before they had expired. The chocolate-coloured Russian Blue was sniffing and pawing experimentally at one of the corpses.

As they entered, the cat leapt clear of the tangle of antique furniture which lay at crazy angles, fractured arms and legs like a grotesque mockery of a holocaust scene.

The chaise longue had been the only piece to survive unscathed. On it lay the Vietnamese manservant, moaning quietly and holding a surgical dressing to his thigh. A steady drip of blood was forming a pool on the floor.

"Please see Ahn," Nadirpur begged, rushing over. "They beat him badly and I don't know what to do." His voice was cracked with emotion.

115

"Good God, what happened?"

"He is shot in the leg," the Iranian replied as D'Arcy crossed the room. "Dear Ahn, he put up such a brave fight for me."

"I can see that," D'Arcy murmured as he knelt and gently prised Ahn's hand away from the wound. Beneath the pad he found the small entry wound; the larger exit hole had gone unnoticed beneath the man's leg and was draining the lifeblood from him. "When did you call the ambulance?"

Nadirpur peered worriedly over D'Arcy's shoulder. "Ahn asks me not to. He does not like hospitals."

D'Arcy turned in anger. "Don't be so bloody stupid. He's been happily dying here since you phoned me."

The Iranian shifted uneasily. "Ahn has no *carte de séjour*. No papers."

Realisation dawned. "An illegal. I see." Deftly he covered the lower wound with a clean handkerchief and raised the limb on some cushions to discourage the flow of blood.

Chantal said: "Let me telephone a friend of my father. He will be able to arrange for a private clinic, so there will be no problems with the police."

D'Arcy nodded his agreement. Sometimes it paid to have friends in a country's security services. "Mr Nadirpur, please hold this firmly in place. If it continues to bleed, I'll have to apply a tourniquet."

"That is bad?"

"A last resort. I need more dressings and bandages."

"I have only a small medical kit. But you will find linen in my bedroom." His eyes were filled with tears. "Please hurry, Mr D'Arcy, Ahn is very precious to me."

Five minutes later, using strips of cut bedlinen, D'Arcy had virtually stopped the bleeding. A feather duvet warmed the patient and helped to check the effect of shock. His condition appeared to have stabilised. Chantal announced that a paramedic team was on its way.

Nadirpur said: "I thank you so much for saving Ahn's

life. I do not know what I would have done if you had not come."

D'Arcy stood back from the patient and lit himself a small cigar. He could think of better ways to start the day. "Tell me, Mr Nadirpur, is this anything to do with what we were discussing yesterday?"

"Please, call me Nader, it is only right." A benevolent smile. "I am afraid it was. Mr Azadi from the Iranian Embassy. He called with another gentleman. I say gentleman, but I suppose he is just an official thug."

"And you let them in, despite my warning yesterday?"

Nadirpur blushed. "They *looked* so respectable. They both wore good suits and spoke in a very reasonable tone. I could hardly refuse to speak to such a good customer on the basis of your suspicions – however correct they turned out to be. At least, I made sure that poor Ahn stays in the room with us."

"As well you did," D'Arcy said, wondering what the hell might have happened had the manservant not been present.

"But as soon as Mr Azadi is inside, his attitude changes. He becomes quite angry. He says that the Iranians had planned to have one of their frigates intercept *Clarion Call* on the approaches of the Strait of Hormuz, to provide safe escort. He says that the ship is now forty-eight hours overdue and he wants explanations."

"What did you say to that?"

"I explain that there could be many reasons. Engine or steerage problems, bad weather and so on. But like you, he has been talking to my shipping office in Monaco and learns that there has been no communication for four days. He accuses me of a double-cross. To make it look as though the ship is lost at sea. I said it was preposterous, but that made him even angrier. He said that when he tried to contact the Spidex company in Paris – who supplied the cargo – it has disappeared. He says that I am in collaboration with them in a swindle against Iran. That he has evidence that I am a pro-monarchy subversive. That I work against the Imam Khomeini –"

Nadirpur broke off, his body trembling with delayed shock, his forehead beaded in perspiration.

Chantal brought coffee from the kitchen and, after several long draughts, Nadirpur had regained his composure sufficiently to continue.

"Azadi said that I had just twenty-four hours to provide him with the exact location of the ship – or else I would be executed. He said his thug would stay with me during that time." His eyes closed as he recalled the confrontation. "I told them both to get out. That I will tell them everything I can find out. But they refuse to go. It is then that Ahn stepped forward to protect me. Dear, sweet Ahn –" His eyes shifted to the prone body on the couch. "The thug drew out a gun. But he did not expect the rice-flail, you know, the sticks joined by a chain. Ahn snaps it across the man's wrist – breaking the bone, I think. The gun flies and there is a terrible fight. Azadi reaches the fallen gun, aims at Ahn and fires. I throw myself at this Azadi and we wrestle like children in the mud. It seems it is for hours, but neither of us are fighters. At last I manage to throw the gun out of the window.

"Azadi takes fright and then calls off his dog. Despite his wound Ahn still fights like a tiger, but is badly beaten and reeling. The thug obeys but he is reluctant. Already he has smashed poor Ahn's body to a pulp and is disgusted that his master will not allow him to finish."

Nadirpur's hand delicately traced a line across Ahn's perspiring brow. "I am devoted to this boy, Mr D'Arcy. He has given me nothing but total loyalty and respect at a time when I needed it most. France is not the most hospitable country to foreigners; it is easy to be lonely here. Isolated in an ivory tower, as you English say. He is my friend." His eyes were moist as he turned to D'Arcy. A small smile of affection curled the delicate lips. "Unless you count my treacherous Czarina, he is my only friend. I do not expect you to understand."

118

D'Arcy nodded sympathetically, felt uncomfortable. "I think I do, Nader."

A slow look of horror showed in the Iranian's eyes. "Do not think that we are lovers, Mr D'Arcy. Understand that. His loyalty and our mutual affection are far deeper than such things." He cleared his throat. "Do you know that he also saved my life at the very time we met?"

"You hadn't told me."

Nadirpur looked at Chantal, almost for the first time. "Sweet and very beautiful lady, forgive me what I am going to confide. It is not for your ears." He turned to D'Arcy. "When I first come to Paris in 1979 I am desperately lonely. I have French business contacts, but socially I am a leper. Some will come to my home for drinks, but never is the invitation returned. I feel I am wanted only for what business I can bring their way. One night – a Friday – I drove down to the Bois de Boulogne. There are some very beautiful young men there. I leave my car to talk with them, and suddenly I am attacked, my wallet taken. They would have stolen my car, too, but for Ahn. He was standing there, also, under the trees. Waiting to earn some francs to pay for some soup and some bread. Waiting to sell his young body. He saw what was happening and comes to my rescue. In doing so he lost the only friends he had here in Paris, such as they were. He has been with me ever since."

It was then that the private ambulance arrived from the clinic on the outskirts of the city, and Ahn was stretchered out to the waiting vehicle.

"Allah be praised," Nadirpur said. "Now I know Ahn will live. I owe you a very great personal debt."

D'Arcy came to a decision. "Listen to me, Nader. You were very lucky that Ahn was with you when Azadi called. But they're likely to be back at any time. You are going to be in great danger until you have positive news of *Clarion Call*. Will you let me take the necessary precautions?"

"I do not want to put anyone else at risk – including you."

"It's my business, Nader. It's what I'm paid for, and my services don't come cheap."

A gentle smile. "That is supposed to ease my conscience? Very well, what do you suggest?"

"If we are dealing with the *Pessarane Behesht* then we're up against some very dangerous and unpredictable people. So it's imperative we get you away from here. I have a friend who may be able to provide accommodation, someone they would not associate with you."

Nadirpur looked at his watch. "The office will be open now. Let me telephone Monaco. Maybe none of this will be necessary."

But when he made his call there was still no news. He gave vent to his anger and lambasted the shipping manager for not having alerted him that *Clarion Call* was overdue.

After that, D'Arcy called Dave Forbes in London to put him briefly in the picture and to tell him to liaise with the ship and cargo insurers at Lloyd's. He added: "You'd better phone Pauline Wilmot, too, and tell her the ship's overdue. But don't be alarmist, because I'm sure there's a perfectly rational explanation."

When he hung up, Nadirpur said: "I think I must call on the offices of Spidex myself. As that man Azadi said, the people who answer the phone say the company has gone. I have tried myself. If that is so, I can at least understand his anxiety – if not his way of showing it."

D'Arcy agreed. "But I don't want you going near those offices – Azadi's people could have it staked out. I'll take care of that. But first I think we should phone Azadi himself and tell him in no uncertain terms that we are as unhappy about this as he is. We *must* convince him that we are doing everything we can to trace the ship and the people running Spidex."

However, the call to the Iranian Embassy did not produce much in the way of satisfaction. Firstly the telephonist denied the existence of anyone of the name of Azadi. Then, on D'Arcy's insistence, he was passed from extension to extension. Finally one unnamed diplomat, whilst claiming that the name meant nothing to him, showed an unnatural willingness to make a note of D'Arcy's message "should he be able to trace such a man."

"May I inquire as to your rôle in this affair, Mr D'Arcy?" the voice asked. It was pitched reasonably enough.

"I am simply Mr Nadirpur's security adviser, which is one reason why any threat against him will be counter-productive. One of my staff is also aboard the *Clarion Call*, advising on maritime protection. So you can see that I, too, have a vested interest in locating the whereabouts of the ship and crew."

"And cargo?"

"Of course," D'Arcy replied. He had not mentioned the nature of the cargo.

"I fear I cannot help you," the voice concluded smoothly. "But I shall nevertheless pass your message on to the appropriate departments in case this Mr Azadi becomes known to us."

"You do that," D'Arcy replied and hung up.

Nadirpur put down the extension. "What do we do now?"

"Show them we mean what we say. I'll visit the Spidex office. But first I must call on an old friend."

# 5

Victor's was a smart *brasserie* and bar sandwiched between two elegant boutiques in a narrow back street off the rue Pierre-Charron. The faded opulence of its *belle époque* styling, with gleaming brass, mirrored walls and ceiling murals, suggested that it had seen better times in the long distant days of Renoir and Toulouse-Lautrec.

While the pavement tables attracted some passing trade from those who could find no restaurant seats on the Champs-Elysées at suppertime, the inner bar remained a more-or-less private sanctum for Victor's regulars.

It was here the *patron*, an ex-sergeant of the *Légion Étrangère*, held court whilst providing both drinks and homespun philosophy in equally generous measures.

D'Arcy parked Nadirpur's BMW outside and left Chantal with her motorcycle to keep watch for any unwelcome followers. He led the Iranian through the elaborately etched glass doors.

They were greeted by the solid smell of furniture polish, blending with the mouth-watering aroma of melting cheese as a *croque monsieur* sizzled under the grill. At the bar Victor was busily dispensing kick-start coffees and hair-of-the-dog cognacs to a huddle of regulars taking late breakfast or early lunch.

He looked up at the newcomers outlined against the bright light of the street. The small dark eyes crinkled in their walnut bags; the magnificent profusion of handlebar moustache, grown long ago to compensate for a balding pate, bristled with the start of a smile.

"Monsieur D'Arcy?" The voice was rich and fruity, oiled perpetually with calvados and coarsened with Disque Bleu. Heads turned in curiosity.

"Hello, Victor."

"It *is* Monsieur D'Arcy! I do not believe it!" Big hairy hands wiped grease over the wide belly of his apron, before reaching out in greeting. The grip was warm and fierce, suggesting that he retained much of the strength of his youth.

D'Arcy grinned. "How d'you French barmen do it? I haven't see you for almost a year, Victor, and you recognise me the instant I step through the door."

Victor roared with good humour. "With you, *mon ami*, it is always the walk. Unmistakable. Like John Wayne!"

"I wish I hadn't asked," D'Arcy replied, trusting that Victor's observation really was just a joke.

As lavish as always with his hospitality Victor began dispensing free cognac and coffee in celebration of what might have been a prodigal son's return, introducing his regulars to D'Arcy and he to them.

"And your friend?" Victor asked, eyes squinting as he made one of his instant character assessments which were rarely wide of the mark.

"This is Nader," D'Arcy said. "A client of mine. In fact I am here on his behalf – to ask a favour."

Victor's joviality was a mask. "And I think it is my fine menu that lures you back."

D'Arcy smiled. "A word in private?"

The *patron* moved to the corner of the bar, clear of everyone's earshot, and began drying glasses. "Anything, Rober', you know that. We go back a long way."

That was true enough. They had first met fifteen years earlier when a small cadre of SAS men, led by D'Arcy, had visited the Mont Louis Commando Training School close to Andorra for an exchange visit. Ever since Victor had saved his life on the deadly ravine-wire crossing they had become firm friends.

"I wouldn't put on you if it wasn't very necessary," D'Arcy said.

Furrows creased the heavy brow. He read the tone. "I know that, Robert. What is it you want?"

"Two things. First a room for my client here. Somewhere that is secure and that has a telephone."

Victor breathed on the glass in his hand, and buffed it until it gleamed. "Your client is wanted?"

"You could say that."

"By *les flics*?"

"No, not the police. By a business contact who has made serious threats."

Victor looked pained. "So what is your client? An embezzler? Or a man who cannot meet his bills? Since when are you involved with such people? Do not treat me like an idiot."

D'Arcy savoured his brandy and studied Victor for a moment, before deciding exactly how much to tell the Frenchman. "I have reason to believe that Nader's business contact could be involved with a terrorist organisation. They suspect – wrongly – that they've been double-crossed."

Victor's facial expression didn't change. He continued blowing on the glass, and D'Arcy smelled the aftermath of yesterday's garlic. "Do I assume your friend is innocently involved?"

"If he wasn't, I wouldn't be working for him. And I certainly wouldn't be asking you for favours."

"You cannot go to the police?"

"This needs careful handling, Victor. If I can just get my client out of harm's way for a day or two this whole problem should resolve itself. But if the police handle things badly it could ruin my client's reputation and start a lot of unwelcome investigation. You've met my partner, Roquelaure?"

"*Le générale de brigade*? Yes, I remember him."

"Well, he has the right sort of contacts in the government. As soon as he's back from abroad, he can handle this. In the meantime –"

"A roof for your friend's head?" A gentle smile. "And the other favour?"

"I need extra manpower until I can get spare staff over from London. Someone who can act as bodyguard and chauffeur for the next two days. I thought you might have an idea."

Victor placed the glass carefully on the bar top. Since he had left the French Foreign Legion his bar had become the Paris watering hole for old comrades-in-arms. A place of recreation and reminiscence, as well as a discreet job centre that worked the 'old boys' network. "Go and speak to Saint-Julien – the big bastard in the corner who looks as though he would kill his own grandmother for a couple of francs. Ignore his rude behaviour, looks can be deceptive. He is a good man beneath that façade. While you talk to him, I will think about where your friend can stay."

D'Arcy left Nadirpur perched on a bar stool with a glass of Victor's best vintage champagne and made his way across the room to where a large figure in black suit and shirt was seated, almost invisible in the dark alcove.

He sat broodily, staring at his untouched coffee. It appeared to hold a mesmeric fascination for him as his dark, red-veined eyes watched the rising curlicue of steam. His elbows were on the table edge, his heavily ringed fingers idly scratching at a thick black beard as though it aided his concentration.

Only the eyes moved, suspiciously, as D'Arcy's shadow fell across the table.

"Saint-Julien?"

A pause, an appraisal. "Who wants him?" He spoke in English, the accent was unmistakably Corsican.

"My name's D'Arcy. Victor says you might be interested in a couple of days' work."

At last the head moved, following the malevolent gaze of his eyes, and D'Arcy could see the hair swept back off

125

the sallow forehead, gathered in a ponytail at the back. He didn't look effeminate, even when you considered the plain gold ring that pierced his left earlobe. The man just looked plain unsavoury, D'Arcy decided.

Another pause and the Corsican said: "Victor should learn to keep his mouth shut."

"Victor and I go back a long way. We met in the Legion."

A raised brow and an almost imperceptible softening of tone. "You were in the Legion? I don't remember you."

"I met Victor during joint training. I was with the British SAS."

A longer pause this time as the words were absorbed, the meaning registered. The lips parted; it could have been a smile. "The hooligans from Hereford."

"Can I buy you a cognac?"

The eyes softened. "It'll be my privilege to let you buy me a cognac. I was beginning to think I'd have to drink this coffee."

"A hard night?"

A flash of anger in the eyes. "Perhaps."

D'Arcy ordered, then took the seat opposite. "I need a good man, reliable, for a couple of days' bodyguard duty. It could be dangerous. There's a real threat. But the money will be good."

The eyes glanced in the direction of Nadirpur sitting demurely at the bar. "The fairy?"

"My client's in serious trouble."

"Boyfriend problems?" A sarcastic laugh.

"I said serious. And if you work for me you'll take it seriously. Very seriously."

Saint-Julien pursed his lips, mouthed something but didn't speak. He turned his head away and picked up the newly arrived cognac. He sniffed appreciatively. At last he said: "You want someone who doesn't have a drink problem."

"Do you have a drink problem?"

The Corsican lowered the cognac, unsampled, and

pushed the glass away. Reaching for the coffee, he said: "Not any more."

"When can you start?"

He downed the coffee in one. "I've started. Will I need a firearm?"

"Have you got one?"

"It will cost you."

"Illegal?"

"What do you think?"

D'Arcy wasn't convinced that Saint-Julien was suitable. Certainly the man wouldn't have been his usual choice, but under the circumstances he was obliged to take Victor's recommendation at face value. "Do you have a criminal record?"

The eyes smouldered for a moment at the impertinence, then he seemed to see the funny side and chuckled hoarsely. "Nothing recent. As a kid I knocked about with *la pègra*. I know my way around. Sometimes I've done the odd job for *la parallèle*," he said simply, as though it explained everything. It was the name given to the rumoured private army which was reputed to have run dirty tricks campaigns for successive Interior ministers. One man's secret service with an awesome notoriety.

"It would be advisable to be armed," D'Arcy decided. "If you do hit trouble it will be from an Iranian terrorist organisation. You should know that."

Saint-Julien shrugged; it was nothing. "And you. Do you want a weapon?"

D'Arcy shook his head. "That shouldn't be necessary. Besides which I don't want any shooting unless it's an absolute life or death situation."

The Corsican rose to his feet. "I'll be back in fifteen minutes with everything I need."

As the man left Victor beckoned D'Arcy to the bar. Besides Nadirpur only one person now remained. A stunningly attractive woman in her late thirties, she sat on a corner stool nursing a Campari on ice. Beneath an open beige silk trenchcoat she wore a red Louis Féraud dress;

her legs were long and sheathed in fine black nylon. D'Arcy recalled the exquisitely made-up face beneath the tumble-cut red hair. The name escaped him.

"You remember Claudette," Victor said.

D'Arcy smiled. "How could I ever forget? *Enchanté, madame.*"

The offered hand was long and slender, her scarlet nail polish exactly matching the painted lips. "It is *mademoiselle*, Monsieur D'Arcy," she corrected gently. "How nice to see you again. And how flattering that you remember me."

"Claudette has an apartment upstairs," Victor explained. "It has two rooms and she is willing to let your client move into one of them for a short period. There is a telephone, a bathroom and a kitchenette."

D'Arcy smiled. "You're a genius, Victor."

"If what you say is true, we cannot take chances. I will have the rear exit barred and bolted. So the only access will be through the bar here. Again I shall keep that door locked. Anyone will have to come past me to get in. And – tell me, Saint-Julien will work for you?"

"He's agreed, yes."

Victor smiled with satisfaction. "Then he can sit in his favourite alcove and keep constant vigil, while everything appears as normal as usual."

D'Arcy turned to Nadirpur. "How does that sound, Nader?"

"You are all too kind. I have not known such kindness since I am in Paris."

Victor reached over the bar, taking Nadirpur's slim white hand in his great hamlike fists and shaking it vigorously until D'Arcy seriously wondered if the fragile bones might break. "You are safe amongst friends. And any friend of Rober's is a friend of ours."

"I am most grateful," the Iranian replied, anxiously withdrawing his hand from the Frenchman's grip. "And the lady, it is especially kind of her to allow me to stay."

Claudette smiled, clearly flattered by such unaccustomed graciousness. "It will be a pleasure to share my home with such a gentleman."

Victor whispered loudly in D'Arcy's ear. "Till yesterday she lives in with Saint-Julien, but they have another of their rows. Now he leaves again – like he leaves her every few months. Always he gets angry when she takes customers home."

"I heard that, Victor!" Claudette said sharply. "Please do not discuss my private affairs in public." She tilted her nose imperiously. "Actually I have a new job as a hostess at *le Chat Noir*, so there will be no disturbance to Monsieur Nadirpur." She turned to D'Arcy. "Nor to Rober'. You will stay, too, I hope –" a tinkling laugh, "– to chaperone us?"

D'Arcy felt the perspiration gather round his collar. The look in her eyes filled in the unspoken words in her sentence. "Er, no mademoiselle, I do not imagine so."

As Victor shook his head in despair at the incorrigible woman a slim black-leathered silhouette came through the door. Chantal carried her bulbous crash hat under one arm.

The *patron* let out the long slow whistle of a kettle coming to the boil. "I think we are invaded by Martians . . . They are not little green men after all – thank God."

"I think you forget me," Chantal chided.

"I'm sorry. I didn't think we would be so long." D'Arcy cast a glance at the door. "No sign of anyone following?"

"Nobody that I could see."

"Good, because Victor and Claudette have agreed to let Nader stay here. You remember Victor?"

"Of course she does!" the Frenchman gushed before she could answer. He hugged her to him and insisted that she had a drink on the house.

"She is a personal friend, Rober'?" Claudette asked D'Arcy absently.

"Very personal."

She didn't attempt to hide the look of disappointment in her eyes.

The midday sun glinted against the bronze bas-reliefs of famous battle scenes on Napoleon's column as Chantal steered the Harley-Davidson through the place de l'Opéra and turned down the busy rue de la Paix.

On the pillion D'Arcy counted the street numbers on the succession of shop fronts – mostly expensive jewellers, furriers and goldsmiths – until he found the one he wanted. He tapped Chantal's shoulder and she slowed into the kerb.

D'Arcy looked at the bland doorway sandwiched tightly between two fashion boutiques. An array of brass plaques were mounted on each side of the entrance.

"It doesn't look a big enough building to house this lot," D'Arcy observed.

"No, Rober', the rents around l'Opéra are *astronomique*, a very prestige area, and the offices are so small. Companies pay many hundred francs just for a nameplate. These will mostly be box numbers. The companies themselves will be in the modern la Défense development in the west suburbs, or maybe Montparnasse." She ran her finger down the row of names. "Ah, *voilà*! Here is the company. Spidex International Trading."

A narrow stairway led up to the third floor where an unmarked door opened onto a plush modern office reception area with a deep-pile fawn carpet dotted with pot plants.

D'Arcy sensed Chantal's critical eye roving over the décor. "It is so tasteless," she hissed in his ear. "So – so, nothing."

At the black ash reception desk a thin, middle-aged woman, with a bright gash of a mouth and hair in a severe French *coupe*, looked up sharply from her word processor.

"Monsieur – Madame – May I be of assistance?" Her voice was stiffly polite, the eyes wary.

D'Arcy smiled with as much charm as he could muster. "I have business with Spidex International Trading and I wonder if there is someone here I can talk to?"

The expression on the heavily powdered face softened

and she managed a sympathetic smile. "Monsieur, I am so sorry. You are at least the third person today who calls to inquire. Some people were here yesterday, too, and became quite angry. So much so that I had to threaten to call the police." She shrugged. "You see, we are just an accommodation address. We either hold or pass on letters for clients. We also have a small selection of offices for daily hire and a conference room. Out-of-town businessmen use our facilities, especially when they wish to impress important clients."

"And Spidex?" D'Arcy pressed.

"They had a small office suite in la Défense."

"You have the address, madame?"

"I can save you a trip. The office was on weekly rental. Three days ago they vanish. A cheque for the amount outstanding for our services arrived yesterday. It is most embarrassing for us, but we have no idea where they have gone."

At that moment the door to one of the partitioned offices opened and a stout, smartly suited figure emerged. It took D'Arcy a few seconds to connect the familiar face in the unfamiliar surroundings. Not unnaturally Chantal got there first.

"Papa!"

Roquelaure registered surprise, and the grim expression on the broad tanned face transformed instantly. "Chantal! Rober'! What a surprise to see you both here."

D'Arcy was suspicious. "Is it, Pierre? It shouldn't be a surprise at all. I gather *you* introduced these Spidex people to Nadirpur. Are you going to tell me what the hell is going on?"

Roquelaure waved him to silence. "Not here, Rober', please." He turned to his daughter. "What marvellous news about Philippe, eh? You get all the news from Jean-Paul?"

Chantal's face lit up with such obvious joy that D'Arcy felt decidedly uncomfortable. "Oh, Papa, yes. It is so wonderful. I couldn't wait to speak to you about it."

131

"I wanted to tell you myself, but I was out of the country." He looked up at D'Arcy, trying to gauge the Englishman's mood. "Listen, I am about to go to lunch. Why don't the two of you join me. A little celebration of Philippe's good fortune – and not before time."

The Vaudeville on rue Vivienne had always been a favourite of Roquelaure's. The art deco style *brasserie* attracts discerning customers from the *Bourse* stock exchange at lunchtime and theatregoers in the evening who ensure that it keeps its standards high. It was loud with business chatter and general bustle as they entered. Roquelaure was recognised instantly by the head waiter who took them straight to a reserved corner table.

With neighbouring diners sitting too close to have a conversation without being overheard, D'Arcy contented himself with the family small talk whilst he made the most of the lobster *fricassée*.

When the crowds later began thinning and the adjacent table cleared, Roquelaure leaned forward over his port glass. He spoke earnestly: "I am very sorry about this Spidex business, Rober'. More sorry than you might imagine. When you and Chantal arrived at that accommodation agency I had just been talking to the proprietor. As no doubt you have gathered, the company was just a front for some people of dubious nature."

"What sort of people?" D'Arcy asked.

"Arabs," Roquelaure replied shortly. "The so-called chairman was a Jordanian. He used the name Abdullah Hayira. But he had co-directors of several Middle Eastern nationalities."

"How the hell did you get involved with them, Pierre?"

Roquelaure toyed with his napkin. "Quite simple. Hayira approached our *Ministère de la Défense*. He had a contract to supply arms to Iran and wanted our help in setting up the deal. Exocet missiles et cetera. Not unnaturally it was handed to me, now being officially outside the *Ministère* and a recognised arms dealer. I liaised with the DGSE to organise everything – to fix Commission approval to export. French items on the list were shipped to Brazil which supplied other wanted items."

"Weren't you suspicious that Arabs wanted to supply arms to Iran?"

The générale looked pained. "I'm sure you did not mean to sound so naïve, Rober'. Businessmen are businessmen the world over – regardless of their nationality. And oil prices are slumping badly at present. There is an urgent need for Arab states to boost their income. Besides, do not imagine that every Arab state hates Iran. Some despise Iraq just as much, even more. Some feel it better to support the moderates in Teheran in order to achieve better relations in the future. Others would prefer just to fuel the war – and make a quick buck at the same time. They reason that while Iran and Iraq are fighting each other they have no time to look for adventures elsewhere in the region."

D'Arcy couldn't disagree with Roquelaure's assessment. "Presumably you checked out this Abdullah Hayira character before you did business with him?"

"We are not fools in France, Rober'. Everything checked; it was very professional. But remember this, in our own secret service every man who joins undergoes an identity and name change as a matter of course. To find out who one of our own DGSE agents really is –" He waved his hand dismissively "– is a near impossibility without inside information. No, all the directors of Spidex and the company itself, had bona fides and apparently legitimate histories."

"And all of them false," D'Arcy observed scathingly.

Chantal shook her head in disbelief. 'And poor Monsieur Nadirpur. All the trouble he has because of this. It is so sad."

"Trouble?" the general queried.

"He had a visit from some Iranian heavies this morning," D'Arcy said. "Put his minder in hospital, and now I've got Nadirpur in hiding."

Roquelaure registered no surprise. "I suppose it was about the overdue ship."

D'Arcy was stunned. "You know about that?"

"Of course. I was the first person the Iranians contacted. After all it was I who recommended them to use Nadirpur."

"Why for God's sake?" D'Arcy demanded. Then pulled himself up short before he inadvertently mentioned Bliss's warning that the shipment was destined for an Iranian terrorist faction.

Roquelaure shrugged. "Why not? I knew Nadirpur. I knew he was a good client of ours. I knew he was reliable and himself an Iranian. It made good sense."

For the first time Chantal became angry with her father. "And did it not make good sense to tell Rober' what is going on?"

"I am your partner," D'Arcy added pointedly.

Roquelaure took a Gitane from a slim gold case and lit it. "I was not in the position to discuss Secret Service matters with you, Rober'. It is *Ministère* and DGSE business. Your involvement and Nadirpur's was pure expediency – plus a little profit for IAP. I did not know that this is going to happen."

D'Arcy said: "And what exactly do you think has happened, because I haven't a clue?"

"That makes two of us."

"So who is behind it?"

"Because it is so carefully planned – with all that fake background setup – I think it has resources from some government. It is *someone*'s secret service operation, of that I am sure. That means it is essentially political in motivation. Profit is not the reason."

"Where does that leave Nadirpur?" D'Arcy pressed angrily. "Not to mention one of *our* staff members, Tom Wilmot, gone missing with that bloody ship."

Chantal flashed D'Arcy a reproving glance, but Roquelaure continued as though he had not heard: "We must think where it leaves the French Government, Rober'. We

134

are now suspected along with these Spidex people of double-crossing the Iranians."

D'Arcy was scathing. "So what?"

Roquelaure was taken aback. Not so much at his partner's tone, but at his apparent lack of understanding. "Because, Rober', the French Government is anxious to do business with Iran. Between you and me the Gulf War may soon be over, and there are vast contracts to be won. To rebuild after the devastation, will require huge construction projects. Not to mention re-equipping their armed forces. All through this war we support Iraq. We have only one Frenchman staying on in Teheran. But Iraq has exhausted its treasury reserves. Iran is where the money lies now."

D'Arcy was exasperated. "And any such deals are off if the Iranians suspect the DGSE of a double-cross?"

"Precisely, Rober'." Thankful that he had finally got through.

"It is time, Pierre, for you to get your priorities right," D'Arcy replied evenly. "While you work with me the interests of IAP and its clients come first. *Nothing* else."

Roquelaure glared. Then slowly the expression of resentment melted, and he smiled. "Forgive me, Rober'. Sometimes the perceptions of us French are different from you English."

"I understand all about French perceptions," D'Arcy retorted. He had long appreciated and respected the historical and cultural differences between the two nations. France had survived over the centuries by its sheer pragmatism. It was an entire nation of pragmatists, each individual swaying with the prevailing wind to ensure his or her own future. It was the one reason why France was unlikely ever to be truly subjugated by mere force of arms. Its society would simply absorb, reshape and adapt to ensure the fate and prosperity of the individual. It was sometimes mistaken for moral weakness. That was a concept that never had, and never would, be understood by the British.

135

"In this case," Roquelaure reasoned, "the interests of France and IAP coincide completely. The DGSE want to trace the people behind Spidex as much as Monsieur Nadirpur does. And especially they want to find that ship." A slow smile crossed his lips. "Why don't you start now? I can give you all the information I have. It will be a worthwhile contract for IAP."

"We're not bloody private detectives," D'Arcy snapped, aware that the scar was pulsing on his cheek. "This is a job for the DGSE, or some other security agency."

Roquelaure stubbed out his cigarette. "I think not, Rober'. You are well aware of the interdepartmental and political rivalry in France. It will be in someone's best interest to leak it all to the press. No, this is *exactly* a job for IAP. It is why you have been so successful for us abroad. You are British – one big step removed."

Sensing the mounting friction between the two men, Chantal rose to her feet. She couldn't bear to witness her father and D'Arcy falling out. This meal was meant to celebrate Philippe Chaumont's imminent homecoming. "Forgive me, I must go and powder my nose. And then I have to leave. I have a hair appointment at Carita's. Maybe I can give one of you a lift?"

As she moved away Roquelaure seized his opportunity. "Listen, Rober', while Chantal is gone. Everything I have told you is the absolute truth. But there is something more."

"Yes?"

"When we were approached on this deal we used it to tie in with the release of one of our hostages held in Lebanon."

"I thought you didn't negotiate with terrorists."

The pale eyes narrowed, the pupils near pinpricks. "That is our public posture, as well you know. On mainland France, we follow that policy strictly, in line with our European allies. Abroad we are sometimes able to be more flexible. This is one such occasion. But this business of the missing ship and what lies behind it puts the whole negotiation in jeopardy. And that negotiation affects every one of us at this table. Me, Chantal – and you."

"How so?" But even as he asked the question, D'Arcy already knew the answer.

"The hostage in question is Philippe Chaumont."

Azadi was trembling as he replaced the handset of the telephone.

This was not the sort of situation he liked at all. Like most Iranians he was by nature a gentle, courteous man. He had originally been appointed as a junior cultural attaché, and saw his rôle as influencing the Western view of the Islamic Revolution through the promotion of traditional Persian arts and crafts, the country's rich historical treasures. Silverware, woven carpets, calligraphy and architecture. They were his chosen weapons to achieve an understanding with the enemies of Allah.

An intensely private man, he was never happier than when sitting quietly at home with his family reading aloud the works of Iran's many respected poets. He had even attempted to write verse himself.

No, he did not like this at all.

He had not asked to be made 'controller' of the *Pessarane Behesht* cell in Paris. He had been called on to take the job in the name of the Imam and the survival of the Islamic Republic. It was a directive from the Department for the Export of Revolution. It would not have been wise for his health, or that of his wife and three children, to have turned it down.

In consequence he was a man in battle with his own conscience. He survived by being efficient at his work, if not deliberately unimaginative at times. When occasionally he read in the newspapers of atrocities attributed to the *Pessarane Behesht* he persuaded himself that they were lies manipulated by the Great Satan. In his mind the CIA had become an evil, many-tentacled monster that was trying to strangle his young nation by every means possible.

When he knew for certain that a particular shooting or

explosion was due to the very cell that he controlled, he consoled himself that it was the will of Allah.

After all, closeted anonymously in the Iranian Embassy on avenue d'Iéna, it was easy to distance himself from events beyond its railings.

Today though had been different. Today he had seen violence at first hand. His suit was still stained with the blood of the Vietnamese manservant of Nader Nadirpur.

It had been his baptism in the struggle for survival of the Islamic Revolution. Now he was in the front line. And it frightened him. Yet, at the same time, he felt a strange exhilaration at being part of the movement. No longer need he consider himself a charlatan, an impostor.

When he had received news that morning from Teheran via Geneva that the ship he had chartered had gone missing, he indulged himself in genuine anger. It was fuelled by intelligence information that Nadirpur was a suspected sympathiser of the late Reza Shah. He was consumed by indignation that there had been so many attempts to swindle his country in its attempts to gain arms to protect itself from the aggression of Iraq.

Once he and his henchman had been obliged to leave the wrecked apartment on the avenue Foch, he had been filled with apprehension at having to report his failure direct to Teheran. He had only twice before ever spoken to the man they called Sabbah. On both occasions, after he had finished talking, he had been a perspiring, gibbering wreck. His leader's menace and awe was able to transmit itself thousands of miles over a telephone line, such was his presence. Perhaps, Azadi ruminated, there was some truth in the popular rumour that Sabbah was indeed a sorcerer of immense supernatural powers.

This time had been the worst of all. Yet, thankfully, his leader's rage was not directed at him, but at the conspiracy of Nadirpur and the French and British Governments to steal the arms shipment that was rightfully the property of Iran. His leader did not believe for one moment the protestations of innocence. It was all a smokescreen to make them believe that the *Clarion Call* had been lost at sea.

Vengeance must be exacted. Pressure must be exerted. The shipowner must be forced to reveal the whereabouts of the ship. Sabbah gave his directive, and Azadi dutifully noted down the orders in his neat, precise script.

It had seemed so straightforward then. But looking down at the words now, it did not appear so simple.

How did you apply pressure to a man you could not even find?

After the incident on avenue Foch, Azadi had left a man to watch in a surveillance car. But the man was a fool, a low-grade *Pessarane Behesht* attachment who had been foisted on him by some egocentric mullah operating from Geneva.

The man had attempted to follow Nadirpur's BMW car and the girl motorcyclist when they left later in the morning. But he had been easily outwitted in the tangled back streets of Paris.

Once again Azadi thumbed through the intelligence report for some inspiration.

The shipowner had no relatives remaining in Iran, and none in France of whom they were aware. Some in the United States had changed their names after they had fled Teheran and had successfully disappeared. He had no friends, except the Vietnamese manservant.

His business contacts were being checked, but it seemed unlikely to Azadi that any of them would have been in a position to spirit the shipowner away at a moment's notice.

The only clue had come in the late morning. A telephone call from a man claiming to be Nadirpur's security adviser. A man called D'Arcy. Not an uncommon name in Paris.

Idly he turned to the London addendum that had been recently updated while the shipping contract had been under negotiation.

He read the personal notes again, and this time he raised an eyebrow. It had meant nothing to him at the time, but now . . .

Very slowly an idea began to form at the back of his mind.

He leafed over another page. Attached to the inventory of *Clarion Call*'s true cargo was the photocopy of a letter from a company called IAP in London. It confirmed that it would supply a sea-marshal and all necessary protective equipment and training to satisfy the ship's insurers for safe passage in the Gulf war zone.

One of the directors on the letterhead was Pierre Roquelaure, the man who had arranged Azadi's deal.

Another was Robert D'Arcy.

Carefully he wrote out the letters on his pad. D'-A-R-C-Y. His suspicions were confirmed.

Angrily he underscored the name with his pen. The point tore through the paper.

He reached again for the telephone, this time excitement replacing his fear. "Get me this Teheran number," he demanded.

## 6

The hot and humid weather that had been suffocating Paris continued the next two days. It contributed to D'Arcy's increasingly bad mood as he scoured the city in his search for the directors of Spidex International Trading.

Roquelaure arranged for him to visit DGSE head-quarters on the boulevard Berthier ring road. Colloquially known as *la piscine*, so named after the nearby disused les Tourelles swimming pool, the complex of modern and antiquated buildings was hidden behind an eighteen-foot high wall.

There D'Arcy met an affable, mild-mannered man whom Roquelaure introduced simply as Hubert. In his early forties with thinning curly hair and a ready smile, his dress was in marked contrast to the usually sober attire of British security service personnel. A colourful seersucker summer jacket covered a yellow polo shirt and a gold bracelet clung to his wrist.

"Sheikh Abdullah Hayira was definitely Jordanian," Hubert pronounced, tapping the file with a certain theatrical air. "His banking and legal references all checked out. They still do, except that the bank officials will no longer tell us anything. Decidedly unhelpful. That makes me think he must have connections with the Jordanian Government – he probably works for the Jordanian Secret Service, either full time or in some ad hoc capacity. I doubt that it is his real name."

"Where does he live?" D'Arcy asked.

Hubert waved his hand with a flourish. "That's a good

question. He claims to have several houses – in Switzerland, London, Rome and a rented apartment in New York. He was always on the move, he said. But they weren't checked because at the time he was renting a suite at the Crillon."

That figured, D'Arcy thought. The fabulous Crillon, with its marble columns, crystal chandeliers and tapestries, was probably the most exclusive hotel in Paris. One wouldn't normally suspect the credentials of anyone who could afford to stay at such a place.

"He said he was planning to buy an apartment in the city," Hubert added with a sly smile, "as soon as he found somewhere suitable."

"How did he pay his bill?"

"I spoke to the hotel yesterday. It was settled by charge card, and that was always debited from his bank in Jordan. The same bank that no longer wishes to speak to us."

"What about his fellow directors?"

"Alas I only met them once. They were apparently all jet-setters like Sheikh Hayira. Always flying from one business deal to another. At least that was the story. However, we insisted that all board members should attend the initial meeting to agree the deal. Anyway there are details of each in the file."

"Was there anything at all about them that struck you as odd?"

"Not odd as such. It later occurred to me that almost every one of the board members was of a different nationality. That I thought a little strange. I mean, as the company had its origins in Jordan, you might expect a preponderance of Jordanians on the board. But no. There was just one, then an Iraqi, a Saudi, a Kuwaiti – and an Englishman."

D'Arcy sat up. "English?"

"Yes, a quiet man. Did not say anything during the meeting." Hubert squinted as though at some object in the middle distance as he tried to recall. "In fact I remember he nearly didn't make the meeting. Said that urgent business had cropped up and tried to cancel his appearance at the last minute."

Roquelaure, who had been silent until now, said: "I insisted that he attend. That, or else no deal. He came."

D'Arcy glanced at Hubert's dossier. "Cupplewaite. George Cupplewaite, is that him?"

"Yes, that's him. Gave the name of his solicitors in London as his contact address. If anything he was more secretive than the others. Said he was nearly always travelling."

"Did he mention any countries in particular?"

Roquelaure said: "I remember Kenya, Hong Kong and the Sultanate of Oman."

A bell rang somewhere in D'Arcy's subconscious. "Oman?"

Hubert was surprised. "Is that significant?"

D'Arcy shrugged. "Just that it's the region where *Clarion Call* appears to have vanished. Tell me, do you have a photograph of these people?"

"Only Sheikh Hayira, and that's in the file," Hubert replied. "They insisted that they held the meeting at a place of their choosing and only told us at the last minute. It wasn't practical to take photographs. We thought we'd have an opportunity at subsequent meetings but, as I've said, it was to be the only time that we all met together."

"George Cupplewaite," D'Arcy said. "What did he look like?"

"He was in his late fifties, I think. But very slim and of average height. And a moustache, I remember a moustache."

"And very tanned," Roquelaure added.

"But he said very little," Hubert recalled. "However, he had very alert eyes. I don't think he missed much. He looked very –" he searched for the word, "I think, furtive. He looked furtive."

Roquelaure studied his fingertips. "And now we know why."

*　　*　　*

143

*"Sit near my tomb, and bring wine and music – Feeling thy presence, I shall come out of my sepulchre – Rise, slowly moving creature, and let me contemplate thy beauty."*

Jalal Shamlou woke with a start. Her sweet words were still echoing in his ears as he came slowly back to reality.

The Iran Air jet must be nearing Paris because there was an undercurrent of activity as passengers sorted out their belongings and talked excitedly to one another. To his embarrassment he realised he had an erection and moved quickly to place a copy of the *Teheran Times* on his lap before the stewardess reached his row.

She offered him the tray of boiled sweets. There was a hint of a smile on the pale, unmade-up face that was surrounded by a black *maghnéeh* hood.

He shook his head, blushing. She reminded him vaguely of the woman in his dream, and he felt sure she had noticed the tent the newspaper on his lap had formed.

"But you did not eat earlier," she said kindly.

Again he shook his head. It was true he had had no stomach for the pallid lamb chops that he had been offered for lunch.

"The sweets will help your ears when we land," she insisted.

Reluctantly he took one.

"And your friend?"

He glanced sideways at Ahmad. He was asleep now, his unlined face peaceful like a baby's, except that his mouth hung loosely open as he snored lightly. At the *Pessarane Behesht* camp the young man had been known as Matchsticks because he was very tall and thin, with long monkey arms which he moved in an uncoordinated fashion that amused his comrades. He was almost without shoulders, reminding Shamlou of a tenpin skittle.

He took another sweet from the stewardess. "How long now?"

"About half-an-hour before Paris," she answered, and he was relieved when she moved on down the aisle.

Just half-an-hour to Paris. Just half-an-hour until he

began the mission. The type of mission for which he had trained so long at the camp, for which he had endured so many indignities. A mission for which he had been chosen personally by Sabbah.

It had all happened so quickly that he could still not believe it. Only that morning he had been summoned to the tent of the bearded one. He had been told very little, and even that he had difficulty in remembering because he was so filled with excitement and anticipation. It did not occur to him that he might also have been frightened.

Pack a small bag, he had been told, you are going to Paris. There is a job to be done. Our members there have need of someone very special. To wreak vengeance on those who would betray the Islamic Revolution. You, Jalal Shamlou, are that very special someone. And you have had the dream.

He noticed the change of pitch in the engine noise and the slight tilt of the aircraft as it began its descent.

Shutting his eyes, he pressed his head back against the seat, recalling the words he had been told. Getting it clear in his mind. Making sure he understood what had happened, what was expected of him.

A consignment of vital arms for the war with the accursed President Sadeq of Iraq had been paid for by Teheran, to be delivered by ship. That ship had suddenly disappeared in placid waters without trace. A modern ship with the most modern communications. While in Paris the Arab arms dealers who had arranged the deal had also vanished with half-a-billion dollars of Iranian money.

The shipowner had protested his innocence, claiming that the loss of his ship was genuine. The bearded one did not believe his treacherous words, but gave him the benefit of the doubt and twenty-four hours to reveal the whereabouts of the vessel. When that time was up an envoy from the Iranian Embassy in Paris had been violently beaten up when he called at the shipowner's apartment. Then the shipowner had gone into hiding.

Attempts to find him by a local *Hezbollah* cell had failed.

Jalal Shamlou was to change all that. This called for the expertise of the *Pessarane Behesht*.

And he had to admit that it was a clever plan to winkle Nader Nadirpur out of his hiding place and force him to tell the truth. It had been made possible by the officers of the *Vezarat-e Ettelaat Va Amniyat-e Kishvar*, the Ministry of Intelligence and Internal Security, who kept detailed files on all Iranian exiles throughout the world, whether or not they supported the new Islamic order. Shamlou's assignment would be coordinated from the Iranian mission to the United Nations in Geneva. They would direct his 'controller' whom he would shortly meet in Paris.

He had felt so proud when he had said goodbye to the veteran Hamman. His new-found friend and ally had looked at him strangely, questioningly, but had asked nothing of young Shamlou's mission. No doubt he was aware of the vow of silence.

He had taken the boy in his arms like a father saying farewell to his son. He had hugged him closely and Shamlou had felt the warm rough texture of the bearded cheek against the smooth skin of his own. He'd felt the tightening in his throat and tasted the salt of his own tears in his mouth.

Hamman had stood back then, and held up the tattoo above his right wrist. Shamlou read the words again. *To God and Yourself be True*.

"Do what you have to do, Jalal. But whatever you do, do it for Allah and for Islam. Not for anyone who uses His holy name for their own ends. Do you hear me, Jalal?"

In tears Shamlou had croaked: "I hear you, Darvish Hamman."

Then the old veteran had gone.

Shamlou was in no doubt that this would be a dangerous operation. Dangerous, that was, to himself and to the snoring Matchsticks beside him. It would require animal cunning, zeal and the utter ruthlessness demanded in defence of Islam. At least danger meant nothing to Shamlou now. He knew a place awaited him in paradise. By the

146

side of the woman who had read him poetry. The woman who had loved him. The only woman who had ever loved him. It was a cruel trick that she had been a dream, that he could not join her yet.

Matchsticks stirred, his snore becoming a sudden snort that woke him up. It took several moments for him to orientate himself and wipe the sleep from his eyes.

Protruding teeth showed as he smiled. "Hello, Jalal, surely we must be nearly there."

Shamlou found himself irritated by his comrade's gormless manner and unkempt hair. Matchsticks would have been the last one at the *Pessarane Behesht* camp he would have chosen to accompany him on this mission. "If you hadn't been asleep all this time, you'd *know* that we are nearly there."

The young man scratched his head and looked around the cabin. He appeared unaware of the rebuke. "I hate Paris. It's full of blasphemy and decadence. The streets are full of harlots, there are live sex shows around Pigalle . . ."

"Shut up," Shamlou snapped. He wasn't in the mood to hear of such things.

"Just look at them," Matchsticks muttered in disgust as he watched his fellow passengers. "Treacherous *taghouti*, every one of them."

Shamlou turned his head. It wasn't exactly true; they weren't all rich and middle-class Iranians who had learned to survive the Revolution by paying lip service to it – then bending the rules to suit themselves. There was also a group of male students; three soldiers on their way to have some specialist medical treatment, and a number of older couples of peasent stock who were probably visiting their well-to-do offspring in Paris. But he knew what Matchsticks meant.

Most of the men who earlier had transformed the small areas of carpet beside the emergency exits into makeshift mosques now sported neckties – the most blatant symbol of Westernism. As though by magic virtually every *chador* cloak and *hejab* headdress had disappeared, the women having changed into smart dresses and tailored suits in the privacy of the toilets. Everywhere mascara was being rolled and lipstick carefully drawn.

"We are not even off the plane and they are playing into the hands of the Great Satan," Matchsticks sneered.

Shamlou hissed: "I will not tell you again to keep quiet. Do not draw attention to yourself. Say another word and I will not have you on this mission."

The other man shrugged and fell silent. To be deprived of his place on the mission was one thing that he was not prepared to let happen.

Shamlou experienced a glow of satisfaction. This was the first time he had exercised his authority and it had worked. The tiresome Matchsticks shut up like a clam. He knew his place, Shamlou mused contentedly. After all, he was 'chosen'; his comrade was not.

Jalal Shamlou was seething.

He felt shamed and humiliated by the officious treatment he received at the hands of the pompous men at Immigration. Standing with their noses in the air. As though he had something bad-smelling on his shoes. For an hour and a half they had kept him standing. Clearly amused at his discomfort and his mounting anger. Questions and more questions. Poring over the sparse details he had been obliged to enter on his landing card. It had been with supreme effort that he had controlled his temper.

That temper was raised higher still when he was finally allowed through and found Matchsticks already waiting, idly smoking and flicking through a copy of *Lui*.

He snatched the girlie magazine from his comrade's hands and tossed it on the seat.

Matchsticks looked shocked. "You didn't have to do that. I just wanted to see what filth they were up to now."

"Come on," Shamlou snapped, and led the way towards the exit. "Our boys should have finished the bombing back in '86. Blown the lot of these French bastards up. Who do they think they are?"

"Friends of Satan," Matchsticks agreed. "I told you so. Do we catch a taxi?"

Shamlou stopped dead. "In the name of the Imam, use what little brains you've got. We've trained together, you know the routine."

"This case is heavy."

"Then you should have packed a smaller one – as you were told to do!" He stalked off to find the airport bus to take them to the SNCF railway station at Roissy, leaving Matchsticks to struggle after him as best he could.

At the station they fought their way through the crush of travellers to join the ticket queue which already numbered some three hundred people. Finally, hot and irritable, they squeezed onto the train for the rapid journey to the capital. Shamlou was gratified to find themselves jostled by so many foreign students, many loaded down with rucksacks, clearly in Paris for cheap hostel holidays. He and Matchsticks blended in perfectly as had been predicted back in Teheran.

Rather than alight at the Gare du Nord railway terminal, they stayed on for another stop, leaving at Châtelet in the centre of the city. There they transferred to the Métro, taking the rubber-wheeled underground train on the Neuilly line to the west of the city.

Following instructions they left at Clemenceau station, emerging after a short climb of steps in the bustle and noise of the Champs Elysées. Shamlou was immediately struck by the difference with Teheran. Here everything was bright with colour, the walkers on the tree-shaded boulevards relaxed, content to stroll against the frenetic background of racing, hooting traffic. The elegant shops were filled with every type of produce, from unimaginable foodstuffs to high fashion and jewellery; the seats of the pavement cafés were filled with people happily eating and drinking and watching the world pass by; queues waited expectantly outside cinemas offering the very latest movies from around the world.

It was a far cry from the city of Teheran which Shamlou

had last seen when paying a visit to his mother before going to the Sabbah camp. Always dirty and drab under the Shah, the streets now showed signs of actual decay and neglect. Many shops were boarded up, their owners having perished in the war or at the hands of the Komitehs, or been bankrupted by the collapsed economy. Every available wall space was covered with graffiti and fervent slogans, or the accumulated remnants of countless religious posters. The pavements were cracked and uneven. There was little colour to be seen in people's clothing now. Dull greys and browns predominated and black was much in evidence. But worst of all was the atmosphere. Not the choking fumes from the traditional traffic jams. It was a pervading atmosphere of sullen oppression that cocooned the place; few smiles and friendly words were exchanged. Everyone got on with the business at hand, preoccupied with the problems of food shortages, lack of funds and compliance with the rules of the Islamic order.

Shamlou put it down to war weariness. Surely the citizens of any country at war would be the same? No family, he knew, had not suffered the bereavement or tragic maiming of someone near and dear. His own family had been no exception.

He and Matchsticks found the Elysées Roundpoint on the north side of the avenue. It was a glitzy split-level shopping centre with brightly lit window displays of expensive fashions. They took the escalator down to the lower level and the Grillapolis café. The décor was all polished glass tiles and gleaming brass.

They sat at one of the marble-topped tables and ordered coffee from a bored waitress who scarcely spared them a glance. Five minutes passed before contact was made.

"Is this chair free?" the stranger asked. He was a quietly spoken middle-aged man whom anyone would find difficult to remember. A grey man, thought Shamlou. Grey suit, grey hair and a greyish complexion. The only dab of colour was a dark blue pocket handkerchief. Otherwise, Shamlou mused, he resembled a photographic negative.

When the waitress had served their orders and moved away, the grey man said softly: "I am Azadi. I am your controller for this mission." He opened his briefcase and pushed a large buff envelope across the table. "These are your new identities. Passports, permits, identity cards, student passes."

Shamlou looked at them dubiously. "Are they genuine? The British authorities are very thorough."

Azadi did not let his irritation show. "They belong to two genuine Iranian students here in Paris. Your photographs have been substituted by our experts."

"What of the real students?" Matchsticks asked.

"They are not your concern."

A hard edge crept into Shamlou's voice. "Tell us."

Azadi sighed. "They were supporters of Reza Shah," he said, as though that explained everything.

Shamlou caught the nuance. "*Were?*"

"They have disappeared today. They will not be found."

"How can you be sure?"

"Bodies fed to pigs are not found."

Inwardly Shamlou shuddered, but Matchsticks thought it was a huge joke and laughed loudly.

Azadi looked at him scathingly, then turned to Shamlou. "A note has been left at the flat where they lived, advising friends that they have gone to London for a vacation. There will be no queries, and if anyone from Britain were to check back here then everything will tally."

Shamlou nodded his understanding.

"Now let me have your own passports and anything that might give a clue to your true identities."

Both men placed their wallets on the table; in accordance with their instructions, all documents and tickets had been kept together. The grey man scooped them into his briefcase and snapped it shut. Shamlou picked up the buff envelope and stuffed it in the pocket of his windcheater.

"In there you will find two tickets for a coach trip to London," Azadi explained. "Go to the Eurolines station at Porte de la Villette. The journey takes about eight-and-a-half hours. Try to get some sleep. You will arrive at the Victoria Coach Station in London at dawn."

"Do we go to the embassy?" Matchsticks asked.

Azadi tried not to show his despair. "Of course not. That is the last place you must go. Make your way to the Pizzaland restaurant in Gloucester Road by twelve noon. There you will meet a man who will brief you on the details of when and where the operation will take place. You will recognise him because he will be sitting alone reading a paperback edition of the Holy Koran."

Shamlou's eyes narrowed. "Who is this man? Is he *Pessarane Behesht*?"

"Certainly not. He is merely a student from Imperial College in Exhibition Road. It is he who has been instructed by our intelligence people in London how to conduct the operation with three friends."

"How do we know they can be trusted?"

The grey man smiled and Shamlou noted how white and perfect his teeth were. "They have families in Teheran. Families who have now been taken into Evin prison. If the students fail, or disobey in any way, they know their families will not come out again. Besides, they are just impoverished students. They will welcome the money we will pay."

Shamlou exchanged a glance with Matchsticks. All seemed satisfactory.

"Do these people know the whereabouts of the safe house?" Shamlou asked.

"They know nothing of your part of the operation. Only our London intelligence people know of the safe house. The address they have selected is in that envelope. The owners have not been approached. That will be entirely up to you."

"Tell me about them."

"He is a wealthy Iranian, an art dealer, who is now a naturalised Briton. He is married to an American woman. They have a son who is at boarding school. As you might imagine, the family is at pains to have no contact with our

152

embassy whatsoever. In fact he has had no contact with our officials since the Shah fled Iran in 1979. He is selected for that reason, because he will not be suspected by the police."

"He will not be co-operative," Shamlou thought aloud.

"It is up to you to make him co-operative," Azadi replied softly. "He still has an elderly mother living in Yazd. The point is that he has a suitable house in north London. It is detached in an acre of ground with high walls. There is an integral garage from which you can gain direct access to the cellar. You will not be overlooked by anyone."

"If he has no contact with the embassy, how do we know all this about him?" Matchsticks asked suspiciously.

Azadi was becoming exasperated by all the questions. He was used to being obeyed without demur. He trusted the curiosity of these young men was an indication of their special training for the task. "Our people have met him in the social life of the arts world. Nothing to do with official embassy business." Anxious to conclude the meeting, he added: "Everything else you need to know is in that envelope – that includes any funds that you may require. They'll be available to you through a special bank account in London. There is one more thing. A *Pessarane Behesht* sleeper cell has been activated in London to assist you. Originally it was planned for them to eliminate enemies of the Islamic Republic, but this mission was deemed more important. They will have the weapons you will need. They know Britain well, and will be of great help to you. But, remember, you are in command. You are responsible."

Shamlou's dark eyes held him in a contemptuous gaze. "I shall not fail. I am chosen." Roughly he pushed back his chair and stood. "*Allah akbar.*"

Without another word he turned and strode towards the escalator, leaving Matchsticks to struggle after him with his heavy case.

\* \* \*

153

"Answer that, will you, Beth!" Ali Christie called out.

He was in the dressing room adjoining the master bedroom, wearing just his socks and silk boxer shorts, when the doorbell rang. The wearing of boxer shorts was just one of the many American ways he'd adopted over the years. Like his new name, changed by deed poll nine years before. Otis Christie – very American. And a wise precaution in 1979 when conducting business in the USA. At that time – even now – a Persian name like Ali Tabrizi was a positive liability. Especially when American hostages were being held in Teheran.

Only his American wife and close friends still called him Ali, pointing out that while Otis might be a great name for a black jazz singer, it was hardly suitable for an art dealer.

"Can you hear me, Beth?" he called again as he hurriedly extracted his golfing slacks from the rack. He liked to get a few holes in before work. "Will you answer the door?"

"Okay, okay!" came the voice from downstairs. It was followed by a stifled yawn.

Christie shook his head in despair. Dearly though he loved his wife, her early morning lethargy never failed to rankle. He would be up with the morning chorus, while Beth was happy to mooch around for hours in her nightdress, drinking black coffee, smoking cigarettes and watching breakfast television. He had never yet seen her washed and dressed before he left for his game of golf on the way to the small art gallery that he owned in Brook Street.

However, this morning Beth Christie was brighter than usual; she planned to shop for the dinner party she was holding later in the week.

She peered through the security peephole in the solid Edwardian oak door. As Harrow-on-the-Hill had one of the highest burglary rates in London, it was understandable that residents of the numerous private roads should be cautious.

Half-expecting it to be the milkman, she was mildly

irritated to see two young men standing on the steps outside. They were both smartly dressed in casual clothes, although the taller one had rather untidy hair.

"I hope they're not bloody Jehovah's Witnesses," she muttered to herself as she bent to release the chain, a cigarette clamped between her teeth.

She swung the door open. "Yes?"

"Good morning," the shorter of the two said with a charming smile. "Is it Mrs Christie?"

Beth was surprised he knew her name. Instinctively she ran a hand through her dishevelled hair, smoothing it into some kind of order. He was quite handsome with an olive-skinned, boyish face. But it was the eyes that drew her attention, dark and smouldering with lovely long lashes. She wished she'd already applied her make-up; she was still good-looking without it, she knew, but at thirty-eight you had to expect a few flaws.

She hid her cigarette behind the door. She didn't want him thinking she was a slag. "Yes, I'm Mrs Christie. What did you want?"

The young man continued to smile. "We are business acquaintances of your husband. We wanted to have an urgent word with him on an important matter."

She laughed lightly, sensing his interest in her. "Ah, so you *are* Iranian. I thought so. Such nice manners. I'm sure Ali will be pleased to have a quick word before he leaves." She opened the door wider and noticed the mustard-coloured van parked on the drive; there were two other men sitting in the back. "Do step inside – and please excuse my dress. It is rather early."

They followed her in, closing the door behind them.

"Ali!" Beth called up the stairs. "Two gentlemen to see you." She gave their names.

"Who?" he shouted back. "Never mind, I'll be down."

The young man smiled sheepishly. "I expect he forgets our names. He must know many people."

Beth shuffled her feet in the awkward silence and found herself looking at the second man more closely. He was tall and gangling with a slack mouth and appeared to be holding something behind his back. She guessed it was a briefcase.

Ali Christie was straightening his tie as he reached the bottom of the stairs. He viewed the two men with curiosity. "I'm afraid, gentlemen, you have me at a disadvantage. I don't seem to recall –"

Shamlou smiled. "Perhaps, sir, this will remind you."

He reached inside his windcheater while Christie watched, expecting a wallet and business card to be produced. He certainly was not anticipating the snub-nosed automatic pistol that was suddenly pointed at his forehead.

"God!" Beth gasped, stepping back.

"Is this some kind of joke?" Christie demanded, not believing his own eyes.

Shamlou looked at the man with disgust. "Joke? I'll show you what sort of joke!" He turned to Matchsticks. "Do it NOW!"

Matchsticks nodded and stepped towards the woman. In panic she stumbled backwards, twisted round and tried to run into the living room. Matchsticks gave chase, catching her in mid-stride. She fell heavily, landing on the marble hearth of the fireplace and shattering the display vase of flowers.

Her legs splayed inelegantly and with her mouth wide and dry with fear, she stared up at the stranger. For the first time she saw the red tin container he had been hiding behind his back. Realised what it was.

"NO!" she screamed as the stench of petrol reached her nostrils.

Christie stepped forward to intervene. He was stopped by the snout of Shamlou's pistol, jammed hard under his chin.

"SHUT UP!" Matchsticks bawled at the hysterical woman and began slopping contents from the petrol can over the front of her dressing gown.

"The business!" Shamlou snapped. "Tell them!"

Matchsticks grinned malevolently as the room began to

156

stink. "Pavilion Gallery!" he shouted his well-rehearsed reply. "Brook Street."

"And the boy!" Shamlou hissed, his eyes fixed on Christie's blood-drained face.

"Greenhill Private School, Hampshire!" Matchsticks answered sharply. "Gregory Christie! Fifth form!"

Beth shut her eyes and opened her lungs, the scream reverberating round the house like the cry of a soul in torment. Then the fumes caught in her throat and her yell petered into a racking cough. Her body started to tremble, totally beyond her control, as she felt the astringent liquid soak into her skin. And she began to sob.

Joyously Matchsticks pulled a lighter from his pocket, rolled the flint with his thumb and watched the flame leap into life.

"Don't!" Christie croaked, his Adam's apple crushed painfully against the thrusting automatic. "P-please d-don't!"

Shamlou smiled gently. "No more," he warned. He did not trust his comrade not to kill them all in a fireball.

He lowered the weapon and pushed the man roughly back against the living room door. "Listen to me, Mr Christie, and listen *very* carefully. You have betrayed your country and your religion. You have turned your back on your people and consorted with the Great Satan, America. You have even married this whore of a woman, and consorted with other traitors."

Christie's eyes widened. "I have not –"

"Shut up!" Shamlou snarled, clearly controlling his anger with difficulty. "Now, all this will be forgiven, we are not barbarians. Allah forgives those who repent. But first you must pay penance."

The art dealer opened his mouth, uncomprehending.

"You will do what we say, and that is very simple. For the next few days – for as long as it takes – you just continue your life as though nothing has happened. That is all. Nothing else." He seemed calmer now, and smiled widely so that Christie noticed how white his teeth were.

157

"See, simple, yes? And when it is over, we will just disappear from your lives and Allah will wash His hands of you for ever."

Momentarily the pounding eased in Christie's chest and he struggled to find the courage to speak. "When what is over?"

Shamlou's smile vanished as fast as it had come. "No questions! There are four of us. Always at least one person will be with you at all times. If anyone asks who we are, you say you are having your house decorated. Meanwhile you go to work as usual."

Christie's mouth was now quite dry, and he had to gather saliva before he could speak. "What about Beth?" he asked in a hoarse whisper.

Shamlou looked down at the cowering woman in the hearth, the petrol-sodden gown clinging to her body. "Your dear wife stays with us. If you tell anyone of what goes on, or call the police – anything – she goes up in flames."

"WHOOF!" Matchsticks said suddenly. He began to chuckle.

Shamlou lowered the automatic. "And after that it will be the turn of your gallery and your boy to be destroyed at any time of our choosing." His gently mocking smile returned. "Not to mention your mother who still lives in Yazd."

Christie fell back against the door, his eyes closed. This just wasn't happening. Wasn't, wasn't, wasn't! It was a nightmare from which he would awaken at any moment.

Shamlou turned to his comrade. "Go and fetch the others. Have everything brought in and taken down to the cellar. And I want the explosives set as soon as possible. We haven't much time."

Matchsticks sneered down at the shaking woman, then turned nonchalantly towards the front door.

Shamlou said: "Now you go to work, Mr Christie."

The nightmare had not passed, and the art dealer forced

himself to open his eyes, to face the bleak reality. "H-how can I?" he whispered. "I am shaking. Look, I can hardly stand."

Shamlou stepped back, and when he spoke all the anger and passion was gone from his voice. Again he was the charming young man who had knocked at the door just ten minutes earlier. "Oh, I think you can, Mr Christie. You are assured no harm need befall you or your wife. You are safe. There is no threat – as long as you do exactly as you are told." His voice was the texture of syrup, his tone consoling. "And that starts with going to work, perfectly normally."

Christie swallowed hard and nodded. He let go of the door he was clutching for support and tested the muscles in his legs. Ignoring the fluttering sensation of his calves, he walked slowly and stiffly towards the sofa where his briefcase lay.

"See, it is not so difficult," Shamlou mocked. "Now leave and get in your car."

A voice wailed from the hearth. "Don't go, Ali! Don't leave me!"

Christie couldn't bear to look at his wife; he only half-turned. "I have to, Beth, for both our sakes. Be brave. I'll be back tonight. Usual time."

Shamlou smirked with satisfaction. "You get the idea. That is nice."

"P-p-please!"

The door slammed shut, and Shamlou felt himself relax. It had gone remarkably well; his intensive training had paid off handsomely. The application of shock tactics to bend the will of the unwilling. To instil such fear that total domination and obedience is guaranteed. He looked down at the woman. She was a pitiful sight, still lying where she had fallen, too terrified to move an inch. Ashen-faced, she was gibbering quietly to herself, her petrol-sodden hair plastered to her head and her dripping gown showing her legs almost to the crotch.

Shamlou began feeling an immense sense of power, and

was aware of his loins stirring. Momentarily he had a vision of the woman in the garden.

Beth caught sight of the strange light in his eyes, and was frightened. In a tremulous voice she whispered: "Who are you people?"

He looked down at her contemptuously. "Allah's chosen. We are the *Pessarane Behesht*."

"What?" She didn't understand. "My Persian isn't very good."

He looked around the room absently. "We are the Sons of Heaven."

*My name is Philippe Chaumont.*

*Just a few days ago I was foolish enough to allow my hopes to rise. For the first time in nearly three years someone spoke my name. Spoke my name and told me that I was about to be released.*

*I was taken from the cellar in Beirut and enjoyed the warmth of the sun on my skin for the first time in a thousand days. It was a short-lived experience before I was nailed into a coffin and transported by car across the rubble-strewn streets of this war-torn city. On the journey I heard sporadic gunfire and by listening to snatches of conversation between my guards, gathered that Amal guerrillas were fighting yet again with Shia militia, the Hezbollah.*

*Only the day before I might have prayed for a stray round to puncture the car and my coffin and put me out of my endless misery. But with my release so close I think the angels themselves might have wept if I had perished.*

*When the car stopped I knew exactly where we were. Don't ask me how. When one is blind the other senses conspire to compensate. My hearing is painfully acute, and my sense of touch and smell quite profound. I have even developed another faculty not normally considered as one of the five senses. That is a sense of direction. No matter how many twists and turns that vehicle made, I was able to keep track.*

I had come to know Beirut well before my incarceration and various clues of sound and smell enabled me to pinpoint our destination. It was logical really that I should be brought from my anonymous safe house to the Hezbollah's Hay Madi barracks. This was confirmed when I heard a Syrian soldier talking at a roadblock we encountered. I think my guards bribed him to let us pass.

I knew the single-storey building from memory, standing as it did close to the dividing line with the Amal-controlled suburb of Chiyah in southern Beirut. No doubt the flat roof of the shattered and shell-pocked building was still guarded by Shia militia, ever watchful behind their sandbag emplacements. No doubt, too, the tattered flag of Iran still fluttered from its mast. In the surrounding debris of apartment blocks more militia would be crouched, forming the outer defence ring of the beleaguered stronghold.

Although encircled by its enemies, I knew just how impregnable it was. The location had often been discussed at my embassy. In those days it was estimated to be guarded by some three hundred Hezbollah fanatics and, despite being a single-storey construction, it was known to have several basement levels. It would have taken a battalion to root the fanatics out, and the casualties would have been horrendous.

On my arrival my coffin was carried to one of those lower levels before I was allowed out. I was kept in a small, square concrete room which had rat-droppings on the floor. Although I was shackled to a radiator, my blindfold was removed and I was given a cup of water and a sweetmeat. I could only attribute my captors' sudden change of attitude to the fact that they were pleased to be getting rid of me. That they were pleased with whatever deal they'd made for my release.

The door was left slightly ajar, and there was much coming and going; much excited chatter.

161

*My brain became a sponge, suddenly spurred into action. After three dormant years it began humming like a computer, sucking in information of which it had been starved, until my head began to hurt physically with the effort.*

*I gleaned several things. The Hay Madi barracks appeared to be divided into three sections. The first was the sleeping and messing quarters of the Hezbollah streetfighters. The second, where I was held, was filled with Amal prisoners taken in the fighting and with local Lebanese hostages.*

*But the third, deep in the bowels of the earth, was kept mysteriously locked at all times. It was protected by special guards of the Pessarane Behesht, recognised by their blue headbands inscribed with Farsi script. Even the Hezbollah militia and the Revolutionary Guards were clearly wary of them.*

*It was simply guesswork that it was in that place that some of the Western hostages were kept. Such detail might prove invaluable to French Intelligence at any debrief after my release.*

*And during all this time I kept getting flashing pictures in my mind of Chantal, like a magic lantern slide. It was as though someone had turned on a current of electricity, and with every second that passed the image became brighter and stronger. The flickering individual images came closer and closer together until it was one continuous picture. It was so close that I felt I could reach out and touch her. So close I could see the pores of her skin, the delicate green threads in the irises of her eyes, the moist velvet warmth of her mouth. Smell the fragrance of her hair. She was smiling, pouting, pulling faces, striking poses like someone not knowing what to do in front of a family cine camera . . .*

*And then the door fell open.*

*I knew it was bad news. The image of Chantal vanished instantly as though someone had thrown a switch.*

*My two guards stood in the doorway. Behind them was a tall, bearded man I did not know.*

*The first guard said: "Your release is cancelled."*

162

*That was all. No hint of apology. Of regret. No expla-
nation.*

*I was manhandled to my feet, unchained, then led down
a flight of steps, lit by bare bulbs, to the inner section. A
single steel door was opened. Beyond there ran a damp,
crumbling brick passageway with a low ceiling. Several
doors ran off it, two now open as prisoners were being
moved from one to the other. No doubt to make room for
me.*

*My heart and spirits sank like a stone in a lake. I was
filled with dread, and with paralysing fear.*

*Then, in that mean, ill-lit corridor I collided with another
prisoner being pushed the other way. We were jammed
together, shoulder-to-shoulder, in the narrow confines. He
was a tall, heavily built man, and I had to look up to see
the bearded face.*

*Momentarily our eyes met. His were dark, fluid and
compassionate. In that brief fragment of time he smiled
down at me.*

*And then he was pushed roughly on, and suddenly,
inexplicably my mind was filled with a vivid picture of Christ
looking down at me as I stood at the foot of the cross.*

*I felt the spiritual strength that had deserted me flowing
back as a warm glow that welled up inside, filling my being.
Lifting my heart with a strange, ecstatic joy.*

*I said to myself, my name is Philippe Chaumont.*

## 7

Ashi Nadirpur laid out the clothes that she was going to wear that day on the bed.

This might be summer, but it was also London. Sometimes she thought her Persian blood would never acclimatise to the damp, cool climate. She settled on a plain pleated skirt in burgundy wool, a cream blouse and a lightweight cashmere sweater.

Lastly she made her selection of lingerie: fragile, feathery lace with thin straps. That was her style. It suited her diminutive stature and delicate features. Had it not been for the honey pigment of her skin, any one of her small circle of friends might have described her as a porcelain doll.

"Mummy, are you ready yet?" The impatient voice of her seven-year-old daughter. "I mustn't be late again."

Ashi glanced at the carriage clock on the dressing table. A present from Nader, it was never slow. Eight thirty.

"Don't worry, darling," she called back. "There's plenty of time."

"If you're sure," returned Sousan's voice from downstairs.

Bless her, she was such a little worrier. Late just once because the car wouldn't start and Sousan was in a panic. No doubt that was due to the ticking off she had received from that strict harridan of a teacher at the small private school in Kensington. It had been clear from the start that the spinster had taken an instant dislike to both Ashi and her daughter. Single-parent families were to be treated with suspicion; it was a status she believed lowered the tone and moral values of the school.

As Ashi dressed swiftly her eyes were drawn back to the carriage clock. Every morning, and each night before switching off the light, she would look at it. And each time it reminded her of her husband. Still the sadness weighed heavily in her heart; she wondered if those precious dreams of what might have been would ever leave her alone.

That teacher would have had a different attitude if Nader had been around. Ashi had no doubt the woman would have been as rapt at his polite charm and elegance as she herself had once been. And the teacher, too, might have made the same terrible mistake that she had made back in Teheran all those years before.

Ashi had met him during the height of the oil boom, when the late Shah was pouring the country's new-found wealth into creating an entire new infrastructure for a land that had hardly changed since biblical times.

Even now she vividly recalled the first time she saw Nader at the exclusive Royal Club, a dining, gambling and sports centre. It was a magical, velvet-warm night at the open-air poolside restaurant. Candles flickered and flower arrangements floated on the lacquered surface of the water, and the music from a string quartet filled the scented air.

It had been a special eighteenth birthday treat for Ashi. Although her father was a well-to-do market trader, his wealth was modest by comparison with that of the new jet-set. Descended from a devoutly religious family, he was mildly disapproving of Iran's high society pleasure-seekers. By nature a man of moderation and thrift, he would limit visits to places like the Royal Club to occasions of celebration. Yet, although he drank only fruit juice himself, he would say nothing if his family chose to indulge in a bottle of wine. He was tolerant, too, of his daughter's passion for the latest Western fashions. Only if the dresses

165

became too tight or too short would he make a gently reproving comment.

That night had been particularly joyous, because Ashi felt that at last her family was allowing her to blossom fully into womanhood. The jokes between her father, mother and older brother had been adult, almost *risqué*; she had been allowed several glasses of champagne without a reproachful look, and her rather revealing *décolletage* had passed without comment.

Then, while the waiters in their black ties and white gloves were serving the meal, she noticed the man at the adjoining table watching her.

He was petite like herself, but strikingly handsome. Almost pretty, she thought. With the blackest hair she had ever seen, swept straight back off the forehead. And a neat moustache which gave him a slightly rakish, debonair look.

As their eyes met he raised his glass to her, and smiled. Ashi had blushed deeply.

Later she had been surprised to learn that he wasn't in his late twenties as she had guessed, but almost a decade older, thirty-seven. Not that his age mattered to Ashi; in Iran a tradition of arranged marriages meant that maturity in a man was something to be respected. Nowadays it was almost fashionable, not least because an older man was more likely to be wealthy and successful.

The problem was finding such a man who wasn't already married. And Nader Nadirpur, Ashi discovered to her delight, was not.

Once, on a rare occasion before their marriage when they were left without a chaperone, she had asked him why he hadn't married before?

Nader Nadirpur had smiled in his usual disarming way. "I had just not met the right woman before I met you that night. You looked so happy, sweet and gentle. I thought you might be the one who was right for me."

She had sighed contentedly at his answer.

But it was not to be like that.

Although Nader Nadirpur was a considerate and attentive husband, one aspect of their otherwise perfect marriage was far from right. Behind closed doors it was a disaster.

Only once or twice did he ever become aroused enough for them to make love. More usually it left him ashamed and angry, despite his wife's kind words of consolation, and Ashi herself in an agitated state of dissatisfaction and unhappiness.

As the months passed he spent more and more time away on his growing shipping business. Their attempts at lovemaking dwindled to the point of non-existence, until there was an unspoken agreement not to try any more. He buried himself in work, while she filled every hour of the day playing tennis or golf at the Royal Club, or discoing at the Key or the Cheminée with a group of friends. Despite numerous opportunities, she loved her husband too much ever to betray him.

The momentous events that led to Ayatollah Khomeini's triumphal return to Teheran in 1979 had long overtaken the problems of Ashi's private life. With many connections in high places, Nader had seen the writing on the wall. Two years before the final fall of the Shah, he had begun transferring his wealth and business interests to Paris.

On the day Khomeini flew in to Mehrabad Airport, she and Nader Nadirpur flew out of Teheran for the last time. They were never to return.

But their new life in Paris was not to prove the dream they had both hoped it would be. They had few friends in France, and without them the dazzling night life meant nothing. Evening after evening Ashi found herself alone in their avenue Foch apartment while Nader was out on business. She took to drinking more than she should, and most nights she would cry herself to sleep, thinking of what might have been.

Her husband, too, became more withdrawn. His business was in some difficulties and, while in no danger of collapse, his fleet of ships had shrunk from eight to three against competition from the Far East.

Then, a year to the day after their arrival in Paris, came the night she would remember always. Nader Nadirpur came home late having been for a drive along the Bois de Boulogne to calm his nerves after a particularly bad day.

She remembered how different, how happy he had been when he returned after midnight. A man transformed. He had joked and they had laughed together. He opened a bottle of champagne and before she had a chance to realise what was happening they had been making love. Ashi was in ecstasy.

The next morning she had awoken happily and full of hope. Sure that, at last, their marriage was coming right.

But it was to be a cruel illusion.

Just two weeks later Nader Nadirpur broke down in tears. He confessed that he had finally come to terms with the fact that he was a homosexual, after a lifetime of denying it to himself. She learned with sadness in her heart that their recent one night of love had been after he had met a young Vietnamese man.

Together they sat by the balcony overlooking avenue Foch and cried in each other's arms until the early hours.

Yet fate was to play a strange card. On that one night of their lovemaking since moving to Paris, Ashi had conceived. Baby Sousan had been a gift from Allah, a blessing, a reward for the affection of two people for each other who were never meant to be together.

"MUMMY!"

Ashi Nadirpur jumped as her daughter appeared at the bedroom door.

"Mummy, you said you wouldn't be long." She was a beautiful child with her mother's fine bone structure and her father's black silken hair.

"I'm ready now, darling, I'll just put my scarf on."

Sousan looked pained. "No one wears headscarves in London, Mummy. It's very old-fashioned."

Ashi smiled as she knotted it at her throat. She knew she wore the scarf through a sense of guilt, a gesture to her family to say that she hadn't forgotten her religious upbringing. Silly really, because her family had no way of knowing that she still covered her head. That she still believed in Allah and prayed regularly at the nearby mosque.

After all, if it hadn't been for Him, she wouldn't have a lovely daughter. Nor a sweet and tragic husband who, despite everything, still loved them both dearly.

Indeed, if anything, spiritually they had become closer over the past seven years. Although Nader's visits to London were infrequent, his allowance was more than generous. It enabled Ashi to run a very pleasant Knightsbridge apartment, to pay for Sousan's education, and was sufficient for her not to have to work.

"Don't forget your satchel!" she reminded as she started down the stairs with Sousan skipping at her heels.

"Of course not, Mummy." Patronising.

"Did you pick up your lunchbox from the kitchen?"

"Yes!" Exasperated.

The front door opened onto a residential street. It was a beautiful cloudless morning and the canopies of the plane trees were lush and transparently golden with sunlight. Only the air was tainted by the fumes from the slow-moving cars that used the street as a short cut.

Ashi cursed silently as she crossed the pavement to the bumper-to-bumper row of parked residents' vehicles. It would take her ages to manoeuvre back and forth and force her way into the relentless stream of traffic. Then her anger was roused again as she saw that a van had double parked alongside her yellow Metro City. It totally boxed her in.

Sousan recognised the problem. "I *knew* we'd be late, Mummy!"

"We shall see!" Ashi replied testily, and marched round to the driver of the van. He was reading a newspaper, apparently oblivious to the contribution he was making to the traffic chaos. Angrily she rapped on his window. He looked up and she was mildly surprised to see that he had a youthful Middle Eastern complexion. She thought he appeared nervous as he wound down the window. As well he might, she thought, if he suspected the dressing down she was about to give him.

"What do you mean by parking like this?" she began. "Please would you move so I can get my car out."

He didn't seem to hear; his eyes were darting about, looking anxiously around.

"Will you please look at me when I'm talking to you," Ashi fumed.

Then she was aware of the coolness of a shadow falling across her back, the presence of two men behind her.

She turned, suddenly alarmed.

Two faces grotesquely disfigured in nylon stocking-masks. The shock of it choked the scream that tried to form in her throat. For a split second the two men hesitated. Ashi's eyes were averted to the pavement where little Sousan stood, open-mouthed. Even as her mother watched, a fourth man swooped from nowhere like a bird of prey and snatched the girl into his arms.

It was like some scratched old movie running at half-speed, a bizarre dream sequence. Ashi found herself rooted to the spot in disbelief as she watched the threshing legs of her daughter. While in her head the urgent sounds of the traffic had become a strangely muted cacophony, shutting her into a world of sudden deafness.

Then the hands of the stocking-masked men were on her, their fingers digging into the tender flesh of her arms. She was propelled roughly along the side of the van, squeezed between its side and the traffic. The questioning face of a passenger in a passing car stared up at her. Puzzled eyes and gawping mouth behind a window like a goldfish. Helpless to assist. And then it was gone.

Frogmarched to the open rear doors, she met the fourth man coming the other way, his arms struggling to restrain the squirming, yelling child.

170

Abruptly the dream finished and she was plunged back into reality. The street sounds rushed at her, filling her head with the roar of engines and angry hooters. People were shouting. Everything was moving, fast, bright and glittering in the sunlight. At last she found her voice, and her lungs exploded in a scream that could be heard even above the noise of the London street.

Someone brusquely pulled the headscarf down over her face, stifling her cry, cutting off her vision. She was launched into the back of the van, wincing as her knees cracked against metal. Powerful arms thrust her forward. The skin of her legs flayed along the hard ribbed floor. She felt the suspension sink as the men followed her in. The doors slammed, locking out the world.

The floor trembled beneath her as the engine was brutally gunned into life. She slid helplessly when the vehicle lurched forward, punching its way into the line of traffic. Brakes squealed and car horns blasted indignantly.

"Mummy . . ." Sousan whimpered from somewhere close by.

Ashi tried to reach her daughter in the darkness. But someone had his weight firmly pressed into the small of her back, pinning her like a butterfly in a case. She wriggled one hand free and stretched it out, searching. It found the small cold fingers of the child. They closed around Ashi's hand for comfort.

"It's all right, darling," she mumbled through the material of her scarf.

"QUIET!" a voice shouted. The van screeched round a bend at speed.

Ashi smelt something strange. A clinical smell like solvent that reminded her instantly of the time in hospital when she gave birth to Sousan. With dear Nader waiting anxiously outside . . . The stink of chloroform overwhelmed her as the wad was jammed hard under her nose. She tried to resist, to hold her breath. But the fumes seeped in until she was forced to gulp for air and she plunged into a deep and haunted sleep.

By the time the van had reached Hyde Park Corner and began heading north up the Park Lane carriageway, Ashi Nadirpur and her daughter had both lost consciousness. For the first time the three students in the back began to relax and pull off their nylon masks. It appeared as though they had got away with it. And that was really all they were concerned with. Not one took any delight or pride in what he had done. Just shared relief that their relatives in Iran would be left in peace and that they would be allowed to resume their studies.

The van sped into the Marble Arch roundabout with tyres whining. One of the students banged his fist loudly on the partition separating them from the driver. Their friend understood the message and slowed at once. He was shaking with nerves, anxious to put as many miles as he could between them and the scene of the abduction. Now he took a deep breath and forced himself to keep calm. Hadn't they all agreed to keep to a nice, steady speed after the immediate getaway? To attract no unwanted attention. He smiled grimly to himself. Already they were making good stop-go progress through the traffic lights of the Edgware Road. And all the time the line of north-ward-bound traffic was becoming lighter and faster. Now the Brent Cross Shopping Centre was approaching, and the start of the M1 motorway to the north of England.

Soon it would all be over for them, with no trace of a clue for the police to follow. The van had been stolen the day before, resprayed a nondescript grey overnight and fitted with false numberplates obtained from two separate sources.

No, if only their courage held, they would be back in time for the lecture at twelve noon, each with a solid alibi.

Nevertheless nerves were still frayed half-an-hour later when they pulled into the Scratchwood service area. The driver sought out the agreed parking space which was as far away as possible from the canteen and shop complex. He pulled up, climbed out, and removed the plastic cone that had kept the space free. Returning to his cab, he reversed in until he was backed up to a smaller, mustard-coloured van in the adjoining space behind. Both sets of rear doors were thrown open to form a screen between the two vehicles.

It took just ten seconds to transfer the limp bodies.

The doors slammed shut and the grey van drove off towards the exit, rejoining the northward rush of motorway traffic. At the next junction it turned off and rejoined the Edgware Road running back south. Finally it was abandoned in a back street in Kingsbury, and the four students thankfully made their way on foot to Wembley Tube Station. Each was two thousand pounds richer for his troubles.

Having left Scratchwood a few moments after the other vehicle, the mustard-coloured van, its roof rack carrying a decorator's ladder, also turned off at Junction 4, but then picked up the Uxbridge road before turning south towards Harrow-on-the-Hill and the home of Beth and Ali Christie.

Meanwhile Ali Christie was sitting in the Pavilion Gallery in Brook Street staring morosely at the gilt-framed picture of his wife on the desk. Next to it was the faded print of a wizened old lady almost totally obscured by a black *chador* – his mother standing proudly in her rose garden in Yazd.

He looked up as someone rattled at the front door of the shop; irritably he waved them away. He had tried to do as he had been told by the *Pessarane Behesht*. As normal he had opened the gallery, but when the first customer came in, he just could not concentrate. In the end the customer walked away, obviously considering Christie to be a gibbering idiot. So he had put the 'Closed' sign up.

Now he looked across at the telephone. How easy it would be to dial 999.

He ruminated on the idea and nervously plucked a cigarette from the green onyx box beside the telephone. He lifted his lighter and paused. A hand-engraved, gold Dunhill – a gift from Beth many years before.

Again he looked at the telephone and lit the flame of the lighter. He smelt the trace of petrol in his nostrils.

At once his mind was filled with the awful picture of his wife lying in the hearth, the petrol-sodden nightclothes clinging to her body.

He didn't look at the telephone again.

D'Arcy had been watched throughout the meal.

The silver-framed photograph of Philippe Chaumont had appeared for the first time since he had known Chantal. Now it sat behind her on the sideboard. It was as though he had joined them at the table, and it wasn't doing D'Arcy's appetite any good at all.

Chantal, too, was picking at her plate without enthusiasm. Hardly a word had been spoken between them. He knew what was on her mind, but there was nothing he could say to ease the uncertainty she must be feeling.

His own mood was blackening with each day that passed. It was a week now since *Clarion Call* had vanished and, despite backup from Roquelaure, he had failed to make any progress in tracing the whereabouts of the directors of Spidex International Trading. Every vague lead had drawn a blank.

Until he had a breakthrough, Nadirpur would have to remain in hiding – and Tom Wilmot's wife would have sleepless nights not knowing whether her husband were alive or dead. Not only that, but only the same breakthrough could bring about Philippe Chaumont's release now. The burden of sharing Roquelaure's secret was proving a hard one to bear.

The incident at Nadirpur's apartment had clearly brought home to Chantal the sort of people who were holding her fiancé in Beirut. She had never before been

174

exposed to the ruthless face of terrorism. And now she knew that those responsible were Shi'ite terrorists from Iran, while Philippe Chaumont was held by Shi'ite terrorists in Lebanon.

Perhaps he should have been expecting her question. Perhaps he was, she was nobody's fool. But it still came as a surprise when she angrily pushed away the unfinished lasagne and stared at him directly. "Rober', tell me something. Is there any connection between this trouble with Monsieur Nadirpur and the release of my Philippe?"

D'Arcy was momentarily fazed. "Has someone been talking to you? Your father?"

She peered at him curiously from beneath her fringe of blonde hair. "Papa? Do you suggest that he knows something? Something he will not tell me?"

He could see no way out of it. "Your father's been trying to keep it from you. He didn't want you to worry."

"Worry about what?"

He took a deep breath; perhaps it was better this way. "That this deal he set up with the Iranians through Nadirpur – part of the arrangement was that Philippe be released – in return for French arms."

Her green eyes fixed him accusingly. "And now that the ship has disappeared?"

"The Iranians suspect a double-cross, as you know."

She shook her head slowly in disbelief. "So no ship, no deal. Is that it? And Philippe is left to rot?"

He reached across the table and took her hand in his. "Don't fret. We *will* find that ship, I promise you. Once we do that, the deal's back on. That's why your father didn't want to dash your hopes unnecessarily. There are a lot of people anxious to find out what's happened to it – not least your father. And you know the resources he has at his disposal. The entire French Secret Service."

She gave a snort of derision, and snatched her hand away. "And you, Rober', how hard do you try to find this ship? If there is no ship there is no Philippe for you to worry about, is there?"

175

The scar on D'Arcy's cheek flared. "Don't talk nonsense, Chantal. I've got one of my staff on that ship. And, as for Philippe, I don't like the thought of the poor sod held captive in Beirut. Him or anyone else."

He saw the hurt and anger in her eyes. "But he is not just anyone else, is he? He was – is – my fiancé. Would it not be convenient for you if he was never seen again?"

D'Arcy didn't trust himself to speak. He pushed back his chair and stood, turning away to the drawing room. In a sullen silence he lit a cigar and helped himself to a stiff measure of brandy.

Stupid bitch, he swore beneath his breath. Did she really think he would stint his efforts just because his success would mean competition for her affections? Didn't she realise how painful an accusation of that magnitude was? Sometimes she was still a stranger to him.

He stared out of the window at the lights of the cars streaming along rue du Faubourg-St-Honoré at the end of the street.

He drained the brandy in three hard gulps and felt calmer for it. Who was he kidding? Oh yes, he had done everything possible to find out just what was going on. But it sure as hell wasn't for Philippe Chaumont's benefit. The Frenchman's release was going to be a bitter pill to swallow if it was the price to pay for finding *Clarion Call*.

He wasn't blind. He'd seen the change that had come over Chantal since the news that Philippe was still alive. He knew that the embers of whatever she had once felt for her fiancé still glowed. Almost forgotten once, perhaps, but now suddenly rekindled. And he was under no illusions as to what might happen to their relationship if Philippe Chaumont returned. The one relationship that had ever grown to mean anything in D'Arcy's life would be in dire peril. On the line the only affair that hadn't been ruined by his previous, all-consuming life in the SAS, or destroyed by his own turbulent and possessive nature.

At last he had mellowed, or so he liked to think. With Chantal there had never been any need for pretence. Despite being so many years his junior, she had instinctively known how to handle him. Giving as good as she got, in bed as well as out. Yet all the time gently showing him that there was another way.

Christ, how he wished he'd had the courage to ask her to marry him before all this. Wished he hadn't been so damn scared that she'd turn him down. If only he had listened to what his friend Dave Forbes had been telling him . . .

"I'm sorry, Rober'. That was a stupid thing for me to say."

He turned away from the window. She looked so young and vulnerable, her head tilted to one side, waiting for forgiveness.

He said: "Not so stupid, kitten. I want Philippe out of Beirut. But I don't want him back into your life."

She smiled sadly. "I know that. It is understandable of any man." She hesitated. "You know, sometimes I am very flattered by your jealousy. Back there, I thought you were going to strike me."

D'Arcy's laugh was bitter. "I'm trying to give it up."

She moved towards him, looked up into his eyes. "Sometimes our relationship frightens me a little. Our feelings seem almost too powerful, the sort that burn themselves out. I wonder what sort of future we have together."

He gripped her arms. "Do we have one, a future?"

Her eyes clouded. "You mean if Philippe is released?" She looked away as though reluctant to think about it. "I don't know, Rober'. How can I say? Truly I don't know what to think about anything any more."

His grip tightened. "Look at me, Chantal." Reluctantly she obeyed. He could see that her lower lip was trembling and that her eyes were moist. He said: "Think about marrying me."

"You are crazy!" she said, astonished, half-laughing,

half in shock. "All this time I know you and you never once suggest it. Now – because you know Philippe is alive – you ask me to be your wife." She pulled away and returned to the dining room to find her cigarettes.

She came back slowly, thoughtfully, and stood a few paces in front of him as she lit up. "You are still the same jealous man, Rober'. You ask me to marry you because you think, if Philippe is released, we will continue with our wedding plans."

"And am I right?"

Chantal looked uncomfortable, as though forced to consider the matter for the first time. "I don't know, Rober'. I am very confused, yes? You understand? When you are very much in love with someone, and then believe that they are dead . . . That love does not die. It burns like a candle in a church." She drew heavily on her cigarette, searching for the words. "Then suddenly you are told he is alive. You ask yourself if you are not just in love with a ghost."

A silence fell between them. Then D'Arcy said: "I'm sorry, I shouldn't have asked you. I know how difficult it must be. Believe me, I've been wanting to ask you how you felt about us, trying not to . . ."

She smiled, understanding. "Dear Rober'. It is hard for you too. But until Philippe is standing in this room again, there is no way of knowing how I will feel."

"Of course."

Regaining her composure, she sat on the sofa and patted the seat beside her. "Forget about Papa and trying to protect me from the truth. I want to know. Do we stand any chance of finding that accursed ship?"

D'Arcy poured two glasses of brandy and joined her. In truth he was relieved to change the topic; he hated heavy emotional arguments.

"I'm afraid at the moment it doesn't look good," he said. "I thought we had a good chance of tracing the Spidex people through London. You remember there was one English board member, calling himself Cupplewaite?

Well, Dave Forbes has made repeated phonecalls to his solicitors in the City."

"And?"

"It was a waste of time. Dave got promises of return calls, all that sort of thing. Nothing. They're stonewalling."

"Didn't Davey visit the solicitors' office?"

"He did that yesterday morning. Some dragon of a receptionist refused to let him see her boss without an appointment. And clearly such an appointment wasn't going to be given."

"Surely Davey can make them say –"

He shook his head. "If the elusive Mr Cupplewaite's solicitors won't play ball, there's nothing we can do to make them."

She stared glumly down at her brandy glass. "Then we have no progress at all. The ship is lost – and so is Philippe."

D'Arcy tried to sound encouraging. "Not necessarily. We've been able to alert people in the area where the ship was last seen. Dave's old SAS commander – a Major Hawksby – is now serving with the Sultan's forces in Oman."

Indeed the legendary 'Hawk' had led Dave Forbes on the never revealed mission to Iran in 1980 to rescue a British hostage. That mission had cost Forbes his leg and his Army career.

"Dave was given an assurance that both the Sultan's navy and air force will be alerted to keep a lookout for *Clarion Call* or any ship that might resemble her."

"That at least sounds promising."

"We couldn't hope for more. Both use expat British officers and they have a mean reputation in the area, despite their small size."

But Chantal was aware of the enormity of the problem. "There are many miles of coast and empty sea involved, no? It is still what you call a long shot?"

"I can't deny that." He glanced at his watch. It was

almost midnight. "I'd better turn in. Want to make an early start tomorrow."

"Still trying to find someone from Spidex?"

"It's our best hope – we just need a lucky break. If we find them, we can start putting on the pressure to locate the ship. Or confirm it is a genuine loss at sea."

She reached out and took his hand in hers. She studied it carefully as though it were some unfamiliar object she was seeing for the first time. When she spoke her words clearly weren't coming easily. "Forgive what I said earlier, Rober'. I know you are doing everything you can . . ." Her voice trailed. "And forgive me if I ask that we do not sleep together tonight – and maybe for a while – until Philippe is home . . . You understand?"

She was thankful that he said nothing to express the inner rage he must be feeling. As he hugged her brusquely to him, she was aware of the tense muscles of his jawline against her cheek, and knew what an effort he was making to hold himself in check.

Desperately she wanted to reassure him, but could find no words. It was suddenly as though the passion had been drained from her, her juices drying up like a desert stream in summer.

It was guilt, she recognised that. However irrational, she knew that her love for him had somehow betrayed Philippe. Blindly she had accepted her father's word that he was dead. Where was the intuitive faith of the wives and lovers of those other hostages in Beirut? You saw them on the television – they never gave up hope, campaigning and running lonely vigils in the long nights.

Yet she had abandoned Philippe – not just physically, within months of meeting D'Arcy. But more importantly she had buried him in her heart. She could not even claim the innocence and impetuosity of youth.

D'Arcy's grip tightened round her shoulders as he felt her hot tears against his skin.

And to think that once she had accused him of having

a shard of ice in his heart – some wound from previous love affairs that prevented him from ever revealing his real feelings to any woman.

How she regretted those words now, however true they might have seemed at the time. The surprised way he had looked at her when she said it suggested that it had not occurred to him before.

After that she had detected an almost imperceptible but important change in him, and their love had ignited with a power of body chemistry that sometimes disturbed her. D'Arcy had opened her up, exposing her raw emotions, giving no quarter and taking none.

It was a far cry from her naïve and youthful engagement to Philippe – two constrained and formal lovers from the same highly respectable social background. Looking back now they might have been playing out the rôle of characters from some nineteenth-century romantic novel.

She the heroine entrapped by family expectations; he a faithful and stoic, if unimaginative hero.

For all that, had she been right just to abandon him pitilessly for the first dashing knight to pass her way?

She took a deep breath to stop the tears and opened her eyes. Above her, she saw that D'Arcy was staring towards the open dining room door and the silver-framed photograph on the sideboard.

A handsome, well-groomed young man with a boyish, carefree face smiled back at them.

The telephone purred on the coffee table. Chantal prised herself from D'Arcy's grasp and found herself eagerly reaching for the receiver.

"It's Davey for you." She sounded disappointed as she passed the handset to him.

Forbes dispensed with niceties. "Have you heard, boss, we've got problems?"

"What?"

"Obviously you haven't. Mrs Nadirpur was kidnapped in London this morning."

The words stunned D'Arcy; he was tired and drained. His friend was talking rubbish. "Kidnap? What Mrs Nadirpur?"

"Apparently it's been splashed all over the *Standard* this evening. I didn't see it, I've been working at the office. The first I knew was a call from your old chum Roy Bliss not ten minutes ago."

Still Forbes wasn't making sense. "Which Mrs Nadirpur, Dave? For Christ's sake, you're talking in riddles. Do you mean his mother – or what – a sister-in-law?"

"No, boss, I mean the bastard's got a wife – lives over here. Didn't you know?"

The blood drained from D'Arcy's face. "Oh my God. I had no idea. He never mentioned a wife, and I just assumed . . . Never mind, give me the full sitrep," he demanded, slipping instinctively into Army jargon.

For the next ten minutes the line hummed as Forbes recounted how the Iranian exile and her daughter had been seized in the middle of the morning rush hour. A van had been used, and the only clue to the identity of the stocking-masked kidnappers was an eyewitness's vague description that the driver, whose face was not covered, was of Middle Eastern appearance.

D'Arcy was now fully awake. "Dave, I want you to stay at the office. Pull in any of our available teams for full manning. Make sure everyone's fully aware of kidnap drill. Call up Brandy and interrupt her beauty sleep."

"Police?" Forbes asked.

"Not till I've spoken to Nadirpur. This isn't even part of our remit – yet." Thinking aloud, he said: "You realise who's behind this?"

"It's got to be, boss. You've taken Nadirpur out of circulation. You left them thrashin' at thin air. They had to find a way of drawing Nadirpur out. Well, they've found the one weakness in our armour all right. I tell you what though, boss, with those sort of resources, we're not just dealing with some terrorist splinter group. This is a mainstream mob with powerful government backing. Our Mr Nadirpur has gone and upset some very undesirable people."

After another brief exchange, D'Arcy hung up.

Chantal had managed to follow most of the conversation, her expression one of horror.

"The poor woman."

"And her daughter, just seven years old," D'Arcy added, thumping his fist on the coffee table. "The bastards!"

"What do they want with an innocent woman and child?"

"To force Nader to come clean about the ship."

She stared at him in disbelief. "But he doesn't know anything."

"Obviously they don't believe that."

"So what will happen next?"

D'Arcy lit a fresh cigar. "With most criminal kidnaps you could expect a long wait. Time for the trail to go cold and the victim's family to get desperate. But in this case, my guess is they'll move fast because they need answers quickly themselves."

"You will want to inform Papa?"

"Yes, but first I need to see Nadirpur."

"If you can face the thought of my driving, Rober', I shall take you."

D'Arcy looked at her closely. "Are you sure you want to get involved in this. Your father – "

Chantal was defiant. "Papa still thinks I am six years old. This poor woman and her child are in exactly the same position as Philippe. They may even be held by the same people. I could not sleep knowing that I have done nothing."

Only when the mustard-coloured decorator's van pulled up outside the wrought-iron gates of Ali Christie's house in Harrow-on-the-Hill had Shamlou's heart slowed its thudding beat.

Driving through unfamiliar London streets had been nerve-racking enough – vehicles and flashing lights seemed to be coming at him from all angles – but with two kidnap victims in the back, his brain refused to function rationally.

He stepped out onto the private road and threw open the gates. A gravel drive swept between manicured lawns to the portico of the imposing Edwardian house. There was no sign of activity except the slight movement of a curtain on the first floor. Shamlou gave a thumbs up sign, then returned to the van.

By the time he had driven through, the door of the integral garage had been swung up and open by those waiting anxiously in the house. It was with immense relief that he drove in and killed the engine.

As he alighted the garage door came down again, snuffing out the daylight like a guillotine. The place stank of oil, solvent and the sweetish smell of garden chemicals.

"How is the American woman?" Shamlou demanded.

The man he knew only as Hamid was one of the two-man London cell. He was in his late twenties with pale skin, prematurely thinning hair and wore a pair of steel-rimmed spectacles which made him look studious. Shamlou gathered he had aspirations to be a cleric.

"She is calmer now," Hamid answered quietly. His manner was self-assured, but wary of this stranger sent from Teheran. "She's been crying all the time. Kamal is with her now."

Kamal was the second half of the London cell. Of similar age to Hamid he was distinguished by a thick black beard. Likewise he appeared quiet and unassuming; the quiet and unassuming character of both men would never lead anyone to suspect their rôle in the Sabbah network. Indeed they had cultivated many English friends. Shamlou guessed that was the reason they had been chosen as 'sleepers'.

A sudden scuffling sound came from the back of the van. Instantly Shamlou recognised the cry of anguish from

Matchsticks, and he winced as he opened the doors to hear the soft thud of flesh against flesh.

Matchsticks almost fell out, stepping back awkwardly like a badly constructed puppet. "Bitch!" he snarled into the van. He turned to Shamlou for sympathy. "The chloroform has worn off. She's started fighting like a cat."

Shamlou turned to Hamid. "Help get them to the cellar."

"KEEP BACK!" Ashi Nadirpur screamed, an animal protecting her offspring in the shadow of a steel cave. "BASTARDS!"

They dragged her by her arms as she shouted, twisting and turning in their grasp. A livid bruise welled on her cheek where Matchsticks had struck her. The burgundy skirt was smeared with grime and buttons were missing from her gaping blouse.

Shamlou stood before her, and for the first time looked properly at his victim. At the woman who showed all the signs of Western decadence, of betrayal of her faith. His eyes flickered to the small heaving breasts in the decadent lacy brassière as she resisted. Then he noticed the dark eyes, smouldering with hate at him from beneath tangled strands of black hair.

Her spittle caught him full in the face, caught him off guard.

He was incensed, stunned, at her action, and stood rigid with anger as he felt the slime roll down his cheek. Without warning his right hand swiped in retaliation at her mouth, splitting her lip. Instantly she recoiled, and coughed and spat again. This time to clear the blood and the chip of white tooth that landed on the concrete floor.

"Bend her over!" Shamlou snapped. "So I can tie her hands."

But it didn't prevent her struggling, and he noticed how tiny her wrists were as he tightened the cord until it bit deep into her thin flesh.

"Take her down!" he ordered, and watched as she floundered and kicked at the man on each side of her.

When she was gone he looked around. In the darkness of the van the whites of Sousan's eyes were wide with fright and incomprehension. A small, terrified child clutching a satchel with both arms as though it were her most prized possession.

Shamlou smiled. "Come, little one," he coaxed.

"YEOW!" His hand shot back, the ring of tiny teeth marks red and bright. "Get out!"

He hauled her bodily from the van in his rage and hurled her in front of him, through the kitchen to the hall, and down the steps that fell away sharply to the brick-built cellar.

The low vaulted roof stretched for some forty feet until it met the blank wall at the far end. The acrid smell of coal lingered, seeping through the heavy partition of railway sleepers along one wall which separated the coke store. During the morning the accumulated household junk had been stacked in piles beside the steps. The wine racks had been systematically emptied, the contents poured down the sink and the bottles thrown into dustbins by the front door.

A wooden cage frame had been hastily constructed by Hamid and Kamal to split the area in half. To it had been hammered rolls of heavy-gauge chicken wire. A rough hinged wire door had been fashioned in cheap soft wood, only eighteen inches square. It was just big enough for an adult to pass through on all fours.

It was not, however, so easy to persuade an angry, kicking woman even as tiny as Ashi to go through without a desperate struggle. Finally Matchsticks ducked through first and pulled the woman in, screaming, by her hair.

Sousan looked on in terror and scampered quickly through after her mother, anxious to be at her side.

The turmoil continued until Ashi's mouth was taped firmly with wide plastic parcel-tape and her feet tied with cord like her hands, leaving her on the floor propped against the wall.

"Get out now," Shamlou ordered the other two terrorists and waited for them before he entered the makeshift cage.

Now that it had been draped by thick blankets stripped from the beds upstairs it was very dark. He took a flashlight from his pocket to shine it down on the face of the petrified child who clung to the side of her mother. He then played the beam on Ashi's head. Her sullen, long-lashed eyes squinted against the brightness.

"Listen to me, woman," Shamlou said. "You and your daughter are being held because your husband has betrayed his country. He has taken things that belong to us. That debt must be repaid. When he has met our demands both of you will be released. Do you understand me, woman?"

Ashi stared dumbly at the misty figure behind the blinding aureole.

"Answer me, woman!"

A stifled mumble and a weary nod of the head.

"I will require your co-operation. If I do not get it, your daughter will be beaten to death before your eyes. Do you understand?"

Another slow nod. Shamlou smiled. He could see the fight had drained out of her.

"I am going to take the tape from your mouth. If you don't want your daughter to suffer then you will remain silent. You talk to me only when I ask a question."

He leaned forward. Instinctively she drew back against the damp cellar wall, willing herself to fuse into the crumbling, whitewashed brickwork. His breath was grunting in her ear as he stooped to find the edge of the tape, and she could smell the sweat and youth of his body as he worked.

Without consideration he ripped the tape from her skin so that she winced with the searing pain.

She gulped for breath, her eyes only inches from his. She noticed that his eyes were very dark and intense, with long black lashes. There was an immature moustache above lips that were pretty enough to belong to a girl.

Those pretty lips filled her vision, and as he spoke she could see the pink membrane of his mouth and tongue, the very whiteness of his teeth. "I want something from you that your husband will recognise. Something that there will be no doubt belongs to only you."

She blinked, unable to think, her mind paralysed. "I don't know . . ."

"A scarf? A purse?" he snapped. "Jewellery?"

"My ring," she gasped, and immediately wished that she hadn't. Of all things most precious to her, it was the wedding ring she had received from Nader. Especially now. That ring was the most important thing in her life.

"Which ring?"

"I don't know," she hedged. "I have several, as you see . . ."

A slow smile crossed Shamlou's face. "Ah, yes. A wedding ring. That is something your husband will remember, yes?"

He arched her roughly forward so that her head was crushed against his stomach, her face just inches from his groin as he reached for the hands bound behind her back. She felt her finger being bent against the joint, the vicious twist as he wrenched the ring free.

She fell back hard against the wall and shut her eyes, her head full of the young man's odour. When she opened them, the wedding ring was held before her as Shamlou shone the torchlight on it.

"Your husband must be a very rich man to give you such a ring," he said, turning it between his thumb and forefinger. "It even has a stone inset. A diamond."

"A sapphire," she breathed. "My birthstone."

"And an inscription. That is good. It can only be yours." Carefully he dropped it into his pocket. There was an expression of curiosity on his face. "Is that why you married him?"

188

"What?"

"Is that why you married him? Because he is rich? Is that why you married a supporter of the Shah?"

She looked away.

"Is it?"

"I don't know." Her voice was scarcely audible.

Shamlou grunted. "Now I want a name. The name of someone who knows you here in London. Someone you can trust?"

"I have relatives –"

"No, no relatives. No close friends. No one the police may now be in close contact with since you are missing. Someone responsible who you feel you could trust."

For no particular reason she suddenly thought of Sousan's severe-faced school teacher. She told him.

"The name of the school?" he demanded.

She gave him that too.

He appeared satisfied and pulled away from her, climbing to his feet. The beam of the torch wavered as he did so, and she cringed, praying that he would not notice.

But he did, as he played the beam over her prone body. He could hardly fail to see that the delicate shoulder strap of her brassière had snapped during her earlier struggles. Now her left breast hung free. A tender fruit. Brazen, humiliating. She closed her eyes in dread.

A pink tongue darted uncertainly over his lips and he swallowed hard. He glanced behind him, afraid the others could see. But the thick blanket over the wire cage hid him from view.

Her eyes still closed she waited, expectant and drained of all emotion. Waiting, and then it came. She felt his fingertips, cold and clammy with perspiration. Felt her nipple brush against his palm, harden involuntarily as a pebble. She turned her head away.

Then surprise. Surprise at the gentle way he lifted her breast as though it were not part of her. Cradled it in his palm like a small injured dove, and let it fall softly back into the silk cup.

She breathed relief and opened her eyes just in time to see him disappear through the wire gate. The blanket fell back into place.

On the other side of it Shamlou found himself alone. He stared down at his palms. They were trembling.

He thought of the woman in the garden, heard her voice, listened to the words of her poem, felt the powerful stirring of his loins.

# 8

The lights were still on in Victor's when Chantal screeched her motorcycle to a standstill outside.

She and D'Arcy had scarcely dismounted before the door swung open. Saint-Julien was taking no chances, his acquired Smith & Wesson discreetly out of sight as he allowed them in. He then checked up and down the street before closing and bolting the door.

"On the telephone you sound like there is big trouble," the Corsican said.

"There's trouble all right, Saint-Julien, but on the other side of the Channel."

Victor was sitting on the wrong side of the bar with Claudette, nursing a calvados nightcap. "So what sort of trouble do you bring me now?" he called over laughingly.

"It's no joke, Victor." D'Arcy glanced around at the deserted tables. "Where's Nader?"

"Upstairs, as always. Watching television."

"He keeps himself to himself, that one," Claudette added.

D'Arcy said: "You'd best all be in the picture. I am afraid Nader's wife and child have been kidnapped in England."

Claudette stared in amazement. "His *wife*?" The others shared her incredulity.

"Yes, I'm afraid Nader has been a bit of a dark horse in that respect."

Saint-Julien said: "I guess there is no doubt it is the Iranians?"

"It's a certainty – they're trying to flush Nader out of hiding."

"What animals would do this?" Claudette murmured in disgust.

Victor shook his head. "Those bastards do not give up so easily, eh? Listen, Rober', if there is anything we can do – I think we are now the nearest thing your friend Nader has to a family here in Paris."

"That's good to hear, because right now he's going to need all the friendship and support he can get."

Chantal touched his arm. "Let me come up too, Rober'. You are hardly the one to share Nader's tears. I know just how he will be feeling."

It was to prove a wise decision. D'Arcy had never been comfortable in the presence of a crying man. It ran contrary both to his upbringing and personal code of behaviour that men should show emotion. So he was thankful that Chantal was on hand to comfort Nadirpur when he broke the news.

Victor, sensing that there would be little sleep but much talking and soul-searching that night, thoughtfully brought up a tray of coffee and a bottle of cognac.

Finally the Iranian's tears began to subside. He blew his nose vigorously, straightened his dressing gown and made a determined effort to regain a measure of composure. He looked up at D'Arcy, embarrassed. "I am sorry, Robert, please forgive me. I am behaving like a stupid child."

D'Arcy poured him a brandy – under the circumstances champagne hardly seemed appropriate. "Forget about me, Nader. I've seen the toughest soldiers break down and weep. It's best to let it out," he said kindly, aware that he had rarely followed his own advice.

Nadirpur took the glass in both hands, as though his life depended on it. He took a deep swallow and closed his eyes as the liquid burned its way down.

Quietly D'Arcy said: "Why did you never mention that you had a wife and child when I was asking about relatives or friends who might be in danger from these Iranians?"

Nadirpur looked sheepish. "To be honest I wanted to

keep them out of all this. Somehow I never dreamed that they might get involved, especially as they are in London. And I think that if I don't tell you about them, well, I guess that no one would ever know. You see, in truth, they are hardly part of my life now. Usually I only see them every three months or so. And then it is to satisfy myself that Ashi and Sousan have everything they need. My wife is a very undemanding woman, Robert, she would never ask me for anything." He looked up with moist eyes. "It is perhaps difficult for a man like you to understand. But I ruined my own life – and more importantly I ruined Ashi's too – because I refused to admit that I was what I was." He found the words difficult to say. "That I was not heterosexual. And all that time poor Ashi suffered in uncomplaining silence, whilst the best years of her youth slipped by."

"You had Sousan," Chantal reminded softly.

Nadirpur nodded, a small smile of pride lightening his face. "That was very ironic, because she was – er – conceived just before we separated. So even though we are apart, poor Ashi is always reminded of me." He turned to D'Arcy, an expression of hopelessness in his eyes. "Tell me, is there *anything* at all that we can do?"

"There might be quite a lot we can do, Nader. But not yet. The ball is in the Iranians' court. It is up to them to make the first move."

"But if they kill dear Ashi –" His eyes were wide with dread "– or little Sousan?"

D'Arcy smiled with grim reassurance. "They won't do that. Well, certainly that won't be their immediate plan."

"How can you know that?" Chantal asked.

"Because the whole point of kidnap is to put on pressure to get your way. Usually it's for money, or sometimes for political advantage. It might be to get a criminal or terrorist prisoners released," he explained patiently. "In this case it's because they believe you've tricked them over the supposed disappearance of *Clarion Call*. It is the threat to the hostage that provides that pressure, not the killing.

Once a hostage is dead, the pressure's off. They no longer have a hold over the victim's family. Then the kidnappers have lost as well."

"So there will be a threat against Ashi and Sousan?" Nader asked slowly, his mind clearly imagining the unthinkable.

"Almost certainly – unless, of course, by some remarkable chance this is nothing to do with the Iranians. But frankly I think you can discount that."

"When?" Nadirpur pleaded. "When will we hear?"

D'Arcy said: "Normally it could be months. In this case I think it will be soon. Probably a telephone call to your office in Monaco. That is why we must work out our strategy. I am sorry, because you're shocked and upset, but it must be done. A mistake now and all could be lost."

"Strategy?" Nadirpur was bewildered. "What strategy? We must give them whatever they want."

"That's our problem," D'Arcy pointed out quietly. "The ship is not ours to give."

"But they must *know* that by now!"

D'Arcy shook his head. "They know nothing of the sort. Look at it from their point of view. The Arabs from Spidex, who set up the deal, have vanished with the Iranians' money and, they suspect, their arms shipment. As Roquelaure was involved, they think the French Government was in on the business, perhaps with revenge as their motive. Who knows? A punishment for holding several French hostages in Beirut perhaps? That leaves you and your protests of innocence. In their shoes, I'd have doubts about your involvement."

"So what *can* we do?" It was almost a wail of anguish.

"For a start I think we must move to London. That is where your wife and child are being held, so it will shorten the lines of communication. I have a secure office where you can stay and, besides, I'll have more staff resources available to me."

Nadirpur saw the wisdom of that and nodded sagely.

"But that does not help what we can say to the Iranians. What *do* we say to them?"

"We persuade them that we are acting in good faith. *And* that we are making progress in locating the ship – whether it be sunk or pirated."

"But we are not making progress, Robert, are we!" His voice had an hysterical edge to it.

"We can't afford to let them know that, because now they've *changed* the rules. Once they believe you really are an innocent party – or cannot be useful to them in finding the ship – then they've no reason to keep your wife and daughter alive. And I've no doubt they'd kill them without a second's thought if they no longer served a purpose. If only because they could be witnesses. I'm sorry, but there it is."

Chantal suddenly said: "Money, Rober', couldn't we offer them money? You know, to the value of the lost shipment?"

Nadirpur's eyes widened. He was grasping at straws. "That is a wonderful idea!"

D'Arcy hated to bring him down to earth, but it had to be done. "That cargo was valued at half-a-billion dollars, Nader, and you know the insurance company isn't going to pay out. So what liquid assets do you have available?"

The expression of optimism on Nadirpur's face died. "I do not have half-a-billion dollars in assets. Liquid or otherwise." He stared morosely at the carpet. "So these damnable people hold all the cards?"

"Not quite." D'Arcy unravelled the cellophane from one of his small cigars as he marshalled his thoughts. "You see, now that they've got your wife and daughter they have, as I said, changed the rules."

"So what do we do?" Nadirpur repeated in despair.

"We negotiate."

Nadirpur stared in disbelief. "Negotiate? How in the name of Allah do we negotiate with nothing?"

"Because now we have demands – just like them."

Chantal frowned, as uncomprehending as the Iranian.

195

D'Arcy lit his cigar and aimed a long stream of blue smoke at the ceiling. "You see, from now on our demands are that your wife and child remain unharmed and are eventually released unharmed. That is our demand. Curiously enough – and tragic as it is – your negotiating position, Nader, is actually better than before the kidnap. Then they did hold all the cards."

Nadirpur gradually began to grasp what the Englishman meant. "But that is hardly consolation!"

"You make it sound like a game," Chantal said angrily, "with your talk of rules and negotiation."

D'Arcy was unmoved. "That's exactly what it is. And if they're professionals they'll know it, too. But with any luck it will take them some time to realise that we know how to play it better than they do."

"Do you have to sound as though you're enjoying it?" Chantal protested.

That earned her a withering glance from D'Arcy before he continued: "Our first job will be to seize the initiative from them. Make them understand that they're not going to have it all their own way. And we'll do that by constantly demanding to know that Ashi and Sousan are alive. Proof on our terms, not theirs. If we keep our nerve long enough it may give the police time to find out where they are being held."

Nadirpur almost had apoplexy. "Police! I don't want police involved in this! Sweet Allah, all I want is my Ashi and baby Sousan safe. No police!"

D'Arcy decided to let that one ride. Whether Nadirpur liked it or not, it would be impossible to keep either the British or the French police out of the affair. Not when the kidnap had taken place in broad daylight and the story had already been splashed across the front page of London's evening newspaper.

He said: "We can cross that bridge when we come to it. All we can do for now is wait for the kidnappers to make contact. In the meantime, we have to step up our efforts to find this damn ship. That's important so we can feed

196

bits of information to the kidnappers – even if we have to invent some."

"But we are already doing everything," Nadirpur said. "Do you have any other ideas?"

D'Arcy didn't want to raise false hopes. Cautiously he said: "It's worth considering getting one of our own men out to the Gulf to investigate – hire a ship if necessary to search . . ."

The idea appealed to the Iranian and he was dismissive of the cost involved. "Is there anything else I should be doing?"

"As a precaution I suggest you look at what assets you can liquidise quickly. If we can't give them what they want, a cash offer might have its uses. Do you have an accountant you can trust?"

Nadirpur nodded slowly, as though coming out of a trance. "Yes, my company secretary is a good man. I shall telephone him at home before he leaves for work in the morning. Tell him to be discreet, to see what amount we could raise and how long it would take."

D'Arcy smiled encouragingly. "That's excellent, Nader. Don't worry, we'll get your wife and child back unharmed. Trust me."

The responding smile was well-meant but understandably limp. "I am sure you will do everything you can, Robert. You have already shown how efficient you can be. I do not know how I could have coped without you and your friends here." He sipped delicately at his brandy, felt it giving him strength. "Believe me, I love Ashi and my dear Sousan as much as any husband or father. I don't know if you can understand that?"

D'Arcy felt a sudden insane anger at the *Pessarane Behesht* and all it stood for. Nadirpur had explained in simple, uncomplicated words his confused feelings and emotions. The feelings and emotions of any human being, however bizarre the relationship with his own wife and daughter had been. A sad, tragic man trapped by an accident of birth. Somehow that made the kidnap all the

197

more obscene: as if the little family, broken yet strangely bound together by the same tragedy, had not suffered enough.

"I understand more than you think," D'Arcy said. "You must get some rest now. It'll be a busy day tomorrow."

Chantal was still clutching Nadirpur's arm. "Would you like me to stay for company?"

He shook his head. "No, thank you, dear lady. I need to be alone. To come to terms with everything."

D'Arcy and the girl left then. Nadirpur climbed wearily to his feet and walked to the window. He drew the curtains and peered into the night. Outside it was raining gently, the Paris streets wet and shiny.

He pressed his brow against the coolness of the pane, and shut his eyes.

"Why?" he murmured. "In the name of Allah, why?"

Dawn came all too quickly.

It seemed to D'Arcy that his head had only just hit the cushion on the settee in Victor's flat when he was shaken awake.

"Hey, you've got a visitor," the *patron* whispered hoarsely. His breath was thick with stale Disque Bleu and garlic.

D'Arcy swung his feet to the floor and rubbed his hands over his face. "Who, for God's sake, Victor?"

A familiar voice came from the door. "I see we have some developments, *mon ami*."

Roquelaure looked fresh and newly shaven, his suit as immaculate as ever with razor sharp creases.

"Hell, Pierre, you didn't waste much time," D'Arcy observed.

The Frenchman sniffed disdainfully at the fug of stale smoke and sweat. "I came as soon as I received your message. Shall I open a window?" Without waiting for a reply he crossed the room. Bright sunlight and the din of early morning traffic rushed in. "I couldn't afford to wait – not with the story of the London kidnap splashed all over the early editions of *Figaro*. It won't be long before the DST starts sniffing around."

"You're not going to be able to keep them out of this. It's too public."

Roquelaure raised his hands defensively. "Believe me, Rober', I am all too aware of that! But I would prefer not to alert our Ministry of the Interior – given that this has been purely a secret service matter of the DGSE until now. It could lead to many awkward questions being asked."

D'Arcy felt instinctively irritated that the générale seemed more worried about scandal than their client's predicament. "What sort of questions?"

"Oh, just the small matter of the DGSE turning a blind eye to arms sales to Iranian terrorists in return for the release of our French hostages in Beirut." He raised an eyebrow. "As you said yourself, hardly in line with official government policy."

"And someone in the Interior Ministry might blow the whistle on you?"

"*La guerre des flics* is alive and well," Roquelaure confirmed, referring to the notorious rivalry between the police and the security organisations, including the *gendarmerie*, which came under the Ministry of Defence. "And there are many politicians with scores to settle."

"And, of course, there's the question of your future son-in-law's life being in the balance," D'Arcy pointed out unkindly.

Roquelaure looked at him steadily before replying slowly. "Indeed, Philippe Chaumont's life is in the balance. Whether or not he will ever be my son-in-law is a matter for Chantal. She is here?"

"Next door, in the spare room of Claudette's apartment."

"And Nadirpur?"

"Sleeping, I hope. Though I doubt it. This business has broken him up badly."

Roquelaure stared out of the window and absently lit

his fifth Gitane of the day. "So what are you going to do?"

D'Arcy said: "Well, you can rest easy on one score, Pierre. We're catching a midday flight to London. I'd prefer to be on my own patch to handle this one."

A smile of satisfaction creased the Frenchman's face. "That is very wise."

D'Arcy's eyes narrowed. "I'm not doing it for you, Pierre. And I've told you once before – you either work for our company or for France."

Roquelaure shrugged. "There is usually a middle road."

"One day there might not be. What then?"

"We shall see. But just now it works for all of us that these *Pessarane Behesht* have taken it into their heads to seize the woman and child."

"The hell it does."

"Because it gives us time to stall them," Roquelaure came back sharply, "until we track down that Arab cartel or locate the missing arms shipment." His eyes were fierce. "Time, Rober', time."

"And Nadirpur's wife and daughter?" D'Arcy demanded. "Are they of no consequence to you?"

"It was not I, *mon ami*, who kidnapped them."

D'Arcy spent the first hour of the morning arranging for a private aircraft to fly them from le Bourget. There was just a risk, however minimal, that the Iranian Embassy had people watching at the main passenger termini. Unfortunately the Docklands Airport did not accept private flights, so Biggin Hill in Kent was the nearest alternative.

Nadirpur spoke to his office in Monaco and left instructions for contacting him at the IAP offices in London.

The shipping office was the only line of communication with Nadirpur available to the Iranians, but no call had yet been received from the kidnappers.

That silence left Nadirpur's nerves frayed despite reassurances from D'Arcy and Chantal, and endless coffee and bonhomie from Victor.

An attempt to play cards was abandoned; no one could

concentrate. All eyes were on the clock as the hands dragged themselves, with agonising slowness towards noon and time to leave for the airfield.

D'Arcy had invited Saint-Julien to join them; the Corsican had struck up a strangely abrasive relationship with Nadirpur, who appeared comforted by his mildly sarcastic wit and no-nonsense approach to the situation in which they found themselves. Perhaps he just had confidence in the man's obvious abilities as a bodyguard. At least in London Saint-Julien would be a familiar, if not over-friendly face.

It came as a surprise when Chantal volunteered to return to London, too. But it was a surprise that D'Arcy welcomed.

"I would prefer to be of help to you and Nader," she explained, "rather than wait around for news of Philippe that may never come."

The blurting ring of the telephone caught them all unexpectedly. Nadirpur stared at it as though it were a rattlesnake, his face quite drained. Chantal ran the tip of her tongue over her lips and exchanged a glance with D'Arcy as he picked up the receiver.

It was Forbes. He didn't mince words. "It's a contact, boss. Through our office here."

"Our office, how the . . . ?" His voice trailed as he recalled giving his name to the anonymous diplomat during his earlier call to the Iranian Embassy in Paris.

Forbes spoke rapidly: "It was a woman calling on instructions from the kidnappers. I gave her your number and told her to give me five minutes to warn you first. I'll hang up now and clear the line."

"Thanks, Dave."

D'Arcy replaced the receiver and turned towards the expectant faces. "It's a contact. We'll get a call in the next few minutes."

Nadirpur breathed again. "It is the kidnappers themselves?"

"An intermediary, I think."

201

Again the telephone rang. D'Arcy pointed to it. "Take the call, Nader. I'll use the extension."

The Iranian's hand was trembling as he lifted the handset from its cradle. The line was bad, the strident female voice crackling with static on the long-distance line. "I want to speak to Mr Nadirpur, please."

"You are speaking to him."

"It is Miss Dalrymple here."

"I am sorry –"

The voice was impatient. "I don't believe we've met. I am your daughter's teacher. At school here in London."

"Oh yes, of course. I have heard of you." He recalled Ashi bemoaning the strict attitude of little Sousan's spinster teacher at the Kensington private school.

"Well, look, Mr Nadirpur, first I apologise. I had no idea that Sousan's mother was – er – was still married. And secondly I am so sorry about the terrible thing that happened yesterday morning. You have heard?"

"Yes, I have heard," he replied flatly.

"Well, something else has happened, and frankly I am worried sick. I really don't know what to do."

"What is it, Miss Dalrymple."

She hesitated. "I suppose it is all right to talk?"

"Please."

"It's a package for you."

"What? A package?"

"In class this morning there was a telephone call for me. I took it in the headmistress's office. It was most strange. A – er – foreign sounding gentleman. Very polite but – well – sort of quietly menacing. He said there was a package in the school yard for you – from your wife. He gave me a number to ring in London. He told me to use a call box." Her voice gathered speed and, listening on the extension, D'Arcy heard her veneer of calm begin to crack. "And he said if I told the police – or anyone else – there would be a bomb thrown into our playground. Godfathers, Mr Nadirpur, I really don't know what to do."

202

D'Arcy left the extension, crossed the room and took the receiver from the bewildered Nadirpur. "Listen, Miss Dalrymple, I'm Mr Nadirpur's security adviser. Let me first thank you for your help, and assure you that you need have no fear."

"But this package is from little Sousan's kidnappers, surely?"

"There's no doubt of that. It's their first contact. But don't worry, just do what they say and tell no one."

"Not even my headmistress?"

"Not anybody. If you do it could result in little Sousan's murder. Trust me. It is not in anyone's interest for you to contact the police yourself. Leave that to us."

"But I must get this package to you. This is a Paris number, isn't it? Do I fly over?"

"No. Do you have a home telephone number?"

"Yes."

"Will you be there this evening?"

"Y-yes." Guarded.

"I'll arrange for someone to collect it and take it to my London office. I'll be in touch later."

"Oh, thank you." The relief in her voice was evident. She gave her number.

"Thank you, Miss Dalrymple." He replaced the receiver.

Nadirpur looked perplexed. "What does all this mean?"

D'Arcy smiled grimly. "It means we're in business."


It was early evening when the French registered, twin-engined Piper Aztec dipped low over the softly lit Surrey meadows on its final approach to Biggin Hill.

To D'Arcy it came as a relief to be back in England where he would have tighter control over the situation and the full backup of his headquarters team.

Nadirpur, too, he suspected would feel happier knowing that he was closer to his wife and child; somehow it helped.

As soon as the propellers came to a standstill the passengers disembarked onto the parking bay in front of a small terminal building.

D'Arcy knew Dave Forbes had been in contact with New Scotland Yard as he had instructed, but he was surprised to see the shabby, raincoated figure of Roy Bliss standing behind the Immigration officer.

"We meet again, Rob," the SIS officer said. He smiled uncertainly, remembering the acrimony of their previous meeting.

D'Arcy handed his passport to the Immigration officer. "You don't miss a trick, Roy, I'll give you that."

Bliss said: "Get through Customs and I'll take you to the reception committee. I can tell you the boys in blue are pleased you've turned up. With Nadirpur in France and the press here baying at their heels, there was precious little they could do. At least now they can get their act together. See you."

The immigration procedures, even for Nadirpur, were a mere formality, and in under ten minutes all four passengers were through to the arrivals lounge.

Dave Forbes was waiting and swiftly intercepted D'Arcy before he could meet up again with Roy Bliss.

"I've got the first demand from the schoolteacher, boss. I haven't mentioned the contact to Bliss. Thought you'd like to keep a step ahead."

"Good man," D'Arcy replied. "We'll keep it to ourselves until we see how the land lies. I gather there's a meeting laid on."

It was a six-mile drive to the country hotel where D'Arcy pulled the company's silver Jaguar XJS in alongside Bliss's road-weary Sierra. After an envious glance, the SIS man led the way straight through reception to a small, windowless conference room.

It was overfilled with a huge walnut and chrome table and ranks of black leatherette chairs. Two used coffee cups and an ashtray full of cigarette ends suggested that the two men who awaited their arrival had been in long and deep discussion.

Bliss made the introductions, beginning with the taller of the men, both of whom wore the nondescript dark suits traditionally favoured by high-ranking police officers.

"Rob, I don't believe you've met Commander Bob Tanner," Bliss began conversationally, as though he and D'Arcy were the oldest and best of friends. "Bob, this is Major D'Arcy."

As the man rose from behind the conference table, D'Arcy realised just how tall he was. A good six foot six, with broad coathanger shoulders and a massive hand that completely covered D'Arcy's when he shook it.

"Bob is Head of SO13 Anti-Terrorist Branch," Bliss advised.

D'Arcy's surprise showed in his smile. "We are honoured."

Bob Tanner's dark eyes were stern beneath the thick beetle brows that complemented the precisely cut head of black hair that was starting to silver at the temples. "It's not a matter of honour, Major. I'm afraid it's a matter of necessity."

There was a trace of a Dorset accent in the voice, which had sufficient gravity in its tone to let D'Arcy know that he took himself and his position with the utmost seriousness. And expected everyone else to do the same.

"And his deputy, Detective Chief Superintendent Reg Roman," Bliss continued, introducing a mild-mannered, lightly built man. He was about D'Arcy's age although, with his fair hair and ready smile, he could have been much younger.

"We've spoken before," D'Arcy said, "but not met. Over a previous kidnap case."

"Good to put the face to the voice," Roman replied.

As they took their seats Tanner began: "I'm afraid, Major, that this case isn't at all like the one you worked on before with Reg Roman."

Instantly D'Arcy read the message. Tanner, as Commander of the Anti-Terrorist Branch, was stamping his authority on the meeting from the outset.

"Let me explain to all of you why this case is so different," Tanner continued, hunching his huge shoulders, his big hands spread before him on the table. His sombre eyes seemed to address each individual personally, in the way that a schoolmaster delivers a final warning to wayward pupils. "This case is different because it appears not to involve the usual criminal fraternity. The kidnap has apparently been perpetrated by a cell of international terrorists, and that automatically makes it a matter for state security. Whilst Reg Roman here is responsible for the day-to-day running of our investigation, he reports to me. In turn I answer to the Assistant Commissioner of Specialist Operations who has a seat on a specially convened COBRA sub-group. That, for those of you not familiar with such things, is Cabinet Office level. It is being treated that seriously. And, as such, any actions taken require the sanction of that sub-group. In short any action that we or you take will have to be in accordance with current government policy."

D'Arcy sensed trouble. "What specifically are you saying that might affect the handling of this case?"

The beetle brows knitted together in foreboding. "That in any case involving a terrorist-inspired kidnap, it is British Government policy not to negotiate. Certainly not in terms of granting kidnappers political or financial reward. Nor, of course, immunity from prosecution."

At the far end of the table Nadirpur almost yelped in anguish. "But it is my wife and child's lives at stake!"

"Quite so," Tanner replied. "I can see from where you are sitting that is difficult to appreciate."

Reg Roman stepped in quickly. "It's not quite as black as it seems, Mr Nadirpur. We have a very experienced police organisation at our disposal. Every attempt will be made to open up dialogue with the kidnappers and to stall them long enough to trace where your wife and daughter are being held. Then appropriate action will be taken."

"And if the kidnappers lose patience?" Nadirpur asked gloomily.

Roman attempted to be reassuring. "I'm sure we can keep them optimistic enough."

D'Arcy said: "As you are no doubt aware, the purpose of this kidnap is to put pressure on my client to reveal the whereabouts of a missing ship. For a while, at least, I think we can offer them assurances that we are taking steps to locate it. Enough to buy some time."

Roy Bliss shifted in his seat and studied the tip of his cigarette grimly.

Roman said: "That's a sound idea, Major. We have to establish contact with the kidnappers and try to exchange something, even if it is just information. Because – you must all understand – it is only when an exchange is made that we can narrow down the area of search to concentrate our resources. Otherwise they could be hiding out at any one of the millions of properties in Britain. But an exchange puts both them and us into a geographical funnel towards the meeting point."

D'Arcy decided to take a new tack to loosen the strait-jacket he could foresee Tanner placing on his options to negotiate. Turning to the Anti-Terrorist Branch commander, he said: "We're not even sure terrorists are involved in this. After all it was a *legitimate* weapons cargo, however much Britain might disapprove. Maybe just some Iranian hotheads getting upset because they think they've been subjected to a con trick by the arms dealers. It's happened before." He turned pointedly to Bliss. "What do you think, Roy?"

D'Arcy watched with interest. After all it had been Bliss who had warned him that Nadirpur was embroiled with the *Pessarane Behesht*, Bliss who had informed him that the real cargo was arms. What else did he know?

To his credit the SIS man took the hot coal landing on his lap without flinching. Perhaps he knew D'Arcy well enough to have been expecting it.

"I'm afraid we have to assume the worst." Bliss turned to Tanner. "The problem dealing with Iranian or Lebanese Shi'ite terrorists is that we know comparatively little about them. And what we do know is often second-hand, usually from Israeli sources. Not only are these terrorist groupings highly fragmented, it is not always clear either who controls them or what their motives are on specific occasions. Unlike many terrorists, Iranian or Iranian-linked groups often do not claim responsibility for atrocities they commit. It's all part of their game to keep us guessing. Helps build up their mystique."

Tanner nodded gravely.

Roman looked at D'Arcy. "What about this ship? If it's been lost at sea, then why shouldn't the Iranians believe it?" He smiled gently. "Accept the will of Allah, so to speak."

"They don't believe it any more than we do," D'Arcy replied, "because, given the size of the ship and prevailing weather, hijacking is the most likely explanation. There have been over a thousand acts of piracy in the past ten years. Usually the cargo is broken down and sold off, then the ship reappears with false papers reregistered under a Honduran or Panamanian flag of convenience. Add to that the fact that the Paris-based company that supplied the cargo has vanished into thin air, and it starts to look very suspicious." As he spoke he could almost feel the dagger looks from Bliss piercing his back.

Tanner appeared to come to a decision. "Well, gentlemen – " He nodded recognition at Chantal "– and lady, we cannot yet know the ins and outs of this business. Clearly there is some chicanery going on and perhaps in due course we will find out the truth. Meanwhile we will have to treat this at its face value. A kidnap for purposes not entirely known. But Mr Bliss is right that we have to assume that the abductors are politically motivated terrorists – "

"I don't agree," D'Arcy interrupted. "As you have said yourself, that will restrict the options open to my client to negotiate. I propose that it should be treated as a case of criminal kidnap until we have evidence to the contrary."

Bliss's cheeks reddened. D'Arcy was throwing down a

direct challenge for him to come clean, and he knew it.

Roman looked sympathetic. He understood that D'Arcy was after the best opportunity to get his client's wife and child back alive. But if he knew his Commander as well as he thought he did, there would be little chance of that. Tanner disapproved of kidnap insurance and companies like D'Arcy's which negotiated for hostage release. In the eyes of the conservative-minded Dorset policeman, it just encouraged kidnappers – criminal or terrorists – to try it again.

As it was, Tanner opted for neutral ground. "I tell you what, Major, we will keep that aspect under review. See exactly what they want first. I take it that you have not yet received a demand?"

"I've seen nothing," D'Arcy answered truthfully.

"And you'll co-operate fully with Reg here?" Tanner asked, knitting his brows together in stern warning.

"*We* contacted you," D'Arcy reminded. "Of course we'll co-operate."

Roman nodded and smiled at D'Arcy. "It'll be a pleasure working with you again, Major."

Tanner rose to his feet, and all eyes upturned. "Right. I'll leave you in Reg Roman's capable hands. He'll keep me informed. We'll meet again in due course." Picking up his heavy hide briefcase, he swept out of the conference room.

It did not escape Roman's notice that his Commander had neglected to offer a word of comfort to Nadirpur and he acted swiftly to compensate. "Don't think we're uncaring, sir. Far from it. Things seem hopeless at the moment, but it's not our policy to let kidnappers get away with their crimes."

Nadirpur looked straight into Roman's eyes. "I do not care about the kidnappers. I just want my wife and child back safe."

"Of course." Chastened, the officer turned to D'Arcy. "Here's my card. You'll phone me as soon as they make contact?"

"You'll be the first to know."

As the group made its way into the reception area, Bliss tugged at D'Arcy's sleeve.

"What is it, Roy?"

Bliss lit a cigarette, cupping it in nicotine-stained fingers. "About your idea. Trading off information about the ship to keep Nadirpur's family alive."

"What about it?"

Bliss inhaled deeply. "You won't find it, pal."

"We can try."

Bliss shook his head. "Not a good idea."

D'Arcy was suspicious. "There's Tanner saying no money, and now you're saying no ship. We've got to offer the bastards something."

"Sure," Bliss said. "Go through the motions of searching for the ship. But don't look too hard, pal, eh?"

The scar on D'Arcy's cheek pulsed. "What do you know about the ship, Roy?"

Bliss tapped the side of his nose. "Just remember – you want to stay in business."

"I've got a man on board that ship."

Bliss shrugged. "He'll come to no harm."

"Is Century House involved in this setup, Roy?"

"I've said too much already. Just take it from me that it's not in your best interests to go hunting around for the ship."

"And Nadirpur's wife and kid?"

"That wasn't anticipated," Bliss conceded. His grey eyes fixed closely on D'Arcy. "But this can be a dirty game, pal, as you well know. Don't worry though, the cops will sort out that side of things. Just know who your friends are. *Caio*."

Bliss turned on his heel and, pausing only to toss his cigarette end into one of the fire buckets, sauntered out of the hotel lobby.

D'Arcy drove his passengers back to London in a mood of suppressed fury. Just who the hell did Bliss think he was? Lying to him, lying to the police running the kidnap inquiry. Concocting any half-truth that suited some hare-brained plan dreamed up by the spooks in Century House.

They lived in a world of their own, that lot. He knew well enough, because once that had been his world too. Well, in part. Standing on the sidelines, carrying out orders. Up the sharp end when all their clever ideas came unstuck and they needed some poor mug to stick them back together again.

But that was then. This was now. He was no longer part of their treacherous, scheming world with its labyrinthine plots and counterplots. This was his world now, helping poor bastards like Nadirpur who had become ensnared by accident.

He swept up to the gates of the converted Flax Wharf warehouse and sounded the horn. Someone checked the car through the closed-circuit monitor and the gates opened, allowing him to drive into the courtyard.

After the crumbling Victorian brickwork of the exterior, IAP's ultramodern nerve centre came as a shock to both Nadirpur and Saint-Julien. They gazed in awe at the hive of activity against the muted background clack of typewriter and word processor keyboards. D'Arcy recognised the faces of several ex-special forces personnel whom he had not seen for some time. Most were writing up reports between assignments, or busy making arrangements by telephone. A number of hands waved in his direction.

On Forbes's 'throne' by the VDUs sat the queen bee of admin, weaving order out of the potential chaos of paperwork. Brandy Slade looked up, tossing her curly mane of chestnut hair and showing a perfectly white New York secretary's smile. "Hi, boss!"

Her gaiety and enthusiasm for work was infectious; nothing seemed to get her down. And she was always turned out with the meticulous make-up and clothes of a Barbie doll, an arch exponent of power dressing with padded shoulders to her grey suit and a tight pencil skirt that drew attention to her long, shapely legs. D'Arcy felt better already.

Once Nadirpur and Saint-Julien had been introduced, everyone settled down around the large 'Ops Room' table while Brandy organised coffee and biscuits.

D'Arcy said: "Right, Dave, let's have a look at the kidnappers' demand."

With a suitable sense of occasion Forbes pulled on a pair of rubber gloves and lifted a sealed plastic bag from his briefcase. He opened it carefully and extracted a padded brown Jiffy bag. Tilting it to one side he allowed the object to clatter onto the table.

Nadirpur gasped.

"You recognise it?" D'Arcy asked.

The Iranian nodded. "It is Ashi's wedding ring." Gingerly he reached out to touch it; it might as well have been a physical part of his wife's anatomy, like an ear or a finger. "See, the sapphire. Her birthstone. And the inscription."

Forbes tugged at the thin wad of paper protruding from the bag. It was a single sheet that had been folded neatly into four. The big hands spread it out.

"Typewritten," he observed. "In capitals."

D'Arcy said: "They're in a hurry. That's a good sign."

"How do you know, Rober'?" Chantal asked.

"Because typewriters can be traceable. If they had the time they'd have cut words or letters out of magazines. Or maybe used a plastic stencil."

Nadirpur stared at the paper as though it were contaminated. "Why didn't they make Ashi write it? To prove she's alive?" He looked at D'Arcy wide-eyed. "It doesn't mean – ?"

"No, it doesn't," D'Arcy replied more sharply than he intended. "If a victim is asked to write, then he or she will know what's going on. That can be dangerous for the kidnappers. Ashi might be able to interfere with the negotiations at her end. Or even write some sort of clue into the message."

"You are sure?"

"A typewriter is normal," D'Arcy assured.

"I'll read it," Forbes said.

"NADIRPUR – YOUR WIFE AND CHILD IS HELD IN THE NAME OF ISLAM. OUR SHIPMENT MUST BE RETURNED OR THEY WILL DIE BOTH. SMITTEN BY THE SWORD OF ALLAH. IF YOU DO NOT FULLY CO-OPERATE YOUR DAUGHTER WILL BE MUTILATED . . ."

# 9

"OBEY THE FOLLOWING INSTRUCTIONS," Forbes continued reading, his voice flat and without emotion. "DO NOT CONTACT THE POLICE OR ANY PERSONS ELSE. INCLUDING THE NEWSPAPERS OR TELEVISION. DO NOT TRY TO FIND US IF YOU WANT TO SEE YOUR WIFE AND DAUGHTER ALIVE. PUT THIS ADVERTISEMENT IN THE *EVENING STANDARD* NEWSPAPER OF LONDON. ADD A SAFE TELEPHONE NUMBER THAT CANNOT BE TRACED BY POLICEMEN." He looked up. "That's it. Just ALLAH AKBAR. No signature."

Nadirpur dropped back in his chair, his eyes closed. That was it; at least now he knew the worst. Chantal squeezed D'Arcy's arm for comfort as the horror of it sank in.

"Not the best grammar," Forbes observed. "But the sort of mistakes a foreigner would make rather than a poorly educated Englishman."

D'Arcy said: "I don't think we've any doubts about who sent it, Dave. As Bliss kindly pointed out, groups like the *Pessarane Behesht* don't leave calling cards."

"What is the advertisement?" Saint-Julien asked.

Forbes glanced down at the sheet. "A small ad about villas for sale in Portugal. The telephone number is left blank."

"You will give your number here?" Nadirpur asked.

D'Arcy toyed with a fresh cigar. "Yes, we're at the centre of things here."

"But the police?"

"They'll want all calls on tape," D'Arcy confirmed. "And on a case like this they'll tap any line they think we might be tempted to use."

"They don't trust us?"

"They know the pressure you – we – are under."

Nadirpur splayed his slender white fingers on the table and studied the bitten nails. "And you *want* to co-operate with them?"

D'Arcy said: "We won't find your wife and daughter without their help, Nader. They have access to the entire British police force, computers and experts in this sort of crime. They are probably the best in the world."

Nadirpur stared at him. "But do they care about Ashi and little Sousan?"

"They care."

The Iranian returned to the study of his fingernails. "And will these people mut –" He couldn't bring himself to use the word. "Will they hurt my little Sousan?"

"Not if we don't give them cause." D'Arcy did his best to sound convincing. He added: "They'll know that it's historically proven that the surest way to get co-operation is to carry out that threat. Mutilation is a powerful and emotive weapon. We must convince them it isn't necessary this time."

"How can we do that?"

"By proving we mean business." He turned to Forbes. "Dave, I made this decision in Paris. We have to get someone out to Oman to search for *Clarion Call* on the spot."

"I've been thinking on the same lines myself," Forbes admitted. "It's all very well getting a bloke like Alan Hawksby to put the word out for you, but there's nothing like having someone on the ground." The grin broadened beneath the shaggy *bandido* moustache. "My bag's packed."

D'Arcy appreciated the gesture. "I need you here, Dave."

Forbes tapped his artificial leg. "No job for a cripple, you mean."

D'Arcy couldn't resist a smile. "Dave, old son, you wouldn't be a cripple if you had *no* legs. I mean it, I need you here. Even if you do speak Arabic like a native."

It had always struck D'Arcy as incongruous that the bluff ex-SAS sergeant had a natural flair for languages that even exceeded his own considerable talent.

Saint-Julien said cautiously: "I can handle that lingo, *mon ami*. And I know my way around the Gulf. Besides, I've nothing else planned."

Despite his initial misgivings, D'Arcy had grown to respect the professionalism of the taciturn Corsican; besides which his staff was still seriously overstretched.

"I guess a guy who's served in the Legion's Amphibious Section would be appropriate," Forbes admitted grudgingly. "Incidentally, something Alan Hawksby mentioned when I phoned. An old chum of yours is operating out of Muscat at the moment. Remember Rick Clay?"

"Clay?" D'Arcy took a second to recall. "You mean 'China' Clay? The bootneck?"

"That's him," Forbes confirmed. "Ex-Special Boat Service. He does a bit of salvage work and diving for the oil companies, that sort of thing."

"That could be useful, Dave," D'Arcy conceded. He turned to Saint-Julien. "See if you can make contact."

"So I get to go?" Saint-Julien asked.

D'Arcy laughed. "Weren't you ever taught never to volunteer?"

At least now there was a slight air of optimism that had been missing the night before in Paris. With contact established everyone had a feeling that things were moving. But D'Arcy was under no illusions that a tortuous route lay ahead. This was a time of comparative high, and it would be one of the inevitable number of highs and lows they would experience for as long as negotiations lasted. He and his team would undoubtedly share Nadirpur's moments of elation and deep despair, but it was part of his task to ensure that their client never gave up hope. For if that happened, all would be lost.

After advising Reg Roman of the Anti-Terrorist Branch that contact with the kidnappers had been made and the note kept safe for forensic tests, he telephoned the *Evening Standard* to place the advertisement as instructed. They then adjourned for a quiet meal in an Italian restaurant. The mood remained expectant and bright under the circumstances when they returned to Flax Wharf, where Nadirpur had his best night's sleep for days on D'Arcy's sofa.

First on the agenda the next day was for D'Arcy to ring the Sultanate of Oman at an hour when he stood a chance of catching an old friend in the Omani Government.

Virtually closed to individual tourists, every visitor to the country required a 'No Objection Certificate' issued by the government. And to obtain an NOC meant being sponsored by a resident businessman or official, and having a valid reason for the trip. It certainly did not include searching for missing ships that might have been hijacked. That smelled of trouble and was something the government was determined to avoid.

"I even knew a bloke," Forbes said, "who had a hell of a job getting an NOC because his name was just plain William Brown. Only two names, see? And to the Omanis – who have names as long as your arm – anyone with just two names must be up to no good!"

Added to the vagaries of Arabic whim as to whether or not an NOC would be granted was the length of time it took to arrive at that decision. Even with full co-operation from the Omani Embassy in London, it was a record for a certificate to be granted in under four weeks. And that would be too late for Nadirpur and his wife and child.

Seven o'clock would be eleven in Oman, allowing D'Arcy an hour to try and get through to His Excellency Shaykh Aziz bin Saud bin Nasir al Zufar before his Ministry closed down for the day at noon.

D'Arcy had known Shaykh Zufar since the days of the civil war in the early seventies after the repressive Sultan Said bin Taimur was deposed by his son Qaboos in a virtually bloodless coup.

The young Qaboos had been educated in Britain and had passed through Sandhurst to be commissioned in the British Army. During that time his father had continued his inept rule, stifling desperately needed development and blindly repressing any dissent. This merely served to encourage Communist infiltrators from neighbouring North Yemen to stir up trouble amongst the already resentful tribesmen of Dhofar in the mountainous interior.

After banishing his father, it had taken the new Sultan Qaboos bin Said six years to win back his country with a highly effective 'hearts-and-minds' campaign developed by the Special Air Service Regiment.

Today Qaboos still ruled with the pragmatism and wisdom of a benign dictator, successfully holding his nation together, although little-reported trouble with the North Yemenis still flared from time to time.

But it had been in the days of the bitter Dhofari campaign that D'Arcy had first met Shaykh Zufar, a wily, mischievous and thoroughly likeable tribal leader whose scheming and plotting would have run rings around any Western politician.

Zufar's only real concern was the welfare of his people, regardless of who might hold authority in some remote air-conditioned office hundreds of miles away. He was healthily scathing of everything and everyone who interfered with his land and his people's way of life. Politicians, rival tribes, religious leaders, foreigners and soldiers were all wittily and unceremoniously cut down to size by his incisive tongue.

Despite the fact that he strongly suspected Shaykh Zufar of secretly supporting the rebels, D'Arcy had hit it off with him instantly. Many a night they had spent by the fire under a cold desert moon discussing far-ranging subjects. Even now he could visualise the wizened, nut brown face of indeterminate age, with its greying, scented beard and one blind eye, wrinkling expressively to show either glee or irritation.

Once they had been in dispute as to whether Zufar giving a goat to a group of retreating Yemenis constituted helping the enemies of the Sultan. At the same time the shaykh learned that a well-boring scheme was coming to his area and he wanted one for his village.

"How can we discuss this," D'Arcy recalled saying sternly, "when you have been aiding Qaboos' sworn enemies? Now you ask for his help."

Zufar had smiled, his one eye twinkling, and reached for the accusing document in D'Arcy's hand. He took it and placed it between some brass pots to one side.

He rejoined D'Arcy and poured some green tea. "There, Mr Robert, now there is no dispute between us. Let us settle the matter of the new well. Afterwards we can resume our dispute."

The village got its well.

After the troubles Qaboos had carefully divided most tribes, elevating members of each to important positions in government so that they had a vested interest in maintaining the status quo. Recognising Shaykh Zufar as a potential source of aggravation, if not trouble, he had created a Ministry of ill-defined purpose, combining economic and cultural development, which in itself might be considered a contradiction in terms.

Nevertheless the ministry was still flourishing with typically labyrinthine Omani bureaucracy, as D'Arcy was passed to one officious young Arab after another. Each in turn demanded to know the nature of his call, insisted that the minister was in conference, on holiday, or out of the country.

Finally, he suspected by accident, he was put through to another line which Shaykh Zufar himself picked up.

"Your Excellency?"

"What? I can't hear you!"

D'Arcy shouted. "Your Excellency?"

"Aziz Zufar here. Do speak up!"

"Aziz, you old rogue. It's Mr Robert here."

"Who?"

"Mr Robert," D'Arcy repeated. "From England. You remember?"

D'Arcy imagined he had disturbed the Minister dozing in his office, but the penny appeared finally to have dropped. The old boy hadn't changed, and the years flooded by in minutes until mentally D'Arcy was back again in the *jebel*, by the fire beneath the cold moon.

He explained carefully that he was planning to go to Oman, but a friend and business colleague would be coming over first on a matter of utmost importance and confidentiality. As he had guessed it would, the hint of conspiracy appealed to Zufar who immediately dismissed any problem of obtaining an NOC.

"I shall deal with it myself, Mr Robert. My driver will meet your friend from the airport in a Ministry car. Just tell me what flight. He shall be my guest. Any friend of yours will be a friend of mine!" he promised. Then, lowering his voice, he asked: "And does your friend share your taste for Christian Milk?"

D'Arcy laughed. That had been his explanation of the contents of his hip flask many years before, when Zufar had developed a liking for fine twelve-year-old malt. "I'll see that he brings you some."

Taking note of Zufar's private number before hanging up, D'Arcy strolled back into the living area where Chantal was serving up hot toast and coffee.

"All settled. Saint-Julien will get his NOC." He turned to Brandy. "You can book our new recruit on the first available flight."

Shortly after Detective Chief Superintendent Roman arrived with a couple of technical officers to begin wiring the telephones with voice-print analysers and tape recorders, including one sealed unit that would be produced 'guaranteed untampered with' for evidence should the case ever reach court.

"We'll be monitoring down at the local exchange, of course," he explained. "And as soon as we get a contact call we'll put a trace on it. Try and keep them talking."

Over coffee he studied the kidnappers' note carefully, reading it several times. "I'll get the make of typewriter analysed. Meanwhile, have you decided on your initial response, Rob?" His attitude was far more informal and relaxed without the brooding presence of Bob Tanner.

"Mr Nadirpur has agreed that we will refuse any negotiation until we have evidence of his wife and child's safety."

"Very wise," Roman agreed. "And not a little courageous." He smiled at Nadirpur. "Believe me, it's worth it if you have the nerve to stick to your guns."

"I thought of demanding something they wouldn't have immediately to hand," D'Arcy continued. "Maybe a tape recording."

Roman nodded. "Anything they have to go out and buy is favourite. That puts them at risk and slows things up a bit. Try and take the steam out of things, get them to realise that there's going to be no rush."

Nadirpur didn't like the sound of that. "I do not want to prolong this terrible ordeal for Ashi and Sousan, Mr Roman."

The policeman shook his head. "No, sir, you don't quite understand. Unbearable though it seems, that is exactly what we have to do. To give time for us to find out who and where they are. Especially as it seems you are unable to give them what they really want."

"How do you even begin to set about finding them?" Nadirpur asked.

Roman took a sip of his coffee. "Obviously we must start on the assumption that this *Pessarane Behesht* group is responsible. But it could easily be some surrogate terrorist faction acting on their behalf. That happens a lot nowadays.

"Nevertheless there are some 25,000 Iranian nationals living in the UK at the moment, many of whom are students. We can probably narrow the most suspect ones down to a thousand. That's those with direct connections with the Iranian Government – embassy staff, journalists, workers in trade missions and those known to have strong pro-Khomeini leanings, et cetera. But then we can't pull them all in for questioning. It's not a question of our manpower resources, it's just that they wouldn't tell us anything.

"Besides, a professional operation such as this is unlikely to be conducted by anyone who might be regarded as remotely suspect by the British authorities. Now we believe the *Pessarane Behesht* has some sleeper cells in the country – mostly established to hunt down their own dissidents. It's possible that one of those has been activated for this kidnap. Equally it is possible that a hit team has been sent in especially to do the job."

"Where do you begin?" Chantal asked. "It seems impossible."

"We've already begun," Roman answered. "There are between fifty and a hundred trained ex-Anti-Terrorist Branch detectives now serving in other police jobs who will be recalled as the need arises. In addition the National Co-ordinator of the Regional Crime Squads will be briefing the nine Regional Crime Squads around the country as the investigation progresses. Descriptions of the kidnappers – such as they are – and the van used in the abduction have already been circulated. Copies of this demand will be circulated for possible identification of the typewriter used."

"It still seems an impossible task," Chantal observed.

"That is why time is needed," Roman explained. "But

also we need to arrange as many contacts with the kidnappers as possible. Because that is the time they have to show their hand. And remember, Mr Nadirpur's wife and child have to be held somewhere. At a remote farm, in some flats, in a house, a derelict building. Someone somewhere will eventually notice something, however small. Often it is something simple that gives them away. Some silly, small oversight. You'd be surprised."

Chantal nodded. "I would, these people seem so professional, so determined . . ."

"These people do not hold the monopoly on determination and professionalism," Roman retorted, more harshly than he had intended. He tapped the tiepin on his chest. "See this?"

She squinted at the small enamel badge. "A man's head with a pipe and – what you say – deerstalker hat?"

"That's it," Roman said proudly. "Sherlock Holmes. See, HOLMES is an acronym of Home Office Large Management Enquiry System. It's a state-of-the-art computer which can be dedicated solely to a case like this. Full text retrieval on up to ten thousand statements. The machine can pick up any one of a number of similarities we request. You know, five people see a man with a green nose driving a red car with a registration number beginning ABC in five different towns. That type of thing. Technical wizardry. We've already started going through lists of Iranian residents held by the Immigration Office as well as any temporary visitors here on limited visas. We're also running through other past kidnap crimes for any similarities."

Nadirpur was impressed, and said so.

Reg Roman smiled his appreciation. "It is a good setup. But I'll make no bones about it, we're dealing in long shots here. We're in the hands of the gods."

Nadirpur nodded. "In the hands of Allah."

The first editions of the *Evening Standard* hit the streets of London at eleven that morning. They carried the small ad for a villa for sale in Portugal and the telephone number of D'Arcy's office.

Tension mounted, anticlimax adding to anticlimax as Brandy replaced the switchboard receiver each time, putting genuine routine calls through to one of the other extensions. She would look across at the row of expectant faces around the table and shake her head.

At eleven thirty there was a false alarm, followed by two others in rapid succession. Callers who really did want to buy a villa in Portugal. Politely Brandy told them it had already been sold.

D'Arcy tried to clear some of the backlog of paperwork, but found that he just couldn't concentrate.

Lunchtime came. Still nothing. Everyone was becoming twitchy, irritable. Attempts to lighten the mood with humour just made matters worse. Around the table a sullen silence developed. Sandwiches were brought in, but remained untouched on the plates. Coffee, too, had lost its appeal.

Lunchtime went. It was like a sophisticated form of Chinese torture. On the far wall the clock times around the world above the map inched towards the passing of another hour. It left a hollow, drained feeling in the gut.

D'Arcy lit a cigar, and almost immediately stubbed it out. His mouth tasted foul from too much smoking, his throat dry.

"Maybe they just want to make us sweat," Reg Roman said, echoing D'Arcy's own thoughts.

"IT'S THEM!" Brandy suddenly shouted from the switchboard, her hand over the mouthpiece.

D'Arcy's heart began to thud. "Right, put them through. Take your time."

Roman stared at the spare telephone that was patched directly through to Scotland Yard's communications technician at the local exchange. As soon as a trace was made it would ring.

"I'm sorry, I'm getting no reply from Mr Nadirpur,"

Brandy was delaying smoothly. "I'll try his other extension." It all added worthwhile seconds.

The phone on the conference table trilled. D'Arcy took a deep breath and picked up the receiver. "Hello?"

"Mr Nadirpur?" The voice was polite, almost soft.

"Who is that?"

"I want to speak to Mr Nadirpur." A hint of annoyance now. "It's very urgent."

"I'm afraid Mr Nadirpur isn't well. My name is D'Arcy. I'm Mr Nadirpur's adviser and a personal friend."

"You know what this is about?" the voice demanded. "It's about his wife and daughter. I need to speak to him now – " Venom suddenly bubbled forth " – if he wants to see them alive again!"

D'Arcy's voice was millpond calm. "You can talk to me. He's authorised me to speak on his behalf."

"Put me through to him!"

"I have my instructions," D'Arcy replied quietly. "What is it you want?"

The phone went dead.

"It was them?" Nadirpur asked anxiously. "What did they say?"

D'Arcy smiled. "Not a lot." It had gone well.

"Is that good?" Chantal asked.

"Good enough. They know now they won't have it all their own way. They'll want to think it over. Decide whether they'll talk to me."

Nadirpur shook his head, unsure. "Perhaps I should have spoken to them. I don't want to aggravate them."

"They'll phone back," D'Arcy assured. "And don't worry, you haven't refused them anything yet. If we can pull it off, it's better they talk through me."

Nadirpur had to agree there. He was used to thinking on his feet when making business decisions, but this was something way out of his league. All he wanted to do was to plead and give them everything he could. And the stupid thing was he had absolutely nothing to offer.

The spare line rang and Roman snatched up the

handset. He looked disappointed. "Sorry, folks, no trace. It was just too short. Maybe we'll get lucky next time."

There was now a distinct relaxing of the atmosphere around the table. Contact had been made; the spell had been broken. Suddenly the curling sandwiches looked appetising and the desire for coffee returned with a vengeance. Nadirpur even managed an unsure smile.

D'Arcy glanced at his watch. The kidnappers would need time to consider their position before they called again. Time enough for a shower and a change of shirt, he decided.

He emerged from the cubicle to find Chantal seated on the bed, talking on his private telephone extension. She looked up, smiled and waved. From the snatches of conversation in French he guessed to whom she was speaking.

He controlled the sudden flare of anger he felt. At the very first opportunity she was on the telephone to Pierre Roquelaure. Making sure he was the first to know what was happening. Keeping the DGSE ahead of their grubby little game of catch with the Ministry of the Interior.

Bliss's hint that Chantal might be working for her father burned in his ears.

She waved the handset at him. "Papa wants to speak to you."

D'Arcy pulled on his trousers and crossed to the bedside. He snatched the receiver, covering the mouthpiece with his hand. She looked up at him, startled. "*Pourquoi?*"

"Don't you think it would have been courteous to ask me before you go bleating to your father?"

She looked hurt. "Bleating? I phoned to see if there was news of Philippe. What is so wrong?"

D'Arcy hadn't thought of that. He was so immersed in the problem of the Nadirpur kidnapping that he'd completely forgotten about the poor sod held in Beirut. How stupidly insensitive of him! He'd really let Bliss's warning get to him. That little grub of doubt had been growing into an evil maggot in his subconscious and he hadn't even realised.

"I'm sorry," he said, and lifted the handset to his ear.

Roquelaure was in good humour. "Dear Rober', Chantal tells me you have contact with the kidnappers, that is good. But please do be careful how you handle this. A false move and our French hostages in Beirut could also be put at risk."

"I've told you, Pierre, as far as I'm concerned our clients come first."

"Yes, yes, quite, I think I have received that message. Besides, I am sure you will handle negotiations bearing in mind all the possible consequences. At least by going to England you have taken the matter away from the hands of our Ministry of Interior. Now there will be no awkward questions. After all, that has always been the special strength of IAP."

"This isn't a secure line," D'Arcy warned. "And we have the police in."

Roquelaure picked it up. "Ah, of course, yes. Let me know about any progress, will you?"

"Naturally."

D'Arcy hung up and looked across at the shower cubicle where Chantal had decided to follow his example. He studied her pale outline through the frosted glass.

Just what the hell was he doing? If he thought about it, he was doing everything he could to drive her away from him. He should have listened to Forbes's frequent advice to marry her. Christ, she was the only woman he'd ever met that he'd wanted to keep for ever. Sometimes his desire for her burned with a ferocity that was almost physically painful. So why the hell did he hold back?

Perhaps it was fear. Fear of becoming too committed, too vulnerable. Leaving himself wide open to be hurt again. Betrayed.

Because, when he on rare occasions allowed his mind to dwell on such matters, he knew that was how he felt. Since childhood, when his mother had deserted him and his father for another man. With good reason, he knew now. His father had been a difficult man, a professional soldier in the British Army. But also a violent man when he turned to drink, and he had turned to drink steadily and more frequently when he was repeatedly passed over for promotion.

But to the young D'Arcy it had seemed as though his mother had betrayed him, despite her protestations of love and the wetness of her hysterical tears in his hair.

It was a pattern that was to be repeated in later life. On the two occasions that he truly opened his heart to a woman, it had ended in disaster. Once, when as a humble warrant officer in the Parachute Regiment, he had met the girl of his teenage dreams.

Starry-eyed, he had spent all his savings on a crippling mortgage to buy her the house she wanted, and then struggled to provide the luxuries for which his young wife yearned.

Then, within the year, she had met what she had always wanted – an officer with an impeccable aristocratic background and an inheritance to match.

It had been that which drove him on to become an officer and then to apply for the Special Air Service Regiment. He could admit that now. It had all been to prove something to himself, and somehow to spite her.

Yet he had seen her again, just a couple of years ago. A woman spreading to middle-aged fat with two obnoxious teenage sons in tow. A rather vulgar woman she had seemed to him, with a coarse laugh and a too loud voice. A voice which told her friends how big her house was, how prosperous she was, how well her sons were doing at college. A voice that her husband, D'Arcy was amused to note, was keen to avoid, huddled with his fellow Guards officers in a corner, pretending she was nothing to do with him.

It was funny really, after all those years. Only then had he realised what a favour she had done him.

But it had been over his next encounter that the hurt had lingered most.

For many years he had avoided emotional entanglements. His affairs were occasional, fiery and brief, invariably allowed to die through neglect when he was posted overseas.

Only once, when he was stationed for a year in Singapore, he allowed himself to fall in love. She was Chinese. Sweet, tender and beautiful as only Chinese girls can be. Bright and intelligent, but beguilingly innocent. Or so he thought.

When she announced she was having his child, he had broken down and wept with happiness. It was the first and last time in his life he could ever remember doing so.

There was talk of marriage, a time of heartfelt promises and hope.

That was until he discovered by accident that she was no more than a sophisticated hooker. Moving on from one wealthy live-in lover to the next.

D'Arcy was discarded for one of the fat cats, a Hong Kong businessman, when she was three months pregnant.

Much later he heard she had borne a son who was abandoned to an orphanage.

A son. His son. Somewhere ten thousand miles away in the Far East. But God knows how he could ever be found.

D'Arcy shook himself from his memories and roughly wiped the moisture from his eyes with the back of his hand.

Suddenly he felt angry with himself. Was his irrational fear of betrayal any damn reason for him to hand Chantal over on a plate to a bloody ghost? Because, the way things were going, he doubted that Philippe Chaumont would ever see daylight again.

She came out wearing his terry towelling robe which swamped her slender frame.

"And is there news of Philippe?" he asked.

She flicked the wet blonde hair from her forehead. "You've just spoken to Papa. Didn't you ask him?"

"I didn't think to."

Her eyes narrowed, momentarily reminding him of Nadirpur's cat. "Are you naturally such a bastard, Rober'? Or do you have to work at it?"

"I'm asking you for God's sake."

She looked down at her feet. "No, it has all gone quiet." Then she tossed her head quickly, staring hard at the ceiling as she tried to prevent the tears. Her mouth worked but she couldn't find the words. Two salty streaks glistened beneath her eyes, mingling with droplets of water from her wet hair.

He reached for her cigarettes on the bed and threw them to her.

"*Merci*," she muttered, fumbling at the pack.

She glanced at him across the flame as he flicked his lighter for her. Slowly she exhaled, forcing herself to relax. "He won't be released now, Rober', will he? Not unless that damn ship is found."

D'Arcy didn't want to talk about it. "They'll always be open to other deals."

He could see in her eyes that she didn't believe him.

"Let me go with Saint-Julien," she said suddenly.

"Saint-Julien?" He was stunned. "Go to Oman?"

She sat beside him eagerly on the bed. "It is driving me crazy here! I can do nothing. Just sit and watch while you try to save Nader's wife and child. And all the time my Philippe is held hostage too. And for him I am doing *nothing*! Your police cannot find him in Beirut. Only that ship can get him freed."

D'Arcy said: "You'd be no help to Saint-Julien. You'd just be a hindrance."

Her green eyes flared with an angry light. "That is not true. Two heads are better than one. I can drive, I have been around boats all my life, I am an aquadiver. I even speak a little Arabic. What more do you want!"

230

"A woman in a Moslem world," D'Arcy reminded, acidly. "You'd be a hindrance."

"Arabs are men, too, Rober'," she retorted. "Or are you scared to leave me alone with a big butch Corsican?"

D'Arcy took to his feet, turning sharply to look down at her. "Who told you to ask, Chantal? Your father? Go to Oman and watch what D'Arcy's boys get up to? Is that what's going on?"

Her small fist swung at his groin. "*SALAUD!*" she swore.

Sidestepping he caught her wrist and thrust her arm to one side as his body fell onto hers. He felt the sharp rush of her breath against his face. "*Salaud!*" she repeated, her free arm flailing against his naked back. "Bastard, bastard, bastard!"

"Tell me the truth," D'Arcy hissed.

Her eyes were close to his, wide and green with fiery gold flecks of rage. He watched her mouth, aware of the whiteness of her teeth. He saw the tendons in her neck tighten and pulled his head back just in time as she snapped at his face like a piranha.

She laughed suddenly at his shocked expression. "You are lucky I did not take your nose off, you bastard."

He laughed too then. "You little bitch. I don't know what to make of you."

She frowned up at him. "I am not a spy. My father's or anyone's." Her eyebrows rose. "I can go to Oman?"

"You can go to hell."

Through her laughter she said: "And I'll take you down with me, Mr bastard D'Arcy!"

Christ, I love you, he thought. And for once he told her.

It was more like rape than lovemaking. Not in her token resistance, but in the shared brutality of their passion and the intensity of her response which left him shaking.

It was several long minutes before he pulled himself from her, leaving her in the last throes of orgasm.

He traced a finger down the valley of her breasts,

flattened by gravity almost to the point of non-existence. As he reached her navel she groaned, opened and closed her legs involuntarily as another wave passed over her.

"Marry me," he said.

Her body went still. She lay like a corpse, her eyes closed. Just her belly moved fractionally as she breathed.

"Marry me."

Still no movement. Then, slowly, she opened her eyes. Lifting herself onto her elbows, she glared at him in challenge. Amber damp hair was plastered to her brow. "Why should I marry a bastard?"

"We need each other."

She grunted, pulled the gown from where it had fallen off her shoulders, and drew it protectively around her. Without looking at him she said: "You cannot ask me that. Not now. Not with Philippe in Beirut."

"Sod Philippe." He hadn't meant to say it. The words were out before he could stop himself. But he was damned if he was going to apologise. "You and he were then. We are here and now."

She scowled at him, and shook her head slowly in disbelief.

"Marry me."

"I'll think about it in Oman."

He grinned. You had to hand it to her. In her way she was every bit as determined and uncompromising as he was himself. "Listen, kitten, I want Philippe freed as much as you do. I just don't want him free to marry you."

"Now you make me feel as though I have just betrayed him," she scolded.

"By being true to yourself?"

"You're being a bastard again."

In the living quarters below the door opened. It was Saint-Julien. "Hey, chief, it's the kidnappers!"

Grabbing his shirt, D'Arcy leapt the steps to the lower level leaving Chantal to dress hurriedly.

Down in the 'Ops Room', Brandy waved to him from

232

the switchboard as he entered. At the table Nadirpur and Reg Roman waited expectantly.

"Put it through," D'Arcy ordered.

"Hello – Mr Nadirpur?"

"This is his adviser – D'Arcy. Tell me what you want."

"Listen, you bastard –" He blinked. That word was starting to sound familiar. "– I know who you are. Listen, D'Arcy, I do not mince with my words. You have ten seconds. Otherwise I hang up – and that is IT! Understand me? You get two corpses floating in your famous Thames river. Okay? No mess. One, two, three . . ."

D'Arcy waved to Nadirpur. The Iranian smiled weakly, patted his script, and nodded. His face was bloodless. "All right, I'll put you through."

Up on the computer deck, Brandy switched the lines through. Nadirpur picked up his own telephone. "This is Nader Nadirpur."

"We have your wife and daughter."

"I know that."

"You have our demand. If we do not have information of the location of the ship, your daughter will be mutilated."

"Pardon?" Nadirpur was confused. The man was speaking too fast for him.

"Mu-ti-la-ted." The voice spun out the word with relish.

Listening on his extension, D'Arcy's scar showed white against his tanned skin like a scimitar. He jabbed his finger at the script notes in front of Nadirpur. The Iranian nodded. Yes, he knew what to do. His nerve was holding. D'Arcy smiled, trying to indicate that this sort of thing was only to be expected. Nothing to worry about.

Swallowing hard, Nadirpur managed to get his tongue around the words. "Yes, I understand. Listen to me. I have told your people my position before, back in Paris. I am as anxious to find the ship as you. I have my people trying to trace it – and the arms dealers who sold you the shipment."

"We don't believe you."

Nadirpur glanced at his script notes. "I do not care if you believe me or not. It is true and already we have made progress." He took a deep breath. "But I will not tell you this information until I have proof that my wife and child are alive and well."

"You do not make demands, *taghouti*! You tell us —"

D'Arcy raised his hand in signal. Nadirpur replaced the receiver.

There was a stunned silence in the room.

"That was very brave of you," Chantal breathed.

Nadirpur shrugged, he wasn't sure of anything any more.

D'Arcy said: "You did well, Nader. That will make them think. I doubt they'll phone back right away. They'll want to move districts in case we've got a trace on the call."

Reg Roman was already onto his technical officer to see if they had had any luck. In theory a modern electronic exchange can track a call in as little as ten seconds. Reality was slightly different and, again, the call was too short.

However, there was not long to wait before the next opportunity. It was just twenty-nine minutes later when the caller rang again.

"All right, Nadirpur, we agree," the voice said quickly. "Tomorrow we'll take a photograph of your wife and child holding an edition of the morning newspaper."

D'Arcy shook his head. But the gesture was unnecessary. Nadirpur remembered what he had been told. How in previous cases, cynical kidnappers had actually stored a hostage's dead body in the family freezer. It was taken out and propped in a chair, holding a newspaper. Even the fingers had to be broken at the joints so that they could be positioned realistically.

"No," Nadirpur said. "That is not sufficient. I want a tape recording of my wife and daughter actually reading tomorrow's newspaper."

"We do not have a tape recorder."

"That's your problem," Nadirpur snapped back with real and sudden anger. "And I want it within two days or there is no negotiation on anything."

"This is the idea of your security person," the voice challenged. "The man called D'Arcy. You get too smart with us and they die."

"And you don't get your cargo," Nadirpur snarled, his pent-up rage charging him with confidence now. "That I promise you."

A pause at the other end. Then: "You will have your evidence."

Nadirpur looked at D'Arcy, then said: "No doubt you will tell us where to collect."

Abruptly the line shut down, leaving a discordant high-pitched tone in their ears.

Nadirpur smiled, actually smiled. The script had worked; somehow he no longer felt so helpless. No longer did the kidnappers seem so all-powerful. Gradually D'Arcy was manoeuvring them into a frame of mind where they no longer expected everything to go their own way. Slowly but surely the kidnappers' ground was being shifted beneath their feet – from a position of making dictatorial demands to accepting a form of negotiation and compromise.

In that respect at least it had been a good day.

It was made even better for Chantal when D'Arcy was able to get through to his old friend in Oman – Shaykh Aziz bin Saud bin Nasir al Zufar – and secure the promise of a second NOC entry visa.

"Thank you, Rober'," she said later when they were alone together. "You do not know how much it means to me. I will not let you down."

"I know you won't." He hesitated. "Have you told your father that you are going?"

"No. I thought you would not like it."

He smiled, proud of her determination despite himself. "Then perhaps you should. You see, for the sake of Philippe, I think he should know that I believe the British

235

Secret Service is looking for a very different outcome to this business from the French DGSE."

"What do you mean? Don't the British want you to recover the lost ship?"

In his mind's eye D'Arcy could clearly see Roy Bliss giving his enigmatic warning in the lobby of the hotel outside Biggin Hill. "I think the British – in some way – have been responsible."

"For the missing ship? *Pourquoi*? For what reason?"

D'Arcy shook his head. "That is something I do not begin to understand."

# 10

The time had come. Tom Wilmot had decided it was now or never.

As he sat in the darkened storeroom, illuminated only by a bar of light from the scuttle high above his head, he heard the receding footsteps of the Jordanian commando. It would be another two hours before they made a check if they stuck to the routine that had evolved on *Clarion Call* over the past few days.

After the incident with the Sarbe radio beacon he had again been isolated from the rest of the crew. There had been no display of rancour from the hijackers. Rather a half-smile from their leader which suggested he recognised a fellow professional when he met one, and appreciated that Wilmot was doing no more than was expected of him.

That respect, however, meant that he was no longer trusted, and he was confined to a locker beneath the stairs at the base of the aft superstructure. It had been cleared of anything he could use to make good an escape. He lay on a folded pile of mildewed canvas and used a pile of rusty paint tins to form a stool, plus a couple of columns to hold the tray on which his food was brought twice daily. Toast or cereal and coffee in the morning, and a simple dish rustled up by the Gambian chef after sundown.

That had caused the biggest setback to the plan. He had to lose weight rapidly, but without seriously undermining his strength. Therefore he had been selective about what he ate, taking only lean protein, like fish or poultry, in small quantities and a spoonful of vegetables. That left potatoes and rice and vegetable scraps to be hidden.

He could not throw them out the scuttle because the debris would attract fish, including shark, and draw attention to what he was up to. Instead he buried the scraps under the piles of canvas. But, after several days in the stifling heat, it was beginning to hum. Now the constant buzz of flies was driving him to distraction.

Exploringly he ran his hands over his belly and flanks. He was fortunate that he had maintained a constant weight since his SBS days, when it was critical to the fit of his diving suit, and fitness and weight control was something his new boss D'Arcy insisted on. Normally Wilmot carried a mere half-inch of tyre round his waist, but now even that had vanished. If he usually weighed eleven-and-a-quarter stone, he estimated that he was down to eleven. And he needed to have lost at least that for his plan to succeed.

Rearranging his stack of cans he was able to give himself sufficient height to gain a foothold on one of the horizontal hull strengthening spars. Then, by drawing himself up to his full height, he could reach the scuttle. The glass was encrusted with accumulated filth and well-rusted, having never been opened since the day it was installed. He had spent hours gouging away at the rust and old paint with a bent nail to get it free. Now he released the catch and pulled it inward on its creaking hinges until the hot salt air of the sea hit his face.

He stood, braced like a climber by his toes and knees, gulping down deep draughts as he peered out. There was room for his head and ears to clear the circumference of the porthole, but with only millimetres left to spare. He wouldn't have believed it possible, but he remembered an instructor's voice carrying down through the years: "If you can get your head through a gap, then you can get your whole body through. Provided you're supple and don't have a bleedin' great beer gut."

It was one of those myths you never seriously expected to put to the test. Looking at the rim of the porthole now, he had to admit he was sceptical. Still, he had to try.

Over the days of his imprisonment he had studied how the Jordanians set about protecting *Clarion Call*. He could see the cork buoys bobbing on the surface. They would be keeping a monofilament net in position, an underwater fence that encircled the ship. Beneath the water it would be virtually invisible to the human eye and would ensnare any unsuspecting diver the Omani Navy might send to investigate.

He had seen the machine gun positions, which would deal with any surface intruders, hidden in the ship's camouflage drapes.

No doubt hand grenades would take care of any swimmers. There was no point in wasting ammunition against an elusive underwater target, when one grenade would act as an invitation to every shark in the area. There was no shortage of the brutes around the peninsula, fat and lazy on the plentiful supply of fish. He had never heard of anyone having problems but he knew that, rather than deter, the crash of a grenade would attract them in seconds.

It was imperative that he should get clear without being seen, not least because the commandos had at least two rubber inflatables with which to give chase. They also put down regular frogman patrols which could be a problem.

Wilmot climbed back down and sought the rusted can of anchor grease. He stripped off his shirt, trousers and underpants and began working the evil-smelling stuff over his torso and limbs until he was completely covered. He grinned suddenly to himself, aware how ridiculous he must look, and imagined his wife Pauline creased up with laughter at the sight of him.

No, he told himself sharply, that wouldn't be her reaction at all. She would have been horrified at the thought of what he was about to attempt.

Twilight was rushing in now with tropical suddenness, snuffing out the remnants of the day. But the small drop in temperature scarcely registered as he felt his sweat transforming the grease on his body into a sticky gel.

It was time. Carefully he once again scaled the inside of

the hull until he was able to push his head through the scuttle. He glanced left to the stern and right along the cargo deck to the bows. He knew there was a sentry there. Somewhere. But the light was so poor now that there was no definition left.

Beyond the hull the coast of Oman was just a dark, jagged frieze below a hazy aquamarine sky with a dusting of early stars.

It was intensely still and silent. The distant lethargic slap of the inky water against the hull was the only sound to reach his ears. He almost convinced himself that his thudding heart could be heard right across the inlet.

He deflated his chest and hunched his shoulders inward, pushing his bare feet against the rivets in the hull for grip. The steel of the open scuttle rubbed against his flesh, tightening like a vice as he squirmed and wriggled into the aperture.

The metal mouth closed around his back and shoulders, scouring the grease from his flesh until he felt his skin begin to flay. Sweat dripped into his eyes as he struggled, gasping for breath. Again he pushed. Again and again. Now he was well and truly wedged, his shoulders biting into the rim of the porthole, his lungs crushed so he could not breathe. So much for that bloody instructor and his sodding dangerous theories. Not only couldn't he go on, he doubted he could get back. He fought to stem his rising sense of panic.

For a moment he rested, drawing on his reserves of strength for a final effort, strung out like a serviette in a ring.

That was when he heard the heavy footfalls on the steps outside the locker. The clump of commando boots was unmistakable.

His heart began racing again and he wriggled and twisted like fury, his toes raw from the exerted pressure. Christ, his flesh must be scraped to the bone! He'd need to be a skeleton to get through. At any second he would hear the lever handle on the locker hatch being turned. Why the hell did they have to change their routine today!

And then, suddenly, the rim of the porthole made contact with unscraped grease, and he realised he had moved. Actually moved. Fear had provided the final spur. He began edging forward vigorously now, freed from the tight constriction of the widest point of his shoulders.

Behind him he heard the sound of boots pass by and continue on down into the bowels of the ship.

There was no time to savour the sense of relief. He knew now he could make it, but there was a long way to go and a hell of a swim ahead of him.

By twisting his arm he was able to free one hand and then the other, pulling the rest of his body after him. With an awkward movement he gripped the edge of the porthole with both hands and lowered himself towards the outer companionway below. He dropped the last metre, his bare feet making no sound on the steel decking.

For several long seconds he crouched in the shadow. Listening and watching. Feeling the sultry air wrap itself around him. The water of the inlet was as black as lacquer, showing only occasional phosphorescent ripples as a wave broke over the floats of the monofilament net. And the stars were now bright enough to illuminate high points on the surrounding crags, as well as his own pale, naked body.

The muted sound of voices and laughter drifted from the superstructure above him. It was impossible to tell if it was Mános and his crew in the mess or the Jordanian commandos. Whoever it was, it persuaded Wilmot for the first time that he really could pull it off. Everything was calm, the commandos unsuspecting.

Slowly he made his way towards the bows – just as far from the bridge and the chance of detection as he could get. It was difficult going, crawling beneath the drapes of camouflage netting that had transformed the massive ship into part of the rocky coast itself.

Then disaster almost struck. He was saved only by the coughing of one of the commandos in a two-man observation post halfway along the cargo deck. The blood froze in his veins; he had been about to stumble straight into them. He shrank back into deeper shadow. He could smell a faint trace of methylated spirits in the air. They must have had a brew going. Angrily he admonished himself for being so bloody careless.

It necessitated a time-consuming detour, working over the steel catwalk that spanned the cargo holds, to the far side of the ship. Only then could he resume his inch-by-inch crawl towards the bow. Once there his plan was to descend to the water by one of the retaining ropes which held the monofilament net in position. He would jump the last few feet to land on the other side of the net. Then it would simply be a slow, steady swim of some four miles to one of the shingle beaches on the far side of the inlet. Assuming his estimate of the distance to be correct, he would arrive before daylight. That would give him enough time to find shade from the full slam of the desert sun. He was confident that the Jordanian commandos, with their limited manpower resources, would stand little chance of finding him.

Once fully rested, he would use the cover of the next night to find one of the fishing villages he knew must be somewhere in the area. But he had no illusions as to how difficult that would be. Without shoes and without clothing the abrasive rock of the *jebel* would cut his unhardened skin like razor blades. He had no map and no knowledge of the area; he had no water and no food. It was not a prospect that he relished.

He pushed the concern from his mind. It was diverting his concentration as he approached the foredeck with its array of anchor winches and neatly coiled ropes.

From the shadow of the hold coaming, he planned his route across the exposed area. It was in full view of the bridge, and the stars would provide sufficient illumination for an alert guard to spot any careless movement.

Moreover the commandos were well-equipped and might well have night-viewing devices. Not that they would need them, considering that he was as white and naked as a newborn baby!

He inched forward on his belly towards the first of several stanchions, the ropes from which trailed over the landward side to hold the ship fast beneath the towering black cliffs.

It was a slow process to reach cover. But he knew that infinitesimal movement over a long period was less likely to be detected than a sudden rush across an exposed area.

Regaining his breath, he prepared for the next leg towards the anchor-winch housing. That took another five agonisingly slow and uncomfortable minutes before he fell back against the steel shell in relief, physically and mentally drained.

It must have been that one careless action that disturbed the dozing sentry.

Wilmot heard the sudden rustle of clothing on the other side of the winch housing. A dry cough and a stifled yawn. Wilmot sprang to his feet, turning as he did so.

For what seemed an age both men stood facing each other, scarcely two metres apart across the housing. The Jordanian confronted by a stark naked, grease-smeared man; Wilmot, paralysed with shock, staring at a black-clad commando wiping the sleep from his eyes. The shortened M16 carbine was held in a loose grip by his side.

Wide awake and keyed up, Wilmot's reflexes had the edge. He leapt up and forward, bouncing one foot on the housing to give him momentum. Wilmot's chest caught the startled commando full in the face. The force propelled them both towards the ship's side as the Jordanian's knees buckled under the sudden weight.

The man's back slammed heavily against the steel deck-plates, with Wilmot sprawled across him like a wrestler going for a shoulder press. Miraculously the M16 had slipped away, momentarily forgotten, as the commando tried to prevent the naked madman from strangling him. He brought his knee up hard into Wilmot's groin, and the grip eased for a second. It was sufficient for the commando to force his forearms between Wilmot's and prise away the deadly grip.

But Wilmot recovered fast, now sitting astride the commando and trying to avoid the flailing blows. Wilmot raised his arm, took aim, and struck. The hard edge of his right hand chopped into the man's windpipe with the full carry-on force of an axe blow.

It was like a power cut, and the Jordanian's lights went out instantly. His head cracked back against the deck.

Breathlessly Wilmot unseated himself from the prone body and ran his hands over the dead man's belt order. A carbine was no good to him, but the diver's combat knife might prove useful.

A voice called out in a stage whisper. It came from the direction of the observation-post halfway along the hull.

Wilmot cursed. He had been about to strip the body and take the clothes and deck shoes. That was out of the question now.

Carrying the knife he made for the ship's rail in a crouching run.

The voice called again, this time a hint of concern in the tone. Boots creaked on the deckplates.

Wilmot clasped the knife between his teeth, and swung himself over the side where the rope played down to the net. Grasping the thick twisted sisal with both hands, he dropped, swinging like a string puppet above the choppy black water.

Inch by inch he let gravity slide him towards the surface, feeling the coarse fibres of the rope rub into the skin of his palms.

Above he saw the beam of a flashlight. It was followed by a gasp of surprise. They had found the corpse.

He knew he had only seconds before he was discovered. Relaxing his grip, he allowed the rope to slide more rapidly through his palms and winced at the sharp sting of his scorched skin. The oily blackness of the water raced up to meet him. He registered the bobbing cork floats and gauged the position of the net below the surface. It was a split-second decision, and he let go, swinging out and willing his body to clear the net.

With a single short, sharp splash he entered the water and plunged below the surface. The clear tepid liquid closed in over his head, blotting out the sound of voices raised in alarm.

With relief his outstretched fingers found the invisible monofilament threads. For a few moments he trod water while he collected his bearings and cleared his mind. He was out of practice, but a year ago he had still been able to hold his breath for a full three minutes underwater. He might now still manage two. That should take him clear of the throw of a torch's beam, if not heavy-duty searchlights.

With a gentle kick he broke surface, his head full back to allow himself a deep lungful of air without offering a target. He was aware of frantic activity above, the shouting of orders and the sound of boots running over deckplates. More flashlight beams played out across the water.

Then they were gone and he was back in his black, wet and silent world. A duck dive took him to a depth of some six feet. What he wouldn't have given for a pair of fins and a scuba pack, he thought grimly, and concentrated on slow, powerful movements to propel him away from the ship. Panic was easy for him to contain; years of diving experience had taught him the value of calm control whatever dangers were faced. Yet the knowledge that the white blur of his body would be clearly visible below the surface, left him feeling horribly vulnerable.

As the seconds passed by his anxiety ebbed; each stroke was taking him farther and farther away from danger. And the longer he remained undetected the larger would be the area that the commandos would have to search. Thankfully this was one hell of a big inlet.

At last his lungs had emptied. Gently he slid to the surface, sucking in deep draughts of air as he glanced around.

There had been no strong tide or undercurrent and he had cleared a good fifty metres from the towering slab side of *Clarion Call*. Even at that short distance the camouflage drapes made the shape almost indistinguishable from the steep wall of the fjord. Several lights wavered indicating frantic activity, and he could hear someone yanking at an outboard lanyard. The engine spluttered, coughed and died. A curse and another pull. A repeat cough, a belchlike sound, and suddenly it caught. The engine shrieked painfully as the throttle was revved.

Wilmot slid gently back beneath the water and continued his swim. Just occasionally lights from the surface would scatter across the water and momentarily illuminate the tiny eyes all around him in the darkness. There must have been hundreds upon hundreds of curious, watching fish.

By the time he surfaced again, some hundred metres from *Clarion Call*, Wilmot was convinced he would make it. He felt fit, strong and remarkably calm in the circumstances. The water was warm and pleasant; in fact the swim was almost a pleasure.

Then he heard the whine of the outboard reverberating across the inlet. His eyes followed the sound until he picked up a torch beam from the rubber inflatable. The commandos had travelled halfway out across the inlet and were now working back towards the ship in a sweep to cut him off. He was suddenly aware of a second outboard, then a third. Christ! How many did the bastards have?

Someone yelled an order, and the three heavy-duty Nitesuns came on in unison, the dazzling daylight blaze blinding Wilmot instantly. He ducked rapidly, cursing the time he had wasted on the surface.

Clearly someone had taken the decision to risk being seen by a passing fishing dhow. And it was a risk because, even in the desert, gossip had an uncanny way of travelling quicker than the fastest vehicle.

The sudden shock wave of displaced water sent him reeling as the first explosion came. His eardrums rang with pain.

As he struggled desperately to maintain his position, Wilmot realised what was happening. The Jordanians were

246

using grenades to force him to the surface. In the same way that depth charges are used against submarines.

A second and third grenade detonated in close succession and the Nitesuns floodlit the water, creating a silver phosphorescent ceiling above his head. All around him brightly coloured fish floated limply or twitched in their death throes. Others spun and turned in a frenzy of indecision, unsure which way to go to avoid the rippling shock waves.

Wilmot broke surface, gasping to refill his lungs. He heard a shout of alarm, aware that he was only metres from one of the inflatables and caught amid the searchlight glare.

He plunged back again into what had now become a crystal daylight world, lit like an aquarium. With rising panic he looked around for some way of escape. But the inlet was very deep and offered only an ominous void below the searing beam of Nitesuns.

Then he saw it, and his heart sank.

It must have been twenty-five feet in length. The lean gunmetal flanks glistened in the light as it emerged from the disturbed clouds of sediment like a space cruiser from another galaxy. Running just ahead of its flat snout was a ten-inch pilot fish with vertical black-and-white pyjama stripes. It was leading the giant brute unerringly in Wilmot's direction.

In his career as a diver he had encountered a hundred sharks, and rarely had they shown the slightest interest, despite the popular legend. Mostly they were too wary or too lazy to cause trouble, especially when the water was as rich in marine life as it was in the Arabian Sea.

Yet Wilmot sensed that this shark was different. He couldn't identify the species, and didn't try. Its movements, he noticed, were agitated. The snout moved from side to side with a thrash of the massive pectorals and an irritable sweep of the tail. And the eyes. Not the steady and appraising eyes of the cautious professional predator, but somehow wild like the eyes of a madman.

Another grenade crashed.

The shark turned suddenly away from the concentric ripples of the shock wave, twisting and turning, driven crazy by the pain, seeking somewhere to wreak its vengeance.

Again it thrashed its tail, the mighty dorsal resembling the conning tower of a hunter-killer submarine as it circled ten metres away. The wild red eye had Wilmot fixed as though with the steady pulse of a homing sonar.

He knew he shouldn't surface. That was the last thing he should do. To leave his legs hanging like tempting soft fruit before the demented, tortured creature. But he had no choice.

He broke, gasping and spluttering, through the glass ceiling into the dazzling incandescence of the three focused searchlights. The inflatables were closing in on the turbulent whirlpool of activity.

From the corner of his eye Wilmot saw the huge dorsal fin, a glittering blue-grey blade carving a circular fluorescent wake, and closing.

Instinctively Wilmot drew his legs up to his chest. The circle grew smaller.

He waved at the nearest inflatable and yelled for help. He would rather be recaptured than left legless and bleeding in the dark waters.

"HELP ME!" he screamed again. But he could see nothing through the blinding aurora of the Nitesuns – just the vague outline shapes of the black-clad commandos.

The three inflatables were together now, line abreast, and his heart sank. They were no longer moving, the outboards throttled back, the craft bucking gently on the swell. The commandos were watching, dispassionately, for nature to take its inevitable course. Bored, faceless spectators at a gladiatorial fight to the death.

"BASTARDS!"

The dorsal fin dipped suddenly, the huge tail fin breaking surface, whipping in one powerful movement that drove the monster down.

Wilmot submerged to meet it head on. The huge flat snout filled his hazy vision, the red gimlet eyes fixing him with their hypnotic stare.

With morbid fascination he watched the gigantic jaw lift like a drawbridge, registered the portcullis of razored and rotten teeth, saw the pink cavern of its mouth, raised his fighting knife, saw Pauline, didn't see their unborn child.

Jalal Shamlou was furious.

He left the call box without a backward glance and stalked down the suburban north London road, his hands thrust deep inside the pockets of his windcheater.

Dammit, he was being used. Manipulated. Who the hell was the betrayer Nadirpur to give him orders, to tell him what to do?

He knew, of course. Hadn't it been drummed into him by his Sabbah instructors back at the camp? Hadn't they warned him of all the tricks police and international companies use when negotiating with kidnappers? Yet, even with that knowledge, he was helpless to resist. Although he recognised that there was a battle of wills in progress, he still had to submit.

If Nadirpur demanded a tape recording, he would have to provide a tape recording. Because if he didn't, what recourse did he have? To kill the woman and child? Then it would all be over and the shipowner would have no incentive to reveal the whereabouts of the missing ship. And he would then have failed in his mission. Failed the bearded one, failed Allah and the Islamic Revolution. Failed his mother and his dead brother. And he knew what the bearded one demanded as the price for failure.

He would not fail.

He had reached an arcade of shops. A launderette, a newsagents, and a grocery store. An estate agent.

He purchased a final edition of the evening paper then continued walking. The last shop in the arcade was a small electrical retailer. Amber cellophane covered the window to protect the motley collection of appliances from the

249

sun. Some new goods and some second-hand. Televisions, radios, food-mixers – a cassette recorder.

He did not even know if the house of Ali and Beth Christie had a record player or a tape recorder. Anyway he was not very familiar with such things. Part of the equipment that had been organised by the London cell had been a Polaroid camera. That had been what he planned to use for proof that the hostages were alive. He had never thought of a tape recorder.

A decision made, he moved towards the door. But he was just in time to see the shopkeeper put up the 'Closed' sign. Shamlou rattled the handle. On the other side the man shook his head. Again Shamlou rattled the door.

The man pointed at his watch. Five thirty.

Shamlou kicked the door, cursed, and trudged off in the direction of the bus stop that would take him back to the Christie household.

No recorder, no tape. A day lost and another day for the police to get nearer to discovering where the hostages were held. For he was under no illusions about that. With all the publicity that the kidnap had stirred, there was no way that the British police would leave it alone. With or without Nadirpur's permission.

He reached the deserted bus stop beside a public park and stared moodily at the children's playground. Beyond the railings a young mother was pushing her small daughter on a swing. In other circumstances it might so easily have been Ashi Nadirpur, and the little Sousan who had bitten him.

He rubbed subconsciously at the tiny scabs on his knuckles where her sharp little teeth had punctured his flesh. Even the child showed him no respect, no fear. Like Nadirpur, the bastard, giving orders. He frowned. No, not Nadirpur. He wouldn't know what to do. It was the man he'd spoken to first. The man with a French name; the same one whose company was shown on *Clarion Call*'s documents as advisers of maritime security.

That was why he was having difficulty. He'd been inadvertently pitched against a professional. Someone as well-trained and schooled as he had been.

Momentarily he was transported back to the dusty desert hut of mud blocks where he had been lectured. He heard the voice, ringing in his ears; "Use shock tactics. Create fear and respect by any means. By creating fear you gain control. Because your opponent never knows what you will do next. Your unpredictability will be your strength."

He found himself watching the mother and child on the swing intently. Suddenly the woman noticed, scowled at him. She took the child's hand and led it away, still looking back over her shoulder as though she suspected that he was a child molester.

An idea was forming in his mind. To create fear, to create respect.

His own words echoed in his head. Mutilation. That had been his threat over the telephone. He had deliberately drooled over its enunciation when he spoke, letting them know that he would enjoy doing it. That he just waited for the opportunity. That was how he had been taught at the Sabbah school.

But in truth he did not have much of a stomach for the idea. Not to chop the finger from an innocent child, or to slice off an ear. Several kidnappers in the past had done such things, he knew. Even the woman, even she he would find it hard to disfigure. He hadn't felt like that when he started on his mission, but he did now. Ever since he had held her small breast in his hand, feeling its warmth and the frightened pulse of her heart. Since she had reminded him of the woman in the garden of his dreams.

He looked up as the red double-decker bus approached. Yes, he resolved, he *would* use the mutilation weapon if necessary. He would order Matchsticks to do it; that cretin would actually enjoy it.

First he would adopt another approach.

After changing buses twice, he picked up the mustard-coloured builder's van for the final drive back to the Christies' house. By that time he had decided how he

251

would wrest the initiative back from Nadirpur and his damned adviser. And how he would deliver his next message.

There was nothing amiss as he drew into the gravel drive and parked outside the front door. As he climbed out he noticed the pile of paint cans and ladders stacked neatly beside the stone steps. A nice touch, he thought. Made it clear that the Christies had decorators in; it would explain the coming and going of strangers. It wouldn't have been Matchsticks' idea; he was prone to brainstorms not brainwaves. The London cell of Hamid and Kamal would have dreamed that one up. He had already been impressed by their quiet professional manner. Was envious of their training by Iranian Intelligence.

He used the heavy lion's head knocker. Almost immediately the door was opened by Matchsticks.

"Where is Mrs Christie?" he demanded as soon as he was inside. "I've told you she must always answer the door. I could have been the postman, or someone from the gas. Even a friend."

Matchsticks was agitated. "I forgot –" A hesitation " – besides, she doesn't look so good."

"What?"

"There is a problem," Matchsticks offered lamely.

Shamlou pushed past him and into the living room. The wallpaper at the far end of the room had been half stripped and white dustsheets covered the floor and furniture. Another touch from Hamid and Kamal.

In the front half of the room Beth Christie sat with her head buried in a cushion as she sobbed.

"Look at me!" Shamlou demanded.

Her shoulders shook as the sob became a flood of tears. She didn't hear, wouldn't or couldn't bring herself to obey.

He was filled suddenly with rage, angry that she too had no respect. Fear and respect. He grabbed her hair at the back of her head and twisted it fiercely in his grip. Forcing her to face him, he took in the livid bruise on her cheek.

"How did this happen?"

252

"We have a problem," Matchsticks repeated uncomfortably. "This afternoon she tells me she has a dinner party for tonight. They have friends coming to eat. At eight o'clock."

"What?"

The woman stared pleadingly up at him, her red eyes and her face running with tears. "It's true," she croaked.

"I did not believe her," Matchsticks said. "I think she lies. It is a trick."

"So you hit her?"

Matchsticks stood his ground. "Yes." Defiant.

"So now she answers the door looking like that? You are a fool, Ahmad."

The other man looked deeply offended at such open criticism in front of the woman. He turned away resentfully.

Shamlou glared at Beth Christie. "So why did you not say about this dinner party before?"

She dabbed at her face with a handkerchief. "I am sorry. I don't know. All – all this – it slipped my mind. You can understand that."

He had to admit he could understand very well that she had forgotten; for the past few days she had been reduced to a gibbering wreck, trembling each time Matchsticks looked in her direction with a malevolent grin. Her heart stopping each time he taunted her with the red can of petrol.

Disturbed by his silence she said: "I am telling you now. I said as soon as I remembered."

He nodded. "It will have to be cancelled."

"But the people are due in just a few hours."

His eyes blazed at her. "Well, they can hardly sit in here and eat, can they? You will telephone them. Now!"

"They'll think it strange."

"Then you will make up some excuse. Say you are not well. You are sick."

"If that is what you want."

"How many?"

"How many what?"

"People. How many people do you need to telephone."

She found it difficult to think. "Er, six people. Well, three couples. Three phone calls."

"Right, come." He grabbed her arm, forcing her from the sofa and across to the telephone table by the staircase. Pushing her into the chair, he extracted the automatic pistol from inside his jacket and jammed the muzzle against her cheek.

"I listen to every word you say. One thing wrong and I will blow your mouth out. Understand?"

She nodded numbly, and fumbled at the pages of her telephone book.

Two of the numbers that she rang answered. Taking a deep breath, she told her friends that she had contracted German measles, she felt absolutely awful, and that it wouldn't be fair to her guests. She was so sorry at the short notice, but it had only just been confirmed by the doctor. She would arrange another date soon. Both women at the other end were sympathetic and offered their best wishes for a speedy recovery.

There was no answer from the third number.

"I remember now. These people – Jane is visiting a friend. Her husband is picking her up after work and they are coming straight here." She looked horrified.

Shamlou eyed her suspiciously: he hoped that Matchsticks was wrong, that the woman wasn't playing tricks.

When Ali Christie arrived home from his gallery ten minutes later, he was bound and gagged in an armchair.

"When these guests arrive," Shamlou instructed, "you tell them what you told the others. Any attempt to give them a warning and your husband dies. Be very, very careful."

Just as he finished talking Matchsticks signalled from his position at the front window. In the unnerving silence that followed they all heard the tyres rolling to a standstill outside.

Shamlou joined his comrade at the drapes. The car was

254

a dark blue Audi. The passengers were a man in his early fifties, wearing a pinstripe business suit and a woman of similar age with tightly permed hair and a fur jacket which, at that time of year, must have been worn purely for show. She snapped something irritably at her husband, who returned to the car and extracted a bottle of wine. Together they mounted the steps.

Matchsticks crossed the room and sat beside Beth's trussed husband. He poked the snout of his gun menacingly under the man's chin.

"Remember what I told you," Shamlou hissed as the doorbell chimed and he pushed Beth into the hallway. He positioned himself in an alcove by the door, released the safety catch on his automatic, and nodded.

"Hi, Beth!" the woman with the perm began. Her voice was ugly and raucous.

"Oh, hello, Jane." Beth responded quickly. "Look I am sorry – I've been trying to reach you. Ali and I have had to cancel the party tonight."

The woman's mouth dropped.

"I am sorry," Beth repeated. "I'm going down with German measles. The doctor's just confirmed it. Isn't that silly? I must have picked it up at my son's school the other week."

Her guests, somewhat flustered, tried to hide their disappointment. "You look tired, Beth. Very pale. And that's a nasty bruise."

She nodded, smiled. "I was feeling woozy. Slipped and fell. I feel really lousy. It's very contagious, you know, so I really do have to cancel."

"Of course," the woman said. "No spots then?"

"Pardon me?"

"Spots. You have spots with German measles."

Beth laughed awkwardly. "All over my body. Awful."

"You should be in bed," the man added. "Let Ali answer the door – unless he's got it too? He wasn't at the golf club again this morning."

Christ! She had completely forgotten about her

husband's routine nine holes before work. She thought fast. "No, he's been looking after me."

"He's such a considerate man," the woman said, glancing at her husband as though to suggest he wasn't. "And there was me thinking you'd had the party without us." She indicated the dustbin at the bottom of the steps.

"I'm sorry?" Beth saw that the lid was off, the mouth of the bin stuffed with the bottles that Matchsticks had emptied down the sink. Her laugh was brittle. "Oh that, just a clear-out . . ."

"And it can't help having the decorators in when you're trying to rest," the man observed. He'd noticed the ladders and the stack of paint cans.

"No," Beth agreed, smiling weakly. She put her hand to her head. "I really must get to bed."

But the woman was inquisitive. "More decorating? I thought you'd finished the house. What is it this time?"

"The dining area," Beth answered without thinking. Immediately she bit on her tongue.

"But really, Beth, you've only just had that done!"

Beth looked sheepish. "Ali said he couldn't stand the pattern."

"Men!" the woman commiserated. "More money than sense."

"Not enough of either, I'm afraid."

The man decided they should leave their friend to her sick bed. As Beth closed the door relief flooded through her, and she fell back against the door. Her knees were trembling so much that she didn't think they would support her weight.

Shamlou resheathed the automatic in his waistband. "That was foolish about the dining room. I hope you were not deliberately trying to make them suspicious?"

Suddenly she was flushed with anger. "Are you joking? *Want* to make them suspicious? Do you think I want my husband killed? Do you think I want your crazy friend to burn me alive? Well, DO YOU?!" she shouted at him.

The young Iranian's eyes narrowed. He was tempted to

smash her other tear-stained cheek. In time he stopped himself. There were other matters that needed his attention. He said: "Do you have a tape recorder in the house?"

Beth was surprised, relieved at the abrupt change of tack. "Er – well, yes. There is a tape in our music centre – er, but we don't have a microphone." She thought, trying desperately to be helpful. "My husband's dictating machine! There will be one in his briefcase."

Shamlou said: "Fetch it and a tape."

She scurried to obey, smiling nervous encouragement at her husband as he sat, still gagged and bound. But his eyes remained empty of hope, drained of all emotion.

"Here," she said.

Shamlou took it in his palm. It was a small Olympus microcassette player recorder. He turned to Matchsticks. "Come. Bring the Polaroid camera," he snapped.

In the cellar he found Hamid and Kamal quietly playing cards on an upturned packing case. He felt irrationally annoyed by their professional calm. Kamal looked up, his beard making him look like some philosopher who didn't know what all the fuss was about; Hamid had the bland expression of an uncomprehending student. He sent them upstairs to watch over the Christies.

As they left Shamlou heard the whispered words of comfort from Ashi Nadirpur to her daughter behind the blanket.

"Hold the torch," he ordered Matchsticks and threw aside the makeshift screen.

It was the stench of urine and faeces that hit him first. It came from the yellow plastic bucket in the corner. Then the rancid smell of unwashed bodies.

Ashi was seated with her back to the brick wall, her knees drawn up, her daughter cuddled protectively at one side. The whites of two pairs of frightened eyes were like marbles in the torchlight.

There is fear here, thought Shamlou. Fear and respect. How different the woman looked now from when she had first arrived. Then she had been a proud, arrogant woman, spitting with indignation. Her clothes had been expensive, clean and carefully pressed. Her face made up like the Western whores Shamlou had been taught to despise. But the woman cowering before him now was little more than an animal, wallowing in her own filth. And like an animal her first instinct was to console and protect her young.

"Clear out that bucket," Shamlou said. "It stinks in here."

Matchsticks brushed past him and lifted the plastic container with a distasteful wrinkling of his nose. He glanced sneeringly at the woman and her child.

"Thank you," Ashi murmured, and studied Shamlou with a mixture of curiosity and trepidation.

In his hands he held the power of life and death, she knew that. The power to feed her and her daughter, or to let them starve. To let them grovel in the waste products of humanity or to allow them a semblance of dignity. She remembered the awful moment when he had held her breast. She had been so sure he would be rough, malicious even, considering her to have been provoking in some way. Yet he had been as gentle and respectful as a small boy with a dead pet. His momentary tenderness had saved her from shame and humiliation.

Why did he look at her in that strange way with those dark, long-lashed eyes? What was passing through his mind? He watched her with such intensity that it gave her an uncomfortable crawling sensation in her groin. She noticed the perspiration above his upper lip and the black down of the immature moustache. He can hardly be out of his teens, she thought. A boy-man. Why had they sent a boy-man to do this job?

The tip of Shamlou's tongue moistened his lips nervously. Quietly, reasonably, he said: "I should like you to remove your daughter's clothes."

Alarm flashed in Ashi's eyes, and Matchsticks, still holding the bucket, jeered.

Shamlou rounded on him. "Get out, you. Get some fresh water."

The other man shrugged indifference, turned and left the wire cage.

"Thank you," she found herself saying again.

How she hated that other man. He made her cringe just looking at him. What vile atrocity would he not be capable of perpetrating. Again she was thankful for the young man who stood before her now. Who showed some sign of humanity.

"Please," Shamlou ordered.

He was going to allow the child to bathe, she realised suddenly. Her captor was once again, reluctantly, proving that he was not quite the monster he pretended to be.

"It's all right, darling," Ashi assured as she unbuttoned the child's blouse, unbuckled the stained, pleated grey school skirt and let it fall.

"Everything," Shamlou said hoarsely.

Ashi glanced, momentarily unsure, in his direction, then did as she was bid.

She stood up to her full, diminutive height.

"And now you."

"What?"

"You too. Take off your things."

Her eyes widened, her anxiety flaring again. "While you stand there? Please?"

"Just do it." A harshness had crept back into the tone.

She swallowed hard. God, how she needed to bathe! She was being foolish. Sometimes in life you just had to accept such indignities.

Although she did not look up as she undressed she could feel his eyes on her, probing, exploring.

"Look at me," he said. "And take hold of your daughter's hand."

He felt a pain over his eyes, and heard the rush of the garden fountain in his ears. He opened his eyes again and saw the pale alabaster figure standing naked and vulnerable before him. At its side an undeveloped replica in miniature.

"Stand together and face me," he said.

"I don't understand."

"Just do it!"

In his head he heard the flutes playing, heard the woman's voice. *"Sit near my tomb, and bring wine and music – Feeling thy presence, I shall come out of my sepulchre – Rise, softly moving creature, and let me contemplate thy beauty –"*

The flash of the Polaroid camera blinded Ashi and her daughter.

# 11

A melancholy chant from the nearby mosque was calling the faithful to morning prayers. The sound intruded on her troubled dreams as she drifted towards consciousness.

There was a sharp knock on the bedroom door and instantly Chantal Roquelaure was awake, momentarily unsure where she was. The large, boxlike room, equipped with telephone, television and mini-bar, could have been in any Holiday Inn hotel around the world.

Then she felt the hot air from the open window on her face. Remembered turning off the refrigerated air-conditioning the night before. Remembered she was in Muscat.

Another knock. Scrambling from the bed she slipped on a short silk kimono to hide her nakedness, and opened the door to the white smile of the Filipino floor waiter. "Breakfast, madam."

His cheerfulness was infectious. "On the coffee table, *merci*."

Even at this early hour the heat of the sun was blistering and, as soon as the waiter left, she turned the air-conditioning back on. Saint-Julien had warned her that Muscat claimed to be the hottest capital city on earth, and now she could well believe it.

Sipping at an iced orange juice, she looked down over the yellow patch of scrub to the nearest collection of two-storey stucco houses. Beyond them rose the forbidding side of the *jebel*, jagged and unfinished, as though God had tired of the job and left it half-done.

She and Saint-Julien had arrived in the Sultanate of Oman the night before on the British Airways flight via Riyadh. Shaykh Zufar had been as good as his word, and they were met by a Ministry driver called Mahmuwd. A scrawny, bearded Arab, dressed in a white *dishdasha* robe and untidy turban, he was brandishing their precious 'No Objection Certificates'.

His efforts to cruise imperiously past the Immigration queue merely antagonised the Omani duty officer and resulted in a lengthy wait until, not only had all the passengers gone, but also the aircrew, who were stopping over.

As they sat in the spotless and deserted terminal building, the ubiquitous portraits of the Sultan watched Chantal and Saint-Julien with benign indifference. They were beginning to have serious misgivings about the delay when Mahmuwd reappeared from a side office, still grinning. In tow was a tall, handsome Arab in the smart khaki uniform and peaked cap of the Royal Oman Police.

He was serious and unsmiling. "I am sorry you have been delayed. There was a small misunderstanding. The Ministry is closed at this time, so I have to check with my superiors."

Saint-Julien smiled graciously and nodded. He never was to find out what it was that had to be checked.

"You are here on business?" the policeman asked with a British public school accent.

"Business with His Excellency Shaykh Zufar."

"What is it that you sell?"

"Advice," Saint-Julien replied blandly.

"What sort of advice?"

"Security matters."

The officer looked uncertain. "This is not the Security Ministry."

Saint-Julien saw that he was in danger of talking himself into trouble. "Asset protection, *mon ami*. How to secure and protect your investments."

It wasn't exactly a lie, depending how you interpreted the word 'investment'. At least it successfully steered the policeman into thinking along lines of insurance and finance. He glanced at the papers in his hand. "Ah, I see you represent InterCon Asset Protection."

The Corsican smiled. "That's it. Private consultations with His Excellency."

"I see." The policeman seemed satisfied. "That is all in order."

There followed a silk-smooth ride to the hotel in a Ministry limousine, a huge black air-conditioned Chevrolet Caprice Classic with plush velour upholstery. Mahmuwd continued chatting incomprehensibly, but his friendliness drew the line at demeaning himself by helping to carry or stow the luggage.

But now, as Chantal watched the new day begin, she wondered what in God's name had induced her to persuade D'Arcy to let her come?

In truth she doubted her value to Saint-Julien. Loners like him – like D'Arcy himself – operated better that way. Alone. They were tough, resourceful and determined, and she wondered if she were really any of those things.

No way must she allow herself to be a hindrance, as D'Arcy had warned she might. It was vital they discover the fate of *Clarion Call*. Give some answer to those bastards in Teheran, so that Philippe's release might once again be on the agenda. Might, if it suited them.

And that poor woman and child in London; the torture her husband was going through. For all their sakes she must not hinder. Perhaps she'd have been wiser to remain in London. Nadirpur had found her compassion and understanding like a balm, D'Arcy had told her. He could be a very perceptive man. Sometimes.

For some inexplicable reason, the last time that they had made love flashed through her mind, and she felt the thrill shoot along her nerve tracts like an electric shock. She gave a small gasp of surprise, and sat down quickly, unsteadily.

"D'Arcy, you bastard," she said aloud, and smiled to herself. "Even here you reach me."

And she knew then the real reason she had wanted to come. It wasn't just that she wanted to help Philippe. If she'd stayed, her confused emotions might have destroyed her relationship with D'Arcy for ever. Either that or she would surely have betrayed Philippe again.

It would be a fine welcome home, to find that his fiancée had abandoned him for another man – without giving him a chance. In fairness to them both, and herself, she had to get away.

Another sharp rap on the door interrupted her thoughts. When she answered it she found Saint-Julien waiting. "I could smell coffee."

She laughed. "Come in."

He shambled through the door and dropped his large frame into one of the easy chairs. "Last night I just crashed out. Never thought to order breakfast."

She poured coffee. "That's why you need a woman with you, Saint-Julien. We think of these small but important things."

He sipped at the cup and wrinkled his nose in distaste. Why was it no one outside France could make decent coffee? He said: "Listen, *ma petite*, ten minutes ago I get a call. From Shaykh Zufar's Ministry. We have been summoned to a meeting."

"Really?"

"Mint tea and sweetmeats at eleven."

"You do not sound very enthusiastic."

Saint-Julien shrugged. "Zufar is an old friend of D'Arcy, not me. I was hoping not to see him."

"We cannot do that, not after we used him to get the NOCs. If he is a powerful man, he might be able to help," she suggested.

The Corsican began to demolish a croissant. With his mouth full, he said: "Our chief reckons he would not trust this Zufar as far as he can spit. Unless the old boy sees something in it for himself or his own tribe. Cantankerous old *salaud – pardon moi*! – well, so D'Arcy says. He has this low-key Ministry to keep him sweet and off the Sultan's back. So not so much influence or power, eh?"

"Oh."

"So we will play it real careful." He grinned at her. "There is no problem. Also I leave a message with the chief's other friend. The man who runs the marine salvage business. 'China' Clay? He's out of port till around midday. Then we see what he has to offer." He glanced at his watch. "We can expect the Ministry car about ten thirty. Better I let you get dressed." He helped himself to a second croissant and left.

She showered and dressed, selecting grey silk boxer shorts and a camisole top for coolness, then chino slacks and a military-cut shirt. With her hair pinned up, she glanced in the mirror. Make-up? She overruled her previous resolution. To hell with it, a touch of mascara around the eyes wouldn't hurt. She reasoned that, regardless of cultural sensibilities, a wizened Arab shaykh was the same as any old man anywhere in the world.

She had just planted a straw fedora on her head and adjusted it to the right jaunty angle, when the telephone rang.

"Saint-Julien here. The car is arrived. See you in the lobby."

It was Mahmuwd again. He stood in his sandals, *dishdasha* and turban in the centre of the vast, cool lobby and grinned his crooked-toothed grin as his charges approached. The vigorous handshakes followed, after which he led the way to the limousine, all the time giving Chantal sly, curious glances. It occurred to her that he was under the impression she had changed sex overnight.

It was a short distance from the hotel to the capital area suburb of Ruwi, where the Ministry of Economic and Cultural Development was situated in splendid lawned grounds alongside other equally impressive ministry buildings. However, the journey became excruciatingly long as Mahmuwd refused to exceed thirty mph on the motorway.

Only when he repeatedly glanced at the car clock, did it dawn on Chantal that he was early and determined not to arrive a minute before the appointed time.

The building itself was in sweeping modernistic style with a few token concessions to traditional Arabic architecture. Inside the endless lobby there was no reception desk, just an Indian cleaner mopping his way across the vast marble floor.

Mahmuwd led the way past the recirculating fountain to the first floor, peering en route into several offices. In almost every one was a young, well-heeled Omani seated at an empty desk in front of a telephone. There was no sign of any paperwork.

It was clear that Mahmuwd had lost himself in the endless corridors of power.

At last he stumbled into a room where an Indian sat in an immaculately ironed shirt and sober tie. In contrast to the other offices, the desk in this one was obliterated by neat columns of papers and documents.

After a brief, irate exchange the Indian dismissed Mahmuwd and rose from his chair. "Mr Saint-Julien, is it? How nice to see you." Brisk handshakes. "And Miss Roquelaure."

"His Excellency is expecting us?"

"Yes, please." The man's head shook from side to side with sincerity. "As a matter of fact he is a little concerned you are lost."

"I think our driver was," Chantal said.

The Indian shrugged discreetly. "I expect so. Omanis are only good for driving, and then only in daylight. It is we Indians, and of course Filipino immigrants who run this country, really speaking." More smiling. "But then you know that, I expect. This way, please."

They followed into a spartan antichamber which was dominated on the far side by two mahogany doors impressively carved in filigree.

As the aide knocked and opened the mammoth doors the hot air rushed at them after the air-conditioned chillness of the rest of the Ministry building.

It was a large, marble-floored chamber with a vaulted ceiling. To one side was a massive kidney-shaped desk; it was awash with state papers, some of which had been scattered by the central fan above their heads. Beneath the opened window three Arabs sat on low chairs around a table laid out with a plastic thermos and delicate china cups with palm tree motifs picked out in gold.

The fourth man, with a wrinkled nutbrown face and grey scrub beard, stood rocking gently over an electric fan placed behind him on the floor. Small gnarled hands held the grubby *dishdasha* up so that the cool air could pass unhindered.

"Your guests, Excellency," the Indian announced, and everyone rose in respect as the old man crossed the room with a spritely gait that was almost a dance.

One good eye peered up over the big Corsican's chest to focus on his face. "Ah, *sabah il khair*, Mr Saint-Julien."

"*Sabah in-nur*, Your Excellency," the Corsican replied in kind as he shook hands.

"*Ahlan wa sahlan*," Zufar welcomed, as he scrutinised Saint-Julien's ponytail with open curiosity. "*Kaif halak?*"

"I am well, Your Excellency, thank you." He turned to Chantal. "May I introduce Mademoiselle Roquelaure."

Zufar frowned; he didn't like the name, couldn't begin to pronounce it.

"Please call me Chantal," she smiled.

The shaykh took a cautious backward step. "A woman's voice!" he said, momentarily puzzled. "But she is dressed like a man!" He squinted at her, trying to get a fix with his poor eyesight. "Yes, definitely a woman!" he chortled.

Chantal removed her straw fedora. "Is this better?"

"Ah, to hide such wondrous beauty! Come, my child." He took her hand and led her across to the sofa, while dismissing his henchmen. As he sat he said with a mischievous chuckle: "In Arabia it is not always a good idea to dress as a boy. Sometimes it is safer to be a girl!" He cackled merrily at his own quip. But he didn't let go of her hand; the awful idea crossed Chantal's mind that he thought she was a gift from his old friend Mr Robert.

They exchanged pleasantries until a fresh plastic thermos of coffee and a plate of dates arrived. As he poured it Zufar apologised for the warmth in the room, despite the fans. "I cannot stand all the air-conditioning," he explained. "I am Bedu, you understand. Of the mountains and desert. A tribe of nomads who seek their wealth from the silver of the stars," he chuckled at his overpoetic description of the harsh bedouin lifestyle. "Now we have houses instead of tents. Tarmac instead of tracks. Cars instead of camels." He leaned closer to Chantal until she could smell the incense in his scraggy beard. "Do you know, my child, our abandoned camels are now causing big problems – eating all the grazing for our cattle!"

"That is remarkable."

Zufar grunted. "That is folly, but other ministers will not listen. Modern, modern, modern! That is all that concerns them. They will not be happy until the whole of the Gulf is like that New York place! Bah! Woe betide the man who forgets his heritage, is that not so?"

Saint-Julien smiled weakly. "*Mais oui.*"

The Arab's milky brown eye twinkled. "But that is not why you fly for eight hours – to hear an old man regret the passing of history. What is it I can do for the friends of Mr Robert?"

"You have done much already, Excellency. And Mr Robert is very grateful," Saint-Julien said and handed over the flask of Christian milk that D'Arcy had given him. The shaykh sniffed appreciatively at the old malt. "A token of our thanks. Your co-operation has allowed us to get here quickly to deal with our business."

Above their heads the noise of the gyrating fan filled the silence. "And that is *it*?" Zufar asked.

"It allows us to make a quick start on our business," Saint-Julien repeated vaguely.

"I am a member of the Council of Ministers," Zufar

said slowly. "There I have the ear of many friends. There can be little business which does not benefit from reaching the ears of friends." The tone of disappointment was unmistakable.

"Not this business," the Corsican stated firmly.

Zufar's smile showed a crooked row of discoloured teeth. "Mr Robert mentioned this was a matter of importance and – that word – confidential, yes?" The good eye blinked. "Confidential even from friends?"

Saint-Julien nodded.

"And this is not a criminal affair, I imagine?"

"I think you know Mr Robert better than that, Excellency," Saint-Julien replied.

"It is my experience that those who travel in secrecy have something to hide. And if they hide the truth from friends, then it is because the truth may harm that friend." The smile returned. "Unless, of course, knowledge of that truth alone may harm that friend."

Saint-Julien said: "Mr Robert would wish to protect his friends."

Zufar studied his gnarled twigs of fingers. "Usually, it will take a month or longer to issue an NOC certificate. Here, when people fall foul of our law, it takes less than twenty-four hours to rescind it." He looked up at the Corsican. "Can you complete your business in twenty-four hours?"

Saint-Julien swallowed hard. This is downright blackmail. Zufar was affronted at not being trusted and, as D'Arcy had warned, was clearly intrigued at the prospect of some conspiracy. He did not want to be left out. Saint-Julien glanced sideways at Chantal and caught her expression.

"Very well," he said. "Mr Robert runs a company that protects shipping, supplying advisers like myself. One of our ships is steaming to Bandar Abbas when it disappears. Disappears in these waters."

The old man's eyes were now wide and alert with interest. "It sinks or is pirated?"

"That is what we have to find out. But it is unlikely that it has sunk."

Thoughtfully Zufar poured more coffee. "There are reports of piracy in the areas around Arabia, my friends. But pirates do not usually choose these waters. His Majesty the Sultan's Navy enjoys a formidable reputation, trained by your own British officers."

"But it is not impossible?"

"Nothing is impossible," Zufar conceded. "But tell me, this ship is bound for Persia – er, Iran, such names! – so should I guess that there were arms on board?"

"I cannot confirm this."

The Arab's eyes crinkled. "Wars demand many arms, my friends. A large ship, yes? Filled with arms belonging to Iran disappears around Oman?' He pursed his thin lips. "You are wise to keep this to yourself. For many reasons. I will give you just two. These arms could be used for insurrection against our Sultan by dissidents. We still have problems with Yemen in the south. Even last year there was trouble around your Christmas time. An incursion with troops and tanks. Mr Robert's men – your own – er – SAS they call it – repels them. Tragically there are several dead. And the Iranians have also tried to topple the emirs of the Gulf to the north. Here too. So far without success."

"And the other reason?" Saint-Julien asked.

"We have a tradition of friendship with Iran from long before the Ayatollah Khomeini comes to power in Persia."

"Yet they have tried subversion here."

Zufar nodded sagely. "Storms do not last for ever, my friends, although sometimes it does not seem that way. This storm too will pass. Sunshine days of peace will return. It is hard for the tribes of Oman to forget that soldiers of Iran came to our aid during our war of survival in the last decade. We remember that. So His Majesty walks a tightrope in relations with Persia during these past nine years while they are at war with Iraq. We are friends, but not too much friends. We are friends, but our Navy has been known to take on the big ships of Persia when the need arises. Otherwise we are neutral but friendly. And behind the scenes His Majesty has put in motion the wheels of diplomatic negotiation. Very few people know this thing. But I can tell you that before this summer is passed, so too will be the war between Persia and Iraq." He smiled a broad smile that creased his face until he resembled a self-satisfied rubber gnome. "That is why you are wise to keep your secret. Whatever the truth lies behind your missing ship, it is not good for Oman or for His Majesty Sultan Qaboos bin Said. For that reason alone, if the purpose of your mission here was known, you would be kicked out with the speed of a mule." He laughed and flicked his bony sandaled foot in demonstration.

"Now you understand my caution," Saint-Julien said.

"And now you know why I cannot help you," Zufar replied, his eye hardening. "As a member of the Council of Ministers I cannot act against the interests of the state."

"What are you saying?"

"Dear friend that Mr Robert undoubtedly is, I cannot put him before what is best for my people – before the security of the Sultan himself." He hesitated. "You may indeed have to conduct your business in twenty-four hours."

"Your Excellency," Chantal interrupted suddenly, "there is something I should like to tell you."

He grinned benevolently again, picking up her hand and patting it. "Tell me, pretty child."

"The cargo of arms on the missing ship was supplied by the French Government –"

"Chantal!" Saint-Julien warned.

She turned. "No, Saint-Julien. I speak as a French-woman. Not as an employee of Robert D'Arcy's company."

"D'Arcy won't –"

"Rober' is not here," Chantal snapped, then looked back at Zufar. "Your Excellency, that shipment is being paid for the release of a French diplomat held in Beirut.

271

That man is my fiancé. He has been held for three years. If that shipment is not found, he may die. My fiancé could be murdered by Shi'ite terrorists."

Zufar blinked, taken aback by the impassioned outburst.

"You should also know that an innocent woman and her small child are being held hostage – under threat of death – if that ship is not found."

Saint-Julien shook his head. "You should not say these things!"

The Arab turned on the Corsican. "Perhaps you, too, should have the innocent trust of a woman sometimes." Without further word he sipped at his coffee noisily for a few moments, then stared at the rotating ceiling fan thoughtfully. Then he glanced back appreciatively at Chantal. She could almost hear the cogs of his mind working as he weighed up his options. If D'Arcy's predictions were anything to go by, his prime motive would be to determine what advantage there was to be gained.

At last he said: "Listen to me carefully. I may look like an old fool, but do not judge by appearance. I know what goes on within and beyond these shores. I am an Arab and know the Arab ways. Mr Robert is no fool either. If he believes your missing ship can be found then he is most probably right.

"In view of this charming and beautiful lady's sad story, what you have told me shall remain the secret of these four walls. You continue your mission with the utmost discretion for a few days, whilst I make a few inquiries of my own."

"Isn't that taking a risk?" Chantal asked.

Zufar smiled. "In the old days of the civil war here, there was an unofficial intelligence 'whisper' network which operates very well in remote regions. It worked through local shaykhs, oilmen, engineers and agricultural advisers who had the trust of the people. It was run by men like Mr Robert. I was part of it. And I tell you, although a little – er – uncertain, and with many people gone or passed over, it still works today. Some think as well as our modern Intelligence Security Service. We shall put it to the test. But I believe that if anything is known about your ship, we will find out about it."

Chantal and Saint-Julien stepped out of the icebox cool of the ministry into the scorching sunlight with mixed feelings. Relief that they had, albeit temporarily, won over Shaykh Zufar, but trepidation that events could now be out of their control.

Mahmuwd was waiting for them by his limousine, a ready smile on his face.

From the corner of his mouth, Saint Julien said: "We must get rid of this driver. If we use the Ministry car he'll be reporting everything back to Zufar."

"Where you go?" Mahmuwd asked helpfully.

"Back to the hotel," Saint-Julien answered.

When they arrived at the Holiday Inn he told the driver that he wouldn't be needed for the remainder of the day. Mahmuwd was clearly delighted and didn't waste a second before driving off towards his home.

"No doubt he's got some young boy to spend his siesta with. Probably a cousin," Saint-Julien observed.

"That is not very kind," Chantal chided.

"Mahmuwd's not married," the Corsican replied matter-of-factly, "so he'll be keeping himself pure for his bride. That's how."

"That's horrible."

"No. That's Arabia. Come on, let's get a cab."

The white taxi with its bright orange roundel on the front door took them through the shimmering heat haze to the harbour of Mina Qaboos. Amid the moored fishing dhows and the naval patrol boats, the *Gulf Bullpup* was unmistakable. A stout workmanlike vessel – with rusted white paintwork and a bright yellow submersible strapped leechlike to her afterdeck – she bucked gently at the quayside. There was no sign of anyone in the wheelhouse as they scrambled over the high gunwale onto the foredeck. A row of scuba diving sets glinted in the sun, and one lay neatly on a towel where someone had been servicing the demand valve.

Suddenly Chantal pointed across the bay to the eastern peninsula where the corniche disappeared from view. "What, *mon Dieu*, is that?"

A small object was creaming a fast and noisy arc around the headland, planing over the waves at a phenomenal speed.

"That's thirty knots," Saint-Julien murmured, fascinated by the strange craft that hurtled towards them.

At first, through the weaving haze, it appeared that the rider was seated in the water with no visible means of support. Only as he closed was it possible to distinguish the shape of the tiny vessel which resembled a two-man scooter mounted on a monoski. The rider throttled back, and at last Saint-Julien made out the strange camouflage paintwork in three merging tones of grey.

"Take a line!" the man shouted, standing astride the skimmer's seat in cutaway denim shorts. His blond hair had been bleached almost white by the sun in vivid contrast to the richly tanned skin of his face and lean, muscled body.

Expertly Saint-Julien snatched the rope and tugged the strange craft alongside the ladder for the man to climb aboard. "That is some boat you have there, monsieur."

The man looked up. His eyes were a pale distant blue. "You haven't seen anything yet." He sprang across the gunwale, landed on the deck, and held up a small plastic bag. "Ideal machine when you're shopping for spare parts. Beats using the roads out here. Safer."

"I'm looking for Rick Clay."

The eyes narrowed. "Who wants him?"

"My name's Saint-Julien. I work for Robert D'Arcy."

Clay stood up and grinned. "So you're the one who's been leaving mysterious messages at the office. Welcome aboard."

"This is Chantal Roquelaure," Saint-Julien introduced. "A close friend of Monsieur D'Arcy."

"Enchanted," Clay responded and eloquently lifted her hand to kiss it. "Now come below. It's a bit cooler and we've some beer in the icebox."

"The best invitation we have had all day," Saint-Julien replied and followed Clay as he deftly negotiated the steps down into the fo'c'sle. Between the bunk tiers a table was laid for two.

"We're not interrupting your lunch, are we?" Chantal asked.

"Not at all," Clay replied. "Join us, there's plenty. Light salad and fresh fish. Caught it ourselves last night."

An inquisitive Japanese head appeared around the bulkhead from the galley."

"Hey, Tokyo, we've got guests."

The man emerged grinning from the galley, drying his hands on a starched white apron.

"This is my partner, Tokyo Joe. Not his real name of course, but I can't pronounce it, so we settled on that to make life simple."

As the introductions were made, Tokyo shook hands vigorously with a formal little bow from the waist. "Friends of China are friends of mine. I am pleased for you to join us in our meal."

His disappearance back into the galley was followed by a sudden scurry of activity. Clay said: "He used to be with some hush-hush diving unit in the Japanese Navy. Anti-terrorist stuff. We met out here a couple of years ago, drowning our sorrows in the same hotel bar after we'd both been stood up on dates. Got talking and found we had a lot in common. Including being cheesed off with diving for other people. So I forgave him the Siam Railway, he forgave me Hiroshima, and we decided to set up in business. Mostly with the oil companies on maintenance work, but also a lot of salvage just lately now the Gulf War's hotted up. We've got an Omani sleeping partner – you have to here by law – but he's no trouble. Just stumps up the funds and let's us get on with it. Came out on *Bullpup* once – sick as a dog he was!"

"Mind you, all this could change too if we get the Jet Raider off the ground."

"Jet Raider?" Chantal queried.

Clay grinned. "My pride and joy. That contraption you saw me arrive on. It's just a prototype."

"Oh, the little sea scooter."

The other man feigned hurt. "Don't you let Tokyo hear you call it that. He's hoping to make his fortune from it as well. We're demonstrating it to as many Arab armed forces as we can in our spare time. There's been a lot of interest in it."

Saint-Julien was intrigued. "What is so special about it?"

"It's not what you can see," Clay replied, quickly warming to his subject. "It's what you can't. She's a stealth technology craft designed for special forces, see? Designed in lightweight Kevlar armour with all sloping surfaces using RAM material. That means it absorbs radar so there's virtually no signature. Less than a standard canoe in fact. And she runs on water jets – totally silent and producing no wake."

"But it made a *terrible* noise," Chantal protested.

Clay laughed. "That's the surprise. Two-engine systems, see. I was using the conventional units to give around thirty knots for a fast getaway, and she can skim in just four inches of water."

Saint-Julien let out a low whistle to show he was impressed. "What can she carry?"

"We can mount a TV camera in the bow and drive her remotely for surveillance work. For reconnaissance a machine gun is mounted for'ard of the first crew member. But her main purpose is to carry a limpet mine fixed to the arse-end pillion. Personally I find that handy for the shopping."

"I'd love to play with it some time," Saint-Julien said wistfully. "I'm not long out of the Légion amphibious section."

"Really? Any contacts?"

276

"We will see. Anyway you should have no shortage of buyers."

Clay grimaced. "That's what we thought. But it all takes time."

Tokyo reentered with four plates of imaginative salad and seafood. "Kingfish steak," he announced proudly. "Very tasty, you like."

As Clay distributed cans of lager he said: "I had a phone call about a week ago from an old mate of mine, Dave Forbes. I understand he's Rob D'Arcy's operations manager. He was very mysterious about it all, and didn't want to give details on an open line. Said you'd fill me in."

Over the next fifteen minutes Saint-Julien brought him up to date with the search for *Clarion Call* and the kidnap in London.

"Christ," Clay said, "you've got your work cut out. And all the time knowing that poor bloody woman and her kid's lives hang in the balance. I don't envy you."

"That is why we *must* make progress. As I said, our people have talked to the man called Alan Hawksby. He has put the word out to the Sultan's naval and air force commanders. And we have spoken with Shaykh Zufar."

Clay winced. "Better watch that old bugger. He'll play it straight while it suits him."

"I have been warned," Saint-Julien answered. "We did not have much choice."

"And Alan Hawksby's a bit of an odd number. He's as likely to put the Sultan's interests first as he is yours. Don't rely on the 'old boy' network with him."

Chantal said: "But we have no such fears with you, Rick?"

He grinned at her. "Me and Tokyo are mugs for a pretty face, no danger. We'll help all we can, but we're just one boat and if your ship's been hijacked, it could be the other side of the world by now."

Saint-Julien shook his head. "We do not think so. When the ship did not turn up the Iranians were quick to get one of their frigates to mount a search. They would have had twice the speed of *Clarion Call*, yet they found nothing. Our client has got contacts in every port in the world and quite a bit of influence. He has put the word out, but nothing even resembling *Clarion Call* has turned up anywhere."

"Pirates today are pretty sophisticated, Saint-Julien. A change of registration, bribery on the spot, a lick of paint, even a change to the superstructure. They're up to all sorts of tricks."

"I am aware of that, *mon ami*. But the fact remains it was off this coast that it disappeared and we have to start somewhere."

"That's true enough," Clay conceded, pushing his plate aside.

"If you wanted to hijack a ship, Rick," Chantal said, "where would you hide it until the heat dies down?"

"That's one bright lady," Clay said with a grin. "What do you think, Tokyo?"

His partner looked up from the fish steak which he had been demolishing with deep concentration. "That is what I wonder while you talk. If I know ship is expected, then maybe I be smart and hide up rather than run. Maybe on the Yemeni coast to the south. Wild down there and very isolated from people.'

Clay nodded his agreement. "I'll buy that. The Omani coast is too well-patrolled. Mind you, having said that, there's a flourishing smuggling trade. Especially toilet rolls and PiffPaff to Iran."

"PiffPaff?" Chantal asked.

"Local flyspray. Those poor bastards in Iran must be in a state over there if they're willing to pay good black market rates for that type of stuff. Mind you, on a more serious note, there's not a little gold smuggling goes on between here and India. Not to mention slavers."

Chantal was horrified. "You are joking?"

Clay shook his head. "It's no joke in Arabia. Many an impoverished Indian family sees selling a daughter or son as their only way to survive. Convince themselves the kids'll have a better life too in some harem or sheikh's palace, I bet. So they ship 'em to Oman, then across the desert by four-wheel drive trucks. I wouldn't say it's a big trade, but it still goes on."

"It is terrible," Chantal said.

"These people," Tokyo said, "such smugglers may know of any hijack to a big ship. There is very little goes on they do not learn about."

"Are they here in Muscat?" Saint-Julien asked.

"Not that I'd know," Clay replied. "Probably some Mister Bigs, but you'd want the guys on the waterfront. The fishermen in some remote spot – they might talk for the right incentive."

"I would try Sur," Tokyo said.

"Where is that?"

"Down the coast near Oman's most easterly point," Clay explained. "Why don't we take you down there. The old *Bullpup*'s for hire, y'know. Gotta earn her keep."

"Don't you have contracts?"

"We're due for a week's leave," Clay replied. "Besides, I could do with a change of scenery. How about tomorrow? It'll take me twenty-four hours to complete some essential maintenance, catch up on the bloody paperwork and stock with provisions. What d'you say?"

Chantal glanced at Saint-Julien and they both smiled. "I think we say *merci* to both of you."

It was with a rising optimism that they left the air-conditioned *Gulf Bullpup* for the thudding heat of the quayside and the return taxi-ride to the Holiday Inn.

There was no warning from the Filipino reception staff when they collected their keys.

"Join me for a celebration drink," Saint-Julien invited Chantal. "And we can telephone the chief with a progress report . . ." His voice trailed off as he reached his room. The door was ajar. From inside he could hear movement.

Chantal frowned. "What is it?"

Cautiously Saint-Julien pushed the door and let it swing open under its own weight.

The man was seated in one of the armchairs beneath the window. His legs had been carefully crossed to preserve the creases in the trousers of his lightweight cotton suit. His elbows rested on the arms of the chair, his fingers interlaced beneath a pinched, very tanned face that sported a moustache that said old military school. The faded sandy hair was well-oiled, combed straight back from the fore-head, greying at the temples.

Eyes the colour of burnt chestnuts watched Saint-Julien dispassionately as he stepped into the room and saw the two Omani policemen rummaging through the belongings scattered over his bed.

"Come in, Mr Saint-Julien." The voice was clipped, very authoritative, very British. "Sorry we had to start without you."

The two policemen, dressed in khaki uniforms and peaked caps, turned round.

Saint-Julien said: "What the hell do you think you are doing!"

The man rose from the armchair. "That'll do," he snapped at the two officers. They acknowledged his order and then brushed past Saint-Julien and Chantal and into the corridor.

"Well?" the Corsican demanded.

"Come in, both of you," the man said irritably. "And shut the door."

Momentarily Saint-Julien stood his ground, then thought better of it. What the hell!

As the door closed the man said: "I'm Major Harry Ingham. I run the Anti-Terrorist Review Board." There was no smile or offered hand.

"Is that supposed to impress us?" Saint-Julien asked belligerently.

"Your NOCs were not issued in the proper way."

"Our what?"

"Your 'No Objection Certificates'."

"Oh, those things."

"Yes, Mr Saint-Julien. Those very important things.

They were issued in an unorthodox manner."

"Really, I would not know, *mon ami*. Are you saying they are invalid?"

The cold brown eyes appraised both the Corsican and Chantal closely. "The purpose of an NOC is to allow all interested parties to examine the names of all visitors and the reason for their coming to Oman to filter out undesirable elements."

"And we are undesirable?" Saint-Julien provoked.

"I should hope not," the man replied tersely. "But when a Minister makes a direct order – under special circumstances – for an NOC to be issued, then the speed of events can mean the papers are not properly examined by all the relevant agencies."

"In this case yours?"

"In this case, Mr Saint-Julien, hardly any. Such was the unseemly haste. It was only brought to my attention this morning by the officer who spoke to you at the airport. He thought it strange at the time. Unfortunately I was out at supper with friends."

Saint-Julien smiled. "I hope it was a good meal."

The man's eyes slitted like a cat's. "That sort of attitude will do nothing to help you."

Sensing big trouble, Chantal stepped forward, at the same time removing the straw fedora. It had the desired effect as the man did a quick double take. He had not expected such a stunning face to be hidden in the shadow of the hat's wide brim.

"Look, Major Ingham, my friend and I are very tired. I am sorry if Saint-Julien seems rude – it is just that we both feel a little irritated and upset at all – at all this!" She waved at the contents of the suitcase on the bed. "But we would like to reassure you about anything that concerns you. Please, what questions would you want to ask?"

The man grunted, apparently mollified somewhat. "Well, you state your business as security advice. I know *exactly* what that means – yet you deliberately led my officer to believe you were talking in terms of financial investments. Why?"

Chantal said quickly, before Saint-Julien could open his mouth: "Asset protection can cover all manner of things, Major, including protection against computer fraud and investigating institutions where money is being invested."

Saint-Julien grinned. You had to hand it to her; she was stretching the imagination, although she'd almost convinced him it was a task IAP might undertake. Perhaps they would?

"And you are doing this for the Ministry?" the major asked in a flat voice.

"It's at the personal request of the Minister himself," Chantal replied with a demure smile. "And I am afraid we cannot discuss individual clients. It would not be ethical."

The major looked at her directly and she could feel his eyes boring into her own. "Do not treat me as an idiot, Miss Roquelaure. I know exactly what InterCon Asset Protection is, and I know its boss."

Chantal's eyes widened hopefully. "You know Rober'?" She was so used to the mere mention of his name opening doors. But this time she was in for a grave disappointment.

"I have crossed paths with Robert D'Arcy a long time ago during the civil war." He did not elaborate. "And I believe I know why you are here."

"Really?" Saint-Julien asked sarcastically.

"Your passports have been taken from reception," the major went on evenly, "and will be held by my office for safekeeping. Meanwhile, I suggest you do not leave the capital area until I have completed my inquiries with His Excellency Shaykh Zufar and others." He handed over a card. "That's my telephone number should you need it."

Chantal was dumbfounded; Saint-Julien checked his rising anger with difficulty.

"I shouldn't unpack if I were you. Yours is likely to be a very short stay." Quietly he closed the door behind him.

# 12

The crockery rattled as D'Arcy's fist hit the table. "Dammit, the Omanis must be in on it too!"

He had received the call from Saint-Julien in the living quarters of the Flax Wharf office just as Pierre Roquelaure arrived unannounced from Paris. Dave Forbes joined them at the dining table.

Roquelaure looked bemused. "I do not understand, Rober'."

D'Arcy lit a cigar to help quell his anger. "We've just had a call from Saint-Julien, he's in Oman with Chantal. They had just started to make inquiries about *Clarion Call* when they were dropped on from a great height by Major Harry."

Roquelaure didn't understand the significance. "Who is this man?"

Forbes tugged at his moustache. "Not that bastard Harry Ingham? Major Harry Ingham." He scoured his memory. "I thought he was dead."

D'Arcy grunted. "Many people who've met him wish he was."

Roquelaure said: "I am sorry, Rober', I am not following this."

"Major Harry – as he is less than affectionately known by the expat community in Oman – is one of those peculiarly British institutions. I had the misfortune to cross swords with him during the Dhofar war in the early seventies. He was a junior officer from a Welsh military family commissioned just before the end of the last war, if I

283

remember correctly. He worked with Intelligence during all those colonial campaigns – he was caught up in some black market racket. He was kicked out of the Army in disgrace but, I gather, kept contact with his old cronies. Then, later in 1970, someone had the bright idea of recruiting him to the team plotting the overthrow of the old Sultan, Said bin Taimur. His son, the current Sultan Qaboos, took over and Major Harry became one of a number he regarded almost as uncles. He joined a group of personal advisers at that time and during the civil war that followed – mostly because there weren't many Omanis at that time whom the new Sultan felt he could trust. Frequently Harry's advice ran contrary to that of the SAS, which brought him and me into conflict many a time."

"And you have seen him since the war ended?" Roquelaure asked, "in – what – '76?"

"A few times. The Regiment still operates out there regularly on exercise. But meetings with Major Harry were purely social – when I couldn't avoid him! He's done very well for himself out of the Sultan apparently. Big villa, yacht, and he runs some sort of consultancy. Jobs in the Caribbean as I recall. Anyway, I haven't a clue what his precise rôle is now. Except –" D'Arcy blew an angry smoke ring and watched it burst over the table, "except that he has no reason to know I've left the Army, let alone that I set up IAP."

"And he knew that?" Roquelaure asked.

"Chapter and verse, according to Saint-Julien."

"Gossip down the old boy network?" Forbes suggested.

"Not if he also knows we're looking for *Clarion Call*," D'Arcy countered sharply.

Roquelaure was surprised. "He knew that?"

"Saint-Julien was sure he did, although it wasn't said in so many words. If so, that suggests he's been talking to someone like Roy Bliss. And recently."

"Ah, Monsieur Bliss," Roquelaure recalled with an air of distaste. "The gentleman from your SIS who I met at the time of the Paris bombings?"

"The very same. Just the other day Bliss intimated that British Intelligence knew all about the ship and warned me against looking for it."

Roquelaure nodded. "Chantal told me that you thought they may be involved."

"And now the Omanis. Otherwise how the hell would someone like Major Harry know we are out there and what we are doing? Bliss or someone at Century House must have tipped him off."

"But *why*?" Forbes asked gloomily.

Roquelaure extracted a Gitane from the pack and twirled it thoughtfully around his fingers. "If it is true, then there is one obvious thought. That the arms have been deliberately intercepted to prevent them falling into terrorist hands. To prevent them being distributed through Europe to Sabbah cells and half-a-dozen other sympathetic groups. Only –"

"Only?" D'Arcy pressed.

Roquelaure smiled thinly. "Only much of that equipment was too large to be of use to terrorists. Missiles, artillery pieces, component parts for aircraft and tanks. It was equipment used for fully fledged armies – otherwise our government may not have supplied it. Of limited use even in Beirut – I can think of nowhere else."

"Couldn't your people at the DGSE talk with Century House?" Forbes suggested. "Tell them they're screwing up your hostage negotiation."

The Frenchman laughed harshly. "In France – as in Britain – we do not negotiate with terrorists. How can we now admit that we are? Besides, your Monsieur Bliss already knows it is the reason for the kidnap of Madame Nadirpur and the child. That has not persuaded them to change their minds. A plea from the DGSE certainly will not. If anything, it will make them more determined."

D'Arcy swore softly. "And to think we used to work for these people."

Roquelaure said: "We must make our own way through this maze."

"You said it," D'Arcy snarled. "A bloody maze, and not one signpost in sight."

"Not quite true, *mon ami*," Roquelaure said with a hint of triumph in his voice. "The reason for this unexpected visit."

"I'm not with you."

"I could not risk the telephone; it was too important. You remember Hubert at la piscine?"

D'Arcy recalled Roquelaure's dapper assistant.

"Well, he has been doing some honest policework. Drawing on help from some personal friends in your own Immigration authorities. He has discovered that the head of Spidex, our elusive Sheikh Abdullah Hayira, is not in France or back in Jordan as we suspected. He is currently living here under his own name. No doubt your own Secret Service has ensured there are no public records of his whereabouts." He lit his cigarette with a flourish.

"Here? London?"

"He has a residence in your fashionable Chelsea. Needless to say his telephone number is unlisted."

For what felt like the first time in days, D'Arcy smiled. "Pierre, you are a treasure. Give your friend Hubert a kiss on both cheeks for me."

Roquelaure guffawed. "It is Hubert who kisses my arse, Rober', not the other way round!"

They laughed together at the inane joke. At last there was a glimmer of hope.

The telephone rang. D'Arcy sauntered to the sideboard and picked it up.

It was Brandy on the switchboard. "Scramble!" she said simply.

D'Arcy dashed down the receiver. "It's the kidnappers," he explained as he rushed for the stairs, aware of the others following close behind.

On the floor below Nadirpur sat expectantly at the conference table. D'Arcy gave him an encouraging pat on the back as he took his seat and picked up the extension.

"Things are looking up, Nader. Some good news. I'll tell you later." He gave the go-ahead and the Iranian picked up his telephone.

The voice at the other end did not wait for confirmation. "Listen carefully. Your proof is ready. Take a car south of London on the A24 road to Dorking. It passes a place called Box Hill by the Burford Bridge Hotel. There are lavatories and a car park. There is a rubbish bin there. Your proof is in a red plastic bag."

D'Arcy wrote STALL on his pad.

Quickly Nadirpur said: "I did not get all of that –"

A click was followed by the dead-line tone.

"Damn," D'Arcy said. "The bastards are getting canny."

"And they're moving around," Forbes observed. "Down in Surrey now."

Moments later Reg Roman telephoned. "We'll get the site watched, Rob, in case they haven't placed it yet. They won't want some old tramp finding it first. Don't worry, we'll keep out of sight."

"Do I go?" Nadirpur asked when D'Arcy hung up.

"No, Nader," D'Arcy said. "I want you safe and sound here."

He left immediately, taking the XJS from the garage. It took forty-five minutes to clear London and a further half-an-hour to reach the Burford Bridge Hotel, which backed onto the steep side of the famous Box Hill beauty spot.

When he arrived the car park was half-empty. A number of holidaymakers and ramblers milled around, making the most of the warm afternoon. He left his car, idly scanning the parked vehicles, noting a few in which the passengers still sat. He thought he identified a possible police surveillance car but couldn't be certain. If they'd seen someone at the litter bin earlier, they'd have been following by now, hoping to trace the kidnapper back to his hide.

D'Arcy sidled up to the bin at the bus lay-by, leaned against it and casually reached back inside. His fingers met with messy ice cream wrappers and cigarette packs before they felt plastic. He tugged it out.

Instantly he knew it was too light. Screwing it into his palm he crossed back to his car, and climbed in. He pulled the plain white postcard from the bag. Sod it!

His car phone rang. It was Reg Roman. "Well?"

"Negative," D'Arcy replied. "Verbatim: Proof is in cistern of male lavatory in The Woodsman public house."

He caught the oath on the other end of the line. "Okay, Rob, I'll check it out with the locals. I imagine it's nearby."

It was. The Woodsman was under three miles away on the Dorking to Reigate road.

By the time he had returned to Flax Wharf there was a full reception committee. Not only was Reg Roman waiting, but also his dour superior, Bob Tanner, Commander of the Anti-Terrorist Branch.

Nadirpur looked pale and nervous. "What is going on, Robert? No one will tell me."

D'Arcy glanced at the gathering uncomfortably. "Gentlemen, give me a moment will you."

Tanner wrinkled his nose, not happy at being given instructions. Roquelaure took him by the arm and reluctantly he joined the others in a far corner of the room.

"They know?" Nadirpur asked, indicating the police officers.

"Yes. I was in contact by phone."

"What is so terrible?"

"You must understand that it is part of the kidnappers' ploy to regain the initiative. To make us bow to their wishes. To frighten us."

"In the name of Allah, what?" He was almost wailing.

"With the tape we requested, they enclosed a Polaroid photograph of your wife and daughter."

"I – I don't understand."

"Both are naked. Standing naked before the camera."

"Oh, Allah help . . ."

Quietly, D'Arcy said: "There is no sign of violence. The kidnappers are illustrating your wife and child's vulnerability. To emphasise that they hold the power of life and death. It is a form of psychological warfare. You must not let it distress you. That will be to play into their hands."

"Have I to look at the photograph?"

"I am afraid you must."

The room fell silent as D'Arcy opened the package and placed the photograph before his client. Slowly the police gathered round. That such evil and such power could be created by one stark, blurred photograph was unimaginable. The white flesh of the woman and child was burned out by the closeness of the camera's flash. No tone. Just palid flesh, drawing the eye to the exposed thatch of black pubic hair. Inviting comparison. The immature body beside it, equally mercilessly exposed. The lack of comprehension in the dark young eyes. The speechless wide-eyed terror on the face of the woman. Two white naked spectres against a black background. Bricks probably. A cellar most likely.

At length Nadirpur said: "That is them." His voice was barely audible. Tears flooded his cheeks.

"I've seen some things in my time," Roman murmured.

Bob Tanner said: "Better hear the tape." The taciturn Dorset accent grated on D'Arcy. He wanted to shout at the man. Tell him to loosen up. Tell him to show some compassion.

Using disposable plastic gloves so that the cartridge could later be dusted for fingerprints, Reg Roman loaded the cassette player.

After a few seconds of scratchy silence Ashi Nadirpur was in the room with them. She began reading the headlines and then the main news story of the previous day's *Evening Standard*. Her effort to be strong, no doubt for the benefit of her daughter, was almost tangible. But she still stumbled over simple words, becoming less confident and more unsteady the longer she read. As he listened, D'Arcy looked down at the photograph on the table and wondered if the woman had been naked when she talked into the microphone. The thought of it made his flesh creep.

Towards the end of the news story her voice fractured and she could not go on. There was a sharp click as someone released the record button.

Roman stopped the tape. Quietly he said: "We'll take it away for tests. We might learn something."

Nadirpur appeared not to hear. Hoarsely he said: "I must do something. Something. I must offer money."

"No," Bob Tanner was adamant. "I have already told you that is out of the question. Terrorists must not be allowed to gain from their actions. Not politically, not financially."

D'Arcy looked down at the photograph again. "We can stall them for a day or two. Say we're not satisfied. That the voice could be of someone else. And we didn't hear the girl talk. We will ask for a video."

"They will be angry," Nadirpur said.

D'Arcy said: "We have nothing else to offer them."

"Money," Nadirpur repeated. "We can offer them money."

"How much is available?" D'Arcy asked.

"Immediately, according to the company accountant, five million francs."

D'Arcy translated. "Half-a-million sterling."

"It will ruin the company," Nadirpur smiled tightly. "People will have to be fired, offices closed. But it will be worth it. To see my Ashi and little Sousan again."

"Are you two deaf?" Tanner demanded. "COBRA will not tolerate any attempt at a buy-off. Our people will intercept any effort at a ransom payment, is that understood?"

"This is crazy!" Nadirpur protested. "It is *my* money."

"At least we could start talking about money," D'Arcy suggested. "Move the goal posts. If nothing else it plays for time."

Roman said: "They have a point."

Tanner rounded on him. "Don't you start, Reg. You

know the rules we're playing on this one." He looked at D'Arcy. "Is there any news of this confounded ship?"

"I've someone out in the Middle East asking questions, but they keep meeting obstacles. Big, blank walls."

Tanner grunted, meshing his heavy beetle brows together in a frown. "Well keep trying, eh? In the meantime we're making some ground in tracing these goddamm kidnappers. I'll let the Detective Chief Superintendent fill you in on that. I'm running late for an important meeting."

The Anti-Terrorist Branch chief collected his briefcase and swept out, his dark raincoat flying behind him like Dracula's cloak.

Roman said: "I'm sorry about that, Rob. He's under pressure from the Cabinet Office. No deals with terrorists."

"I know that."

The detective forced a smile, and extracted a dossier from his case, waved it. "On a brighter note, a short progress report."

Everyone looked expectant.

"Firstly, the grey van used for the abduction has been found abandoned in the Kingsbury area of north London. The lab boys are still conducting tests. It was left in a residential side street. It had been stolen only the night before from a second-hand dealer in Hertfordshire. The false number plates were bought from two different sources. One shop assistant recalled the purchaser. So at least we have a description for the first time. It certainly fits with the scant evidence of the witnesses at the abduction when most of the men wore stocking masks. I think we can confirm that the gang are of Arab or Middle Eastern origin. Two residents in the street where the van was abandoned have given fairly accurate descriptions of the four men who left the vehicle in a hurry. Photofits will be going out to the press, and on the television *Crimewatch Special* programme tonight, together with a request for any further information on that van."

"The kidnappers said no police," Nadirpur reminded.

Roman shook his head. "Don't worry. The press have

had the story from the start. The kidnappers will know the police are already involved."

But D'Arcy shared Nadirpur's apprehension. "I'm not sure it's a good idea – it might badly spook the kidnappers into panic. We don't want them doing something stupid."

"That's a very remote risk," Roman assured. "We're pretty damn certain that a vehicle switch took place. In which case the four who took part in the abduction are a different set from those now holding the hostages. Therefore the programme should not present a direct threat to them. But, anyway, the fact is we need as many leads as we can get – time isn't a friend on this one. Media coverage may prompt someone's memory." He paused. "At least we might already have the identity of two of the kidnappers."

"That is excellent news!" Roquelaure said.

"I said *might*. We have traced all visitors holding Iranian passports who have arrived in the past two weeks. Out of some two hundred, five were not at the hotels, hostels or places of temporary residence given on their immigration cards. Three have since been located, but two are still missing. They came over by coach from Paris."

Roquelaure grunted; that made sense.

"The French authorities are sending over copies of their passport photographs, hopefully in time for inclusion in tonight's television programme." He hesitated. "Only there's a strange thing – the French are quite convinced that these two students were monarchy supporters – in fact they're on file as being anti-Khomeini activists. Doesn't exactly fit in with what we know about the *Pessarane Behesht*. So maybe it's a false alarm."

D'Arcy shrugged. "It's a start, nevertheless."

Roman smiled grimly. "Unfortunately though, it doesn't take us much further forward, yet anyway. You see, any vehicle switch made between central and north London put the kidnappers in an ideal position to take flight up the M1. So the hostages could still be anywhere in the UK."

"All the phone calls appear to have been from London," D'Arcy pointed out.

"And the drop today was in Surrey," Forbes added.

Roman nodded. "I agree *someone* is operating in the Home Counties. But there's such a thing as a telephone."

"Not with the speed they've responded to our request for proof," D'Arcy thought aloud. "They've got to be within a fast drive of London. Or on a good rail link. I reckon at least you could draw a line halfway across the country."

"We'll see," Roman said noncommitally. "We've still got twenty-five thousand registered Iranian nationals to interview and I guess the majority of those will be in London. Mostly students."

"Needles in haystacks," Forbes muttered sympathetically.

Roman smiled grimly. "Well, if Rob is right, we've only got half a haystack to look at. And another line of inquiry. Remember the typewriter they used for their first message? It's been identified as an IBM golf ball."

"How does that help?" Nadirpur asked.

"Those models became obsolete in the early eighties, so we have a cut-off point. Now I admit we're playing the percentages game here, but 80 to 85 per cent of typewriters are financed in some way – lease or hire purchase. Of those, 80 per cent are in the hands of four or five major finance houses. The remaining 30 odd finance houses scramble after the odd 20 per cent of the business.

"With copies of the finance house file tapes, we'll run them through our HOLMES computer, matching purchasers of that IBM model against our list of 25,000 registered Iranian nationals, Iranian government and trade missions in the UK, and any other groups that seem likely." He picked up the tape. "Now let's see what our technical wizards can make of this."

But the high technology detective work was not the main thing on Nadirpur's mind. Once the policeman had left the room he said: "I cannot go on working with those people.

293

They will only be happy when my wife and child are dead. No money, no deals! It is ridiculous!"

"Reg Roman's okay," D'Arcy assured. "He'll do his best."

"But will his best be good enough?" Nadirpur glared. "If I am not allowed to offer money, then I will no longer co-operate with them. I am sorry, but that is my decision. However much I understand their principles I cannot allow Ashi and Sousan to die because of them."

D'Arcy said: "You don't have enough money, Nader. The kidnappers would laugh in your face."

"That is just to start – liquid assets within a few days. Then I sell my ships, my apartment, my contracts –"

"That would take months. Besides, you'd be a broken man."

Nadirpur stood up. "And what am I now?" he demanded. "What do I have to live for, tell me that? No, I have decided. No longer will I co-operate with your police."

"They are the only chance you've got," D'Arcy retorted. "Thousands of policemen, detectives, national resources, computers."

"These things will not be needed if the *Pessarane Behesht* accept my offer."

"So they accept your offer," D'Arcy snapped back. "And *then* kill your wife and daughter for the hell of it. To punish you. And why should they allow the only people who might identify them to live? They certainly won't release them before they've got what they want."

Nadirpur shook his head vehemently. "No more police." Final.

D'Arcy held him in a steady gaze. "Then, Nader, I am afraid that I have no option but to resign from this case."

The Iranian blinked. "What?"

"I am sorry. Either we co-operate with the police, for better or for worse. Or I resign. I'm sorry."

"I – I will double your fee," Nadirpur stuttered. "Treble it! Name your price and help me settle this business."

"ROB!" Brandy called from the switchboard. "It's them."

D'Arcy stood his ground. "Sorry, Nader, I've resigned."

Nadirpur slumped down in his chair, deflated. "I do not know what to do."

Forbes leaned across to him. "Do yourself a favour, Nader, listen to the boss. Trust him. He's all you've got."

"Rob?" Brandy called again. "They're getting impatient."

Silently Nadirpur nodded.

"Put them through!" D'Arcy called, then turned back to the Iranian. "Remember, you are *not* satisfied with the tape. It could be a fake. You want a video. Clear? And tell them that on it you want a personal question answered."

Wearily Nadirpur reached out for the receiver and told the caller what D'Arcy had instructed him to say in a flat, defeated voice.

"What you mean? Not satisfied? You want your child posted to you in bits? How dare you, *taghouti*! This has gone on long enough. Do you take us for fools?"

Nadirpur began to answer, then just didn't have the heart. He couldn't find the words, the meaning. The spirit had been crushed from him. He began to cry.

D'Arcy snatched the handset. "Right, you listen," he said firmly. "Nadirpur's just told you we are not *at all* satisfied. You sent a lousy recording and a photograph that could have been taken before you killed them. Now *we* have news. Good news. Even if the ship cannot be found, we have news that will please your masters. So get a decent VHS video tape of Mrs Nadirpur and the girl, holding tomorrow's newspaper. And answering the question Nadirpur has just put to you." His knuckles were white as he spoke, and the scar on his cheek deepened. "And if they are not both fully dressed and unharmed, then any possibility of a deal is off. Get that? OFF!"

D'Arcy slammed down the receiver.

"Sweet Jesus," Forbes breathed.

"Brandy," D'Arcy called. "Help Nader up to my quarters. He needs rest."

When the Iranian had gone, Forbes said: "You were a bit hard on the poor bastard."

"What else could I do?"

"Rober' is right," Roquelaure interrupted. "He does not have anything like the money that would compensate those Iranians. My people know his financial state. Business has not been good recently." He paused to light a cigarette. "But maybe my government could find the funds. Enough to satisfy them."

D'Arcy found it hard to contain his surprise. "Would they? Is it possible?"

Roquelaure gave one of his best Gallic shrugs. "I can but ask. I am returning to Paris tonight, Rober', I'll see what can be done. Meanwhile . . ." He dropped a torn sheet from his notebook.

D'Arcy picked it up. "What's this?"

"The London address of Sheikh Abdullah Hayira, president of Spidex International."

Dave Forbes parked his red Cavalier in the shade of a mottle-barked plane tree in full leaf, picked up the in-car telephone and called D'Arcy's number.

"In position, boss. But I still say he won't tell you anything."

"Even silences can be telling."

"And that's all you'll get, silence. That or a thick ear."

D'Arcy laughed. "If you see me being bounced by some big black eunuch in a turban, come running."

Forbes hung up and peered out at the imposing white stucco façade of the Regency building. It had the air of bland, conceited charm that only the houses of the fabulously wealthy manage to convey. The sort of house to which visits were strictly by invitation only. Roller-spikes on the garden wall, a burglar alarm, a closed circuit television camera, and an ancient 'No hawkers No circulars' plaque on the gate served to reinforce the feeling.

In his rearview mirror he saw the silver bonnet of D'Arcy's XJS turn the corner and pull into a vacant parking place.

Forbes opened the briefcase on his lap to reveal a compact radio-receiver unit and aerial. Wired to it was a cassette recorder. He settled back.

Meanwhile D'Arcy had left his car and crossed the pavement to the gate. From behind the garden wall, he could hear the sound of children playing.

He jumped the short flight of steps to the front door, pressed the bell and faced the closed-circuit camera.

"*Hello, who is it?*" came a woman's distorted voice from the speaker set in the wall.

"I am a representative of Nadirpur Shipping. I have come to see Sheikh Hayira. My name is Robert D'Arcy," he said politely.

"*Oh.*" A thoughtful silence. "*Will you wait a minute please?*"

A few seconds later she returned. He heard chains being slipped and her hand on the catch.

"Hello, Mr D'Arcy. I am the wife of Sheikh Hayira."

He tended to put good-looking women into three categories: attractive, pretty and, very occasionally, beautiful.

Mrs Hayira was stunningly beautiful. Probably in her late thirties, she wore her hair drawn tightly into a plait at the back of her head, showing off the symmetrical almond face, high cheekbones and flawless olive complexion to perfection. Her eyes were very dark and penetrating as though they had the ability to see right through him. Her teeth, as she smiled, would have been the envy of a top movie star. Only the slight hook to the long nose, made her looks classically Arabic rather than English.

"Do forgive the delay." She indicated the floral silk shirtwaister. A timeless English style. "I had been sunbathing. Isn't it a gorgeous day?"

Momentarily D'Arcy was thrown. This had not been the reception he was expecting.

"My husband's away, I'm afraid." There was no trace

of a foreign accent, Jordanian or otherwise. It was pure English public school. "But do come in. I expect you could do with a drink."

"You're most kind."

He followed her through the star-shaped hallway decorated with what looked like original oils in heavy gilt frames. The reception room was a good forty feet long, furnished sparingly with antique furniture and an exquisite Persian silk carpet. French windows at the far end gave onto a patio and walled garden.

Children were playing on the lawn. A boy and girl of about eight and seven respectively and dressed in swimming costumes were running through the spray of the lawn sprinkler, laughing and squealing with joy.

"Not too much noise now!" she chided gently, and closed the doors. "Do sit down, Mr D'Arcy. And what would you like? Personally I love a gin and it this time of evening."

"A brandy would be fine."

As she busied herself at the drinks trolley, D'Arcy rearranged his plan of attack.

When she handed him his drink, and sat demurely in an armchair beside him, he said: "Your husband's company has set up a deal exporting goods to Iran. The ship has gone missing and so, indeed, has your husband's company. The shipping company I represent is now being held responsible by the Iranians who suspect a double-cross."

The wide eyes fluttered above the rim of the gin glass. "How unfortunate, Mr D'Arcy."

"It is more than unfortunate, Mrs Hayira. It is a very serious and dangerous business. Several innocent lives are at stake."

She lowered her glass. "I mean it," she said. "It all sounds very worrying. But please understand, my husband does not discuss business matters with me." She waved her hand airily, indicating the room in general. "Despite all these Western trappings, my Abdullah is still very much a traditional Arab at heart. Women are for the raising of

298

their children and for looking after the home." She laughed lightly. "We are far too silly and empty-headed to know about business."

D'Arcy didn't believe it for one moment, but there was nothing to be gained by calling the woman a liar.

He said: "Very well, Mrs Hayira, but you should be aware of the situation, because it could result in your husband going to jail for a very long time."

The finely plucked eyebrows suddenly fractured. "I beg your pardon?"

"I'm no policeman, but piracy on the high seas and fraud are arrestable offences, I believe."

She looked genuinely horrified. "Is that some kind of joke – in, I may say, extremely bad taste?"

"Believe me, this business *leaves* an extremely bad taste. That's why I must speak to your husband and resolve this matter. To talk out some kind of compromise. If he doesn't, his whole involvement in this will be revealed to the world press." It was a bluff, but he hoped to God she didn't realise how little he really knew. "Will you tell Sheikh Hayira that?"

She swallowed hard. Whether in shock or in anger at his words, he didn't know. "When I see him, yes, Mr D'Arcy, I will pass on your message. He is out of the country."

He smiled, long and slow. "He is in the country, Mrs Hayira. We both know that."

He killed his brandy in one and stood up. He looked towards the window as the little girl outside shrieked with glee. "A pretty daughter, Mrs Hayira. How old is she?"

Taken aback by the sudden change of topic, the woman hesitated. "Er – Amal is seven. Seven and a half."

"Amal?" D'Arcy smiled. "It's a nice name for a girl. Hope."

"You speak Arabic, Mr D'Arcy?"

He ignored her observation. "My client has a daughter similar to yours, Mrs Hayira. Like Amal she is about seven years old. And like Amal she is very beautiful." He fished

299

absently in his pocket for his cigar pack while he watched the flailing arms of water tossed by the sprinkler. "Not an hour ago, I was looking at a photograph of my client's daughter. Little Sousan. She was standing naked and very frightened beside her mother. A woman a little younger than yourself. Both were naked and very frightened –"

"What?"

"Holding hands as they looked into the lens of a kidnapper's camera." Without asking permission he lit a cigar, aware that Hayira's wife was too stunned to speak. He turned to face her. "They are being held – and we've no idea where – in retaliation for the ship that your husband has had pirated."

"That's preposterous!" The beautiful high-boned cheeks were flushed with indignation.

"Do not tell me what is and what is not preposterous, Mrs Hayira." He leaned down with both fists punched into the arms of her armchair, his face close to hers.

"Your husband's enemies are not my client's enemies. Nor are they the enemies of seven-year-old Sousan or her mother. Imagine, Mrs Hayira, that this morning you received a picture of your daughter. Naked. Held by kidnappers who wanted the one thing in this world you could not give. Did not even know about."

"Please!"

D'Arcy straightened up. "That is why I will speak with your husband. There will be no hiding place for him, not now. I will find him."

Flustered, she spilled her drink on her lap. "I – I will tell him."

"Thank you for your time." He turned sharply on his heel. At the door he paused. "And may peace be with you and your children always, Mrs Hayira."

The door closed.

"Thank you," she muttered, her voice dulled by the lace handkerchief pressed tight to her mouth.

As the front door slammed she heard soft footsteps from the dining room door. She looked up at the man with the familiar neat black beard and the twinkling dark eyes that she loved so much. It was nice to have him home for once, nice to see him relaxed in slacks and a yellow summer shirt.

"That man is dangerous," he said quietly and sipped at the drink he held in his hand.

Mrs Hayira was still unsettled. "He is but one man, my husband."

He moved silently to the window, carefully fingering the net curtain aside a fraction. "He has an army. An army of friends. He once belonged to a British regiment that is known as 'The Family'. It is known as that because, no matter what happens, one always belongs. Like a family there may be disagreements and rows, but you still belong." He let the curtain fall. "It means that our Mr D'Arcy can call on many friends, some in high places, who will give assistance without question. Some will put loyalty to their family before that of their current paymasters."

"Something in particular is troubling you, my husband?"

He looked vexed. "That telephone call I received just before the arrival of Mr D'Arcy. It was from the Sultanate. Already there is someone out there asking questions, calling on old friends."

"I should not have let him in."

"No, we made the right decision. It is best to know a man, to take his measure, if he is to be your enemy."

"And he is to be your enemy, my husband?"

Hayira smiled. "That will be up to him. Now, perhaps it is time to prepare supper whilst I play with our children – before they forget who their father is."

"I thought some *kibbeh nayeh* with a little salad."

"That would be splendid." He opened the French doors to be greeted by the sudden sound of playful laughter.

"My husband."

He turned.

"The man spoke of a woman and a child held hostage by kidnappers . . ."

"It is not for you to concern yourself."

"Will you speak with the man called D'Arcy?"

He took a deep breath and looked out at his children. "*Inshaallah*." If God wills it.

D'Arcy dialled on the in-car phone as he headed the XJS back towards the City. "Did you get all that, Dave?"

"Clear as a bell," Forbes answered from his Cavalier parked opposite the house of Sheikh Abdullah Hayira. "And I'm getting more. And he is there, by the way."

D'Arcy grunted. "I thought as much. Let's just hope our luck holds."

"Where did you place it?"

"Under the coffee table, next to the telephone."

"Not bad."

"Listen, Dave. Stay put until I can get you relieved. I'll pull in a spare team."

"You haven't got a spare team to pull in," Forbes reminded. "Otherwise that Corsican wouldn't be in Oman."

"I'll think of something."

"And get hold of a camera, boss. One with a telephoto lens and motor drive."

"Good thinking, Dave," D'Arcy replied. "One way or another, I'm going to nail that bastard."

It was with a real sense of achievement for the first time in weeks that he arrived back at Flax Wharf. There he found Brandy preparing to leave for home after a particularly long and exhausting day.

"I need backup for Dave," he said. "Who's available for some surveillance work?"

"Me."

"You?"

She showed him all her teeth in what could have been a smile or a snarl. "Okay, bossman, so I'm a woman. Sorry. But there *is* no one else."

D'Arcy grinned at her enthusiasm. "Thanks for the offer, but it could get tricky if you were spotted."

"So it'll cost you double overtime."

D'Arcy thought for a moment. "Just stake out with Dave, that'll be safer. Take it in turns to sleep. You can get the coffee and sandwiches."

"Boss!" Brandy warned, her feminine pride rising.

He laughed and raised his hands in surrender. "It's just safer that way. I don't want you left on your own. And take that camera from the storeroom."

"The address, boss?" She could scarcely hide her excitement. "Just one thing. You'd better phone Dave's wife and tell her where I'm spending the night. She won't believe it from him."

"I'm like a bloody father to you lot," he moaned.

"By the way, you've just had a call from your friendly local spook."

His heart sank. "Roy Bliss?"

"Can you meet him at the Dickens between half seven and eight?"

It was nearer eight when D'Arcy arrived at St Katharine's Dock by Tower Bridge. The soft summer evening had encouraged the mêlée of tourists to linger around the wharves and walkways. The old Charles Dickens pub opposite the bright red lightship was filled with smoke and chatter in several languages.

Bliss was at a window table which looked over the placid green waters of the dock, a half-pint of bitter in hand.

He glanced up as D'Arcy approached. "Still brandy is it?" Brusquely he shoved the glass across the barrel table.

"Thanks. Glad the department's expenses run to five-star."

"It's three-star."

D'Arcy tried it. "You were done. Anyway, what's the problem?"

"You, pal. You're the problem. Have you got a death-wish or something?"

"Tell me."

Bliss ran a hand over his florid, tired-looking face. His only concession to summer was to forgo his tie; the crumpled brown suit and raincoat remained the same.

"After all I told you, the desk has been getting reports of your people snooping around Oman. It's made me look a right chump. I'm supposed to have warned you off."

"I've got a distraught client who's got a frightened wife and child under dire threat, Roy. What the hell do you expect me to do?"

Bliss searched in his pockets for a fresh pack of cigarettes; the full ashtray and squashed packet told its own story. "I've said before. Learn who your friends are. If they close you down you'll be no good to anyone."

"Who's they?"

"My boss. Century House. Who d'you think? And they'll stick enough on you to make sure you get five years."

"For what?"

"They'll think of something."

D'Arcy put his cigars on the table. "Have one of these."

Expressionless grey eyes appraised him for a moment, almost as though they expected a trick. "Cheers."

"There's nothing to celebrate. You know me well enough, Roy. I'd oblige you if I could. I'd walk out on this one if there wasn't some poor bitch and her daughter with their lives at stake. You're saying leave the ship and Tanner's saying no money."

"Tanner's an arsehole."

"So are you," D'Arcy snapped. "Hijacking legitimate ships is not what Her Majesty's Secret Service is supposed to be about."

Bliss glanced nervously at a jostling group of youngsters nearby. "I never said we did anything of the sort."

"But you know all about it."

"I just advised you not to go looking for the bloody ship."

"Thanks for the advice, Roy. Again."

Bliss swigged a mouthful of beer. "You won't get anywhere."

"I have to. I've got maybe two days before those Sabbah bastards start sending Nadirpur bits of his wife and child

304

through the post. So I've got to give them something."

"Money or the ship – money or arms – either will just fuel their terror network."

"That's what you say. I have it those arms and spares we're talking about are big league – probably destined for the legitimate Iranian Armed Forces."

"What do you know?" Sarcastic.

"Why don't you tell me? Maybe there's a way through. A compromise." He reached out for Bliss's wrist. "Listen, you told me you want to get Sabbah. Well, help me extend the negotiation with the kidnappers and you stand a chance of the police catching some of his cohorts. That would be a big step forward."

"It's out of my hands. Out of our hands. There's more at stake. If you could offer me Sabbah – on a plate – there's a chance we'd put that priority first. But that's a wet dream and you know it. Meanwhile what's going on is big, and you can't stop it. If you try, you'll get crushed."

"Another threat?"

Bliss smiled thinly. "You can't threaten a brick wall. And that's what it's like talking to you. No, it's not a threat. It's just a warning for your own good. I've done my best." He stood up. "Thanks for the cigar. Just watch your back, pal, eh?"

And he disappeared into the crowd of drinkers, leaving D'Arcy with an empty brandy glass and a lot to think about.

At the bar the swarthy young man in the navy Adidas tracksuit ordered another orange juice with ice.

"The bastards," Shamlou swore under his breath. "The sons of whores."

He stared at the brand new video camera on the table in the dining area, and then at the tightly set print of the instruction leaflet.

Matchsticks sauntered into the room from upstairs where he had been taunting Ali and Beth Christie.

"What is the problem, oh chosen one?" he mocked.

Shamlou jabbed a finger at the instruction book. "This. How am I supposed to work out all this? My mind is on other things. Look, there is pages of it! Those sons of whores, tricking us again."

Matchsticks sat on the edge of the table. "Then why do what they say? I wonder who pulls the strings. Us or them? Who is telling who what they will and won't do?"

His comrade glared up at the provoking words. "You are an expert, I suppose?"

"I would ignore their demands. I would cut off a finger. Or a hand. Send it to them. They would soon co-operate." He grinned devilishly as another thought occurred to him. "I would send them a video picture of me cutting off the hand."

"And whose hand would you cut off?" Shamlou demanded. "The woman's or the girl's?"

Matchsticks laughed. "Does it matter?"

For one mad moment Shamlou was tempted to tell him to go and do it. To do it that very instant before he had time to change his mind. In one flash he saw the woman standing naked, screaming, clasping the stump of her right arm as the blood spurted over her belly, over her daughter who stood screaming beside her. Over him, Shamlou.

And he remembered the night of the martyrdom of the goats, and the sickly sweet smell of their blood again filled his nostrils.

He looked up at his comrade with disdain. "And how will you staunch the blood without a doctor? Will you kidnap a doctor, too? If you have a corpse, you have nothing to trade."

Matchsticks shrugged. "Well, just a finger then. Or slice off an ear."

"And that is how you will build trust with someone you negotiate with?"

"Huh, what is this trust you speak of?" Matchsticks sneered. "Fear of the scourge of Islam is all you need."

"Trust that if we say the hostages will be delivered unharmed, that is how it shall be."

The other man gave a snort of disgust, and wandered over to the television. He punched the on-button before dropping into the armchair, the knees of his long legs jutting to his chest, his long arms hanging uncomfortably over the sides.

Shamlou noticed the *Crimewatch* programme start then looked back to the video instructions. Still he could not concentrate. For, although he had outwitted his comrade with words, he knew that Matchsticks was right. Had his own instructor not told him that mutilation was the most effective weapon – that it had always, in the history of modern kidnap, brought results. Why then could he not order it to be done?

Again he saw and heard the dulcet incantation of the woman in the garden; and in his mind's eye he could not separate it from the image of Ashi Nadirpur standing naked before him with her child.

Was he failing? Had he failed? Was this why Sabbah himself had chosen him – only for him to fail when his mettle was finally put to the test?

Angrily he thudded the table with his fist and suddenly, inexplicably, recalled the parting words of the veteran Hamman at the camp. *"Do what you have to do, Jalal. But whatever you do, do it for Allah and for Islam. Not for anyone who uses His holy name for their own ends."*

He turned the words over and over in his mind. Hamman was a fearless man, but not cruel. Shamlou found himself asking what the older man would do in his position? The veteran, he was sure, would not mutilate a woman or a child. Not unless he was directly ordered; not unless it was a last resort. Now he felt vindicated; Matchsticks was wrong. Why did he ever think that the imbecile might be right? After all, wasn't it he, Shamlou, who was 'chosen'.

"Shamlou! Come quick!" Matchsticks' excited words

cut across his thoughts. "On the television, look! It is about us!"

Quickly he crossed to where his comrade sat, his eyes bulging intently as he watched the fair-haired presenter talking solemnly to the camera.

The abduction of an Iranian woman and her child in Knightsbridge. Wife and daughter of a wealthy shipowner in Paris. Terrorists. Grey van and men in stocking-masks. Middle Eastern in appearance. Abandoned. Kingsbury, North London. Witnesses.

A strangely surreal, segmented Photofit picture flashed onto the screen. It was followed by three more.

Shamlou thought he recognised one, but he had only met the students who had carried out the abduction for a few moments. During the changeover at the Scratchwood Service Station. He felt a thrill of fear shoot through his body.

Cutback to the presenter. Two more Iranians wanted for questioning. Two students from Paris on short-stay visas. Two names.

Shamlou's mouth dropped. His cover name. His and Matchsticks'. His pulse raced as he waited to see his picture appear.

No Photofit this, but a proper photograph. His cover name. Never before had he seen the blank staring face of the passport photograph that looked directly at him from the screen. A flash. A second picture.

Beside him Matchsticks chortled. "If I looked like him I would kill myself!"

"Shut up!"

Back to the serious-faced presenter. Dangerous men. Do not approach. Telephone these numbers. Strictest confidence.

Shamlou lost the words as his mind tumbled to recall the words of his 'controller' in Paris. The grey man. False passports. "Bodies fed to pigs are not found."

Suddenly he felt release, a heady elation like pure oxygen swelled inside his skull until he began to laugh, and laugh. Matchsticks joined in. Together they laughed until the tears began to stream.

The British police were looking for the wrong names and the wrong faces.

# 13

Rick Clay clambered down the ladder from the wheelhouse of *Gulf Bullpup*. "Glad you could make it. I was just about to send out a search party."

Saint-Julien helped Chantal over the side. "I am starting to think we don't get here, myself," he replied. "Quick, we must get under cover."

"What's this? Sunstroke?"

The Frenchman placed a hairy paw of a hand on Clay's shoulder. "I am not messing, *mon ami*. We have big trouble."

"You know the way."

"Can we cast off?" Chantal asked anxiously. Her face was almost totally obscured by her straw fedora and wide-rimmed sunglasses. "If we are seen boarding by police, we will not reach the mouth of the harbour."

Clay began to realise that both were in deadly earnest. "Get below. I'll be with you in a moment." He returned to the wheelhouse where Tokyo was poring over Admiralty charts.

"What is this sudden rush, China? Why is it I get bad feeling just now?"

"Our friends have problems with the police. Just start her up, will you; I'll cast off. We'll find out what it's all about soon enough."

Within two minutes *Gulf Bullpup* had slipped her moorings, and her white bow was chomping eagerly through the wavelets towards the open sea.

A grey Customs launch passed them from the opposite

direction and its skipper exchanged a friendly wave with Tokyo. The old tug, with her bright yellow submersible creating a distinctive hunchback, was a familiar sight. Slowly the great ships of the container terminal were swallowed up in the sea haze behind them.

Clay called their passengers up to the wheelhouse. "I think we ought to keep Tokyo up to date on this. Seeing as you seem determined to bring the wrath of the Royal Oman Police down on the both of us."

Saint-Julien shrugged. "Well, it appears to be the police. Something called the Anti-Terrorist Review Board."

"Doesn't mean a thing to me. I've never heard of it."

"A Major Harry Ingham?" Chantal added.

Realisation dawned. "That old bastard," Clay said. "Major Harry! Oh dear."

Chantal looked aghast. "Is that so bad?"

Clay laughed. "Well if you've fallen foul of Major Harry, you're in good company. So have half the expat community in Muscat! Virtually accused me of gunrunning a few years back. I ask you! He has this knack of rubbing people up the wrong way. Mind you, I thought he'd retired. Haven't heard much of him for a couple of years."

Tokyo agreed. "I hear he goes Cayman Islands. To make his fortune after he has bustup with HM."

"You mean the Sultan?" Chantal asked.

"Sure, His Majesty."

"Well, I assure you he is back," Saint-Julien growled. "He is waiting for us on our return to the hotel last night. He knows who we are, who we work for, and why we are here."

Chantal added: "We were forbidden to leave the capital area. That's why we were late. We had to leave the hotel through a back way because a policeman waits in reception."

"No problem now," Clay assured. "If there's any trouble you've just gone scuba diving with old friends off the coast. They won't know any different. There's no restriction been placed on us."

Tokyo didn't look so happy. "Do not make light of this, *Clay-san*. Major Harry still a man of much power. Much influence. How else does he work with Oman Police? We must be careful, we still have business to run."

"Yeah, I know, Tokyo," Clay replied. He spun the helm a couple of spokes, grinning with a cigarette clamped between his teeth. "But we won't need Oman soon. Not as the sales of the old Jet Raider start mounting up."

Tokyo smiled and shook his head in mock despair. "My old China, we have not yet sold one."

It was dusk before they'd covered the hundred plus miles to Sur, with *Gulf Bullpup* manfully delivering a steady fifteen knots without complaint.

The livid pink sky provided a stunning backdrop to the ragged lower slopes of the Jebel Bani Jabir heights that tumbled haphazardly towards the sea. Along the shoreline the fishermen's fires burned fitfully in the fast descending twilight. With her diesels throttled back, *Gulf Bullpup* swung gently round to make a westerly approach, nudging her way into the placid waters of the lagoon. All around its shores wooden dhows bucked at their moorings; others lay in stages of construction like the ribbed carcasses of beached whales. Beyond the tarmac corniche the outline shapes of Sur town rose, guarded by the cut-out onion minarets of the several mosques.

"This place was once big port for dhows," Tokyo explained. "They build here and export dates, dried shark and other fish to East Africa. But now trade is all but finish. Only few dhows to be built."

They tied up to one of the mooring poles and took the inflatable Avon dinghy to the shore, leaving Tokyo in charge of security. The smell of seaweed and cooking spices wafted across the tranquil waters on the breeze which carried the mesmeric incantations of the *muezzins*.

It was a far cry from the antiseptic environs of the capital area. After beaching they made their way into the dark and dusty narrow streets, passing windows shuttered with goatskin and torn mosquito nets. Open doorways gave an insight to the cramped and feebly lit dwellings within. The pungent aroma of cooking was stronger now, mingling with the scent of incense and the sharper, salty smell of the nearby fish market.

Women were out to shop and to gossip, vivid silks and gold embroidery glimpsed beneath their black headdresses and *abba* cloaks. At the sight of the strangers, heads would turn, talking stop, and veils would be quickly drawn.

Clay turned down a narrow alley between two mud-brick walls. It was only slightly wider than a man's shoulders; a flyblown sign bore the unlikely legend Street of Grapes. It was very dark, the air thick with the smell of hashish, and Chantal was glad to be in the company of the two men.

An Arab youth with a wispy beard was leaning against a door jamb, idly cleaning his nails with the point of a sharp knife. A scavenging dog, its ribs showing through its mangy pelt, sniffed at food scraps by the man's feet. A babble of conversation and rough laughter came from beyond the doorway.

"*Masa'il khair,*" Clay greeted, smiling.

The youth looked sullen and suspicious. Chantal was reminded of the graceless attitude of a nightclub bouncer. "*Masa' in-nur,*" he intoned the formal reply without sounding as though he meant it.

"*Assif. Ismi Mr China. Tatakallam ingleezi?*"

A shake of the head. "*La.*" He spoke no English.

Clay broke into fast but shaky Arabic, asking to talk to sea captain Nasiyb.

The Arab kicked at the dog which yelped and pulled back, but did not go. "*Ma fi Nasiyb.*"

Clay tried his most charming smile. In Arabic he said: "Yes, there is a sea captain called Nasiyb. Please see if he is inside. I am an old friend. Tell him it is Mr China."

The youth sniffed, scowled, then reluctantly pulled aside the rough blanket that covered the entrance and disappeared. From inside came the sound of much male laughter and talking. They heard the youth say something

313

and an abrupt silence fell as others listened.

The young Arab reappeared. With an incline of his head he said curtly: "*Ta'al*."

They followed as they were bid. A brass oil lamp hung from the low ceiling of the den, lighting the dense blue swathes of smoke above the woven carpet around which the men sat. An old date farmer without teeth sucked with the contentment of a nursing babe on the gypsum waterpipe, inhaling deep draughts of sun-dried tobacco. Only he seemed oblivious to the newcomers; the others, sitting cross-legged in white *dishdasha* robes and woollen turbans, stopped their conversations and looked up.

Nasiyb was holding court, seated facing them as they entered. He was not an easy man to mistake. In his early fifties, he was particularly tall and broad for an Omani. Beneath the beaded skullcap his dark mahogany skin was evidence of his descent from the slaves of Zanzibar. Wary eyes watched from under the deep frown of his brows and his thick lips pursed between separate moustache and goatee beard. A curved *khanjar* dagger was carried in his waistband.

Now Clay understood the earlier laughter and cries of encouragement. Nasiyb had been playing *Huwayliys* with a friend, a fast-moving game involving counters dropped into two sides of fourteen holes. Usually the counters were made of dried camel dung or pebbles. The ones in use were ivory; a sign of the times, Clay decided, a sign of Nasiyb's illegally acquired wealth.

Nasiyb climbed to his feet. "*Ahlan wa sahlan, Mr China. Al-salam alaykum.*" Welcome. Peace be with you.

Clay took the offered hand. "And with you, old friend. And how are your family and friends?"

"Praise be to Allah in good health," the sea captain replied in broken English.

"And life is treating you well?"

"No one complains." Nasiyb looked suspiciously at Clay's companions. "And your friends. You and they are well?"

"They are fine. Tell me, Nasiyb, one of my companions is a female, a dear friend of a friend. Is it permissible for her to join us?"

Nasiyb screwed up his eyes in the poor light. Clearly Clay wasn't referring to the black-shirted bulk of Saint-Julien with his heavy beard and ponytail. The sea captain's eyes shifted to the slender, fair-haired creature in the chino shirt and slacks, with the straw fedora which cast her face in shadow.

"It is permissible," Nasiyb grunted. "Sit. Have coffee."

After much handshaking with the unsavoury-looking but genial seafarers – no doubt smugglers to a man – their host dispensed fresh green dates before pouring cardamom-flavoured coffee from a copper pot. After that a finger bowl was passed around, prior to the arrival of unsweetened red tea.

It was a long but relaxing ritual before Nasiyb considered it proper to bring up the purpose of Clay's visit.

"I seek your guidance, good friend. There is much trouble abroad. No peace."

Nasiyb nodded cautious agreement.

"There is war in Persia, in the Gulf of Oman," Clay said. "You see the mighty warships of the Britishers, the French, the Americanos, the Russians in these waters."

"We have seen them."

"My friends here have a ship. It takes arms to Persia." Nasiyb's eyes lit up. "It is taken by piracy in the waters of Oman. We seek your help in finding it."

Nasiyb's eyes narrowed. "These are arms for the Ayatollah of Qum?"

"To fight his war."

"I spit on the Ayatollah and his war. I spit on the brand of Islam that blackens men's hearts."

Clay was taken aback. "We share those views, Nasiyb, but my friends are men of trade. Does one ask where the gold you transport is destined? Or the slaughter of animals to give you your cargoes of ivory and rhino horn? Trade is trade."

315

The sea captain's eyes darkened momentarily, then he sniffed and sat back, aloof. "When did this ship pass this way?"

"Some three weeks ago."

"What type of ship?"

"Very large. A freighter with this emblem." Clay used his finger to draw the Nadirpur line's motif in the earthen floor.

Nasiyb turned to his companions and asked a question. Then for five minutes there was an excited exchange, much gesticulating, and heated debate.

The three guests drank more tea until the contretemps subsided.

At last Nasiyb leaned forward conspiratorially. "Trade is poor in these times, Mr China. Sur dies like an old woman. We must make our living as best we can. This night I trade in information."

"How much do you ask?"

"Ten thousand rial." Fifteen thousand pounds sterling.

"You joke with me, old friend."

"Arms are a precious commodity to the Ayatollah with the black heart. It is ten thousand rial to buy an old man a new fishing dhow."

"One dhow, not a fleet. Two thousand and he is a scoundrel."

"Ten, and his children starve."

"Five and they will eat well."

Nasiyb smiled and a gold tooth glinted in the lamplight. "Seven, and you will have every fisherman in Sur looking out for your ship."

Clay glanced at Saint-Julien and the girl. They had no idea. "Yes," Clay decided suddenly. The deal was struck.

Nasiyb extracted an ancient, bent-double fisherman with a white beard and pinched face from the crowd of on-lookers. "This man. This man sees your ship. Three weeks ago to the day. He is passing on his way home to Sur with a catch during the last light of the day. Your ship uses its horn, like the voice of Allah, to drive him aside. He ignores

316

the sons of goats. Then he sees a sight that makes him think he has been in the sun too long."

The old man nodded enthusiastically.

"Up out of the sea come two black boats in rubber, like the one you use tonight to come ashore," Nasiyb continued. Through his local spy network he had obviously known of Clay's arrival as soon as *Gulf Bullpup* had sailed into the lagoon. "These rubber boats race towards the bows of your ship, spreading outward." He illustrated with the palms of his hands. "And a line catches across the bows. With the rubber boats alongside, men in black scale the sides of the ship."

"What happened?"

Nasiyb shrugged. "The ship sailed on."

"Was there any shooting?"

The smuggler asked the old man. "He says not."

"And the ship did not change course?"

"Apparently not."

"Thank you, good friend."

Nasiyb leaned forward again. "Something more, for which I will not charge. There are agents of the Ayatollah with the black heart here in Sur. They ask about this ship, but I do not tell them," he said contemptuously. "But be warned, there are agents throughout Oman who say nothing but listen with the ears of a bat."

D'Arcy received the signal from *Gulf Bullpup* on returning from his early morning three-mile run.

He broke the news to Nadirpur over breakfast.

The Iranian was elated. "This is the most wonderful thing to hear, Robert. It is absolute magic to my ears. At last we have something to offer those kidnappers."

D'Arcy didn't dash his expectations immediately. He waited until coffee before gently pointing out: "Of course, the kidnappers may not consider this a tangible step forward. They may frankly not even believe us. We must remember that."

"But we even have a witness!"

"An old fisherman in some remote village in Arabia may not prove the most reliable of people under questioning, Nader."

Nadirpur looked at him curiously. "You are trying to depress me?"

"Not at all. I just don't want you to build your hopes too high. But it could be the start of more good news."

And so it proved to be, but not quite in the way that either had been expecting.

As the clerical staff of IAP began arriving at nine o'clock, Detective Chief Superintendent Reg Roman of the Anti-Terrorist Branch was among them.

"Good news, gentlemen," he announced. "Last night's *Crimewatch* programme was something of a triumph. I think we have our abductors!"

Nadirpur's mouth dropped in astonishment: "You have *caught* the kidnappers! Wonderful! My wife and child . . . ?"

"Steady, steady," Roman said, holding up his hand like a policeman on traffic duty. "I said the abductors – the men who actually seized your wife and child. It is an exciting breakthrough, but there is still some way to go."

"I do not understand," Nadirpur said.

"I'll explain. Last night brought a good response. Firstly the Photofit pictures prompted a number of calls, mostly from Iranian students who are against Khomeini. We have to be careful because there's a lot of acrimony between pro and anti factions, so it could be spite. But two names cropped up several times. Students at Imperial College, London. We made a dawn swoop today. One is keeping quiet, but the other is already singing like the proverbial canary. We are now seeking to arrest two more students."

"Has it taken you any further forward?" D'Arcy asked.

Roman hedged. "Yes and no. As you might imagine there was a cutout. These lads appear to have had threats made against their families back in Iran if they didn't co-operate. At the same time they were offered money. The chap who's doing all the talking says he paid the money to a charity – he wanted none of it."

"That is very sad," Nadirpur observed.

"It's a nasty position to be in," Roman agreed. "I wouldn't want to be faced with such a decision. Anyway, the approach was made by two strangers to them by the names of Hamid and Kamal – whether or not they are real names, we don't know. They just walked into Imperial College one day and asked to speak to the students by name. Obviously they'd been chosen as being vulnerable. Actually selected because of their anti-Khomeini activities. All four collected for Iran Aid. And all those poor buggers are paranoid about being caught by a hit squad from *Hezbollah*. However, these strangers did appear to be well-educated and to know London extremely well. Although they are not on our files as having any sort of diplomatic connections."

"A sleeper cell?" D'Arcy suggested.

"It looks that way. They had organised everything apparently. Had the van and the chloroform supplies, stocking masks, the works. And complete instructions on how and when the snatch should be made. A changeover was then made at the Scratchwood Service Station on the M1. The victims were transferred to a yellow van. There was a ladder on the roof rack which suggested it could have been a builders' van. Our talkative friend couldn't remember the registration number but remembers it began with an H – his own initial – and there were two sixes or nines in the number."

"Very helpful," D'Arcy grunted.

"It all helps," Roman said.

"And who was in this yellow van?"

"Two more men, Iranians. But not the Hamid or Kamal who set the thing up. Two strangers."

An idea occurred to D'Arcy. "Not the two students from Paris who went missing?"

Roman smiled bitterly. "My first thoughts, too. We showed them the pictures sent over by the French authorities, but it definitely wasn't them."

"And have they been traced?"

"No sign."

"So we're talking about a gang of four? The two called Hamid and Kamal – and the two strangers in the builders' van." He thought for a moment. "Or even six, if those two from Paris are part of it?"

"That's about the measure," Roman agreed. "And we've a couple of extra clues from that audio cassette tape. Not a lot, mind you. The Yard's technicians detected there was a fair degree of echo which suggested a room without much furnishing. But then I guess we would expect that. A cellar or an attic. And there was a twenty-second section on the reverse side of the tape which hadn't been properly erased. It was an all male or school choir singing Christmas carols. Poor quality with a lot of rustling and distortion. Definitely a live performance. Sort of thing a doting mother might make if her son was in a concert."

"And that's it?"

"So far that's all we can offer. I'll call back at lunchtime for a further chat."

Roman had just arrived back at Flax Wharf when the kidnapper's next telephone call came at precisely one o'clock. As usual Nadirpur took the call. Listening in, D'Arcy was gratified to note that this time the caller sounded very quiet and confident, almost complacent. Gone was the previous vitriol and hysteria. He sounded very much like a man in control of the situation as he gave instructions for collecting the promised video, which had been hidden behind a telephone box in the suburbs of Birmingham.

D'Arcy wondered why the man sounded so rational? Hadn't he seen the *Crimewatch* programme or the photographs in the morning's newspapers? Surely he had. So why was he suddenly so cocksure? Was he on drugs to keep him calm? Whatever the reason, it hopefully meant that Ashi and Sousan's fate would not be in the hands of some jittery and trigger happy terrorist.

The kidnapper finished with: "This proof will satisfy

you. I shall telephone tomorrow when you will have the information I want." It was a chilling, straightforward statement. The very lack of a hint of threat made it somehow all the more menacing.

Nadirpur, following D'Arcy's script, replied: "If all is in order, you will be given every assistance."

Both parties replaced their receivers. It was almost gentlemanly.

Within seconds Roman received his tracer call. The kidnapper had actually telephoned from the Birmingham area.

Roman grinned widely: "I think you're right, Rob. The bastards are in the south. And in or around London. Calling from Birmingham is just to throw us. Just two hours up the motorway or a fast train from Euston. And the bastard's still there. This is too good a chance to miss . . ."

"What d'you have in mind?" D'Arcy asked.

"He'll be heading back to London," Roman replied, thinking aloud. "I'll get a watch put on the M1 for the builders' van . . . And someone on each London train leaving Birmingham today."

"The caller sounded calm, but he's bound to be hyped up, on edge," D'Arcy warned.

"No, no." He understood the other man's worry. "There'll be no approach. I'll get an ex-SO13 man on each train. He can accompany the ticket inspector in a British Rail uniform. He'll be able to assess how many passengers could possibly be our Iranian suspect. That'll give him time to get descriptions and the right number of surveillance teams in place by the time each train arrives at Euston." He reached for the phone and began to dial.

"But there could be a couple or a dozen possibles on each train," D'Arcy pointed out.

Roman shrugged. "In a situation like this, all you can do is throw money at it. It'll require scores of officers and the Home Office won't like the bill, but – " He was put through then, and pressed the scramble button for the massive covert operation at Euston. He then arranged for a local plain-clothes detective to pick up the video tape from the drop and have it flown down to London by police helicopter.

When he'd finished he found D'Arcy slouched in his chair pensively tapping a tattoo on the conference table with his pencil. "A penny for them, Rob?"

D'Arcy looked up. "Tomorrow is crunch time, Reg. If that video is legit, then we have to offer something. We've made some progress on the ship, but it isn't much."

Roman was delighted. "Really? Give."

"We know when, where and how it was taken. By professionals using inflatable dinghies. Boarded in Omani waters."

"And?"

"Exactly, Reg, there isn't any 'and'," D'Arcy smiled grimly.

"Would that impress you, if you were them?"

"Stall. Say more news tomorrow."

"And chance the little girl's life? If they hang up and decide to make a point, there's no way I can reach them."

"What are you trying to tell me?"

"I've talked it over with Nader. We're going to make a cash offer."

Nadirpur nodded eagerly. "An act of goodwill."

Roman took a deep, thoughtful breath. He stared at the wall, stared at the ceiling, stared at the floor. He grimaced. At last he said, slowly: "I understand your reasoning, Rob. Christ, don't I just! But it's not in the rule book of this particular game."

"I've just thrown out the rule book," D'Arcy said darkly.

"Tanner won't agree."

"He doesn't have to. It's up to him to make his own decision. He's either with us or he isn't. I've got to stall, you're right there – but I have to have *something* to stall with. It'll still give your blokes more time."

"Don't tell me!" Roman snapped back. "It's not up to

322

me. I'm taking my orders from Bob Tanner like he's taking his from the Cabinet Office. No money to terrorists, that's the line. No money and no negotiation."

D'Arcy rose from his seat: "Then we know where we stand."

It was an acrimonious parting which left D'Arcy with a bitter taste. The encounter had left Nadirpur confused and troubled.

At least the good news was, when the video arrived in the late afternoon, that both Ashi and Sousan looked well, apart from appearing dishevelled and unclean. The mother's voice was remarkably steady as she read the headline story from the previous day's paper.

To keep the mood light, that evening D'Arcy booked a table for the two of them at a nearby restaurant. Although he'd telephoned Forbes in the car outside Sheikh Hayira's house to say where they would be, he was surprised when he and Brandy made an appearance at nine o'clock.

The waitress gave a disapproving glare as an unshaven, untidy Forbes helped himself to chairs from an adjoining table. Even Brandy looked less than her usual pristine self.

"Christ, I'm famished," Forbes declared, dumping his camera on the table. "This girl's been feeding me bloody celery and cottage cheese all day. That and Diet Coke, for God's sake."

"It's good for you," Brandy protested lamely.

Forbes poked a fork at D'Arcy's dish. "That looks good. What is it?"

"Osso bucco," D'Arcy replied. "And for God's sake tell me what's happened."

"Same as he's got twice, love," Forbes told the waitress. "And a nut cutlet for the lady."

"Are you going to tell me?" D'Arcy demanded.

Forbes helped himself to wine. "Things started to get a bit hot this evening, boss. Pity we didn't change cars or have the resources to replace Brandy and me. Either Hayira or a neighbour got a bit suspicious of us being parked there all day, I don't know, but someone called the police. There was no hassle, but we had to call it a day."

"Was the bug found?"

"Nope," Forbes replied, "not up until we left. And quite a revelation it provided, too. It's all on the tapes. He used that downstairs phone quite a lot, and mostly talked in Arabic. But he was always a bit cautious when his wife was around. I think he used the upstairs phone for important stuff. But he's been a busy boy. Phone calls to Iraq, Kuwait, Jordan, the Emirates. And to our chum George Cupplewaite in Oman."

D'Arcy raised his eyebrows. "What was said?"

"Well, this was a one-sided conversation I was listening to, mind. But it looks like you really stirred the shit when you paid him that visit. He's calling for a special meeting of the directors in London. All the little creepie crawlies of Spidex are coming to the centre of the web.

"Saint-Julien and Chantal have been creating waves too, reading between the lines. But Hayira mostly listened during that conversation, I'm afraid. But it confirms they know we have a presence there."

He poured another glass of wine, finishing D'Arcy's bottle. "I thought we'd get another car round tomorrow. I've a mate who might help out."

"Good idea."

"And what's been happening back at the fort?"

D'Arcy updated him on the day's events while Forbes tucked into a double osso bucco and chips with gusto.

Brandy, having declined the nut cutlet, finished her chicken salad. "Why don't you just give Hayira's address to the kidnappers and let them get on with it?" she suggested with an air of innocence. "It would be a sort of rough justice."

Forbes grinned evilly. "I like it."

D'Arcy was scathing. "We all know what would happen if we did that. We'd be accessories to murder. Is that what you want? Century House really would have cause to

324

come down on us. And don't think for one minute it would guarantee the release of our hostages."

Nadirpur nodded soberly. "Whatever Hayira has done, I agree nothing would justify that. He, too, has a wife and family."

It was in a more sombre mood that they left the restaurant. Not one of them noticed the young man in the navy Adidas tracksuit waiting patiently on his scooter in the shadows. As, indeed, they had not noticed his discreet surveillance of their Flax Wharf office for the past two days.

As *Gulf Bullpup* was on the last leg of its return trip from Sur, a message was received from IAP in London.

Major Alan Hawksby, a former SAS squadron commander who was now an officer in the Sultan's Special Forces, had contacted D'Arcy with important information. Hawksby had already learned that Saint-Julien and Chantal were in the country – he didn't specify how – and sought an early meeting with them. It had been fixed for eight that night at the InterContinental.

"You'll just make it," Clay observed. "The bar there's a favourite with the British expats. But I'd better come with you, otherwise you'll never recognise the Hawk."

"What do you mean?" Chantal asked.

Clay grinned. "You'll see."

Like most of Muscat's hotels, the InterContinental was staking its claim for architectural supremacy. Glass-fronted lifts glided up and down the central core of the vast domed lobby like something out of a science fiction movie. Below, waterfalls cascaded over black marble feature walls.

The bar was less spectacular and crowded with a mixture of nationalities, including a strong and instantly identifiable contingent from the British community.

Clay glanced around. "He's not here yet."

They were just settling down with their drinks when Chantal noticed the tall Arab enter.

He was distinguished in a flowing white *dishdasha* and

a *shamag* upturned to form a turban. The leather tanned skin covered a strong bone structure with gaunt cheeks and a prominent hooked nose. The trimmed beard was short and very black, edged with traces of silver.

But as he scanned the room, it was the eyes she noticed most, the deepest, bluest eyes she had ever seen.

Clay nudged her. "See what I mean?" He waved. "Alan! Over here."

Hawksby threaded his way through the crowd and joined their table with a curt nod of acknowledgement to Saint-Julien and Chantal.

"Beer?" Clay offered.

"No thanks, I've got to start back down to Salalah as soon as I can."

Saint-Julien had been studying the newcomer curiously. "Pardon me, my friend, but why the Arab disguise?"

Clay winced as Hawksby turned on him. "You live in the Arctic, you dress like an Eskimo. In the desert Westerners dress like Westerners and suffer the consequences. I find the locals usually know best."

"That makes sense," Chantal said.

Hawksby looked at her more closely, the eyes hard and appraising. "You must be D'Arcy's girl."

"Guilty." She smiled.

"And this is Saint-Julien," Clay added.

"I know about both of you," Hawksby said. "The word is out for no one to have anything to do with you. It's like this. A week or so ago your Dave Forbes telephoned to put me in the picture and ask a favour. I sent a round-robin memo to a select group of officer friends in the navy and air force to ask of any news of your missing ship. As a result I received a visit from a certain Major Harry yesterday. He was none too pleased and had an order issued to all British staff, contract and seconded, to deny you all assistance."

"We have met this man," Saint-Julien growled.

"Very unpleasant," Chantal added.

Hawksby's hooded eyes blinked momentarily. "Unpleasant he may be, but he holds considerable sway with

HM. And, to be fair, my request for personal information wasn't strictly protocol. Gone are the days when the Brits could treat this place as if it were a colony. The Omanis are getting pretty strict on such things, especially in terms of security. Even old commanders here on visits have been refused permission to meet their old comrades at barracks. Sounds petty, I know, but there it is."

"But you have come to see us," Chantal pointed out.

"Because I understand a woman and child are being held hostage over this ship. That's the only reason. And before Major Harry's visit, a pilot of one of our Defender maritime patrol aircraft telephoned me. He'd got my memo and recalled a strange incident which occurred a day or two after your ship disappeared. They picked up a distress beacon transmission – Sarbe – but it only lasted a few minutes, then cut out."

"From which area?" Clay asked.

"The Musandam peninsula."

Chantal frowned. "Where is that?"

Clay said: "It's a big knuckle of land that forms the southern coast of the Strait of Hormuz. Remote and isolated from the rest of Oman by part of the United Arab Emirates. All mountains and fjords like someone dropped part of Norway there by mistake."

"The pilot flew up there to recce," Hawksby continued. "Usual emergency search procedure. They came across an American Fleet Viking aircraft looking as well. They scoured the area and came up with nothing. No ships in the area were in distress."

"That would be the place," Clay said thoughtfully. "You could hide a whole bloody fleet up there. I just never thought of it."

"The search was thorough," Hawksby reminded. "A distress beacon is associated with a ship in trouble."

"But now we *know* it was a hijack," Clay said, his mind suddenly racing. "We've established it happened off the coast near Sur. Very professional. Men capable of taking a protected ship without a shot being fired would be quite capable of hiding it around Musandam. Proper camo drapes and the like. I don't believe it sank for one moment."

"Is it feasible to search the area?" Saint-Julien asked.

Clay shrugged. "It's a helluva big area, all inlets and coves, but yes, I suppose it is. Local knowledge would help."

"Don't let me hear this," Hawksby warned.

Chantal said: "Why is it that this Major Harry is so against us searching for this ship? It does not make sense to me."

"Maybe because Oman doesn't want to earn a reputation as a haven for pirates," Hawksby replied, "or to get involved with anything remotely connected with Iran. HM is treading a very careful line. And, young lady, you should be very wary of Major Harry. He'll happily have you put on the next flight home. That's how it happens over here. They don't antagonise the British by imprisoning troublemakers. Drunken drivers have been given just twenty-four hours. Even if you're a rape victim it's often the same principle. You're trouble, so you're out."

"What is this Anti-Terrorist Review Board anyway?"

Hawksby pulled a tobacco pouch and short-stemmed clay pipe from the bag on his belt. "I've not heard of it. Must be separate from the Intelligence Security Service, which is run by a British officer who can't abide Major Harry. Perhaps it has an intelligence-gathering and analysis function, a sort of embryonic MI5 with a direct line to HM. To be honest, Major Harry has always been known for empire building, trying to make himself indispensable to the Sultan. It would be typical. With a little unit like that – officially non-existent and virtually answerable to no one – he can stick his nose into anything that suits him."

"I just hope he's not waiting for us back at the hotel," Chantal said later, as the bar began closing for the night.

As it turned out Major Harry wasn't waiting for them, but a message from him was. Curt instructions to telephone his office or his home.

Chantal made the call in the mistaken belief that her natural charms would prove more disarming than Saint-Julien's brusque Gallic manner.

"Where have you been?" Major Harry snapped. "You weren't at your hotel last night. No sign of you both yesterday or today."

"We were on a boat with a friend. Scuba diving."

"I said not to leave the capital area."

"We didn't, Major. We were off the coast."

"Searching for that confounded ship."

"For conch shells."

"Who was this friend?"

"Does it matter?"

"Your story must be corroborated, Miss Roquelaure."

Chantal hesitated. "Someone called Rick Clay."

A brief silence at the other end. "Now I know you are being less than truthful. It doesn't matter anyway. I spoke to His Excellency Shaykh Zufar today. He says he has completed his business with you. So there is no longer any reason for you to stay. Your visa will be cancelled at midnight tomorrow. No doubt you and your friend will be able to get tickets for a flight between now and then. If not, I'm sure I can pull some strings for you. Your passports will be at the airport. Good night."

The phone went dead in her hand.

"What is it?" Saint-Julien asked.

"That nasty little Arab, Zufar!"

"You said he was a cute little gnome."

"Not *now*!" she flared. "He has dropped us. Told Major Harry his business with us is *fini*. We have till midnight tomorrow."

"*Salaud*!" Saint-Julien swore, pounding his fist on the mattress. "Just as we begin to get close! Monsieur D'Arcy will not be pleased."

"He is not the only one. I am not that pleased either." She lit a cigarette. "So, what do we do?"

Saint-Julien studied the backs of his hands. "Once we leave this country we will not get back in. If Major Harry's intelligence is as good as it seems, then anyone else from D'Arcy's company will be refused entry."

She stared at the window and the stars sprinkled above the ragged outline of the distant *jebel*. What view would Philippe Chaumont be seeing at this moment? A brick wall, a high barred window? And the woman and child in London? She stood suddenly, pacing the room like a tigress in a cage, drawing on her cigarette in growing agitation. Should she phone D'Arcy? What would he say? She knew the answer. He would be afraid for her safety. Exactly the point he'd made when he had reluctantly allowed her to go.

She held up the tip of her cigarette and blew on it gently until it glowed. She also knew exactly what D'Arcy would have *wanted* to say. A slow smile crossed her face as she imagined him saying it. You sweet damned bastard.

"*Pardon?*"

Chantal turned to Saint-Julien decisively. "We stay. It is the only solution."

"The major will throw us out. You heard him."

"He will have to find us first."

"Leave the hotel?"

"Yes," she snapped in reaction to his slowness. "We leave this air-conditioning behind. We take provisions and go to this place, this Musandam peninsula."

"We cannot get there directly without passports, it cuts across the Emirates. We need a boat."

"Rick Clay and Tokyo will help, I know it."

Saint-Julien looked dubious. "D'Arcy would not approve of this. There are big stakes involved, and this could put you in danger."

"You too."

Saint-Julien grinned widely. "That is nothing. I lead the fat soft life for too long already."

"Then we go. We cannot telephone Rober' to discuss it. Major Harry may be monitoring calls. It must be our decision."

"You do not have to ask a legionnaire, Mademoiselle!"

On impulse she reached up and kissed him. Fortunately the telephone rang before he had a chance to react. He answered it.

"This is reception. There is someone for you here on our desk telephone. He will give no name, sir. He requests you come down." The Filipino clerk let it be known what a silly idea she thought it was. "Is that possible?"

Intrigued, Saint-Julien took the stairs to the foyer, quickly pinpointed the plain-clothes policeman who had been loitering for the past two days, and went to the desk.

"Saint-Julien here."

"This is Shaykh Zufar," the voice rasped at the other end of the line. "I call you in secret. That Major Harry has come to see me – we must be careful. I do not trust this modern telephone. Many ears may listen. I need to speak with you for I have news."

"Where?"

"It is difficult. I am not sure who I trust."

Having spotted Saint-Julien, the secret policeman made a pretence of coming to the desk to ask an imbecilic question of the clerk. The Corsican turned away, presenting his huge shoulders like a wall, and cupped the earpiece.

"You must talk, Excellency. Just say when and where."

Zufar thought, sucking on his teeth. "Tomorrow I must go to the fort at Jabrin where the *wali* is holding court. Take the road to Nizwa and then the road to Bahla. Be there by nine o'clock. I shall have my car stop when I see you."

The Corsican felt the surge of adrenalin. "It is agreed. *Fi aman illah.*"

"*Ma'a as-salama,*" Zufar murmured and hung up.

By one o'clock they were ready. Saint-Julien had made the supreme sacrifice and lopped off his ponytail and trimmed his beard to avoid obvious recognition. Chantal telephoned a taxi driver whom they had come to know and persuaded him it would be well worth his while to shake the sleep from his eyes and meet them outside the nearby mosque.

In the lobby there was no one on the front desk and the secret policeman had disappeared. They slipped out into the sultry heat of the night to rendezvous with their taxi.

There was little traffic on the brighly lit road to Mina Qaboos harbour, and there were no lights burning on *Gulf Bullpup* when they boarded.

A sleepy Rick Clay emerged from the fo'c'sle after they knocked. "You two again! Go home, the party's over."

"We want your help," Chantal said earnestly.

"What else?" Clay replied with a weary grin.

Below deck Tokyo made coffee while Saint-Julien brought them up to date, adding: "Our first problem is to find transport that the Omani police cannot trace. Do you have a friend with a car, perhaps? Someone trusted?"

"I suppose hire cars are out," Clay thought aloud. "Most of our mates are really just casual acquaintances. We spend most of our time at sea."

Chantal looked disappointed. "It is a pity you cannot put wheels on your Jet Raider. Like a motorcycle."

Saint-Julien grunted. "This crazy woman drives motorcycles like you would not believe! You should see her."

Tokyo said suddenly: "There is a motorcycle. The one that belongs to Mike. He would not mind."

"We can pay," Chantal offered.

Clay said: "No need, Mike's on leave back UK-side. He's an absolute bike nut. Belongs to the Oman Motorcycle Club on Qaboos Street."

"It is his pride and joy," Tokyo added, as though having second thoughts.

"It's a fine machine," Clay agreed. "Get you anywhere you want to go." He grinned at Chantal. "That is when her ladyship has decided where she wants to go. I suppose it is Musandam after what the Hawk was saying."

"It depends what Shaykh Zufar has to tell us. Maybe it is nothing. In which case, *oui*, we must look there."

Clay pulled a map from the chart rack and spread it out over the table between the bunks. "Look, we must arrange a rendezvous on the coast. Here at Mina Qaboos is no good, it will be the first place Major Harry will look when he discovers you've gone walkabout. We'll give Customs some reason to look us over before we sail, invite them for drinks even, they're good friends. Let them see we're the only ones on board. Then we'll meet you along the coast. Maybe the village of Al Muntaifa, nothing much goes on there. We'll just bring the inflatable ashore tomorrow night. There'll be plenty of time for you to get there after your meet with Zufar."

It was agreed and, while Tokyo prepared for *Gulf Bullpup*'s dawn departure, Clay took them to his absent friend's house where the big Suzuki was stored in the yard.

Chantal grinned with pleasure as she sat astride the monster and gunned it into life. With Saint-Julien a most nervous-looking pillion passenger, she took off at a steady speed towards Seeb International Airport along the coast. The road was virtually deserted in the capital area. She turned at the Tower of Reawakening on the MAM roundabout and took the inland road for Nizwa, a town situated on the far side of the Jebel Akhdar range. Only the occasional long-distance truck from the south hurtled down the twisting road in the opposite direction and buses ferrying workers to and from the oilfields of the desert interior.

She was pleasantly surprised by the surface quality of the road which was regularly dissected by dry *wadi* beds that could flood in minutes with flash storms in the rainy season. Through the whispering, shaggy sentinels of the Fanja palm groves, on through the Sumail gap, and so to a slow incline parallel to the *jebel* that led to Nizwa. There the inhabitants were stirring as a soft pre-dawn light radiated from behind the peaks of Eastern Hajar.

They swept through the main drag of the town, slowing only to negotiate the sparse but chaotic early morning traffic in the centre. They travelled on a further five miles before Chantal pulled over and killed the engine.

A stiff-legged Saint-Julien dismounted and thankfully removed his crash helmet. After the constant roar of the bike engine, the craggy landscape of the Jebel Akhdar foothills was stunningly quiet.

"So desolate," Chantal murmured, sharing his mood. "So beautiful."

Gentle peach-coloured light, reflected off the sand and rising bluffs, began to fill the still, dusty air. The distant summits were sharply focused, three-dimensional against a backdrop of milky blue.

Saint-Julien lit two cigarettes, and handed her one. "Let us just hope that Zufar shows as promised."

The wait was an hour. In that time the sun cranked up its strength remorselessly. Chantal rolled the motorcycle into the meagre shade offered by a stunted thorn tree. Four-wheel drive vehicles, trucks and buses began passing at more frequent intervals. It was nine thirty before the distant dust cloud marked the arrival of a large black Ministry limousine.

It shot past before the driver hit the brakes and steered onto the hard shoulder.

"Stay here," Saint-Julien ordered, and began walking towards the vehicle.

On his approach the rear door fell open and Zufar emerged. Against his natural background of endless desert stone and *jebel*, the bent old man appeared to increase in stature. The big nostrils in the hooked nose flared as he breathed in the hot, dry air and the one good eye scanned the horizon lovingly.

He didn't turn as Saint-Julien approached. "It is rare for me to see my homeland in these days. I tell you something, friend, my fellow ministers do not all share my sense of loss. They are in love with their cool offices, their big cars and the good life in their big villas." He spat contemptuously on the ground. "Every year His Majesty makes us all go out into the desert with him for six weeks, to live in tents, to meet his peoples." He chortled with glee. "How they hate it! Now me, it is the most precious

334

time in the whole year." He nudged Saint-Julien. "Come, join me for a pee."

The shaykh picked his way through the strewn boulders, out of earshot of his limousine and stopped behind a scrawny *najdiy* bush. Unable to squat because of his rheumatic knees, he hiked up his *dishdasha*, revealing thin, bowed legs, and let go a long jet of urine with a sigh of relief. "Busy, busy, busy, that is the life of the Arab today, friend. My life is not my own. Reports, meetings, rush here, rush there. I tell you, the pleasure to stand here with you. To pee together with a friend."

Saint-Julien was dehydrated, managing only a trickle. "It is safe here?"

"You are a friend," Zufar said easily. "A chance encounter on the road. What is more natural?"

It didn't strike the Corsican as at all natural, but he let it pass. "So what news do you have for me, Excellency?"

"There is a man you must speak to. I know him as Mr Keith. An engineer. He has been here a long time. He arrived during the Dhofar War and has been here ever since. He was part of the 'Whisper Service' in those days. He received news that I was seeking the answer to a missing ship. He is working up on the Musandam peninsula now. Lately he has heard rumours amongst the fishermen of a spirit ship that vanished."

"Vanished?"

"One night it passes a fishing boat, heading into a blind inlet. They fish all night. In the dawn they pass the inlet on the way home to their village. As the big ship has not gone by during the hours of darkness, they expect to see it. They are curious. Naturally they wonder why such a big ship should enter such waters. There is no port, no harbour. There is no storm from which it seeks shelter. All these things even a simple fisherman will ask himself. But in the dawn there is no ship. It has vanished, and yet, friend, you see there is nowhere for it to go." Zufar shook himself and let his *dishdasha* fall back into place. His good eye turned on Saint-Julien. "A spirit ship. That is what they say. On board the lost souls who seek endlessly for the paradise they are denied."

The Corsican stared at the horizon, now vibrating in the heat reflected off the scorched rock. "Bull," he growled.

"Bull," Zufar said, repeating the unfamiliar word. "But these are simple people. They lead a life of isolation. They are *Shihuh*, not Arab. They speak a dialect of Farsi. In ancestry they are half Arab from Oman, half Fujara. What is not explained by their knowledge and experience, they make up in their imagination."

"Like spirit ships."

Zufar shrugged.

"It could have sunk," Saint-Julien thought aloud.

"I believe they are deep waters in those inlets," Zufar said carefully. "But if it sinks, there are no survivors."

"Can I speak with the engineer? Telephone him?"

Zufar shook his head. "Mr Keith telephoned me from a town where there is a telephone. Each Holy Day he spends with his woman. Home comforts. A man, even one like Mr Keith, needs the love of a woman." His eye wandered wistfully to the patiently waiting figure of Chantal. "You will need to see him at the village where he works. I have a map. It is only accessible by sea." From the *zajiybah* gazelle skin bag attached to his belt, he extracted a crumpled piece of paper. "My clerk draws this for me from a map. It is not good, but it will help you find him."

"I am for ever in your debt, Excellency," Saint-Julien replied.

Crooked teeth showed as Zufar smiled. His scrawny hand gripped the Corsican's wrist. "Remember that, friend. You are for ever in my debt. And remember this, I have been visited by the man called Major Harry. He makes it clear to me that to associate with you will be much to the displeasure of Sultan Qaboos Bin Said. And I do not wish to displease His Majesty. I do this for old friendship, and for the sad story of the lady who wears a hat like a man."

"It is understood," Saint-Julien replied. "This meeting has not taken place."

"Where will you go now?"

"To Musandam. To find the spirit ship."

# 14

"The bastards," Clay murmured.

Another tanker had been hit in the Gulf. They heard it over the radio as *Gulf Bullpup* steamed north towards Musandam after her pickup rendezvous at Al Muntaifa.

Again it had been Iranian Boghammars, circling the defenceless giant like rabid dogs of the sea. Snapping and snarling, riddling the bridge with heavy machine gun fire, killing the first mate and injuring many others.

Eventually the attackers were driven off by the arrival of an American helicopter gunship.

"Bastards," Clay repeated. "They seem to know just how far they can provoke the Yanks and the British without fear of retaliation."

Saint-Julien said: "They are fighting a war. In war you must disrupt your enemy's supplies."

"The Saudis and the Kuwaitis are not at war."

"In all but name," Saint-Julien answered shortly. "They all fear Khomeini, support the Iraqis."

Chantal sided with Clay. For her the distinction between black and white was clear. "It is wrong to kill innocent seamen of neutral countries. It is not their war."

Saint-Julien was unmoved. "They've made it theirs. They know the score, they know the risk. The money is good. That is why they are here. No one forced them."

Clay understood the Corsican's hard-bitten cynicism. "I'll tell you something to make you smile. The Iranians in the Boghammars, the ones causing all the trouble. We trained them, the British. In Bahrain back in the late seventies. I was part of a training cadre – run by the Special Boat Service, training Iranian divers – based at Bandar Abbas. Of course it was some time ago, but I've no doubt some of them are the same men. At least those who've survived Khomeini's purges."

Saint-Julien shrugged. "What seeds we sow, eh? And the Iranians, what is their calibre as fighting men?"

"It was a long time ago. But okay as I remember. Just lacking in self-confidence. Afraid to lose face. But in the end they turned out pretty good." He screwed up his eyes as he tried to remember." One in particular, I recall. We became quite good friends. I'd have been pleased to have had him in my squadron. Now, what the devil was his name?"

"Land approach!" Tokyo called suddenly from the helm.

The headland of Ra's Sarkān was a dark grey smudge emerging from the heat haze.

"Darvish," Clay muttered absently. "That was his name. Darvish Hamman."

No one else heard. Tokyo was saying: "We must not get too close. No wish to alert anyone on board your ship. China and me, we say drop kedge anchor near headland. Then we take dinghy to find the village."

"That makes good sense," Chantal agreed.

It was to be a long, wet ride. The outboard thrust along at a steady five knots in a careful route between the headlands of Ra's Sarkān in the south and Ra's Dillah in the north. Between them they formed the mouth of a vast enclosed bay named Khawr Ḥabalayn. That bay itself created the southern knuckle of the great Musandam peninsula. Distance between their craft and the landfall on each side was some one and a half miles. It was sufficient, in the early afternoon heat haze, to obscure their approach from the coast.

Two hours after leaving Tokyo alone aboard *Gulf Bullpup*, the heavily laden inflatable chugged into the lee of the *jebel* where it fell sheer away to the sea. The sudden shade was almost chill after the fearsome heat of the sun.

Ahead lay a shingle beach at the apex to the inlet, where half-a-dozen small boats had been pulled ashore. Fishing nets were strung like fences whilst repair work was carried out. Beyond them, a cluster of mud-brick dwellings jostled for a share of the diminishing space before the rocky gradient rose to form a steep pass. A goat watched the new arrivals from his precarious vantage point on a flint track that wound into the mountains. That was the only uninviting landward link to the outside world.

Clay cut back the outboard, the noise reverberating around the canyon walls as it died away to leave just the regular grating of water on the shingle. Slowly the fishermen left their nets and upturned boats to join the small gathering of curious children. Women suddenly scurried for the dark doorways of their mud houses, drawing their veils as the strangers approached.

First ashore was Clay, wading the last few feet to greet whom he assumed to be the village headman. A small, thin Arab with a ragged turban and patterned russet *dishdasha*.

Warily he accepted Clay's offered hand, clearly unsure of the words in Omani Arabic. He didn't smile, but exchanged a few sentences with his fellow fishermen. One of them spoke to a young lad who, grinning widely, scampered back up the beach. Clay watched him run to a small tent which had been wedged in the only available area of nearly flat land. The boy went inside to reappear only moments later holding the hand of a white man.

Clay put his age at around forty, but the sun and the booze had taken its toll, so it was difficult to be certain. He wore jeans and trainers and a check shirt that strained against his beer gut. He was broad-faced and tanned with thinning auburn hair, and the stubble on his chin suggested that he hadn't shaved for several days.

The tone when he spoke wasn't particularly friendly. "What d'you want here? The locals don't speak English. Nor Omani Arabic either."

"I'm looking for a Mr Keith?" Clay replied. "Afraid I haven't got a surname."

"Well?"

"You're him?"

Still no smile. "That depends whether or not you're from the tax office."

Clay grinned. He was certain he'd found his man. "Zufar sent us. Said you had word of a spirit ship?"

"Oh that," the man replied and shook Clay's hand with little more enthusiasm than had the village headman. "Keith Evans."

"Rick Clay. My friends Saint-Julien and Chantal."

Later, as they sat around a driftwood fire outside the tent, Keith Evans explained his earlier reticence. "I thought you were expats joy-riding. Get the bastards everywhere now. Driving their bloody Toyotas and Nissans into the interior for weekend picnics. Wadi-bashing they call it. Make a thorough pest of themselves with the Omani villagers. Same at sea. Racing around with their confounded speedboats, carving through the fishermen's nets . . ." He reached forward and turned the fish he was smoking. "A far cry from when I first arrived here back in '72. The military airfield was under bombardment from the rebels when I arrived. Plane landed, I was bundled out, and it took straight off again. There's me, standing like a bleedin' refugee with my suitcase in the middle of the battlefield with explosions goin' off all round. I knew then things could only get better." He grinned. "Been all over the interior since. Engineering projects like the one here, a freshwater well. In those days the British set up an informal intelligence network of those who worked with the Arabs in remote areas. That's how I met up with Zufar, for my sins."

"Beer?" Clay offered, opening the sixpack of lager he'd brought ashore. Zufar had told Saint-Julien of Mr Keith's weakness.

The engineer sniffed and viewed the can with hostility. "I only drink at weekends."

"Break the habit of a lifetime."

Evans glowered. "Someone's been talking. I take the booze seriously, see. So I take a liquid diet over the weekends, sober up and spend the rest of the working week on the Scarsdale." He patted his paunch and glanced at Chantal. "Gotta keep in trim for the ladies." His smile was nervous.

"Do you ever go home?" she asked.

"This is home. When I take leave I go to Bangkok or Hong Kong. There's nothing left for me in the UK."

There was no hint of self-pity in his voice. It was just a statement of fact. Chantal detected an underlying sense of sadness in his words, but Evans's taciturn manner didn't invite inquiry.

Saint-Julien just laughed. "So like me in *le Légion* you come here to forget, eh?"

Evans granted him one of his rare smiles; instinctively he took to the rough-mannered Corsican. "Search me, I've forgotten!" He turned back to Clay. "So what's so important about this ship to bring you lot out here?"

Clay outlined the problem without reference to *Clarion Call*'s real cargo. At mention of D'Arcy's name, Evans studied the flames of the fire. "I think I remember him – yeah, sure I do. Got a nasty scar on his cheek. Had a set-to with Major Harry about that time. Harry wanted to intern old Shaykh Zufar and D'Arcy reckoned, handled right, the old sod could be persuaded to the Sultan's side."

"And he was right?" Chantal asked.

"With old Zufar, sweetheart, who can tell! But seriously, he's a Minister now, so I guess that speaks for itself."

The barbecued fish was ready and Evans served up the simple fare with a couple of cans of baked beans. Washed down with cool lager under the warm star-filled sky, it was a meal that none of them would forget.

Afterwards, Evans invited the village headman and a couple of older fishermen to join them. The engineer translated as Saint-Julien and Clay asked a series of questions. They confirmed what Zufar had told them in outline. But there was more.

"A few nights back," Evans explained, "they said there were lights on the water around the inlet where the spirit ship had vanished. And deep rumbling noises coming from under the sea. The fishermen who saw it were very spooked and came back to the village. Next day they went out to take a cautious look. Still the inlet was deserted, but hundreds of dead fish floated on the surface. Nothing outwardly wrong with them. No tear marks from nets or hooks, no fungi. They got out of that place as fast as they could."

"The spirit ship?" Clay asked.

Evans swigged at his lager. "What would you think in their position? Angry lost souls, or somesuch."

"Can they pinpoint the location of these dead fish for us?" Saint-Julien asked.

Evans spoke to the headman. "Sure, no problem."

A sudden commotion began at the water's edge. From the light of bobbing hand-held lanterns, they could see the fishing canoe and its two occupants jabbering excitedly. A small crowd was gathering on the shoreline. Instantly the headman stood up by the fire and called out.

Someone shouted back and the headman strode briskly down towards the boat.

"What is happening?" Chantal asked.

Evans grimaced. "I'm not sure. This language is a bit tricky – but I don't like what I *think* I just heard."

Hauling himself to his feet, the engineer led the way to the excited gathering. The canoe had been beached on the shingle and the fishermen were dragging in the net. Something pale and bulky held the other end of it fast in the water.

Others waded out to help pull in the catch.

"Poor sod," Evans breathed. "I was right. Shark."

Chantal turned her head away.

"Not Arab," the engineer observed.

Saint-Julien leaned forward, peering down at the tangled

343

lump of white, rotted flesh. It was unrecognisable until he saw a human head. Just a torso with three pink stumps from which the lifeblood had poured into the sea. Yet the left arm and hand were perfectly intact, as though it did not belong to the rest of the grotesque wreckage of humanity.

"First time I've seen a shark attack in these waters," Clay muttered.

Saint-Julien reached out a hand and ran it over the bloated white flesh of the dead man's back. He studied the tips of his fingers. "Grease."

Clay frowned. "Thick . . . Ship's grease?"

Forcing herself to look, Chantal said: "Like a long-distance swimmer?"

Evans gave her a curious look.

"He has a wedding ring, see!" she said suddenly.

Saint-Julien picked up the rigid limb without hesitation and wrenched the gold band from the finger.

Evans called for a lantern.

"I cannot read the inscription," Saint-Julien said.

Chantal held out her hand and took the ring, turning it carefully against the flickering light. "It is engraved in English. *To my darling Tom. My love for ever. Pauline.*"

"Tom?" Clay asked.

Chantal shook her head slowly. No, it couldn't be. Not this decaying corpse at her feet. Not the handsome, smiling young man she had met months before at Flax Wharf?

"What is it?" Saint-Julien demanded.

"I am afraid it might be Rober's man. Tom Wilmot. Rober's man on *Clarion Call*."

"Wilmot?" The Frenchman blinked. He had only ever heard of the man and had failed to register the connection. "Tom Wilmot, *mon dieu*! Are you sure?"

Chantal swallowed hard, reached to the lolling head and turned the distorted face towards her. She looked long and hard, trying to visualise what the dead man would look like without the overblown flesh.

Shakily, she stood. "I cannot be certain – not for sure, but, yes, I think it is Tom Wilmot."

Saint-Julien looked out at the black void of the inlet. "Then *Clarion Call* is somewhere out there."

Bob Tanner, Commander of the Anti-Terrorist Branch sat hunched over the kitchen table in D'Arcy's living quarters. He had demanded a meeting in private, with Nadirpur the only other person present.

The dark eyes glowered beneath the thick brows which were knitted together in a fierce frown to let everyone know just how displeased he was. "I have just come from a COBRA meeting. I can tell you I was given a stormy ride. As I've pointed out, the government has an absolute 'no deal' policy with terrorists. So your message to Reg Roman yesterday – that you intend to offer money – was not well received."

D'Arcy held him in a steady gaze. "That can't be helped."

"Well, Mr Nadirpur's difficult position was understood. Your view that, if nothing is offered at your next talk with the kidnappers, then a fatality could occur was put forward. Reg Roman agreed with your estimation. The question was referred back to the very highest level, D'Arcy." He swallowed hard as though taking a bitter pill; perhaps he considered that he'd lost his chance of a knighthood for ever. "Luckily for you, we have a very compassionate Prime Minister."

Nadirpur's eyes lit up. "So it is agreed?"

Tanner looked at him scathingly. "Only a compromise has been agreed. You may offer private money, but on the strict understanding that it is not paid. Under any circumstances."

D'Arcy said: "There's no guarantee the kidnappers will even consider the idea yet."

"If they do, it is obviously in all of our interests to spread the negotiations for as long as possible. Each day will get us closer to locating the kidnappers. At the moment we're

345

investigating everyone who has hired or purchased a video camera in the past twenty-four hours. Every shop in the country will be visited by local CID officers." He allowed himself a tight smile. "Be assured, gentlemen, the net is closing."

The words cheered Nadirpur, but D'Arcy realised that the police would also require the almost inevitable lucky break. He just prayed it would come sooner rather than later.

However, any sense of renewed optimism was soon shattered when the kidnapper next telephoned.

"You have the video recording. It is satisfactory." It was a statement.

"Yes," Nadirpur replied, consulting D'Arcy's script. "It is satisfactory for the moment –"

The voice interrupted fiercely: "Then our ship?"

"Listen, listen," Nadirpur said quickly. "We have learned that my ship was indeed hijacked, off the coast of Oman. There is an eyewitness locally. So now we are looking very carefully, but I cannot promise what will be found."

The man at the other end sounded uncertain. After a brief hesitation he said: "You can say that at any time. Why should I believe you?"

"Because you hold my wife and daughter," Nadirpur retorted. "We are making progress, but we *must* have more time."

"There is no time!" the caller snapped back. "Someone will die now. That will speed you up –"

"Don't hang up!" Nadirpur pleaded. "Money! I will give you money for time! To prove my good faith."

"We don't want money!" The voice at the other end was almost a scream.

"Six hundred thousand dollars!" Nadirpur shouted. "Everything I can raise in two days."

D'Arcy glanced at his watch. They'd been talking for nineteen seconds.

"No money!" the man yelled. He hung up.

*　　*　　*

346

Shamlou left the telephone kiosk in the Slough shopping centre and slipped into the passing crowd of lunchtime shoppers, making his way up the steps to the multistorey car park stack.

He was deeply troubled as he gunned the yellow van into life and negotiated the tight turns down to the congested urban dual carriageway. He had not been prepared for Nadirpur's sudden offer of money. It had thrown him, taken control of the situation out of his hands.

At the busy roundabout he narrowly missed colliding with another vehicle and scolded himself severely. His nerves were shot, he knew that. Events the previous day had badly shaken him.

He had been on the Intercity express, returning to London from Birmingham after his telephone call to D'Arcy with instructions for collecting the video. Having spent longer than he had intended on the telephone, he was nervous that the police would be able to get a trace. Yet that in itself did not explain his deep sense of foreboding. After all, that was why he'd taken the trouble to go all the way to the Midlands. And he knew it would take only seconds for him to disappear into the mass of shoppers nearby – long before any policeman on the beat could be diverted to intercept him.

By the time he caught the southbound 125 he felt more relaxed, confident that no one was following. But later on the journey, as he drank his coffee, he became inexplicably disturbed by the arrival of the ticket inspector. There was another British Rail official with him, probably a supervisor. Shamlou didn't like his dour face and penetrating gaze. It made him uncomfortable and he found himself trying to avoid the man's eyes.

His nerves returned with a vengeance. By the time he reached Euston he was physically trembling. Even the fact that there was not a uniformed policeman in sight did nothing to quell his anxiety.

There were so many people just standing around watching the passengers. He became angry with himself. Just people waiting for relatives – like any railway station in the world.

He bowed his head and scurried for the subway that led down to the underground taxi rank. There was a long queue. More people. Everyone appeared to be looking at him. Again he felt the hot flush of fear and unbuttoned his collar. He felt trapped. There was no way he could wait.

He retraced his footsteps, back up to the station concourse, then left by the main exit and set off at a brisk pace south towards central London.

Fifteen minutes later he found himself in the bustle of Oxford Street. He glanced around at the sea of blank faces swimming before his eyes. Everyone was a potential plain-clothes policeman. He scoured the throng for the man in the blue shirt. The one he'd seen at Euston, like the one he'd seen at Gordon Square, like the one he'd seen in Bloomsbury Street. Were they the same man? Or the woman in the grey slacks? Was she still walking on the other side of the street? Or was she hiding in some shop doorway?

And the taxis. Everywhere black taxis. They all looked the same and they were always there. Every time he looked there was a taxi. Dawdling behind him. Parked in this side street, parked in that side street.

It seemed that every cab driver in London was watching him. Suddenly the black taxis took on an air of menace, as though an orchestrated arm of London's secret police. He was in a sweat now.

A bus hooted violently. He leapt aside onto the pavement as the red double-decker thundered past.

That was it. He took to his heels and fled down the nearest narrow street, running for his life into the labyrinth of Soho. He took one turning after another. Occasionally he stopped to regain his breath, to check for pursuit. Still there was nothing.

Eventually he plunged down into the Tube station at Leicester Square. He travelled two stops east to Holborn, then doubled back west to Green Park. He resurfaced on the London streets and checked for the umpteenth time for signs of his imagined pursuers.

He carried out several more deceptive manoeuvres as he had been trained before finally boarding a north-bound Underground train at Baker Street.

When he eventually alighted at Northwick Park where his van was parked in a nearby side street, he was mentally and physically drained.

Now he had this new problem on his plate. The money offer. And it was not a decision that he could make. For the first time since the kidnap he would have to consult his 'controller'.

During his drive back to Harrow he located a kiosk that accepted Phonecards. He rang the direct Paris number of Azadi at the Iranian Embassy.

When he got through, he said simply: "Sword of Islam."

There was a pause and he imagined the grey man thumbing through his notebook for the list of codenames that indicated a series of public telephones situated in different areas of Paris. The French authorities were known to be monitoring all calls to the Iranian Embassy. Eventually Azadi said: " 'Peacock'. Fall-back 'Carpet', then 'Nougat'. One hour."

The phone went dead.

Shamlou looked at his diary and the list of codenames he'd written in the back. Next to each was a Paris number. He wrote them out on another page. His 'controller' would be waiting at the first public box to receive the call in sixty minutes. Then there were two other numbers in case the first was out of order or Azadi was unable to dislodge a chatty caller. Shamlou would try the others at twenty-minute intervals, and then repeat the process if necessary.

But it was not necessary. One hour later Shamlou rang 'Peacock' from another Phonecard box. It was immediately answered by Azadi.

Briefly, using open code, Shamlou brought his 'controller' up to date.

349

At the mention of Nadirpur's money offer, Azadi was very calm, relaxed. "Speak to me again in two hours. Phone 'Carpet', fall-back 'Nougat' and 'Zagros'."

Shamlou understood. He knew that the *Pessarane Behesht* were orchestrated from Geneva. His 'controller', too, would need to consult with a higher authority.

What Shamlou did not know was that the higher authority was already in Paris. Such delicate matters could not be disclosed over the telephone.

Azadi hung up and immediately redialled another number from his coin booth. He did not know the address of the new number, and he did not remember the brusque voice which answered. He did know, however, that he was talking directly to the man called Sabbah.

"I have news."

A pause. "Meet me in half-an-hour. On the quai de Gesvres. There is a pet shop."

Although Azadi did not remember the voice, he had met Sabbah before, so he asked nothing about recognition.

In his apartment in the run-down Arab quarter of the 20th *arrondissement*, Sabbah rose from his easy chair and stared through the open shutters of the window at the shamble of rooftops and television aerials. This area had been chosen so that he could pass in the local community of Middle Eastern and Chinese nationalities without attracting attention.

He had no need for grand hotels. This spartan room was sufficient for his needs. A bed, a telephone and a television. A shower cubicle that had to be shared with cockroaches, and a kitchenette where the sink was piled with unwashed plates and cartons of sour milk. Even this place was a palace compared with the Beirut slum of his childhood.

It should not have been like that. He should have grown up with his brothers in the pretty palm grove village in Palestine where his father was a cobbler. Although his family were minority Shi'ite Muslims of Lebanese extraction living in a Sunni nation, there was no animosity in their friendly village. All had been hard work, sunlight and peace in the dusty palm grove.

That was what he had heard on his grandmother's knee.

That was how it should have been. But the reality had been Beirut.

There he had grown up, witness to the legacy of French ineptitude and high-handedness when it had granted Lebanon independence in 1943. Witness to the results of British partition of Palestine in 1948 into separate Arab and Jewish states. Witness to the Zionists' declaration of the state of Israel one year later.

He had heard all those stories on the knee of his grandmother in the parlour. Had seen for himself the wretched lives of the thousands of Palestinians pouring into Lebanon, squeezed into the squalid refugee camps of Sabra and Shatila. Had shared that wretched life. Freezing in their makeshift shanties in the winter snows. Collecting drips in buckets when it rained. Seeing his father fined for trying to improve his home because the Lebanese Government feared the camps would become permanent. Had seen his own mother die, old before her time.

While all around him Beirut's luxury hotels and clubs were filled to brimming with the *nouveaux riches* of the oil-glutted Middle East, the ports filled with expensive yachts, the beaches crowded with half-naked sunworshippers.

Lebanon had become the jewel of the Arab world while he had abandoned school to sell chewing gum, cakes and cigarettes on the street corners of Ain al-Rummaneh. A child with his nose pressed up against the restaurant window, drooling over flavours he could only imagine.

That was how it was. And for Sabbah it ended early one morning in 1973 when the Lebanese Air Force bombed the refugee camps in retaliation against the PLO guerrillas living there.

He and his two brothers had lifted the body of their dead father from the debris. His blood still warm on their skin.

That was why he had taken up the fight. To be able to return to his homeland. To wreak vengeance on the Israelis who had taken his land, and their American protectors. On the French and the British who had started it all.

He had joined the PLO under Arafat, fast losing patience with the leader who was moving away from the armed struggle to fight on the diplomatic front.

Sitting in the flyblown cafés of the refugee camp, he had learned of the legend of Al-Hasan ibn-al-Sabbah, as highly regarded amongst his fellow freedom fighters as were Robin Hood and William Tell in Europe.

Then one sunny, dusty morning he awoke after an amazing dream, a dream so vivid it was impossible to separate it from reality. He was Sabbah.

He realised that, while the PLO guerrillas might hold the legend in awe, only he had Iranian ancestry. Only he could be the direct descendant of Sabbah, rising to the call of Allah after a gap of centuries. And the more he thought about it, the more he believed.

In 1976 three men crossed into Israel; the next day a small landmine explosion killed an Israeli soldier and injured two more in the patrol. Unusually the *Jerusalem Post* received a note claiming responsibility. The editor did not publish the claim, instead passing it to the security service. The Sons of Heaven were reborn.

He stepped back from the window and closed the shutters on the Paris skyline.

It had not been his dream, but it had become his. It had been the dream of the bearded one. But it was all for one, and one for all. And it had served them well.

He slipped a casual jacket over his shirt, locked the door and took the creaking stairs to the street. It was a short walk to the Père-Lachaise station from which he took the Métro to Réaumur Sebastopol before changing for Châtelet.

The remaining distance to the north bank of the Seine he walked at a leisurely pace. He waited in the leafy shade of the embankment, apparently browsing along the stalls of antique prints and books, from where he could see the cages of the pet shop which spilled onto the pavement.

Azadi pretended to take an interest in the mynah bird, but in his slate grey suit stood out awkwardly amongst the shoppers and tourists.

"Hello, Azadi."

The Iranian jumped. He did not recognise the speaker. "*Agha*?"

"Come, walk with me."

Azadi was uneasy; this man was nothing like he remembered. It wasn't just the missing beard. He looked thinner, shorter and younger. He really could not believe it was the same man.. Yet he had heard the rumours that Sabbah was a master of disguise. Some of the more gullible recruits to the *Pessarane Behesht* swore he had magical and mystical powers, as the legend said. It was true enough that he was often reported to be in several different countries on the same day. The 'controller' did not believe in such fantasies, but he could hardly deny the evidence of his own eyes. Certainly Sabbah was *the* master of disguise.

The leader poked a finger absently through the bars of a poultry cage. "So tell me, what happens in England?"

Azadi quickly told him as they left the pet shop and strolled along the *quai*, finishing with the news of Nadirpur's money offer.

Sabbah laughed suddenly. "That is interesting! Well, why not?"

The 'controller' did not understand. "But it is the ship you want."

"And will we get it?"

"I have a feeling Nadirpur is genuine. He really is trying to locate the ship. I believe he truly wants more time."

Sabbah knew that too. From his agents in Oman he had heard of strangers asking questions. But he did not pass that gem of knowledge to the 'controller'. He said: "Well then, to be realistic, we will give that time." He paused. "But at a price. Not a mere six hundred thousand dollars.

Tell Nadirpur that the price for time will be ten million pounds sterling."

Azadi gawped.

"Tell Shamlou to squeeze for as much as he can as quickly as he can. Don't let up the pressure. We will have the ship *and* the money."

He turned away from the 'controller' then and disappeared into the crowd of pedestrians strolling along the *quai*. There was a smile on his face as he walked. It was not often that you had the chance to screw the French and the British – the countries responsible for the start of all Palestine's troubles.

Momentarily he thought of the man behind Nadirpur's attempts at negotiation. The man whose name appeared on *Clarion Call*'s documentation. Robert D'Arcy. He knew a lot about him now. People in the West sometimes regarded Iranians as fools, he knew that. Tabloid papers gave the impression the country was run by madmen. Again he smiled. Let them, it suited his purpose that they forgot that the country had a sophisticated intelligence system and long-standing relationships with Britain. Like the reputable firm of City solicitors who had hired an extremely efficient private detective to investigate IAP.

Yes, Sabbah knew a lot about Robert D'Arcy. Had the measure of the man. Knew that really the kidnap negotiations were a battle of wills between himself and the man who had once been a major in the SAS.

Without being consciously aware of it, Sabbah had decided that the adversary he had never met had become an enemy of Islam.

As he took a seat beneath the awning of the pavement café in the rue du Pont-Neuf to order a mineral water and ice he realised that he had already decided that Robert D'Arcy was going to die.

Dave Forbes pinned the enlargements on the cork noticeboard and stepped back admiringly.

"Your friend's done a good job," D'Arcy observed.

354

"He owed me," Forbes said.

D'Arcy turned to Roquelaure. "Recognise any of them, Pierre?"

The Frenchman smiled broadly. "These are excellent! We can put a name to every one of these faces." He moved closer to the board and jabbed a finger at the first photograph. "I confirm that's Sheikh Abdullah Hayira, Jordanian, Spidex chairman. These others, all directors. The Iraqi. These two from Saudi. This one is, I think, Kuwaiti. And this one represents the Emirates."

"But still no sign of Cupplewaite from Oman," D'Arcy reminded.

Roquelaure shrugged as he lit a fresh Gitane from the butt of the last. He always chain-smoked when he was excited, and he was extremely excited now. "When were these taken?"

"All through yesterday," Forbes replied. "The shame was our bug was found. The bastards actually had the house swept by a professional firm."

D'Arcy said: "At least we know they're here because of the waves we've been making. Here and in Oman."

"And what progress have the police made in finding the kidnappers?" Roquelaure asked.

"Apparently they got very close to one yesterday. In fact Reg Roman believes they may have him on a video film."

Roquelaure was astounded. "That is amazing good fortune, *mon ami*."

D'Arcy shook his head. "Not quite the good fortune it *could* have been, Pierre. You see, after the kidnapper telephoned from Birmingham yesterday, the police had helicopters up looking for a yellow van returning down the M1, and on all Intercity trains to London. They had Anti-Terrorist Branch detectives on each service in the afternoon to pinpoint any passengers who could fit the bill of our Iranian chums. Details were radioed through to plain-clothes surveillance squads waiting at Euston.

"According to Reg, it was all pretty shambolic while

each team tried to pick out and follow their allocated quarry. Twenty-five suspects in all – you can imagine the chaos with a four-man box following each, plus backup vehicles. Reg reckoned it cost a fortune.

"Anyway, they've since managed to eliminate twenty from their inquiries; three are still under discreet investigation – probably illegal immigrants. And two they lost. One in particular got as far as Oxford Street before something spooked him, and he raced off like the devil was after him. So he's the favourite. Now the police are running back the platform video at Euston to get a positive ID on the man."

Roquelaure smirked happily. "Today big brother always watches you."

"The lead on the typewriter used for the kidnapper's original note came to nothing, I'm afraid. None of the buyers of IBM golf ball typewriters in the early eighties corresponded with the computer list of 25,000 Iranian immigrants or suspect organisations."

"The end of the trail?" Roquelaure suggested.

D'Arcy shrugged. "Looks that way. Reg says they're now adding that list of typewriter buyers to the computer suspect list for any future cross-referencing. Meanwhile local police are following up the yellow builder's van lead through the DVLC in Swansea. But with the likelihood of number plate and colour changes, that's going to be a real plod."

"It seems impossible," Forbes agreed.

"But they'll slip up eventually," D'Arcy said. "For every twenty-five contingencies the kidnappers have thought of, there'll be another twenty-five they've overlooked. And you can't plan for the totally unexpected. It's the unwritten law of policework. The question is, can we wait that long?" He paused. "That's why we've offered the kidnappers six hundred thousand dollars. All Nadirpur can raise immediately."

"I understand," Roquelaure said, "but that is not a lot to satisfy people like the *Pessarane Behesht*."

"It's all his working capital reserve. It'll mean shedding staff and closing offices. He's already put one of his ships on the market. When that's sold – if he gets a buyer – he'll be down to one ship. And one ship hardly constitutes a shipping line."

"That is sad, *mon ami*," Roquelaure said, studying D'Arcy's face closely. "But I may be able to help."

"Yes?"

"The DGSE may agree to funding a cash payment to the kidnappers."

D'Arcy was stunned. "That's marvellous news."

"But, *mon ami*, there is a condition."

"Ah, so what is the catch?"

"That Philippe Chaumont is released along with Mrs Nadirpur and her daughter."

D'Arcy felt the flash of anger. "No, Pierre, that is not on! We're hired to save a woman and child who are in *immediate* danger. Chaumont is not. Besides, to involve his release would be a dangerous complication. It would stink of French Government involvement, which is the last thing I want. As it is, I think I have just about persuaded the kidnappers that Nadirpur really is the innocent party in all this."

"Be reasonable, Rober'," Roquelaure countered. "Even if they accept your paltry offer, it will leave Nadirpur a broken man."

"He already is a broken man, Pierre, if you hadn't noticed. He's lost all interest in his business."

The Frenchman's attitude was hard. "He will recover, and then he'll wish he'd taken this offer. And it is not an offer the DGSE has made lightly. The only reason is that – if their involvement in this sorry business becomes public knowledge – they can claim at least it secured the release of one of France's hostages."

"I've told you before, Pierre, IAP clients come before your government."

Roquelaure showed a rare display of anger. "Others may interpret your refusal as pure self-interest."

"Meaning?"

"That maybe it suits you to have poor Philippe rotting in Beirut. Rober', this may be our only chance for years to get him back. Perhaps *ever*!"

"He has a point," Forbes reflected.

D'Arcy turned. "I don't remember asking your opinion."

Forbes stood his ground. "You got it anyway, boss."

There was still an uneasy stand-off amongst the three men until midday when the kidnapper called again. Nadirpur, who had only just risen, looked tired and emaciated.

His hand was trembling as he picked up the receiver. If they said no deal again, that was it. His wife and child were dead. And his own stupidity and his own misjudgement meant he might just as well have pulled the trigger himself. "Nadirpur here."

"Your proposal, we have decided to be generous," the voice said rapidly. "You have three extra days before your wife and child is killed. Three days."

"It is not enough!" Nadirpur blurted without thinking. D'Arcy nodded his approval.

"If you are telling the truth, it will be enough time."

"Give me a week. I must have a week. There is much area to cover."

A tense pause. "You have five days. I am generous. But it will cost you two million sterling a day."

D'Arcy closed his eyes.

"That is ludicrous!" Nadirpur gasped.

"Ten million. I am generous."

D'Arcy shoved the script back in front of Nadirpur who, in his anguish, was in danger of forgetting it. D'Arcy had been half-expecting this development. But never ten million pounds.

"L-look," Nadirpur stuttered, "I have six hundred thousand now. In two days it can be yours. It will take weeks to raise more. I cannot force someone to buy my ships. And insurances will not be settled for months – if ever!"

"You will think of something. You have had plenty time." Complacent, knowing he once again held the initiative.

Hastily D'Arcy scrawled some figures on Nadirpur's pad.

The Iranian nodded. "Look, maybe I can scrape another two hundred thousand. From friends, a bank, I don't know."

"Ten million sterling." The voice was positively gloating. "In five days." He hung up.

"Shit!" D'Arcy rasped.

Nadirpur was ashen.

"He knows he's got us," Forbes growled.

D'Arcy forced himself to concentrate. "No wait, he'll know we can't agree to that. He'll want to know what we *can* make. My guess is he'll let us stew a while."

Forbes agreed. "There'll be no call tomorrow. Maybe two days."

There was no reason for the kidnappers to ring for news of the ship. If Nadirpur needed to contact them, he had to place a specifically worded small ad in the *Evening Standard*.

Roquelaure said: "There is no way the DGSE will go to ten million. They have already spent millions on the original cargo."

"I said I don't want your money," D'Arcy snapped.

The general smiled gently. "My dear Rober', from what I just hear, our poor friend has no choice."

D'Arcy glowered, but knew in his heart that Roquelaure was right. Additional French money would give negotiations a much needed new lease of life. At least it would give him the chance to 'move the goal posts' and reset new counterdemands that would not be based on extra time, but would include the release of Nadirpur's family and the wretched Philippe Chaumont in Beirut.

He spent the afternoon in conference, planning the strategy. Roquelaure finally agreed on a figure of three million sterling as the maximum to which the DGSE could be persuaded to go. Nadirpur should accept anything under that figure.

When the meeting broke up, he found Brandy waiting for him.

"Hi, boss, you've got a visitor in the waiting room."

"Who?"

"One very beautiful and anonymous lady."

He pushed aside the curtain that covered the two-way mirror. Mrs Sheikh Hayira sat demurely in the plush white kid sofa, flicking through a dog-eared copy of *Elle*. She didn't look as though she was taking in a word.

Opening the door, he said: "This is a pleasant surprise."

She rose quickly to her feet. "Forgive me coming here uninvited, Mr D'Arcy. I had to see you."

"Yes?"

"It was something you said when you were at my house." She fingered her clutch bag as she searched for the right words. "It left me unsettled, worried. I have not had much sleep, wondering if it is true."

"Wondering if what is true, Mrs Hayira?"

"About the woman and her child held hostage."

D'Arcy looked at her steadily. Was this some sort of ploy? Some way of finding out how much he knew? "Follow me," he said, and showed her into the now deserted 'Ops Room'.

He picked up a folder, extracted the kidnappers' photograph of the hostages and tossed it down on the table.

It took a couple of seconds for her to register what she was looking at. No doubt she had never seen anything like it before. She swallowed hard, visibly shaken. Dragging her eyes from the photograph, she looked at D'Arcy. "I don't think I really believed you."

"Now you know. I'm not in the habit of lying. Everything I told you was true."

The dark eyes clouded. "The hijacked ship. I would not believe it of my husband."

"Perhaps he has his reasons. I don't know what his priorities are. Or whether he thinks he's justified in what he's done. I don't really care. All I know is that he is going to pay for his actions."

"Is that what you meant about going to the press?"

Got her worried now, D'Arcy thought. "Only if it is necessary."

"Is that why you placed the microphone?"

He decided to play an ace. "If you will look over there, Mrs Hayira, on the noticeboard. A selection of photographs of the people involved in your husband's conspiracy."

She blanched. "I see." Her voice was faint. At length she turned to face him. "What can I do, Mr D'Arcy? You must understand that I have very little influence over my husband's business affairs."

"If you really want to help, persuade Sheikh Hayira to see me. Let us discuss a way out of this."

"He may not listen."

"Tell him what you've seen here. The picture of Mrs Nadirpur and her daughter. The photographs of his co-directors. Tell him we have tapes of evidence enough to satisfy both the media and the police. Tell him he has twenty-four hours to agree to meet me."

"I will tell my husband."

# 15

*Gulf Bullpup* creaked as she rolled gently with the swell, held fast by her kedge anchor.

Clay and Tokyo had spent the morning aboard one of the fishing canoes wearing borrowed *dishdashas* to get a closer look at the inlet where the spirit ship had disappeared. Although it was too dangerous to go right in, from a distance they had been able to eliminate much of the landscape as a possible hiding place for a ship the size of *Clarion Call*. That left an area some two miles square which was not directly visible from dhows trafficking across the inlet mouth.

"Who will come with me?" Chantal asked.

"You're not going, for a start," Clay said decisively.

"I've been diving since I was a child," she protested.

"Tokyo and I will go. We work well as a team."

"It is not your mission," Saint-Julien challenged.

"It is now, old son," Clay grinned. "You said yourself you're rusty, Saint-Julien, and this could get dangerous. From the evidence we've seen with those fish, someone's got hand grenades or explosives and isn't afraid to use them. Besides, Tokyo and I know how to handle the Jet Raider."

"You intend to use *that* contraption?" Saint-Julien asked. He was 'old school' who thought only in terms of inflatables or collapsible Klepper canoes.

"That's what I designed it for," Clay retorted. "It'll be an ideal test. Meanwhile you and Chantal must stay aboard here."

Reluctantly Chantal agreed. "But it will be just as dangerous for you."

Clay shrugged. "We don't intend to do anything heroic. Just locate the ship – if it's there – and get back. After that it's up to your boss."

"You should have some personal protection," Saint-Julien said.

"Well we won't carry firearms, if that's what you mean, but we'll do our best to look after ourselves."

His best turned out to be two lethal-looking 'shark-sticks'. When the point was jammed into the belly of a predator, the compressed spring was released, firing a 12-bore shotgun round with devastating effect. It would work as well on a human, Clay assured him.

Tokyo produced two superb Gerber 'Neptune' diving knives with double-edged stainless steel blades and serrations for cutting rope. To be worn with them were 'butcher's gloves' of woven stainless steel and Kevlar 29, which enabled the wearer to grasp razor coral or, for that matter, the blade of an enemy's fighting knife.

The rest of the afternoon was spent checking the scuba equipment and servicing the Jet Raider in preparation for the night's mission.

There was just one brief interlude in the activity when Tokyo spotted an incoming craft.

It was a dhow like any other. But her weathered timbers and tatty, faded red sail belied her steady fifteen knots, no doubt assisted by the throaty engine which suggested more power than was usual for a fishing boat.

A tall figure in flowing black robe and turban stood on the prow.

"Ah, Mr China! I think I see you here."

It was Nasiyb, the sea captain from Sur they had met three days earlier.

"What are you doing in these waters, you old scoundrel?" Clay called as the dhow cut back her engine and drifted alongside. "Smuggling more toilet rolls to Iran?"

Nasiyb deftly jumped the gap. "Even ayatollahs must shit, my friend."

"So what are you really doing here?"

"To help you look for your ship." He grinned widely at his own generosity.

"Thank you, Nasiyb, but I can't afford another ten thousand pounds."

A gold tooth glistened in the smile between the moustache and goatee beard. "There is no charge. I am here of my own free will. Two sets of eyes are better than one."

"We can manage, Nasiyb," Clay replied warily.

The sea captain pulled a face. "So you say, but then why are you at this inlet? I can tell you there is nothing here. No place to hide a big ship. No depth."

"You mean draught?"

Nasiyb shrugged. "No space between a deep keel and a coral bed to rip her heart out. If you will not accept my help, at least accept my advice. Go farther north. That is where I would seek."

They parted company then, and Nasiyb's dhow turned away, restarting her engine and running south along the coast.

It was nearly midnight when Clay and Tokyo began changing into the familiar paraphernalia of the diver: black rubber wet suits, sufficient in these warm waters; 'stab' jackets, inflatable waistcoats for 'stabilisation' of depth, which incorporated a backpack harness for the scuba tank; mask; weightbelt and the regulator octopus of air pipes.

By the time the two all-black spectres appeared on deck, Saint-Julien and Chantal already had the Jet Raider in the water alongside, shark-sticks, harpoon guns and fins strapped to its fuel tanks.

They synchronised watches. "We'll take our time," Clay warned, "so don't panic if we're longer than expected. However, I intend we should be back here by five. That's four hours total. Should be ample. If we're in real trouble and you can help we'll put up a red flare. Bring the *Pup* in pronto. "Sure you can handle her?"

Saint-Julien nodded.

"Good luck," Chantal said and kissed both Clay and Tokyo quickly on the cheek. "And take care."

They descended the ladder, climbed onto the bucking skimmer, completed a final check and started up. A mere whisper issued from the auxiliary water jets which were run off the secondary battery.

With grudging admiration Saint-Julien watched as they cast off and the craft melted into the blackness at a steady two-and-a-half knots.

The slow speed meant an hour's run to reach the point they had selected that morning. It was a small rocky outcrop set half-a-mile into the target inlet. On schedule they reached the first slime-covered boulder of the outcrop and cut the silent motor. Tokyo tested the water depth. Five feet saw him all but disappear.

He rose again, thumbs up. A soft silt patch was a suitable bed for the Jet Raider as Clay opened the buoyancy tank and let her slowly sink below the surface. There it would remain, safe from detection, until it was needed for the return trip.

Clay had allowed for half-an-hour's observation from the rocks before deciding whether to abort or go on, depending on what they saw. In the event there was nothing to be found. Even with their eyes fully adjusted to night vision there was absolutely no sign of human habitation, let alone 15,000 tonnes of freighter.

Clay began to doubt his certainty. The fishermen could have been wrong about the ship and the explosions. Perhaps the dead fish had been diseased. They couldn't even be certain that the corpse, now buried beneath a cairn of stones, was Tom Wilmot . . .

"What you think?" Tokyo asked.

Clay smiled. "Maybe this is a wild goose chase. And you?"

"I think we go look a bit. Too dark. Besides, I like a swim."

The Japanese diver had a point. It was a long way to have come just to go back. And he was right, without night vision devices it was just too dark to be certain.

A decision made, they hauled the stab jackets and scuba cylinders back on and donned fins, hoods and masks. After setting the lubber line on their wrist compasses for a point on the far side of the inlet, they struggled down into the water. With their fast diminishing belief that there was a ship, they took only one shark-stick and harpoon gun between them. It made for a quicker, easier swim.

It took fifteen minutes steady going before they were in the lee of the towering wall on the opposite side of the inlet. The area was even blacker and more forbidding than it had appeared when viewed from the other side.

Visibility was a murky ten metres and the two divers closed up in the world of silence that was broken only by the rush of water and the steady stream of bubbles.

Together they broke surface right against the barnacled wall of rock. Farther along, the profile of the fjord side appeared to bottom out to form a shelf, then rise sharply, only to fall away again sheer to the water.

It struck both men as a curious geological feature, but dramatic rock formations were common phenomena in the region. There could, however, be another explanation. That sudden pinnacle rise at the water's edge, seen in cross-section, could also be the shape of a gigantic tethered ship. In the moon's shadow, it was just impossible to tell.

"What you think?" Tokyo asked, removing his regulator mouthpiece.

"If they've used camo drapes, yes, it could possibly be," Clay said. "I'd guess it's about half-a-mile away. That would also give it the right height."

Tokyo whispered hoarsely: "See it straight on, you would never know. Only this angle it looks more possible. We go in?" He sounded keen.

"We'll go in deep. I don't want to take any chances. At

366

half-a-mile we'll either hit solid rock or a rusty hull. I'll go first and take the shark-stick. You cover me, come in above and as far behind as possible with the harpoon gun in case I hit problems."

"I with you, China baby!" Tokyo enthused.

"Whatever you do, if I get into trouble, make sure you get back – one of us must, or else this whole exercise is pointless."

Deflating his stab jacket, Clay allowed the weight of his lead belt to take him gently down again into the viridescent murk. At intervals he held his nose and blew to equalise the pressure in his ears and eliminated the buildup of mask 'squeeze' by exhaling into it. He repeated the process several times before his feet touched hard rock. To his right he could just make out the dense colour of the inlet wall. To his left the bed fell steeply away to the void of the central gorge.

He checked his depth gauge. Fifteen metres. Above him Tokyo hovered, his shape barely discernible at ten metres distance.

Clay added a touch of air to his stab jacket for neutral buoyancy, so that he hung suspended, just above the rock bed. He then began kicking his fins in a slow, relaxed rhythm to take him on a course parallel to the inlet side. He held the shark-stick in readiness, but ready for what he could hardly imagine.

He still could not bring himself to believe the ship was here. And even if it were, he doubted those guarding their prize would suspect the presence of two frogmen in the middle of the night.

But there he was to be proven very wrong.

He was first to sense rather than see the massive black bulk ahead of him. His pulse began to speed with anticipation. In such conditions it could easily be an optical illusion . . . But the vast blurred shape appeared too uniform and rounded to be part of the fjord wall.

Kicking with renewed vigour, he startled a shoal of tiny fish which parted to allow him through. In his eagerness he pulled too far ahead of Tokyo, who almost immediately lost sight of him.

He had certainly not anticipated the presence of the monofilament net which surrounded the ship like an invisible spider's web. The point of the shark-stick went in first, until the firing mechanism caught in the strands.

For a second he could not comprehend what had happened, what held it fast. As he slowed he felt his octopus of hoses snag, threatening to rip the mouthpiece from his face.

Despite his training to remain calm at all times, the flurry of bubbles betrayed his sudden, anxious breathing. As he turned to look for the cause of the obstruction, he was aware of the demand valve of his scuba cylinder catching behind his neck.

Netting! Fine transparent strands momentarily showed themselves inches from his face, then melted tauntingly out of focus. He cursed his own stupidity and thought instantly to warn Tokyo.

Like a fly stuck in a web he twisted to look for his companion. Nothing, just a rippling green and black fog.

He forced himself to keep calm, breathing slowly and steadily until the stream of bubbles reduced to a trickle. Then he reached down his leg for the double-bladed Gerber strapped to his calf.

He sliced out blindly, ripping the razored edge at the nothingness around him. The only way of telling if he was cutting successfully was the feel of resistance against the blade. Then he discovered that his knife arm had been caught in another invisible hold. He cursed.

The warning sound of Tokyo banging his own knife against his scuba cylinder first alerted Clay, the sound carrying sharply through the eerily muffled silence. He saw the plummeting ball of white phosphor trailing behind the black shape to his left, clear of the net. Then another a few metres behind it, as the second frogman dived from the watch boat.

Frantically Clay struck out again at the unseen netting,

desperate to free himself to tackle the approaching intruders. At last he pulled his right arm free, but he had to let the ensnared shark-stick go. Now snagged only by his demand valve, he was able to turn to face the menacing rubber-suited figures, anonymous behind their face-masks.

He heard and felt the thud and *whoosh* of the harpoon gun as Tokyo fired. The barbed dart streaked past his own ear and embedded itself deep in the first frogman's thigh. Clay sensed the pain the man felt as he clutched his limb with both hands. A knife spun away into the depths. Threads of black blood pumped from the gash in the torn suit. The man signalled to his colleague, thumbs up, and kicked himself towards the surface.

Clay braced himself. The second frogman closed in, patient and wary. Confident and professional, a heavy Puma knife with a wicked seven-inch double blade and protective D-guard handgrip in his right hand. He could see Clay's predicament – the entangled shark-stick and the demand valve were stuck fast. He had witnessed the harpoon dart and knew it was a one-shot weapon. Knew his enemy's ally could not reach him in time.

The frogman circled cautiously, studying the trapped diver as he turned with him, looking for a break.

Clay could think of one consolation. The only sure way to win an underwater struggle was to attack your victim from behind. To grab his hair and rip the mask from his face. To slice his air supply or his throat. But a frontal approach put both men on equal terms, each going for a fatal forward thrust.

For what seemed like minutes they eyed each other, waiting the moment.

Suddenly the frogman moved. Forward with a powerful kick of the thighs, feigned, and lunged to Clay's left in a swift outflanking movement. The Puma knife came down in an ice-pick motion, stabbing viciously at the exposed kidneys.

Clay swung to counter, jerked back by the restraining net. Still he struck out with forward thrusts, kept short to defeat the pull of the water. He felt the Gerber blade ring against the metal of the other's cylinder.

The frogman pressed home his attack. Short, sharp thrusts and backcuts, his left hand scrabbling for a grip on Clay's mouthpiece.

The Gerber whipped across the man's knuckles, slicing the flesh to the bone. A burst of bubbles blew from the man's mask as he gasped. Then he renewed his attack with fury.

Clay felt the sharp pain in his side, aware of the knife point breaking the resistance of the rubber suit and piercing his flesh. He twisted away, feeling the suction of the weapon as it was withdrawn. He reached out his left hand and grabbed the blade with the woven steel palm of the butcher's glove.

Surprise registered in the eyes behind the mask and it gave Clay a moment's advantage to slash the Gerber at his opponent's air hose. But the drag of the water threw his aim, the blade glancing uselessly on the steel of the regulator mouthpiece.

Still gripping the frogman's knife, Clay wrestled for all he was worth. But he was aware of the dull pain in his side and the water darkening with clouds of his own blood. His strength was starting to ebb. His muscles were weakening against the relentless power of the frogman, the needle point of the Puma jerking ever closer to his body again. Coming in for the kill.

Then Tokyo arrived. He swept down on the frogman with the speed and dexterity of a barracuda, coming in from behind. It was over in seconds. Fingers came over the frogman's head, grabbing the lower rim of the mask under his nose, jerking the skull back. As the victim thrashed, Tokyo's knife hand came in with one short, sharp and decisive slash deep into the man's windpipe.

Black froth billowed in a mushroom cloud and a burst of bubbles blasted from the man's slack jaw as he released his mouthpiece. Almost casually Tokyo pressed the inflate button on his victim's stab jacket. The limp body rocketed towards the surface like a marionette pulled away by its strings.

Clay's relief was short-lived. Behind Tokyo two more trails of bubbles were dropping down from the watch boat. He waved at his companion to leave him, but the Japanese diver continued slashing at the monofilament bindings. Yet the more he tried the worse Clay became entangled.

The two new frogmen were closing. Clay could see the outline of spear guns. The surface above became a silvered green ceiling as searchlights were turned on. The black outline of inflatables became clearly visible.

Get out, Tokyo! he willed, gesticulating wildly.

At last his companion decided to look, realised there was no time and sped into the murk. The barb of a harpoon flashed in the refracted light as it streamed after Tokyo's wake. It failed to find its mark.

Slowly Clay threw away his knife and raised his hands.

One frogman trod water, covering with his spear gun whilst the other came in to check the prisoner for other weapons. He found the spare diver's knife, threw it away, then began to cut Clay from the net.

When he had finished he jabbed his thumb upward. Clay nodded. Together, slowly and steadily, they began their ascent to the waiting inflatables of the Jordanian commandos.

Clay lost consciousness the moment they surfaced.


"I don't know how you managed it, pal, but I've gotta tell you, you're walking on very thin ice."

Roy Bliss changed down a gear as he spoke, swinging the ageing Sierra into the mayhem of Hyde Park Corner.

"I seem to make a habit of that," D'Arcy replied evenly. "When did you hear?"

"Sheikh Hayira called me about two hours ago. Just said he and his colleagues wanted to talk to you."

"I didn't need an escort, Roy."

"Don't be too sure, pal. Our influence with them is

strictly limited – those A-rabs like to paddle their own canoes. What I want to know is how you found them and how the hell you persuaded them to talk?"

"That's my business."

Bliss ignored the rebuff, instead lighting a cigarette with one hand while he steered casually with the other. "Hayira asked if you could be trusted. If you were a reasonable man."

"And?"

A wry smile. "I'd get my P45 if my boss knew what I said."

"Thanks."

"Just remember – whatever Sheikh Hayira and his cronies tell you, Century House will deny it."

"Is it that bad?"

"The usual wheeling and dealing. Still trying to put the Great back into Britain." Briskly he negotiated the Marble Arch traffic jam, prompting hoots from several taxi drivers. "Whatever you might think, Rob, I'm not immune to the fact that poor sod's wife and child's lives hang in the balance. Do what you have to do, but don't rock the boat more than you have to. I still have to put this country's interests first. And so should you."

"Thanks for the lecture."

Bliss swung the Sierra left up Portman Street, jumping the red light on the corner with Oxford Street. "Well, propaganda never was my strong point. But if you get in too deep, you won't find anyone standing around to bale you out."

He pulled up in the portico of the Churchill Hotel in Portman Square. As the doorman stepped towards the car, D'Arcy said: "Aren't you coming?"

The SIS man flicked his cigarette stub out of the window. "Like I said, pal, don't expect anyone to be standing around. Including me."

The door was opened.

"You want Suite Two."

The door was closed and D'Arcy watched as Bliss accelerated harshly out into the stream of traffic. In doing so he almost knocked a young man in an Adidas tracksuit off his motorcycle.

Roy Bliss was one hell of a strange character, D'Arcy decided as he turned into the airy lemon-and-grey lobby and took the lift. As a secret service field officer the man had the utterly unscrupulous and professional attitude required for the job, but at least he didn't try to justify himself. Sometimes it could be a dirty job, and he just accepted it. Maybe there was a heart – even a soul – beating somewhere beneath that shabby brown suit.

"Mr D'Arcy, how good of you to come."

For some reason he hadn't expected the beautiful Mrs Hayira to open the door of the suite. Also to his surprise there was no burly minder to check that he was unarmed. Obviously Roy Bliss's assurance that D'Arcy was a reasonable man had carried weight.

He followed the woman into a sumptuously appointed lounge where a number of men were gathered. All heads turned as he entered, eyes hard and appraising. Automatically D'Arcy began putting names to the faces of the secretive directors of Spidex International.

Before the fireplace stood Sheikh Hayira. Although stout, he was trimmer than he appeared in the photograph snatched outside his London house. The pale blue silk woven suit helped, in an understated cut that suggested it cost double what you thought it might. Although the neat beard was black, the head of moss-tight curls was thickly threaded with grey.

"My husband, this is Mr D'Arcy." Immediately she stepped back in deference, leaving D'Arcy to respond to the outstretched hand.

"Mr D'Arcy, it is most interesting to meet you."

D'Arcy kept the handshake brief.

"Let my wife get you a drink. We were having Arabic tea, but I understand you may care for brandy." He smiled gently. "You are not amongst Moslem fanatics here."

"Tea will be fine."

Hayira signalled his wife curtly. "Let me introduce you to my colleagues . . ."

"I know who you all are," D'Arcy replied quietly.

The Arab's eyes hardened. "So I understand. Nevertheless I think it only politeness."

There were three other men in suits, from Iraq, Kuwait and the United Arab Emirates. Two others, brothers from Saudi Arabia, wore white robes and headdresses. All the handshaking was perfunctory, the eye contact suspicious.

There was, D'Arcy noted, no one present from the Sultanate of Oman.

"Understandably you and your client Mr Nadirpur feel a little upset at the events that have befallen you," Sheikh Hayira began in a reasonable tone. "And we have decided that you should be put fully in the picture, so that you understand the importance of what we are about.

"You see, we all, in one way or another, speak for our governments. This has been a concerted effort, with the approval of your own government, the French, and the American." He paused for effect. "We have been acting in the interests of both the West and the free Arab world."

"I don't think the French would quite see it that way," D'Arcy interrupted.

"Please, I will explain. When the Iranians first started inquiries about obtaining certain arms, the French were indeed the frontrunners. They had a vested interest in getting one of their hostages released from Beirut as part of the deal. But – " He gestured round the room. "We saw it as a different opportunity. One from which the French, reluctantly, had to be excluded. They wanted their hostage returned, but we had other ideas."

"More important ideas?" D'Arcy suggested cynically.

Hayira blinked, and stared at him for a moment. "Yes, frankly, Mr D'Arcy, I think so. You are not an Arab, so you would not find it so easy to understand. But for the past ten years since Khomeini came to power, there has been nothing but trouble. He creates unrest in every Gulf nation, causes mayhem for the Saudis in Mecca, inflames

374

the situation in Lebanon, and protracts a war with Iraq that could have been settled peacefully years ago."

D'Arcy smiled grimly. "I am aware of the Ayatollah's exemplary record, gentlemen."

"Then you understand why it is so important to us not to perpetuate his régime. We Arabs have enough troubles and misunderstandings with Israel and among ourselves without Khomeini trying to export his revolution to us."

D'Arcy was becoming impatient. "So how does hijacking my client's ship help your cause?"

Sheikh Hayira took a step closer, his expression more intense. "Khomeini is ill, weak. The chances are he will not see out the summer. The moderate speaker of the Iranian parliament, Rafsanjani, has persuaded him to talk about a cease-fire with Iraq, over which the Sultan of Oman is secretly moderating. Our intelligence sources believe that an announcement will be made public very shortly."

"Then your troubles may be over?"

"Rafsanjani is just one man. There are others who would have no time for moderation. Mullahs and revolutionary guards who have had a taste of power and do not want to go back to their mosques or their tenement homes. And the focal point for their fanaticism is none other than Khomeini's son himself, Ahmed. It is he who is known as the eyes and ears and brains of his senile father. It is he who has been steering the course of the revolution." He paused, his face flushed with suppressed anger. "And it is he for whom Sabbah organised the arms aboard *Clarion Call*."

"In readiness for a struggle after Khomeini's death?" D'Arcy considered for a moment. "But these are sophisticated weapons, not suitable for the Revolutionary Guards."

"Exactly!" Hayira said in triumph. "Because Rafsanjani the moderate has control of the Iranian armed forces. Ahmed Khomeini cannot fight them with handguns. He is preparing his own force of Revolutionary Guards and sympathetic elements of the Army to fight his corner when the time is right – spearheaded by our old friends the *Pessarane Behesht*."

"Then I understand what you are trying to achieve. But why not just scuttle the ship, or take her out of Arabian waters?"

"Because those arms are needed by Rafsanjani to equip an élite caucus of the armed forces. They have become a shambles during ten years of war, taking a back seat and stripped of equipment for the Revolutionary Guards to throw away at the front. Those arms will be the insurance policy of the moderates who *must* succeed Khomeini. Over the coming months they will be smuggled across the Gulf to Rafsanjani. We plan that other shipments will follow. So you can see, a delay in the release of that French diplomat is a small price to pay."

"I doubt that the French diplomat would agree with you," D'Arcy snapped. "Nor would Mr Nadirpur."

"Ah, the woman and child." Hayira looked suitably sad. "That is indeed a tragic dimension to the affair. And entirely unexpected."

"What do you intend to do about it?"

Hayira shrugged. "What can we do? It is a matter for your very capable English police."

The scar coloured on D'Arcy's cheek. "I'll tell you exactly what you can do about it. You return the funds that the Iranians paid up front. You keep your bloody weapons and the Iranians save face. I'll use it to negotiate the Nadirpurs' freedom – and maybe even that poor bastard in Beirut."

Hayira smiled uncertainly and glanced around at his stern-faced co-conspirators as though making certain that he spoke for them all. Their expressions were enough.

"You do not understand, Mr D'Arcy. That would be quite impossible. You are talking of billions of dollars –"

"That don't belong to you," D'Arcy interrupted sharply.

Hayira raised his hands in a gesture of helplessness. "We

would never get all these disparate governments to agree."

"They were happy enough to agree to this criminal plot in the first place."

Any semblance of good humour finally drained from the sheikh's face. "They will not agree to surrender funds to perpetuate the Khomeini régime. Nor to encourage terrorism. You, too, Mr D'Arcy, should know better as a former antiterrorist soldier."

"I don't give a stuff who benefits from the money – it was *theirs* in the first place. You're sacrificing the lives of two – correction, three – innocent people in order to back some highly suspect gamble."

"We do not think so."

"You'd be on a safer bet playing pass-the-parcel with a bottle of nitroglycerine."

"I beg your pardon?"

D'Arcy didn't bother to explain. "You've heard my terms for a compromise. It's not ideal for you, but at least you'd have deprived Khomeini's son of the arms he was expecting. That will set back his plans somewhat. You can also get your arms to Rafsanjani. Okay, your governments have had to pay for them, but then if the future of Iran is so important to you, it should be a small price to pay." He turned abruptly and walked to the door. Mrs Hayira looked at him strangely, as though imploring him not to walk out. He stopped and faced back into the room. All eyes were on him. "You've got twenty-four hours to think it over, gentlemen. Then the whole truth will be revealed to the press. Backed up by photographs and tape recordings."

"Don't be foolish," Hayira snarled. "For the sake of peace in the Middle East, see sense."

"Sense to me is a poor woman and a seven-year-old child held in some damp cellar. Face it, Hayira, you've blown this one. You've been tumbled. It's over. Salvage what you can."

"Do not threaten me," Hayira replied darkly. "You are messing with powerful forces –"

The door slammed shut, cutting off the Sheikh's words,

with D'Arcy on the other side. Momentarily he closed his eyes, allowing his seething anger to subside. Then, recovered, he strode down the corridor and took the stairs to the foyer.

As he left the hotel foyer he didn't notice the man in the blue Adidas tracksuit who sat reading a newspaper. The man watched D'Arcy go, but this time made no attempt to follow.

Instead he folded his paper and crossed to the cluster of pay-phone booths. It took two attempts to get through to the apartment in the 20th *arrondissement* of the Paris suburbs.

The young man said: "The vipers' nest has been found."

It was the coded ring. Four bursts, then two bursts a moment later.

This was the first time it had happened, and Shamlou's mouth was dry as he waited for the telephone to ring again in the Christies' hall. The coded ring was to be used only in a dire emergency.

Again it rang and, although he was expecting it, the sound made Shamlou jump.

He picked up the receiver without speaking.

The voice on the other end said simply: "Carpet." The caller hung up.

"What does it mean?" Matchsticks asked afterwards.

Shamlou was irritated. "It means that you ask too many questions." He picked up his jacket. "I'm going out. And make sure the Christie woman takes some Valium tonight. She looks a wreck, and I don't want her doing something stupid."

He left in the van and drove for half-an-hour before he stopped at a telephone kiosk and telephoned the 'Carpet' number in Paris. It was his 'controller'.

Azadi said: "The sword of Islam must strike. There is another mission for you to undertake."

Shamlou began to protest, but his 'controller' cut him short. Instead he gave him a brief set of instructions, then hung up with the words: "Remember that you are chosen. Allah and Islam are depending upon you."

The Iranian kicked open the kiosk door in anger and climbed back into his van. It was a long and tiresome drive through the congested London streets to the south of the city and the area of suburban woodland known as Epsom Common.

His instructions were precise, and it took him no longer than ten minutes to locate the heavy fibre suitcase buried in the soft leaf mould.

On his return to Harrow-on-the-Hill, he virtually ignored his three comrades and went straight to the bedroom he had commandeered. It belonged to the Christies' son, and the hanging plastic aircraft and pop star posters provided an incongruously innocent setting for the items that Shamlou emptied onto the bedspread.

He examined the sealed envelope first. It contained a single sheet of paper with a photograph attached. Typed on the paper was a man's name: Sheikh Abdullah Hayira, followed by an address in Chelsea.

The other contents of the suitcase he had seen once before. It had been demonstrated by a Libyan instructor at the *Pessarane Behesht* training camp. A 9 mm Heckler and Koch MP5K sub-machine gun had been mounted inside a small leather briefcase. Fitted to the top of the weapon was a laser sight for pinpoint accuracy. Two unobtrusive apertures in the side of the case allowed a target to be fixed, and then shot, without revealing the assassin.

He remembered how proud the Libyan had been of his gadgetry, boasting how it had taken years of intelligence from various sources to obtain the original British technology through VIP bodyguards in Saudi Arabia.

He examined the photograph again. It was needle sharp, a stout middle-aged Arab with tight curly hair and a neatly trimmed beard.

The next morning the sword of Islam was to cut him down.

\*     \*     \*

Shamlou couldn't sleep. It was a humid night and he was restless. The picture of the man he was going to kill filled his mind.

For the first time it occurred to him that he had never actually killed anyone in his life before. True, at the war front with Iraq he had shot at enemy soldiers, as they had shot at him. In his thirst to avenge his dead brother he had known no fear. But he had not waited until he saw the whites of another human being's eyes, waited until he could see the sweat in the pores, until he could smell the rank funk of fear before he pulled the trigger. Most of the killings had been long-range, the whipping cut of the heavy machine gun or the distant duel of artillery. That was how his own brother had died.

The only thing Shamlou had ever killed in his life had been an old she-goat. And he remembered vividly and ashamedly how there had been tears in his eyes as he drew the blade across its throat.

Who was this man? The name meant nothing to him. Nor the face in the photograph that stared straight at him. As though daring him to carry out his task.

Enough that he was to be destroyed. An enemy of Islam, an unbeliever. And enough that he, Shamlou, had been chosen yet again by the great Sabbah.

He tossed the sheet from the bed and stood up. Reflected by the mirror, his thin naked body was a delicate statue of pale lilac marble in the moonlight. He thought of the dream. Of the woman who waited for him in paradise.

*"Sit near my tomb, and bring wine and music – Feeling thy presence, I shall come out of my sepulchre – Rise, softly moving creature, and let me contemplate thy beauty."*

He watched in the mirror, mesmerised, as his loins swelled, marble becoming living flesh. Angrily he looked away, snatched his jeans and pulled them on, anxious to cover his nakedness.

He would have liked to talk to Matchsticks, but he heard the fool snoring outside the bedroom where the Christies shared an uncomfortable sleep, shackled to each other.

Shamlou's foot caught the dozing man in the kidneys. "Keep awake! I'm going downstairs, I'll get Kamal to relieve you. We'll leave at four."

Downstairs he roused Kamal from the sofa and sent him upstairs to relieve Matchsticks. In the airless cellar Shamlou found the bespectacled Hamid reading a magazine. A smell of stale urine and body odour pervaded the enclosed space.

"How are they?"

Hamid shrugged, forever the apologetic student. "It is hot tonight. They are restless."

Roughly Shamlou threw aside the blanket. The two creatures in the wire cage shielded their eyes against the sudden influx of light. They lay together in their dark privacy, skirts abandoned in an effort to keep cool, buttons undone. Sweat trickled down the woman's face, glistening, smudging days of encrusted dirt. The once beautifully groomed hair matted and rank like that of a mangy bitch.

She snatched at her skirt to cover herself.

Shamlou dropped the blanket. On impulse he snapped at Hamid: "I'll take over here. But before you sleep get some clothes from the wardrobe of the woman upstairs. Also something for the girl. And some clean water."

Hamid nodded, prepared to leave.

"And take that slop bucket with you."

Five minutes later he returned, then left Shamlou alone in the cellar.

Once again he drew aside the blanket and opened the cage. He placed the bucket of fresh water inside the low gate and tossed a pile of clothing at the woman.

"Get washed," he ordered.

Ashi didn't move. Gathering Sousan close to her, she just stared at him, defiant and proud. He saw no fear in her eyes.

"Do it," he ordered.

She swallowed. "No. Not another photograph. I know what it will do to my Nader. It will destroy him."

Shamlou wanted to shout at her, to scream that the idea

had been exactly that. To destroy her husband, to make him a broken man. Instead he said: "No photograph. Just get washed, and put on fresh clothes – before I change my mind."

She looked at him curiously. "We are to go?"

Anger flashed in his eyes. "You are to WASH!"

Ashi knew better than to argue more. She climbed to her feet, aware that Shamlou was silently watching, and positioned herself to cover his view of the child. Gently, with the skilled patience of a mother with a tired and listless offspring, she removed the girl's stained clothes and sponged her with the water. The replacement garments were a boy's; they looked dated and smelled of mothballs. She dressed Sousan in a pair of grey flannel shorts and a T-shirt.

Then Ashi turned. Shamlou was still watching from the shadows, she could see the glowing tip of his cigarette as he smoked in a rapid and agitated way.

She became angry at having to cower and hide herself from his gaze. In a sudden act of defiance she started to throw off her clothing, ignoring his presence. Delicious cool water sluiced over the contours of her small, slender body as she scoured hard with the sponge until her skin began to burn with the friction. Filth, filth, filth! It felt as though the dirt had soaked into her very bones.

She picked up the clean pants, looked at them, and then laughed aloud.

"What is so funny?" Shamlou snapped.

She held them up. Lacy, scalloped, expensive. "They don't seem to go with – with all this!" She gestured at her surroundings.

"Do not behave like a whore. Have you no shame?"

"Then don't treat me like a peepshow!" she bit back. "Haven't you ever seen a woman before?"

His face coloured. "Of course."

"What would your mother think of you now?"

Shamlou slammed his fist angrily against the wire of the cage, causing Ashi to take a backward step. "She would

382

say you are an inflamer of men's souls. That you were a disgrace to Islam. That you should be stoned —" He stopped himself, swallowed hard. "Get dressed," he said hoarsely, and turned his back.

Ashi dressed swiftly in the furious silence that followed. Again she wondered why they had sent this boy-man with his long lashes. This boy-man who was so quick to anger one moment and could show kindness the next. This boy-man who she was now sure had never made love to a woman. This boy-man who blushed so easily. ·

There was a sudden rush of warmth in her lower belly as the thought pulsed unbeckoned through her mind.

She dropped to her knees, clutching the edge of the wire cage, feeling dizzy, and closed her eyes. When she opened them again Shamlou was standing close by, looking down on her from the other side of the wire. She was aware of the smell of him, remembering from the time he had touched her breast. And she was aware of the closeness of him to her face.

"Why don't you ever wear a mask?" she whispered.

"It is not necessary."

"Because you are going to kill us anyway?"

A sly smile crossed his face. Now there was fear, respect. "That is not for you to know. Besides, when this is over we will be safely away, or we shall be dead. There will be no compromise. There is no higher reward than martyrdom."

"Who would kill us?" It was a thought that had occurred to her before. Not in panic, but by way of quiet curiosity.

He didn't answer, just looked deeply into her eyes as though recognising something for the first time.

"Could you kill a child?" she asked in a small voice.

She seemed to have broken a spell. He blinked. "Death is not to be feared. It is to be welcomed."

Ashi knew it was pointless, even dangerous, to argue against religious fanaticism.

"I have seen it," Shamlou murmured softly, staring at the child who was now curled in a ball, clean and sleeping contentedly.

"Seen what?"

"Paradise," he said simply. Then he reached into his pocket, and drew out a pack of sweets. He poked it through the wire. "Give these to your daughter when she wakes up. And wash her hair with the remaining water. Yours too. It is a shame to see you like this. You are a beautiful woman."

As she took the pack from him through the wire, their fingertips briefly touched.

This strange boy-man who held the power of life and death.

"I do not want to die," she breathed.

"No one wants to die."

And as he spoke the words he knew he'd betrayed himself. Had betrayed the faith that Allah, the Imam and the great Sabbah had placed upon him. In silence he stood and let the blanket fall back into place. In a few hours he was going to kill a man who didn't want to die.


Sea captain Nasiyb was well pleased with himself.

He sat in the shade of the awning on his dhow. The traditional impedimenta for coffee-making were spread before him. All around were his henchmen. And a more menacing, hard-eyed bunch of cutthroats he would hope never to meet. Each armed with a curved *khanjar* and, concealed beneath his robes, a pistol which he would use without hesitation.

On the far side of the spread of brass pots and delicate china cups were two men. Visitors from the Iranian dhow tethered alongside his own on the open sea.

"Then we have a deal," Nasiyb confirmed.

"It is done," the bearded one said. Both men spoke in English so that they could understand each other.

Nasiyb kept the smile from his dark features, but could do nothing to hide the light of satisfaction in his eyes. It was twice the price he had been offered by the Jordanian commandos to offload the *Clarion Call*'s cargo over the next month.

If that English fool Rick Clay – with the French couple – had not told him the nature of the cargo, he would not have known the strength of his own hand.

It had been easy to contact the Iranian spy in Sur and tell him he knew the location of the hijacked ship the mullahs of Teheran sought.

The result had been this meeting on the high seas. Away from prying eyes and listening ears. Away from the dangerous chitter-chatter of gossiping village women.

"There is the question," Nasiyb said craftily, "of how payment shall be made."

The bearded one nodded. He had introduced himself simply as Sabbah. It was a name of no significance to the smuggler. "Payment shall depend on the truth of your words."

"My words are true, and payment should be in gold bars. That is what I told your agent in Sur."

"That is so. And our agreement is equal to five gold bars."

"It is agreed."

"Then I shall place two gold bars upon this ship. You will give me a copy of the chart with the location of the missing ship. Together we shall sail to confirm that location. When I am satisfied I shall deliver the final bars. It is also agreed?"

Nasiyb glanced sideways at the Iranian dhow. It was slow, old, and he had heard its croaking engine with his own ears. No match for his own Perkins diesel.

And his crew. Ten of the toughest smugglers in the Arabian Sea, all armed and happy to use their weapons if it proved necessary to seize the remaining three gold bars. There were only two crew members with the man who called himself Sabbah, a skipper who remained aboard the Iranian dhow, and a powerfully built man with grizzled hair and the face of a seasoned veteran, who guarded his master.

"It is agreed," Nasiyb said. He beckoned one of his henchmen to bring a chart and a pen. Carefully he indicated the dog-leg inlet in the south sector of the Musandam Peninsula and handed the rolled chart to the bearded one.

The other man smiled. "It is done." He rose from his crosslegged position. "My man will bring your two bars." He turned to the veteran. "Get them, Hamman."

Nasiyb watched suspiciously as Sabbah stepped over the gunwales and stood on his own dhow, waiting while his guardian disappeared into the fo'c'sle. The smuggler reached inside his robe, his fingers closing round the polished wooden butt of his revolver. All the eyes of his crew were on the Iranian dhow. The tension mounted.

Darvish Hamman, captain-swimmer of the *Pessarane Behesht*, struggled back onto the deck. In his huge hands he held a small, heavy package.

Relief swept over Nasiyb. He stepped forward, stretching between the two boats to grab his precious reward. He dropped to his knees, tearing at the packaging with his fingernails. Bright sunlight glinted on the gold pigment as Darvish Hamman slipped the ropes, and the two dhows drifted apart.

Crew members gathered around the sea captain, the Iranian vessel already forgotten. Nasiyb lifted the bar clear of the wrapping, its heavy weight belying its comparatively small size.

Not bad at all, he gloated. Twice the price of the ferrying job for the Jordanians for no work – plus the original down-payment of the hijackers' fee. Indeed, as he had told the Englishman 'China' Clay, he was in the information business now. That was where the future lay. He was moving into the modern world. He was happy to take the money from the evil Ayatollah of Qum.

He swung the blade of the *khanjar*, slicing it into the soft precious metal.

Beneath the sprayed gold crust a grey lump of lead clattered onto the rough timber decking.

Nasiyb looked up, across to the receding arc shape of the Iranian dhow. "Does he take me for a fool!" he demanded savagely.

He rapped out his orders to the helmsman and crew. Leathered feet slapped urgently on planking as the men scampered to their stations. The Perkins rumbled angrily into life.

As the dhow straightened up, Nasiyb strode to the prow, his black turban and robe streaming behind him in the sultry breeze. Ahead of him the Iranian vessel was already melting into the glittering haze. He heard the cocking of firearms and the rasp of blades being sharpened as his crewmen's anger grew to match his own.

Swiftly they closed, the other dhow taking form again, falling under the inexorable power of the diesel.

But, Nasiyb thought in his anger, the taste of revenge was not as sweet as the promise of gold. At least he still had his deal with the Jordanians.

"ABAFT!" a lookout yelled in Arabic.

Nasiyb turned his head, straining to see behind the high aft castle of his dhow. Two craft, gaining fast. Low in the water, sleek and menacing, sweeping out suddenly to form a pincer like a crab's claw.

Instantly Nasiyb knew what they were. Knew what had happened. Knew he had lost.

The first Boghammar opened with a heavy machine gun as it drew alongside. It riddled the dhow's hull from stern to prow, blasting fist-sized holes out of the timber.

Next came the grenades from the launcher of the second craft. Two missed but the third struck the centre of the deck, its shrapnel cutting down the crew like a scythe.

Nasiyb was decapitated by machine-gun fire on the second pass, which left the deck awash with blood.

It took a third pass to sink the dhow. Sea captain Nasiyb went to the bottom with his vessel, his crew, and his precious two bars of fool's gold.

# 16

Jalal Shamlou found a parking place at five a.m.

It was only five hundred metres from the smart residence of Sheikh Abdullah Hayira and his wife. But crucially the two streets, which backed onto each other, were separated by a pedestrian walkway. No car could give chase to someone fleeing on foot.

"Tell me what's happening?" Matchsticks demanded. "What is so important about that briefcase?"

Shamlou felt irritated. His heart was pounding like a tom-tom and his palms were sweating, a tiny rash of heat spots breaking out between his fingers. "Something has to be done, that is all. Your part is to stay here and keep alert. I will have to leave in a hurry."

"When will you come back?"

"I don't know. The man I have to see is not a creature of habit. It may take all day."

"What happens if I get hungry?" Matchsticks protested.

"You stay hungry!" Shamlou snapped. "Don't you dare leave this vehicle, for whatever reason."

"I might need to relieve myself."

Shamlou was exasperated. "Piss in your pants. Or get an empty bottle from a milkman. I don't care. Just *be* here."

Matchsticks sat back in the driver's seat, a sullen expression on his face. But his intention to ignore his comrade was defeated by curiosity as Shamlou placed a pair of spectacles on his nose. A fine strand of flesh-coloured electric wire ran from the right ear hook, and Shamlou fed it into the collar of his shirt, down his sleeve and out through the cuff. He placed the briefcase on his lap and pushed the small plug at the end of the wire into a connection socket under the handle.

"Remember everything I've said."

"Yes, chosen one," Matchsticks mocked disagreeably.

Shamlou stepped out of the car, briefcase in hand, and entered the pedestrian walkway. Halfway along he halted and studied the black iron stanchion planted at the far end to deny access to vehicles.

He shut his left eye and concentrated on the fine cross-hairs in the right lens of the spectacles, which fed down the wire to the laser aiming-spot indicator sight in the case. A single spot emblem showed in the lens a few millimetres below the cross-hairs – this was the trajectory indicator of the 9 mm submachine gun. He took a pace forward, then another. As he did so, the spot in the spectacle lens shifted up towards the cross-hairs. They were synchronised to meet at fifteen metres. Another two steps. He stopped. The spot was dead centre in the cross-hairs. Both covered the top section of the stanchion. Perfect.

He felt calmer now. Confident he could handle it. He removed the spectacles, dropped them into his top pocket, then sauntered into the street beyond.

There were few people about as he strolled past Hayira's house twice, allowing a fifteen minute interval. The curtains were drawn and there was no sign of life. A black Porsche was parked on the gravelled forecourt.

He returned to the walkway, counting his paces. Thirty. Thirty steady paces at one second each. Thirty seconds to reach the front of the house.

Taking a newspaper from his pocket, he pretended to read it as he leaned against a high fence by the stanchion. He had a clear view of the front of the house beyond the parked cars and plane trees.

No one took any notice of him for the next three and a half hours. Gradually the parked cars moved away as residents left for work, the traffic passed more frequently.

Eight forty-five. Shamlou was tired now. His legs ached. Would the man never leave the house? For the love of Allah . . .

His heart suddenly upped its tempo. The door to the house had opened. Just ajar. Adrenalin coursed through his body, and he felt the muscles of his gut contract.

Hastily he took the spectacles from his top pocket. He fumbled, nearly dropping them. In anger he tossed aside his newspaper and used both hands to tuck the spectacles over his ears. He picked up the briefcase and began walking, plugging the lead into the socket as he moved.

A lorry crawled past, cutting off his line of vision. He cursed and kept walking . . . Twelve, thirteen paces . . . Fourteen, fifteen . . . The lorry cleared. The man with the beard stood at the top of the steps at the front door. There was no doubt. It was the man in the photograph. He turned and called into the house. He had a smile on his face. A pleasant-looking man.

Eighteen, nineteen . . . Walking over the uneven pavement, his view half-obscured by the parked vehicles.

The man trotted easily down the steps, looking about him. Enjoying the gentle morning sunshine, spotting a bluetit in the branches of the plane tree. Another smile to himself.

Twenty-two, twenty-three . . . Standing directly opposite now, across the street.

The man opened the door of the Porsche, glanced at his watch, called back up to the house.

Twenty-five, twenty-six . . . Road clear, moving forward. Cross-hairs over the man's back. The aiming-spot below, moving up to synchronise.

Twenty-eight, twenty-nine . . . A call from the front door. Two children. A boy. A girl of about seven. Dark blazers, grey flannel shorts and skirt, old-fashioned satchels. A girl like Sousan Nadirpur, dark-skinned with large eyes. Running down the steps.

Thirty . . . Cross-hairs and aiming-spot synchronise

across the target's back. His finger hesitates on the trigger, the girl at her father's side is looking directly at him. Frowning, curious. His heart is trying to burst out of his chest. He is drenched in sweat.

A blasting horn, a squeal of brakes.

He shuts his eyes and squeezes the trigger.

The briefcase leaps in his hand like a living thing, pouring out its lethal venom. Tearing into the expensive material of Hayira's suit like carnivorous moths, shattering the Porsche windscreen, cutting down the children like flowers, spurting vermilion graffiti over the writhing bodies, the car and the gravel.

Shamlou's head filled with the childish high-pitched screams of terror and the screech of brakes as the van on the road swerved to miss him, fishtailed into a parked truck. Cries of horror from passers-by, stunned, shocked, uncomprehending.

He stood, rooted to the spot, unable to move. Watched the anguish of the beautiful woman at the door as she wailed and rushed to the heap of torn bodies on the gravel.

Slowly, slowly he backed away, panic suddenly seizing him. Must run, must run. *Can't* run! One by one he forced his legs to obey, realising that in the strange disembodied world around him, no one knew, no one suspected. No one suspected the quiet man in the spectacles with the briefcase.

Calmly he turned and headed stiffly towards the walk-way, wanting but unable to move faster. Almost there. Out of sight and a sprint to the next street.

The driver of the crashed van staggered across the road. Blood trickled from a forehead cut. He appeared bewildered, shocked. There was a wild look in his eyes.

"Hey, you!" he shouted.

He reached out a hand to Shamlou.

"Did you do that . . . ?" The accusation was made in a voice of disbelief at the evidence of his own eyes.

Shamlou squeezed the trigger again.

The briefcase jerked twice with the recoil of the last rounds in the magazine.

The van driver slumped forward. As though suddenly released from an invisible shackle, Shamlou began to run, pounding down the walkway to where Matchsticks waited for him.

Two hours earlier, on the northwest outskirts of London, Detective Sergeant Ron Wilkins had driven to his golf club.

He was addicted to the game, a very unfortunate vice for a police officer. Golf and the long and unsociable hours required by the job had been the cause of his divorce.

A cheerful, good-looking man in his mid-thirties, he had bottled up the emotional turmoil well, and had begun using his golf as therapy. That had been when their little group was formed. All men with demanding jobs, they took to playing nine holes at first light during the summer months before going to work.

There was the doc, a crusty old medical practitioner who should have been pensioned off years ago. Freddie Phillips, a fussy middle-aged businessman who used the clubhouse to escape the henpecking of his wife. The fourth man of their group was an art dealer, an exiled Iranian called Ali Christie.

Ron Wilkins's spirits dropped slightly when he realised that, once again, Ali was missing.

"Mornin' all," he greeted in the expected British bobby fashion. "No sign of our friend?"

Freddie Phillips shook his head. "Not a dickie. Jane's been trying to phone Beth all week. No one's answering the phone. Must be on holiday."

"He didn't say."

The doc grunted. "Typical foreigners. No sense of dedication. Or good manners." He was as old-fashioned in his bigoted views as he was in his dress – tweed jacket and plus fours.

"You can't say that about Ali," Ron Wilkins protested.

"Absolutely charming bloke. Better manners than most people I come across. Sometimes I think we've become an entire nation of yobbos – of all ages."

The doc didn't see the point of discussing someone who wasn't even there. "I'll tee off, shall I?" His untroubled swing took him straight down the fairway, just outside the green. Not bad for a par three.

Freddie Phillips got halfway there and Ron Wilkins failed to correct his left-hand slice, which landed him in the rough.

As all three strode forward, Wilkins said: "The Christies can't be away. I've just remembered, I saw Beth out shopping yesterday – or was it the day before? We were picking up some poor old dear at a supermarket – usual menopausal shoplifter – when I met her. Wasn't very talkative, but then I was in a hurry. I must say she didn't look well. Very tired and pale." He considered for a moment; he'd always rather fancied Ali's American wife. "Come to think of it, she didn't look her usual smart self. Lost some weight, I reckon."

"Must be that German measles she's had," Freddie Phillips said. "That can take it out of you. Isn't that so, Doc?"

The other man grunted. He had little time for any patients, especially middle-aged women, even if they were as attractive as Beth Christie. Time-wasters all with their petty and coy 'women's troubles'. Post-natal depression, PMT and hormone replacement therapy were not in the doc's vocabulary, let alone his understanding. "I doubt she's had German measles or anything like it," he muttered dismissively. "You know what these Americans are like about their health. Just got to sneeze twice and they call in the doctor, demanding tests or some-such. Always on about food allergy. Put everything down to that . . ."

Freddie Phillips was mildly surprised. "She said you'd confirmed it, I'm sure she did. The day she cancelled a party. You are still her GP?"

"For my sins." So saying he strode off towards the hole, leaving the other two to catch up.

"Miserable old sod," Freddie Phillips said under his breath.

Ron Wilkins agreed. "Perhaps I ought to call round to see them. Find out why Ali's stopped coming."

Freddie Phillips jabbed a thumb in the doc's direction. "You don't have to look far for your reason."

Detective Sergeant Ron Wilkins said no more, but resolved to call in on the Christies that evening on his way home from the station.


D'Arcy heard the news of the murder of an Arab and his two children in London on the midday radio news.

It held no special significance for him, and anyway his thoughts were interrupted by a call put through from Brandy on the switchboard.

"*Chéri*, is it you?"

He grinned at the sound of Chantal's voice. Christ, how he missed her.

"Yes, it's me," he repeated. It was a bad line.

"Thank God. Listen Rober', I have news. I am on the *Gulf Bullpup*. We have found the ship – hidden in the Musandam Peninsula."

D'Arcy was speechless, stunned with disbelief. He could not prevent the tears of emotion welling in his eyes.

"*Chéri*? You are still there?"

He found his voice. "Kitten, that is *fantastic* news! Nadirpur will be over the moon."

He noticed that her tone did not match the excitement of the news. "But, Rober', things are not all good. The ship is guarded by soldiers. Last night your friend Rick Clay and his partner Tokyo went to have a closer look – in scuba gear, you know. Rick is caught. We do not know if maybe he was killed, or else is held on the ship. I am so sorry."

D'Arcy was winded by the revelation. "You've no way of knowing which?"

"Tokyo came back alone. He was exhausted and badly shaken. Apparently they had alarm nets under water and frogmen. He is *so* nearly caught." She hesitated. "And also I think Tom Wilmot is dead, eaten by shark. We find his body here . . ."

"Sweet Jesus," he breathed, his initial elation now completely crushed. Wilmot dead. He just could not grasp it.

"Tell me, what do we do now?"

"Get away," he snapped instinctively. "I don't want any more loss of life."

"Tokyo knows a safe place where he can watch the ship. Rick is his buddy. He wants to keep the ship – that expression? – under surveillance."

He thought for a moment. "Look, kitten, I've no control or influence over this chap, I've never even met him. Just persuade him not to do anything foolhardy."

"He is a good, sensible man. A Japanese special forces diver."

D'Arcy was at least relieved to hear that. "Will you and Saint-Julien keep in contact with me?"

"Yes, we have to stay aboard *Bullpup*. Once we land in Oman, Major Harry will have us thrown out."

"Well, just keep out of trouble. No risks, eh?"

A gentle laugh. "I save myself for you, do not worry."

He replaced the receiver deep in thought.

Despite his promise to the kidnappers that he would give them the location of the ship, there was no way he could do it in reality. To allow the *Pessarane Behesht* to seize it themselves would be unthinkable, putting the lives of *Clarion Call*'s crew and possibly Rick Clay's at risk. The Iranian terrorists were hardly renowned for their humanity to their fellow man.

He just had to make Sheikh Hayira crack. Force him to return the ship voluntarily, or make full restoration to Nadirpur . . . In the meantime he would just have to continue to play the kidnappers along.

At lunchtime Reg Roman made an appearance. He was in an untypically foul mood.

"Someone's been playing silly buggers with me, Rob. I am not pleased, and Bob Tanner hit the roof this morning when he heard."

"Heard what?"

"About a certain Sheikh Hayira, living in London. The head of this Spidex organisation you told me you couldn't trace."

"Ah, well," D'Arcy hedged. "I'm sorry, Reg, but I'm afraid that's down to Roy Bliss and Century House. He didn't want their involvement with the ship's hijack getting out. He wanted you dealing with this Nadirpur case as a straight kidnap."

"So I gather," Roman replied. "I had a visit from him this morning. Events have rather forced his hand to come clean."

D'Arcy was puzzled; he couldn't imagine what on earth would force Bliss to reveal all to the Anti-Terrorist Branch.

"Hayira was shot dead this morning," Roman explained. "And it looks very much as though your *Pessarane Behesht* friends were responsible. I understand you'd met Hayira recently?"

D'Arcy was stunned. He nodded numbly. "Yes, I've seen him. I'm sorry I couldn't tell you."

"So am I. I would guess that the killer traced him by following you. An act of revenge."

"Have they claimed responsibility?"

Reg Roman shook his head. "Not their style, as you know. But we think there's a direct connection between the killing and your kidnappers. There was a witness at the shooting, a passing motorist. He's in hospital now with a bullet lodged in his lung. He was able to give a description and we've been able to fit it together with other statements given by local residents. It seems the killer was hanging around for several hours before he struck. The description fits that of the man on the Euston video. The man on the Birmingham to London train, who we lost in Soho."

D'Arcy frowned. Descriptions of Middle East nationals by whites tended to be vague and simplistic.

Roman read his thoughts. "There's more, Rob. His getaway vehicle was seen. A mustard-coloured van, just like the one at the kidnap switch-over."

"So the killer and the kidnapper could be the same person?"

"At least from the same gang." He hesitated. "One more thing. This guy was reading a newspaper while he waited. He threw it away when he went in for the kill."

"And?"

"It was a copy of the *Harrow Observer*, a local newspaper."

"Is that significant? Surely he wouldn't . . ."

Roman shrugged. "It happens. He wouldn't have been planning to leave it behind, but in the heat of the moment, under stress – it could just be the lucky break we've been praying for."

But the meeting with Reg Roman left D'Arcy far from pleased. Under other circumstances he would have been delighted that the police net might be closing in, but the death of Sheikh Hayira put matters in a different light.

With Hayira dead, he had no one to put pressure on to release *Clarion Call* and Rick Clay – or to agree to pay compensation to the Iranians.

His threat to take his tapes and photographs to the press had always been mostly bluff. It hardly constituted evidence and it would take a team of good reporters weeks to put together a corroborated story. With the skeikh now a corpse and virtually nothing known about the other Spidex members, it was now a non-starter. And if there were no deal, then Nadirpur's wife and child would remain in captivity – at best until some rescue bid was mounted with all the terrible risks that such an operation would entail.

There was also a new dimension. If Reg Roman was right, the kidnappers had now killed. And if they'd killed once they had nothing to lose in killing again. The terrorists would be under mounting pressure, aware that the murder of Sheikh Hayira could give the police more leads. Nerves would fray, paranoia would set in.

When he shut his eyes, D'Arcy could see it all. Could see to where it would all lead. Disaster.

He made a final decision. Snatching up the telephone he dialled Forbes at his home where he was catching up on some paperwork.

"Dave, we need to meet urgently. And somewhere very private."

He returned to Flax Wharf in the late afternoon, following his meeting with Forbes. The sun still had strength and there was a welcome gentle breeze. It was ideal weather for calming the troubled mind.

Two days, D'Arcy thought. Two days since the kidnappers had telephoned to demand ten million sterling in return for a five-day stay of execution of Ashi and Sousan Nadirpur. A five-day reprieve, at the end of which he *had* to be in a position to conclude a deal. That left just seventy-two hours. He was sure the kidnappers must telephone again before the day was out.

Clearly Reg Roman agreed; he was parking his car outside the office as D'Arcy arrived. Together they went up to the living quarters where Nadirpur had spent the day.

"No news?" D'Arcy asked.

Nadirpur shook his head. He appeared more exhausted than ever; D'Arcy had seen that look many a time on survival courses – men physically and mentally drained, having pushed themselves beyond the limits of human endurance.

D'Arcy tried to reassure him. "We'll hear. But if the kidnapper was involved in that killing then he'll have had other worries besides us. Be patient."

Roman asked: "And what will you say if he rings?"

D'Arcy helped himself to the coffee pot. "That depends if we get an agreement."

"Obviously," Roman responded tartly. "But on the last

transcript Mr Nadirpur here offered to up the sum to half-a-million sterling."

"And the kidnappers demanded ten million," D'Arcy reminded, "at which point he rang off."

Roman was visibly losing patience; D'Arcy could imagine the pressure he was under from Commander Bob Tanner and their masters in COBRA. "Everyone is aware of that, Rob. Everyone, including the kidnappers, is also aware that your client doesn't have such resources. They'll have to strike a bargain now, or your time runs out. So what *happens* if you *do* get an agreement? We can't allow you to deliver, especially now we're getting closer to finding the bastards."

"I'll play it by ear."

"Balls!" Roman thundered, in untypical language. "I know you, Rob. You've anticipated every stage of the game. How much will you offer?"

D'Arcy liked Roman; he didn't enjoy doing this to him. "Go home, Reg, and get an early night. If they ring you'll get the tapes from your phone-tap people soon enough."

The policeman blinked and stared long and hard at the man he had considered an ally until now. "I'm staying, Rob, unless you throw me out bodily. And then I'd be back with every official backing I need."

D'Arcy said: "Then you'd better have a coffee."

It was nine o'clock and two pots of coffee later when the kidnappers' leader called.

Nadirpur took a deep breath and put the receiver to his ear. The voice was nervous, aggressive. "You, listen, where is your ten million sterling?"

The Iranian looked and sounded like a zombie as he read his script. "I told you I can't get ten million. But I have raised other finance. I can now raise one million – within seven days."

"Five million!" counterdemanded the voice with scarcely a second's thought.

D'Arcy noted the kidnapper's acceptance of the time extension without protest. Also he hadn't expected the

399

kidnapper to jump down to five million in his first counter-bid. It suggested the gang was now really anxious for a quick resolution. The killing of Sheikh Hayira was beginning to backfire on them.

Nadirpur looked confused.

Gently D'Arcy took the handset from him. "Listen, this is Nadirpur's adviser here. We've spoken before . . ."

"D'Arcy –" The voice almost spat with contempt.

"We make a final offer of two million sterling. Delivered in full in seven days to your instructions." He spoke rapidly, striking hard whilst he had the kidnapper at a disadvantage. "With just two conditions. Proof that Mrs Nadirpur and her daughter are still alive. *And*, the release of Philippe Chaumont from Beirut –"

"Jesus Christ!" Roman exclaimed.

D'Arcy waved him to silence. "Agree this and in seven days you'll have the money and your ship – or full compensation."

"No way!" the kidnapper protested. But there was a hint of doubt in his voice.

"Agree now, or it's off!" D'Arcy snarled at the mouthpiece.

A pause. "It is agreed."

D'Arcy said: "Then ring this number *immediately* . . ."

Roman's face dropped. "Rob, what the hell are you playing at!" Frantically he scribbled the number in his notebook.

D'Arcy hung up. "Sorry, Reg."

"You bastard!" The policeman grabbed at the handset to call the eavesdroppers.

"Save yourself the effort, you're too late," D'Arcy said. "It's the number of a neighbour of Dave Forbes."

Roman's face was scarlet with rage. "And he's passed on a new safe number?" he accused.

"You know the form, Reg."

"Bastard," the policeman repeated under his breath. "And this sudden increase of funds, where does that come from?"

"That's a private matter."

Roman's eyes narrowed. "Nothing to do with the sudden inclusion of Philippe Chaumont in your negotiations, I suppose? Do I detect the dark hand of the French in all this?"

"No comment."

Reg Roman stood up. "Bob Tanner will have my balls for this. And you've just lost yourself the last few remaining friends you've got. You'll find the offence is called obstructing the police."

D'Arcy said: "Just think of the seven-year-old girl and her mother, Reg. And another poor bastard in Beirut. Think of that, and get your woodentops to find the kidnappers. That's your job. I've done mine."

As Roman stormed out, Nadirpur confessed his puzzlement.

D'Arcy explained: "A neighbour of Dave Forbes was given a new safe telephone number – unknown to the police – where Dave himself has been waiting. The kidnapper telephoned the neighbour and will have been given the new number before the police can trace or intercept the call. Now there is no way that they can break in on our new line of communication. Even as we speak Dave should be making final arrangements with the kidnappers."

Nadirpur nodded soberly.

"Smile," D'Arcy said encouragingly. "We've got our deal. We've located your ship. Barring the unforeseen you'll see your wife and daughter within seven days."

"But the ship is not yet in our hands. You now have no contact with Spidex, so how do you get it back to let the Iranians have their cargo?"

"I'm working on it," D'Arcy replied.

"You cannot rely on the Omanis to co-operate. They will not give the arms to Iran."

"I don't want force to be used. There's the crew and Rick Clay to think about. The hijackers must be persuaded to give the ship up peacefully."

"But how?"

D'Arcy wasn't going to be drawn. "Trust me." He crossed to the kitchen and returned with a bottle from the fridge.

"It may be premature," D'Arcy said, "but a small celebration may be in order. Perrier Jouët Belle Epoque – that's a good one, isn't it?"

"Champagne? I haven't touched a drop since this began." Nadirpur stared at the enamelled art nouveau flowers etched on the bottle. He could not really believe that the nightmare might be coming to its end.

"It's one of the best," he tried to say, but the words stuck in his throat as the tide of emotion rose, and tears of joy sprang in his eyes.

Captain Darvish Hamman bore the expression of a sphinx.

The inscrutability suited the face like weathered rock as he stood in the brick office hut of the desert camp near the Iranian naval base of Busheir.

To one side of him, his charge sat at a desk and wrote in neat Farsi script on quality paper. There may have been no lavatory rolls for the citizens of Iran, but there was writing paper for the bearded one. The man they called Sabbah.

Hamman wondered at the mysterious workings of Allah that he of all people – a middle-class *taghouti* – had been chosen as the leader's personal bodyguard and trusted adjutant. But he could guess the reason why.

It had begun after the dream. Just days after young Shamlou had vanished from the camp on a secret assignment to Europe.

The instructor sergeant had not forgiven Hamman for the humiliating climb-down he had been forced to make in front of his recruits. He had directed his sadistic attentions on Hamman in the days that followed. Punishments for invented misdemeanours: carrying a rucksack of rocks on the double, cleaning the cesspit with his bare hands, eating holy dirt.

That was when Hamman turned. Before an entire assembly of recruits, the veteran had cut the instructor sergeant down with a blow behind his knees. With three hard sharp movements he had pummelled the man's face into the stony ground, pulping it beyond recognition. Then Hamman had stood to attention, awaiting the retribution that would surely follow.

Yet when he was summoned to the tent of the bearded one, he had been received like a hero. The instructor sergeant had got no more than he deserved, Sabbah said; after all, the man was not 'chosen'. Hamman was.

Since that moment he had hardly left the bearded one's side. Trusted implicitly, he had borne witness to the dark and dangerous secrets of Iranian high politics.

Sabbah had been pleased with his silent, obedient service which had culminated in his handling of the Omani seadog Nasiyb. It had been Hamman's unit of *Pessarane Behesht* Boghammars which tore into the smuggler's dhow and sent it to the bottom of the Gulf with no survivors.

The bearded one stopped writing. He turned and looked up at his guardian. "I have an important visitor coming now, Darvish. You will kindly remember that you are both blind and deaf."

Hamman's lips tightened imperceptibly. He left the spartan office, shielding his eyes against the bright glare of the sun on the drill square of the compound. On the far side the huge wire gates were being opened to admit a Suzuki jeep. A cloud of dust followed the vehicle across the square to where Hamman stood.

The veteran saluted the single occupant automatically. He recognised him as one of two men who had often been in Sabbah's company at the training camp. Younger than the bearded one, he was clean-shaven and wore a jacket over a collarless shirt.

He mounted the verandah and greeted Sabbah who had come out to meet him. They hugged like brothers.

As they settled down to talk Hamman poured them both

lemon juice before taking up his usual corner position from which he could cover both the windows and the door.

"So what is the news from London?" the bearded one asked.

"They have agreed a sum of two million sterling." The younger man sounded pleased. "For that they have demanded seven days' grace. At the end of that they promise the ship itself or compensation in full. Of course I have no way of knowing whether they can deliver. They cannot stall for ever."

The bearded one smiled. "It is of no importance."

"How so?"

"You may ask our friend here." He turned in his seat and smiled at Hamman. "He has located the *Clarion Call* and his Boghammars have destroyed the scoundrel spy who worked for us. This knowledge is now ours alone. We will seize it back for ourselves."

"And the two million sterling?"

Sabbah relaxed back in his chair and sipped at his lemon juice. "Oh, I think we shall have that too. Our Iranian paymasters can have their arms, but the two million shall be ours. Our war is still for Palestine. Two million sterling will pay to increase the presence of the *Pessarane Behesht* in Lebanon before that traitorous dog Arafat can raise his new army."

"Then you should be aware that a new condition has been laid down for the deal in London."

"Laid down? By whom?"

"By Nadirpur's negotiator. The man called D'Arcy."

Sabbah grunted. "And what is his condition?"

"That, along with Nadirpur's wife and child, the Frenchman Chaumont is released from Beirut."

A fist crashed on the table; lemon juice spilled. "May Allah rot his miserable soul!"

"I believe the two million has been made available by the French Government. Nadirpur does not have such money."

The bearded one's wrath subsided. If it was French

404

money, then he would have to accept that there would be no deal without the release of the diplomat in Beirut. "Then Shamlou has done well," he reflected. He turned again to Hamman. "You will be proud of your brother-in-arms."

Hamman said nothing. He had thought often of the boy, had wondered what had become of him. Whether he was dead or alive.

"No comment, Darvish?"

"I am blind and deaf," he reminded. "And dumb."

"And insolent," said the younger man.

The bearded one laughed. "He is professional. We could do with more like him." He turned back to the other man. "And how will this money be paid?"

"I thought in diamonds. Brought to a neutral country by the man called D'Arcy."

Sabbah frowned. "For what reason?"

"Because, over this business, he has made himself an enemy of Islam," the younger man said darkly.

"Or an enemy of my little brother?" Sabbah provoked.

"Like Sheikh Hayira he should be cut down by the sword of Islam."

"And what makes you believe he will agree to go where you want?"

"Because I will suggest the Sultanate of Oman. And that is also where he believes he will find the ship."

Sabbah stared up at the fan, his mind momentarily drifting back in time to the book he had read in his childhood, back through the centuries to when Al-Hasan ibn-al-Sabbah would disperse his fearless warriors to destroy his enemies. They had failed against Prince Edward of England. The man D'Arcy was no prince, but he would do. "So be it," he murmured.

After further discussion Sabbah called Hamman to stand before his desk. "You and your group are able to take over the ship *Clarion Call* and return it to me?"

"It is what I am trained to do. All the plans are ready. My men are in place. We just need the word."

A gentle, menacing smile. "You have the word, Hamman. Go and do your duty."

Hamman saluted and moved towards the door.

"By the way, there should be no survivors to spread rumours and lies."

The face was stone. "It shall be done."

Another smile. "No wonder Allah chose you, Hamman, no wonder."

He stepped out into the blinding sun with anger burning in his head. Anger that youthful innocents like the boy-man Shamlou should be sent on a divine mission that was nothing but a sham. To manure the fields of martyrdom with his own young flesh to satisfy the evil whims of men like Sabbah.

Anger that he, Hamman, had but one real duty. To his own survival and that of his family. And that required him to obey those who could and would destroy both him and his loved ones.

Because Hamman alone had seen the sham. Had been unnerved by his own dream and had distrusted his memories. Had seen the walled compound that was always out-of-bounds with armed guards and fierce dogs.

He who had stolen out one night after Shamlou's departure, had climbed the wall. Had relived his dream in the empty garden. Had seen the dried-up wine fountains and pipes from the vats. Had seen the wired music tapes and the store shelves of sleeping draughts and syringes. Had seen the actors and actresses. Had seen the actress who had been with Shamlou fornicating with the instructor sergeant.

Hamman, he told himself as he crossed the dry heat of the drill square, you have been chosen all right. Chosen to know the truth. And it was a heavy burden to bear.

"Ron, isn't that list finished yet?" Detective Sergeant Ted Plover asked.

He was starting to crack. Anxiety was beginning to overwhelm his usually placid personality. Having once served in the Anti-Terrorist Branch, he had been the natural choice for local coordinator as the focus of the hunt for the Nadirpur kidnappers switched to Harrow.

"One last check, Ted, I don't want to miss one," Ron Wilkins, his fellow detective sergeant, replied.

Plover grunted. He was beginning to drown in the sea of paperwork despite the arrival of two senior officers from New Scotland Yard. In fact their mere presence increased the pressure.

The list on which Ron Wilkins was working was Harrow police station's contribution to the nationwide check on purchasers of video camcorders two days earlier. In all some five thousand shops would have been visited. Multiples were the easiest as most kept customers' names and addresses as part of the till receipt and proof-of-purchase. That year some 90,000 camcorders were expected to be sold, and between 200 and 400 on the day in question.

Across the country the pressure was on to have them collated and fed into the HOLMES computer. There they would be cross-matched against the list of 25,000 Iranian nationals resident in the UK, and known owners of a particular model of IBM golf ball typewriter.

Since the murder of Sheikh Hayira in London that morning – and the finding of a copy of the *Harrow Observer* at the scene – nowhere had the pressure been greater than in Ted Plover's office.

"Small world," Ron Wilkins said. Harrow station's contribution to the national list was just two names. One of them was Elizabeth Christie.

"What's that?" Plover asked irritably.

"One of the names is Beth Christie. If it's the same one. The wife of a bloke I play golf with."

Plover wasn't impressed. "So she bought a video camera. Happens all the time. But as Harrow is now top of the list they'll want her checked anyway."

"I can look in on my way home," he offered casually.

"Sure, now that list is finished you can push off. Those bastards from the Yard will have me at it till all hours."

407

Wilkins took his jacket from the back of the chair. "Mind if I borrow a copy of the kidnap dossier? Never know, something might gel."

"Be my guest. See you tomorrow."

But beneath his calm exterior, Wilkins was in a sweat. His mind was racing. He had not mentioned several things to Plover. One was that Beth Christie's husband was Iranian. Another was that the detective constable who had visited the retail outlet reported that the camcorder had been purchased for cash. And the address given for Beth Christie was not the same one that Wilkins knew.

He parked outside the shabby terraced house in Station Road, praying that the owner would also have the name Elizabeth Christie. The old lady who answered the door was called Jones; she only owned a black and white portable television.

Why the hell hadn't he told Ted Plover of his suspicions? He knew the answer. Because he could not, would not believe it himself. Ali involved in kidnap? No way. Or the lovely Beth? It was unthinkable. He had to make sure himself. Put his own mind at rest. Despite what they said about coppers, Wilkins valued personal friendships outside the force.

He made the short journey up Harrow Hill, past the sprawling old buildings of the famous school, through the little village and into London Road. There he turned off into the private road.

Almost as soon as he passed through the tall gates to the gravel drive, he began to experience a strange sensation. An uneasiness. He climbed from the car and his professional eye took in the scene. The house seemed unnaturally quiet. Despite the warmth of the early summer evening there wasn't one window open at the front of the house. The lawn looked in need of a mow.

He might have assumed that Ali and Beth were out, except that Ali's Mercedes was parked in front of the garage. Just protruding behind the corner of the garage was the mustard-coloured bonnet of a builder's van. A pile of paint cans, tarpaulin, sacks of plaster and other decorators' rubbish was piled beside the front doorsteps. He couldn't imagine the houseproud American Beth being too pleased about that.

Then he remembered something that Freddie Phillips had told him some days earlier, that the Christies had decided to redecorate the dining area only weeks after it had already been done. Because they had made a mistake and couldn't live with the colours.

Wilkins felt a pang of envy. Some people really did have more money than sense . . .

He glanced again at the van. Seven thirty was a bit late for builders to be working. Still, he had mates in the game and knew they worked long hours in the summer months to make up for winter losses.

He rang the bell and shuffled his feet uneasily. Why did he have this ridiculous feeling he was being watched?

No sound from within. He pressed the bell again. And waited.

He was on the point of leaving when the door inched open. The security chain allowed just enough space for him to recognise Beth's face.

"Hi, sweetheart, it's me. Sorry to disturb you."

Bloodshot eyes blinked out of a pale, drained face. "Oh, Ron." The words sounded more guarded than welcoming. Hardly what he expected from the vivacious American who had played footsie with him under the table on more than one occasion.

As the hairs on the back of his neck began to crawl uneasily, he decided to make no mention of the camcorder. Instead he said: "Could I have a word with Ali?"

"No, I'm afraid Ali's out."

"Ah, I saw his car here and thought . . ."

She just stared at him.

Wilkins took an involuntary step back and shrugged. "He didn't turn up for golf again this morning. I thought I'd just call by."

"Ali is very busy just now. I'll tell him you called."

"Fine, fine." He forced his widest smile. "You feelin' better?"

"Better? Oh, yes. Just a bit run down, that's all." Final. "See you then."

"*Caio*." The door shut.

Wilkins returned to his car, deeply troubled. On his way home he picked up a Chinese takeaway. He ate it in front of the television with a can of lager while he read the Nadirpur dossier.

Then he read it again.

He realised he hadn't touched his drink.

At ten thirty he telephoned Plover's home number. "It's Ron here. Sorry to disturb you, Ted. Perhaps I'm being silly, but I'm a bit worried."

# 17

The dark blue Ambassador 1.7L swept out of Paddington Green police station into the Saturday morning traffic, tyres squealing.

Detective Sergeant Ron Wilkins steadied himself with the grab rail. Things were starting to move fast in more ways than one.

"Thank God you knew the couple," Detective Chief Superintendent Reg Roman said. "Neither would have shown up on the computer because the husband changed his name by deed poll to Otis Christie. On the Iranian immigrant list he was under his original name. Anyway, we ran the Christies through the HOLMES computer first thing this morning. Sure enough he bought an IBM golf ball in 1981 through Mercantile Credit. In the same way her name would have meant nothing on the list of video purchasers. I guess the fact she gave her name to the shop at all was by mistake – she probably wasn't expecting to be asked because she paid cash. Fortunately she bought it at Dixons who include names and addresses on all till receipts as a matter of course. If the terrorists are using her place as a hostage house against her will, then I imagine her nerves are shot to hell. I'm not surprised she made a mistake."

Wilkins said: "She probably didn't realise how important it was."

"I just wish you hadn't gone round to the house yesterday. That could have given the bastards a bad fright."

Wilkins looked suitably sheepish. "I am sorry – I just didn't believe it, you know. But when I read the full report last night it all tallied. Including the first time Ali didn't turn up for early morning golf. I checked back – that was the date of the kidnap."

"Tell me more about the wife," Roman pressed.

"American. Gregarious – suddenly cancels a dinner party at the eleventh hour with the limp excuse of being unwell. In various conversations she's been contradictory about having visited the doctor. And I can personally tell you she looks a nervous wreck."

"And these decorators?"

"That's the clincher," Wilkins replied. "They've got a mustard-coloured van and the postman describes them as looking Arabic. And all this after just having extensively redecorated. I spoke to the original decorators this morning. The guy's done a lot of work for the Christies over the years. He was amazed – said both of them were over the moon at the job he'd done. Reckons they'd never even consider using another outfit."

"What about movement? I mean, do these decorators come and go at regular times each day?"

"That's a difficult one, sir. We don't want to alert all the neighbours to the fact that something's going on. So we've been talking to delivery people. Newspaper girl, postman, milkman, et cetera. And there's no fixed pattern. There are high fences or hedges all the way round the house, so it's not easy for anyone to know. Except that the van's been seen there very early in the morning and late at night."

Roman grunted. "You've done well. We'll want to speak to the delivery people again, and meanwhile pull them discreetly off their rounds. Get our people to replace them. It's holiday time so that won't seem suspicious." He stared out at the busy London streets flashing past. "What other steps have been taken?"

"Detective Sergeant Ted Plover is on discreet surveillance in the road in an unmarked van. He's ex-Anti-

412

Terrorist Branch. But nothing else in the immediate vicinity."

"Local shops? Has she been buying extra food, that sort of thing?"

"No, sir, we've kept away. If we can get to Ali himself, that won't be necessary."

Another grunt. "Good thinking."

"But we are sending someone down to see the boy. He's at a boarding school in Hampshire. Just a precaution." Wilkins remembered something. "That reminds me. He's in the school choir. And I remember reading about –"

"The tape recording? The message from Mrs Nadirpur was played over an earlier recording of a school concert, or somesuch." He nodded with grim satisfaction. "You've done well, Wilkins. Let's see now if we're right."

Roman tapped his driver on the shoulder. "Drop us here and wait."

As the car pulled into the New Bond Street pavement, the two passengers were already out and walking towards Brook Street. They could see no one obviously loitering as they approached the Pavilion Gallery.

It was a simple, single-fronted shop with one window sparsely, but expensively filled with Iranian artefacts set against a background of a hand-made silk Persian carpet. Roman noted the dust on the pottery and the accumulation of dead flies.

The sound of the bell rang in the long, narrow interior. At the far end a man sat at an antique desk. He looked up, startled. He made no effort to move, spoke no words of welcome.

They passed the paintings and carpets that adorned the walls.

The man squinted at the newcomers who were thrown into silhouette by the strong sunlight outside. "Ron? Ron Wilkins?" His voice quavered. "What are you doing here . . . ?"

"Hi, Ali, how are you, old son?" Wilkins said breezily.

"Hope you don't mind me dropping in, but I was in the area. This is a mate of mine, Reg – he's into antiques, relics and so forth."

Roman smiled. "My card."

Taken aback Ali glanced down. On the card was written: IS IT SAFE TO TALK?

The Iranian opened his mouth and closed it again. As he looked up his eyes were wide and white, as though he expected one of them to shoot him dead on the spot. "I-I-er, yes, what do you mean?" His smile was brittle, his eyes glittering with fear. "Of course it is *safe*."

Wilkins seated himself, whilst Roman remained standing.

"Are you *sure*?" the detective repeated, and his eyes said that he knew all about it.

Ali Christie swallowed hard. "You can talk here."

Instantly the tension evaporated and the two policemen relaxed.

"It's okay, Ali," Wilkins said kindly. "We know all about it. You'll be safe soon. It's nearly over."

Ali Christie just stared, his mouth hanging loose. The colour had drained from his face, leaving his skin ashen and his eyes with the desperate look of a man who had been condemned to death.

"Ali?"

Not a flicker from the eyes, just a nervous tic pulsing at the corner of his mouth.

"You're amongst friends, Ali. We're here to help."

Ali Christie stared, motionless. Moisture gathered in the corners of his eyes. Then, slowly, tears began to roll and he started trembling like a man in fever.


At precisely one thirty-five in the afternoon Reg Roman pressed the button. From the Pavilion Gallery he made a direct phone call to Bob Tanner, Commander of the Anti-Terrorist Branch.

It was to launch one of the most experienced and sophisticated crisis management machines in the world. On receiving the message Tanner's first step was to call COBRA – the Cabinet Office Briefing Room – in Whitehall.

The conversation was brief and to the point. The key word was 'covert'. As yet the siege had not 'gone live', and with innocent parties at risk, all police units were to be put on standby. No move was to be made without prior consultation with the highest authority.

"I want to keep the lid on this one," said the voice from Whitehall. "Pull in SO7 for initial covert surveillance."

Tanner added: "In view of the terrorist involvement, sir, may I suggest we alert the SAS to this one from the outset."

"I agree. I'm going to call a meeting now. I'll put Director, Special Forces in the picture and he can alert 22 before he leaves to join us." A pause as Whitehall consulted the clock. "How long before you establish Zulu Control?"

"What's the record?"

Hesitation. "One hour forty minutes."

"It won't be longer."

Ten minutes later, at the Stirling Lines barracks in Hereford, D'Arcy's old friend Major Johnny Fraser – second-in-command of 22 SAS and commander of the Counter-Revolutionary Warfare Wing – was hastily convening a meeting with key members of the Duty Squadron, whose rota turn it was to be on permanent thirty-minute standby. It was cramped in the Squadron Office as the commander, Major Crispin, his second-in-command Captain Seagrave and Sergeant Major Brian Hunt joined the collection of Troop commanders who had been called by personal bleeper.

After the sketchy outline brief the buzz of anticipation was like electricity in the confined space. The first question came: "Where exactly in north London, boss?"

"Harrow-ish," Major Fraser replied. "Anyone know Harrow? Anyone go to Harrow school?"

"Na – try G Squadron," quipped one wag to an appreciative audience, referring to the one unit that recruited almost exclusively from the Regiments of the Guards.

Major Crispin took the direct approach. "While they're sorting out what maps and JARIC1 cover we've got of the area in the library, has anyone got an *A to Z*?"

A scuffle of activity in the packed, smoke-filled room. A dog-eared copy of the street map book appeared.

"Scale's too small," pronounced Toby Carstairs, D'Arcy's successor as second-in-command of CRW Wing. "But here's the road, probably a private estate. Hell, doesn't *anyone* know the area?"

A united mumble of apology.

"Never mind," Major Johnny Fraser interrupted. "We'll get aerial photo coverage soon enough and they'll fax up large-scale maps from London as soon as they're located. Might take a little longer than usual as this isn't central district. Meanwhile I'm flying down in five minutes with Lionel. We'll take the Recce Party with us and get someone established on the ground as soon as possible. It'll also give us a group on immediate standby in case things go pear-shaped at the house unexpectedly."

"Usual team?" Seagrave asked the Duty Squadron commander.

"Yes, you and Sarn't-Major," Crispin confirmed. Seagrave and Hunt nodded in quiet satisfaction. "And two from CRW Wing. Recce, assess and report back." He turned to Seagrave. "Take a SATLINK set and keep in touch. Use Deputy Commander Reg Roman at SO13 for liaison. If it's as tricky as it sounds you might want to link up with Bill Pearson, poacher turned gamekeeper – ex-D Squadron now with SO13."

Johnny Fraser glanced at his watch. "Right, time to go to the party . . ."

Ten minutes after receiving the alert from London the Puma helicopter took off from Hereford with its six passengers.

416

It was met on its arrival just forty minutes later at the Duke of York's barracks in Chelsea by three police cars. One set off with the advance Recce Party for Harrow, whilst the second sped Captain Lionel Witcher of the SAS 'Kremlin' Intelligence unit towards Paddington Green police station.

The third took Major Johnny Fraser the short distance to New Scotland Yard where he was shown to the Operations Room.

There he was introduced to the gathering of representatives from the many branches of police and security services which were already on standby. They included Reg Roman from the Anti-Terrorist Branch; a Special Branch expert on Arab terrorism; a Foreign Office official responsible for Middle East affairs; a Home Office adviser, and a senior Military Intelligence officer.

These men would form the nucleus of the 'Intelligence Cell' which would constantly analyse the situation and advise Bob Tanner who was on the spot at Zulu Control. They would also have access to advice from two police superintendents who had taken a special two-week course at Bramshill on 'negotiation' should that become necessary, and a professor from the London Institute of Psychiatry.

Also standing by for briefing were officers from SO11, police 'Blue Beret' marksmen from PT17, and SO11(2) Technical Support Branch, affectionately known as the 'Dirty Tricks' Department.

While the representatives were taking their seats for the initial briefing and discussion a yellow British Telecom van was trundling down a private road in Harrow. It passed the house of Ali and Beth Christie, and stopped one hundred yards beyond.

While engineers began erecting a striped protection tent over an inspection manhole, Bob Tanner sat amongst the state-of-the-art communications equipment in the body of the van and made his call to the Operations Room at New Scotland Yard.

"MP from Zulu. I am operational. Repeat. I am operational."

It was just one hour and thirty five minutes since COBRA had pressed the button.

At three-thirty in the afternoon Captain Lionel Witcher, a painfully thin, bespectacled young officer with unkempt fair hair, stepped into Paddington Green police station. Even in the smart but subdued Gieves & Hawkes suit, he was no one's concept of an officer in the military, let alone the SAS.

Over coffee he was given a rapid update of developments by one of Reg Roman's Anti-Terrorist Branch detectives, Inspector 'Josh' Amesbury, and a local Harrow CID officer, Ron Wilkins.

"So that's what D'Arcy's up to now," Witcher said.

"You know him?" Amesbury asked.

"Did a lot of ops and exercises together during his time in CRW Wing. Good man. Looks like he's bitten off a bit more than he can chew this time."

"Maybe his old mates can do the chewing for him?" Amesbury suggested with a grin.

"We'll see." Witcher prodded his spectacles back onto the bridge of his nose. Although in his mid-thirties he looked ten years younger, and probably always would. "So any chance I can talk to the houseowner?"

"I've arranged a meet for four thirty. But it'll have to be at his gallery. Sometimes the scrotes ring up to check he's there, and to remind him they've got his wife. Make threats. All pretty vile stuff."

"Is the gallery ever watched?"

"He thinks it might have been in the beginning sometimes, but not now."

"Let's go."

Fifteen minutes later they arrived at the Pavilion Gallery. Ali Christie was watchful and nervous, despite Witcher's quiet reassurances that all would be well.

The Iranian jumped when Inspector Amesbury flicked

his lighter to start a cigarette. "I'm sorry," he said in a small voice. "Since this began I can't stand the sight of flame. You know, lighters or matches?"

"Why's that?" Witcher coaxed.

"They threaten to set light to Beth. It was the first thing they did, douse her with petrol and flick a lighter. They still do it every few days. One of them, Ahmad, he really enjoys it, I think. I'm sure he'd really like to do it. He's foul, tall and gangling with a gormless grin. Beth is petrified of him, we both are."

Witcher held the CRW Wing questionnaire on his knee, pen poised. "Tell me very briefly how it all began," he said softly.

Christie shrugged, despondently. "One morning two men arrived. My wife Beth answered the door. They said they were business acquaintances of mine. When I came down, they pounced. They produced guns and threatened to set fire to my wife. They said if we did exactly as they demanded we would come to no harm. They just wanted the house." He swallowed hard, fighting back emotion. "I had never seen them before."

"Why did they want the house?"

"They never said. But later two more of them arrived, and after that they all pretended to be builders and decorators – you know, as a front. They took over the cellar. I think they are holding people down there. We've heard voices."

"They allow you to go out to work?"

"They insist – everything must appear normal."

"But not for a social occasion. Like your morning golf?"

He held up his hands. They were shaking like tuning-forks. "My handicap is bad enough at the best of times." A brittle laugh. "No, work only. And when I am home my Beth has to go out for them. To buy food. She must always go to several shops, so no one knows she is getting more than usual."

"What do these people call themselves?"

"*Pessarane Behesht*. Sorry, that means – "

"Sons of Heaven?"

"You speak Farsi?"

"A little." A shared moment, a small comfort.

Ali Christie relaxed and went on to give his descriptions of the kidnappers, gradually opening up and becoming more talkative. Occasionally he slipped into his native tongue.

Lionel Witcher made no comment and continued his note-taking.

Then they were onto weapons. He showed a sheaf of photographs.

"Pistols first," Christie said. "Then later, when the other two turned up, these bigger guns appeared. Machine guns, I think." More photographs.

Witcher wrote: 9mm automatics. At least one identified as a Beretta. Two AK 47s seen at the same time. He looked up again. "Tell me, how do they treat you? Roughly, gently . . . ?"

"Mostly politely and formally."

"Is their attitude consistent?"

"No."

"Who is the most inconsistent?"

"Ahmad. Behind his back they call him Matchsticks."

"In what way is he inconsistent?"

"He acts violently and is irrational, moody."

"And they threatened to kill you both when they first came?"

"They still do. Every night."

"Do they watch television or listen to the radio? How do they pass their time?"

"The leader, the one called Jalal, is very tense. He is often going out, but when he's in he appears to do a lot of thinking or making notes. The two quiet ones – I believe they are called Hamid and Kamal – they often read books and magazines, or do the crossword. Sometimes they watch television. Always they watch the news."

"And the one they call Matchsticks?"

"He watches much television. Always he sees *Neighbours*, Beth says."

Witcher disguised his smile. "Do they have a sentry, a guard?"

"Yes, always one."

"Where do they keep watch?"

"At daytimes there is one by the front window in the living room. At night there is always someone outside our bedroom door. Beth and I are kept handcuffed. I would not know others."

"Is there a burglar alarm?"

"Yes."

"Do you know how it works? What make?"

"All I know is it picks up movement. Just the downstairs rooms, including the hall."

"And the garage?"

"No."

"Did these people bring anything with them that might be explosives or grenades?"

He nodded. "There were packets of stuff which looked like putty . . . wrapped in brown paper. I believe that is explosives – there are wires connecting them all.

"There is a small black box with a switch which I think triggers the explosives. There is no wire to it, so I think it must be remote-controlled. Usually the leader has it with him. Otherwise Hamid or Kamal. Never the one called Matchsticks."

"Where are the packages placed?"

"In each corner on the ground floor and by the front door. Also wires go into the basement. I do not know if there are explosives down there, too."

"Do they use the telephone?"

"Never themselves. Only once someone called them. Sometimes Beth and I answer when it rings – if they allow us. But not just lately."

"How many telephones are there?"

"One downstairs in the hall. And a bedroom extension, but they have removed that."

"Do you know what these people hope to achieve?"

"They talk about a ship that has a cargo which they want . . . That they have been double-crossed by a supplier . . ."

"Do you know why they picked your house?"

Ali Christie shrugged. "It suits them, I suppose. It is secluded and has high fences and hedges. I have many Iranian business acquaintants, maybe one of those suggests my house."

"Does your wife cook for them?"

"They would not trust her, no. They cater for themselves with the provisions she is ordered to buy. I think they must give them food downstairs."

"How many people are they holding in the cellar, do you know?"

"I have only heard two voices. On two separate occasions. A woman shouting, hysterical. And some nights later a child screaming, like a tantrum. A girl. That is the only time."

"Do you know what their toilet arrangements are? Are they brought up to your bathroom?"

"I do not think so. In fact, at times there has been an unpleasant smell, you know? On the hotter days."

"These people are Moslem. Do they pray together at any prescribed time?"

"Often they pray before breakfast, but one always guards. It is not a fixed time, but usually between six thirty and seven. But they do this less now. They are more nervous, more keyed up."

"But they are still alert?"

"Very, I would say."

"Unstable, in your opinion?"

"I do not know. More so now, I think. We are very afraid."

"From what you know of them, do you think they might be persuaded to let you, and the people in the cellar, go in return for some other inducement? Perhaps promise of an unhindered passage to the airport and a flight direct to somewhere in the Middle East?"

Ali Christie looked directly at Witcher. "Candidly, I think they would only agree if that was their purpose. I think that escape is not their concern. Just to have their demands met. And I think they are professionally trained – I hear them refer to that sometimes. And I do not think they would believe such an offer from Britain."

"One more thing, Ali. We need detailed plans of the house."

The Iranian nodded distractedly, glanced down at his wristwatch. "It is five thirty. I must go."

"House plans, Ali." Firm.

"They are lodged with my building society, the City & Westward. Architect's drawings."

Witcher smiled. "Thank you, Ali. You can relax this weekend, knowing it is nearly over. But on no account must you tell anyone – even your wife – that you have spoken to us. Your lives may very well depend on it. Just try and reassure Beth, and be calm. Do absolutely nothing to provoke them."

A bitter laugh. "Do not worry about that!"

"We may need to speak to you again on Monday."

They left the gallery then and hailed a cab. As it turned the corner, Witcher glanced back to see Ali Christie locking the door. He looked very small, and very alone.


Since his secret meeting with D'Arcy on the Thursday, Dave Forbes had been extremely busy.

After receiving the redirected 'safe' call from the kidnapper, during which the caller said he would be in contact again with delivery instructions for the agreed two million sterling, he began to work on his plan.

The target: a firm of City solicitors called Mendlesham, Hall & Agnost, amongst whose clients was the mysterious George Cupplewaite. Following the murder of Sheikh Hayira, Cupplewaite was their only tenuous link with the Spidex cartel.

Before midnight he made four telephone calls. One was to a solicitor friend who assured him that, generally, solicitors were not particularly security minded. He also confirmed that really confidential documents were invariably held in a locked safe or strongroom.

The second call was to an ex-Signals Corps friend who in civilian life had become a confirmed radio ham. They arranged to meet the next day.

His third call was to Jack Ducane, an old friend from his SAS days, who ran his own private investigation company. Ducane kept a small printing press in his office for making up business cards and letter headings for any cover identity he or his staff might require. Ducane assured him that his request would present no problem.

The final call was to a Wiltshire farmer, an ex-Green Jackets officer and pigeon fancier.

With a quarter bottle of Scotch inside him, Forbes slept blissfully until his alarm went off at eight the next morning. By nine he had breakfasted, washed and shaved off his moustache.

He telephoned a well-known wigmakers off Tottenham Court Road and made an appointment for a fitting at ten thirty. He settled for a cheap £30 curly brown wig which cleverly transformed his appearance.

He wore it out of the shop. No one gave him a second glance as he searched for a passport photograph kiosk where he took a strip of film.

At twelve he met Ducane at the Duke's Head public house at the junction of Great Russell Street and Bloomsbury Street. After sharing a swift half, Ducane departed with the photographs and left Forbes with a Polaroid camera.

There was just a five-minute wait before Forbes's radio ham arrived with a plastic carrier bag. Inside it was a hand-held PRO-30 radio scanner.

"City police headquarters transmit on 451.775 UHF," his friend said, evidently having relished the challenge. "Mobile patrols and PCs on the beat receive on anything between 154.010 and 156.775 MHZ. I listened in last night to Old Jewry station. I reckon their response time will be piss-poor, especially to a non-priority property like a solicitors'. If it's eight minutes, you're hard done by. You sure it's not the Bank of England you're turning over?"

Forbes grinned. Now that was a thought.

After another half-hour gossiping over old times, Forbes returned to his temporary rented flat in south London. He checked the answerphone. No messages and no tell-tale clicks from callers who had hung up.

He made himself a cheese wedge sandwich and waited. At three o'clock the Wiltshire farmer arrived with a ventilated cardboard box. They shared a joke, but no serious questions were asked.

"If this pigeon doesn't show up at your farm in a week," Forbes said, "I owe you."

"That turkey couldn't find its own backside. Keep it with my compliments."

As the farmer left, Ducane arrived.

"British Telecom identity card. Most useful bit of kit we ever use. Called you Fred Smith – to suit your new hairdo."

"Piss off."

"The check address is right, but I've printed the telephone number you requested. Here's a box of screwdrivers and BT overalls. You might find them a tight fit."

"Cheers, Jacko. For that you can give me a lift to the City."

At exactly four o'clock Fred Smith, telephone engineer, sauntered into the entrance of Mendlesham, Hall & Agnost. It was a tired Victorian building off Throgmorton Street, the inside all chipped tile flooring and panelled walls that cried out for a coat of varnish. The solicitors occupied the entire ground floor and he pushed open the door to the reception area, in which he had previously sat in unhappy defiance for many hours during his unsuccessful attempts to be granted an interview with Mr Agnost.

The puckered mouth of the middle-aged receptionist was unsmiling. "Yes?"

Forbes grinned. "Telecom, love. About the fault." He showed his identity card.

She gave no sign of recognising him. "What fault? I haven't reported any faults."

"Ah, no, it's your clients phoning in, see. Reported can't get through."

"No one's said anything to me."

"Well, they can't, love, if they can't get through, can they? Want to check with my boss, in case it's a mistake?"

Irritated at the interruption, she said: "I don't expect that's necessary."

"Go on, love," he goaded. "To put your mind at rest." He jabbed a forefinger at his card. "That's the number."

He smiled to himself as he watched her ring Brandy's number, scarcely able to keep a straight face as D'Arcy's secretary adopted a variety of voices pretending to pass the caller from one department to another.

That'll teach you, you miserable old cow, Forbes thought with satisfaction as he recalled her offhand treatment of him on earlier visits.

Finally she hung up in exasperation. "Totally inefficient! Nothing changes. Well, if it's any consolation you're at the right address. You'd better carry on."

As he played with the reception switchboard for a few minutes he studied the alarm system. It was an infrared device, chosen as an economical way to cover a large old building with many doors and windows. The red LED light on the sensor above the desk blinked as it picked up his body heat.

He opened the door behind reception. It led into a long corridor with small partitioned offices running off each side. The smaller ones housed typists and secretaries like battery hens producing reams of paperwork, while three larger offices were home to the senior partners.

There was no sign of a strongroom.

He visited every office in turn, noting the position of the infrared sensor in each as he busied himself unscrewing and screwing up the telephone sets.

Nothing he saw referred to George Cupplewaite or to Spidex. All files, he noted, were identified only by reference numbers.

At five thirty, the stream of secretaries moving towards the reception area became a torrent. Most, he noted, carried files. They were laughing, chatting, eager to go home. But first they were taking important files to the strongroom. A small door he hadn't noticed before was open by the reception desk. He listened to the descending clatter of high heels from the stairwell behind the door, then followed the sound down to the basement.

The area comprised mostly a large stationery store with rows of racking plus a dumping ground for obsolete office equipment. The senior receptionist was supervising secretaries at an open door as each entered and returned without the files they had carried down.

Forbes busied himself tracing telephone wires until the last secretary left. He saw the woman lock the fireproof door to the strongroom and leave.

He came out of hiding, crossed the basement and opened the outer door. Immediately inside was another door of grey steel which guarded the concrete inner room.

"What are you doing here?"

He turned sharply. It was the receptionist. "Just a last minute check, love. Can't be too careful."

"Well, you won't find any telephones down here."

He grinned. "So I see."

"I'm about to lock up and set the alarms."

"Of course, I'm sorry. Too conscientious, that's my trouble."

She looked at him suspiciously. "Don't I know you?"

"Alas, ma'am, I don't believe we've ever had the pleasure."

At eleven thirty that night Forbes rendezvoused with D'Arcy in a side street, one block from the offices of Mendlesham, Hall & Agnost.

Forbes switched on the PRO-30 scanner while he showed

427

his boss the detailed floor plan he had made which illustrated the location of each sensor in the burglar alarm system, and explained how he'd decided they should break in. At intervals the scanner would suddenly burst with static and voices as Old Jewry police station and mobile patrols in the City exchanged messages.

On the stroke of midnight, when Friday night became Saturday morning, they left the car and strolled the block to the solicitors' offices, ducking into an alley which ran alongside the building. They passed railings which sealed off the drop to a dead basement area. Later that route would give them access to the strongroom.

Eventually Forbes stopped at a ground floor window. Using a dustbin to gain height, he went to work on the sash lock with a wide, thin-bladed palette knife he had borrowed from his wife's kitchen.

Two minutes later they were in the office of Mr Agnost's secretary. On the far wall the red LED light on the infrared sensor mounting winked on. At that moment the warning would be passed down a telephone line via the security firm to Old Jewry police station.

"See you later," Forbes said, and disappeared into the corridor, making his way swiftly into reception and down the stairs to the stationery stores. He quickly located the flyblown window that gave onto the dead basement area and railings in the side alley. Opposite it, almost immediately above the unmarked door to the strongroom was another infrared sensor unit. As he approached it blinked on.

Using an abandoned swivel chair, he stood and removed the plastic cover to the sensor eye. He then stuck a wide strip of parcel tape over the back of the cover, before replacing it. Undetectable from the outside the sensor was now half-blind. This would allow a direct approach to be made from the window to the strongroom without triggering the alarm again.

Satisfied, he retraced his footsteps to the secretary's office.

Meanwhile D'Arcy had switched on the radio scanner while he took a Polaroid snap of the desk he was about to search. He would use it to ensure that everything was left exactly as found.

None of the pile of papers and files on the senior secretary's desk referred to George Cupplewaite. However, he did find the cross-reference index book which gave the man's file number. He copied it down.

As Forbes had predicted the strongroom key was also in the desk, this time neatly hidden in an unlocked cash box in a bottom drawer. It was obligingly marked FILES. The odd-shaped Chubb key could only be for one place.

D'Arcy grinned. So much for security.

The scanner suddenly burst into action. Old Jewry police station was requesting a mobile unit to investigate a Central Station alarm at the offices of Mendlesham, Hall & Agnost.

Forbes arrived back from the basement. "All done, boss."

D'Arcy held up the key. "Let's go."

They scrambled back out of the sash window, which Forbes then closed, leaving a six inch gap at the top. He took the bewildered pigeon from its cardboard carrier and released it back into the office.

By the time the squad car arrived the men were back in Forbes's car. Police response time from the alarm first sounding had been sixteen minutes.

A long wait followed while the police called the keyholder. An irate Mr Agnost finally arrived from his home in Chiswick to inspect his premises with the law officers.

D'Arcy and Forbes smiled to each other as the voice came over the scanner, reporting back to the duty officer at Old Jewry. "*Another false one, Sarge. Window of premises left ajar and some dozy pigeon decided to make a nest in there. Set off the infrared. No intruders, all in order. Keyholder has attended. Say, Sarge, does your missus know a good recipe for pigeon pie . . . ?*"

D'Arcy and Forbes waited a further half-hour before

returning to the alley alongside the office. They fixed a knotted rope to the railings and let it drop to the narrow basement area. In seconds both men had vanished below eye level. The window catch on the sash yielded to the palette knife without protest, and they were in.

Approaching the strongroom in a straight line, they kept to the blind side of the disabled infrared sensor. The LED warning light stayed firmly out.

The large key turned stiffly in the Chubb lock and the heavy door creaked open. Wall-to-wall files covered the windowless room. Without the file-code number it would have been a hopeless task. With it, the file was located in seconds.

Forbes turned the pages while D'Arcy photographed them with a Minox micro document camera.

Twenty minutes later the intruders left, and it was as though no one had ever been there.

While D'Arcy and Forbes had been making their way to the City late on Friday night, the six men of the SAS recce team huddled in the cramped interview room that had been allocated to them at Harrow police station. It had become the local nerve centre for the operation. Linked to it, and monitoring all radio traffic was the Operations Room at New Scotland Yard.

Major Johnny Fraser, commander of the SAS Counter-Revolutionary Warfare Wing, had spent an exhausting day of briefings with representatives from every branch of the police and security forces on standby. He now knew every aspect of the case including the background and details of the negotiations for the release of the hostages. He was tired, but relieved to be back in the company of his own men.

Captain Lionel Witcher had just filled in the team on his interview with Ali Christie and now awaited their reaction.

It came initially from the 2IC of Duty Squadron, Captain Mark Seagrave. He was 'new school', a redbrick university entrant from a middle-working-class background, who had come to 22 Special Air Service Regiment via the Royal Engineers. He didn't smoke, rarely drank and ran a minimum of five miles every day. He was sharp, bright and transparently dedicated. After two years with the Regiment he was finally, thankfully, developing a sense of humour.

"Well, this one's going to be a barrel of fun," he said with feeling.

"Basements are always bad news," Major Fraser agreed. "Anyone got any bright ideas?"

"This is an old building, strongly built," Sergeant Major Brian Hunt stated. The likelihood was that it would fall to him to lead any assault. "So what's the cellar used for?"

"What d'you mean? To keep wine cool," Seagrave said.

Wine! Typical officer. "What about coal? Those buildings all ran on coal in the old days. And if there's coal there must be a hatch from the outside."

"That's a thought. Can we get a closer look?"

"Have we got access to plans?" asked one of the two CRW sergeants.

Witcher produced them with a flourish. "Took me a hell of a job getting these out of the building society after hours."

"What d'you want – a paper hat?"

The architect's drawings were spread over the table.

"Any modifications since this time?"

"Is this all there is?"

"What d'you expect?"

"You sure our friend remembered everything, Lionel?"

"What about these explosive charges?" Hunt asked. "Could they be booby-trapped?"

"Possibly, but not probably, Brian. There appears to be a command radio transmitter. Usually the leader's got it."

"Just hope it's not that loony – Matchsticks or whatever," said the other CRW sergeant.

"Whoever's got it must be taken out fast," Hunt added. "These Moslem fundamentalists are an unpredictable bunch."

"Could we gain access as gasmen or something?" Captain Mark Seagrave said helpfully.

"Or a coalman?" General laughter.

"Too dodgy," Hunt cut in. "They're already getting twitchy, look at Lionel's interview transcript. We need to take these bastards out quick and clean."

"We have to wait for authorisation," Major Fraser pointed out. "There's going to be no go-ahead unless the situation goes 'bent'. Usually someone's got to die before the politicians panic."

Groans of agreement.

"In this case we can't wait," Hunt pressed. "We can hardly hang about till they twig we're all around them. Then they'll just press the button and take the lot out – themselves, the hostages and all."

"I've advised COBRA of that," Major Fraser said. "I think they took it on board, but they're still passing little pink memos to each other."

"So d'you know *when* we might get the green light, skipper?"

"No, Brian. They want to give themselves – and us – as much time as possible. That might largely depend on how the hostage negotiations are going on."

"I hear Rob D'Arcy's involved."

Fraser said: "I'll be having words with him soon."

"He's all right. One of us," said a CRW sergeant emphatically.

Johnny Fraser wasn't so sure. "Meanwhile the police have established Zulu Control outside the premises with a view of the gate. They've got taps on the telephone, and in an hour or so the Dirty Tricks Department is going to have a go getting probe mikes in. I've got clearance to set up a close OP in the grounds. The air photos from JARIC show good ground cover."

"May I suggest your two CRW sergeants, skipper?"

Seagrave said. "Ted and Shorty. Sarn't Major Hunt and I could do a bit of lurking at the same time."

The thought of action was agreeable after a long and particularly diagreeable day.

"When's the off?"

"Three hours."

"What time does the moon rise?" Hunt asked. "I think it's on the wane."

"Hang on, I've got a clever diary," said Seagrave. Seagrave would. "0220 – great. Good timing."

"Right," Major Johnny Fraser said, happy that things were moving at last. "We need a crew up here. Two Troops at least, maybe three in case it's a long drawn-out business."

"No problem, skipper," Seagrave assured. He turned to Hunt: "Signal HQ for two immediate Troops from Duty Squadron, fully equipped. Helicopter into Northolt. Four drivers to bring our Rovers by road. Also get a couple of four-tonners from RAF Regiment. Set that up, please, and get RMP to provide us with base security – contact the Provost Company in Rochester Row."

The meeting broke up in a sudden burst of activity.


One hundred miles away in Hereford, Major Crispin of Duty Squadron called a midnight Orders Group for Troop commanders and their teams.

"Ground," he began in front of the gathered SAS veterans. "A detached house backing onto open ground in north London. The plan on the display board shows the layout of the house which has been faxed up from London. Other plans and photographs show the layout of the area and grounds. A model of the inside is being prepared and will be available as soon as possible, but probably not until we get to London.

"Situation – Enemy Forces: A terrorist group of fundamentalists have taken hostages at this address and are holding them in the basement. House owner and wife forced to behave 'normally'.

"Friendly Forces: MetPol have established Zulu Control and covert OP in road outside, posing as BT engineers. The telephone is being monitored; so far nothing useful has come up. Tonight we are establishing a close OP in the grounds and by daybreak SO11(2) plan to have surveillance devices *in situ*.

"Attachments and Detachments: None at this time.

"Mission –" Crispin paused, glancing up at his calm, watchful audience. "To ensure the release of all four hostages using minimum force."

He went quickly on, confirming the preestablished plan: "Execution – General outline: The two Troops will prepare to assault the house as directed. One Troop will assault, the other will secure the area.

"Detailed Tasks: Bill – ," he said, turning to the ice-cool, sandy-haired Mather, "your Troop will assault. Brummie, your Troop will provide a secure cordon and OPs as necessary. Benjamin, your Troop will be in reserve, supporting Brummie when needed. Troop commanders to prepare briefings and options.

"Co-ordination and Timing: Captain Mark Seagrave will be in-command and coordinate all action. Security team should arrange OPs prior to H-hour and be in position to provide cover by that time.

"Admin and Logistics: Ammo: Assault team, six full mags per man ('Hocklers'); Doormen, ten solid shot rounds each. Support team, ten full mags (SA80s). All: Brownings with two mags 9 mm. Armoury will open at 0030.

"Dress and equipment: CQB, respirators, flash resist and body armour, plus bergens, plus sleeping bags.

"Transport: Main party plus kit by Pumas at 0600. Advance party of Troop 2ICs and drivers by Rovers 0100.

"Feeding: By rota, Squadron SM to coordinate. RAF Northolt is available as a secure base.

"Medical: Sarn't Belcher will provide initial aid.

"Special Equipment: Stun grenades, CS aerosols for the assault team, plus demolitions and special stores will be held available by Squadron Quarter Master Sarn't Brown, to be based at RAF Regimental Arms Kote at Northolt.

"Command and Signals: Command, conditions for take-over. In command Captain Seagrave. Assault, in command Squadron Sarn't Major Hunt; his 2IC will be WO2 Bill Mather, then Staff Sarn't Joe Monk.

"Conditions for opening fire: Standard Ops Procedures, or as directed by OIC.

"Radio procedure: Captain Seagrave is Callsign 'X-ray'. Coordinate via SO13's OP Zulu Control. Personal radio secure-link only to 'X-ray', who will relay via Northwood." Major Crispin looked up and added: "Any questions?"

The words released a suppressed torrent of queries and ideas.

"So how do we get in?"

"It might be possible to blow the coal cellar hatch."

"Use Foamex. Quick and minimum fuss. And a fast follow-up."

"Why bother, you can just open it," someone pointed out.

Hilarity helps break the tension.

"It's still risky. That hatch is only eighteen inches in diameter, and the scramble in would take too long."

"I agree. We'd be one at a time – like ducks at a fairground."

"What about sneaking in? That back door can't be too strong."

"Time again – too much chance of them opening fire or pressing the explosives detonator. Not to mention the burglar alarm."

"There's no alarm in the garage. Say we snuck into the boot of the house owner's car. This Ali Christie. He doesn't have to know we're there, so his nerves wouldn't give us away. We'd then have one, maybe two, right in the building . . . ?"

A sudden, thoughtful silence.

Assault Troop commander WO2 Bill Mather said quietly: "That sounds interesting. Get Lionel to ask discreetly about it when he sees Ali Christie on Monday."

"Once we've got someone in they can let the rest through, or even secure the main hall while the others blast through the back door. It would save fiddling around with locks."

"There's usually a sentry upstairs – we need two or so to 'negotiate' him."

Bill Mather's voice was flat, without emotion. "Fine, then how about this . . . ?"

# 18

As darkness fell on Friday evening, plain-clothes officers of the Anti-Terrorist Branch had called on the surprised neighbours on either side of the Christies' house.

Intrigued, and not a little apprehensive, the law-abiding residents of Harrow-on-the-Hill had readily agreed to co-operate. They promised to tell no one about their unorthodox guests and to continue to run their lives as though nothing unusual were taking place.

Under cover of darkness sealed boxes of equipment were brought in from an unmarked van. In the privacy of their newly allocated 'quarters' overlooking the Christie house, police marksmen in blue overalls from the PT17 'Blue Berets' began unpacking their weapons. Others from TO7 Technical Support Branch began fitting the thermal imager to its tripod. It would be their 'eyes' – enabling them to penetrate the walls of the house next door and track the images of body heat as the occupants moved around.

Offers of cups of tea and biscuits were politely accepted with the warning: "Remember, ma' am, everything but everything as usual. Just forget we're here."

Still burning with curiosity and excitement, the lady of the house joined her husband in the bedroom. He was already snoring gently, but she knew she wouldn't sleep. She looked out over the rough ground behind the house, a sheen of silver from the moon rippling on the leaves of the trees.

She did not see the four men approach along a rear

hedgerow. She did not see them as they moved amongst the shadows of the willows, rose bushes and azaleas in the next door garden.

At two thirty in the morning Captain Mark Seagrave and Sergeant Major Brian Hunt, who would lead the assault, withdrew. Their initial close reconnaissance was complete. They left behind the two CRW sergeants, skilfully hidden in the herbaceous border with their surveillance equipment and just 9mm Browning automatics for self-protection.

Later Seagrave and Hunt passed their observations and advice onto four figures wearing camouflage jackets and black balaclavas. These were the men who, for now, had the most difficult job of all, the Dirty Tricks Department of SO7.

At precisely three o'clock, the PT17 marksmen, wearing blue flak jackets moved onto the rooftops of the houses adjacent to the Christie residence. Through the nightsights of their sniper rifles, they watched for any sign of movement.

On the ground the four shadows from SO7 slipped through the hedge on the blind side of the hostage house.

Padded lightweight aluminium ladders were rested against the wall. Minute holes were silently hand-drilled into the wooden frames of each window in turn. Through some, tiny sound probes were inserted. Through others were passed microscopic visual lens-heads that ran on low-intensity light which would pass television pictures back down fine fibre-optic conduits to Zulu Control.

One man alone, the 'chief', reached the roof. First he fitted a device to the television aerial. He then crossed stealthily to the chimney stack and slowly lowered another sound probe down on a carefully premeasured length of cable. The probe would hang, just out of sight, in the fireplace in the centre of the living room.

The woman next door did finally get to sleep, but not for long. She awoke with the Saturday dawn and could not resist a peek out of the window. Nothing stirred in the garden next door. The house of Ali and Beth Christie was as quiet and peaceful as all the others in Harrow that morning. She went back to sleep.

D'Arcy had slept deeply after the previous night's work. It had been a welcome reminder of his days in the Regiment, and it had helped to give him some of the answers he needed. Not only did he now have another way to reach the Spidex cartel, but he had begun to understand a number of other mysteries.

He took Nadirpur his breakfast at eight, and the two of them were just sitting down for coffee later when two men arrived outside. Through the TV monitor he recognised Reg Roman; the other visitor managed to keep his face averted from the camera.

As he opened the door D'Arcy said: "Hello, Reg, are we still talking?"

"Just. I believe you know Major Fraser, Commander CRW Wing?"

The man turned towards him, his grin wide.

"Christ, Johnny!" D'Arcy shook his hand. "What a terrific surprise! How's it going?"

Johnny Fraser shrugged, still grinning. "Nothing changes, you know. Hasn't been the same since you walked out of my office."

"How's Toby Carstairs filling my boots?"

"His feet are big enough, Rob. But I still miss having you around."

Roman cut in. "Okay, you two sweethearts, let's get down to business."

As they gathered around in armchairs, D'Arcy introduced Nadirpur to Johnny Fraser.

Roman smiled. "We've got some red hot news for you two. The kidnappers' hideout has been located!"

Nadirpur stared in disbelief.

D'Arcy glanced at Fraser. "So that's why you're here."

"The lads will be in Northolt by now, Rob. The police have been doing their stuff overnight."

"Where is it?"

"Harrow."

"That figures. When do you move in?"

"As soon as we get the word from on high."

Roman said: "That's the problem, Rob, since you pulled the rug from under us. COBRA wants to hang it out, but on the ground we think it's a big risk. If you're about to pull off a deal with the kidnappers, then there's a good chance they'll kill the hostages – destroy all witnesses."

"My aim was to have them released first," D'Arcy said.

"But that's *if* they agree," Fraser pointed out. "You might be forced to accept their word."

"We haven't got to the handover details yet, but you're right. We might have to take some gambles."

"It won't be long," Roman said. "There was a call from Paris last night to the hostage house, which we intercepted. We believe it was a code to instruct the kidnappers to make contact with whoever controls them. The one called Shamlou went out first thing this morning and made a call from a public phone box. So I'm sure you'll hear soon."

D'Arcy said: "They gave us seven days. That runs out end of Thursday."

"Give me the full details, Rob," Roman ordered sternly.

"I can't do that."

"The Frenchman in Beirut?"

"Even if you pull off a rescue, there's still an outside chance that they'll do a deal on Chaumont. I'll have to play it by ear, I can't just let the poor bastard rot."

"I understand," Roman said, "but I doubt Bob Tanner will. You're Public Enemy Number One in his book."

Fraser said: "Will you keep us posted when you make any deal? It'll affect the decision to go in."

"No problem."

The deal came at three o'clock that afternoon in a telephone call to Dave Forbes's temporary home.

The kidnapper's voice was obviously excited beneath

the veneer of self-control. Forbes guessed that the man was elated at having nearly completed his mission, but fearful that something would go wrong at the eleventh hour. "My instructions are that the man D'Arcy – and only him – will go to Oman with the equivalent of two million sterling in uncut diamonds. Then our people can pick up the ship. When they are satisfied, the hostages in London and Beirut will be released."

"We'll want safeguards."

"That will be arranged in Oman, when our people contact the man D'Arcy."

"That's too vague."

"That is how it will be done."

Forbes didn't like the sound of it at all. It was leaving to chance that D'Arcy could get foolproof handover arrangements agreed on the ground in Oman. In a country where he was known to his terrorist enemies, but he did not know them. Thank God, he thought, that the London hostage house was now known. "Okay, it'll be agreed in Oman, but I warn you now, out there it will be the same. No safeguards, no deal."

"You do not warn me about anything!" the voice sneered down the line. "The man D'Arcy flies out on Tuesday night to Oman. During Wednesday our man will make contact with him."

"Do you want an address?"

A sinister chuckle. "We will find him."

I bet, Forbes thought savagely, and as he went to speak he found the deadline tone singing in his ear.

"COBRA's decided," Roman said. "Barring unforeseen circumstances we sit this one out."

Major Fraser's face was a mask. "Is there something wrong with my hearing?"

Roman gave a harsh laugh. "It's to be expected. They're afraid of the political fallout if you go in and it ends in disaster. They've considered the sound and visual scans and reckon there's nothing to suggest that the kidnappers will do anything rash at present. Nerves are frayed but it's all going their way. They've had reports from experienced negotiators and psycho experts. When D'Arcy gets to Oman, there's every chance the hostages will be released."

"When Rob gets to Oman," Fraser replied with restraint, "he'll be up shit creek without a paddle. He'll be in neutral country that suits them. I've had full Int. reports on this *Pessarane Behesht* mob. They are not rational. They are highly dangerous, and vindictive. When they've got Rob out there with the money and the ship, there's nothing to stop them just pulling the plug on London."

"I know how you feel, Johnny. But we've some good soundscans. When the kidnappers have been talking together, there's been no hint that they're not expecting events to run the full course."

"Then let's hope to God that COBRA's got it right."

D'Arcy spent Monday making urgent travel arrangements to fly to Oman and spoke to Shayhk Zufar to organise the visa details. He also had a meeting with a London diamond merchant. Meanwhile the police and security forces devoted the time to refining their contingency plans.

Captain Lionel Witcher paid another visit to the Pavilion Gallery and heard Ali's account of the previous two days' events at the hostage house. Although the terrorists had been reasonably amicable the Iranian, Witcher noted, was decidedly more shaky. The intelligence officer's additional questions touched fleetingly on the garage and the family's Mercedes car.

The assault teams of Duty Squadron went through a dress rehearsal at a similar house nearby posing as a film unit. They tried several variations, adding refinements as they went along. At the end of the day, the regrettable conclusion was that the chances of getting the hostages and the Christies out alive looked ominously slim.

In the houses adjacent to the hostage house, the men from SO7 and PT17 had settled down for a long wait. In the solitary British Telecom van in the road outside, Bob

Tanner of Special Branch and Major Johnny Fraser patiently watched the fuzzy television pictures relayed from the visual probes in the house, and listened to the soundscans. Every word and movement was analysed and discussed on the radio link with backup terrorist and psychology experts at New Scotland Yard's Operations Room.

Night fell, and the long wait for Tuesday to dawn seemed interminable.

In the hostage house Jalal Shamlou awoke on Tuesday morning feeling decidedly cheerful. That evening the man D'Arcy was due to leave for Oman. Thankfully their mission was almost over. No more negotiating telephone calls, no more risk of discovery. Just two more days to wait until he received instructions of when and how to release the woman and child in the cellar.

Then, while Hamid and Kamal returned to take up their normal cover as the London cell, he and Matchsticks would slip quietly out of the country, and back to Iran – to a heroes' welcome.

Perhaps when he was back and could relax, he would have the dream again. He felt his loins stir at the thought.

Dressing quickly he went downstairs and out into the garden. It was still chill from the previous night, but the sky was blue with promise of another hot day. The air was filled with the scent of roses and he sniffed at the open blooms, blissfully unaware that he was standing three feet from the concealed observation post of the two CRW sergeants.

A movement caught his eye, high up at one of the upstairs windows of the adjacent house.

He scolded himself for his carelessness and returned inside. He could not afford mistakes now.

Matchsticks was getting on his nerves again. Shamlou had learned that the previous week, when Matchsticks was out buying supplies, he had actually shoplifted a suit that took his fancy. If that wasn't bad enough, he learned that he'd stolen it from an Oxfam charity shop. To jeopardise the entire mission for a second-hand suit!

Now totally confined, Matchsticks seethed and constantly goaded the others, particularly Shamlou. He had also started making increasingly lewd threats to Beth Christie, constantly taunting her with his cigarette lighter, until both she and her husband were reduced to sobbing hysteria.

Shamlou avoided his comrade and went down to the cellar where Kamal was on duty, reading a paperback copy of the Holy Koran. "I'll take over here. Go upstairs and get some breakfast."

When the other man had gone, he drew aside the blanket. Inside the chicken wire cage Ashi was stirring, rubbing the tiredness from her eyes. He looked at the smooth skin of her legs, gleaming in the torchlight. How pale they were now, without benefit of sunshine for so many weeks.

"Some more sweets for the girl," he said brusquely, and pushed a paper bag under the netting.

Ashi smiled sleepily, her eyes large and luminous. The boy-man again. "She is not awake yet."

Sousan was curled in the foetal position, a thumb in her mouth.

"For when she wakes, then."

"You are very kind."

They looked at each other and she noticed the brooding darkness of his eyes beneath the long lashes. Sensed the strength of his youth. And remembered what she had dreamed. Shamed, she felt the flush of warmth in her lower belly.

"Perhaps it won't be long now."

She held his gaze. "Do you really mean that? What has happened?"

He stepped back. "I have nothing to tell you. Just that it will not be long."

"I see. My husband has agreed something with you? Dear Nader."

"Will you go back – to him? To your husband?" His

voice was hoarse. In his mind's eye he saw her being violated.

"I love him," she replied in a whisper. "But he is my husband in name only. Do you understand?"

He nodded and looked hurt, but did not understand.

"You won't let him kill us, will you?"

He looked at her.

"When this is over," she said, "you won't let your friend kill us?"

"Who?"

"The tall, thin one. He frightens me with what he says. In front of Sousan, too. Don't let him kill us."

"I promise, you will not die. Not now –" He stopped himself. "I have said too much."

"I am pleased you have what you want. Thank you for the sweets."

He went upstairs and sent Matchsticks down, warning him that it would be he who died if he threatened the woman and child again.

"I do believe you've been bewitched by that whore," Matchsticks grinned, and defiantly flicked his lighter.

"Pay no heed to him," Kamal said softly. "Join me for prayers."

The telephone rang. Then stopped. It rang again. Shamlou's mouth was suddenly dry. It was the coded ring. He picked up the receiver. "Listen, it is over," the voice rasped. He recognised his 'controller' from Paris. The man sounded unusually agitated. "You leave tomorrow morning. Hamid and Kamal will know what to do. You and Ahmad take the ferry back to France. You will use your own identities. Your passports will be given back to you by a 'friend' at a café in Oxford Street at noon tomorrow." He gave the name. "Your mission is at an end. You have furthered the glory of Islam."

Shamlou was astounded that his 'controller' was speaking over an open line. The mission must truly be at an end; their safety assured.

"What about the woman and child? And these people who own the house?"

"I just have instruction from Geneva. Dispose of them, you understand? Do it in the early hours of the morning, in the cellar, when all the neighbours will be asleep. Leave the explosives and put them on a time fuse for when you are safely in France. That will destroy much evidence and there will be no witnesses to the identity of any of you."

Shamlou's voice cracked. "But the ship, the deal – tonight the man D'Arcy is flying to Oman –"

The 'controller' cut in sharply. "The hostages are now irrelevant! We have what we want. That is all I know. I do not ask questions. Neither should you. And be vigilant – do not get careless now. *Allah akbar!*"

The phone went dead. Shamlou replaced the receiver in confusion. He looked down at his hands. They were trembling.

At nearby RAF Northolt Captain Mark Seagrave received the signal from Major Johnny Fraser at Zulu Control.

He ran from his temporary allocated office to the empty aircraft hangar that was serving as the holding area for the three assault Troops of Duty Squadron. Amidst the chaotic scene of vehicles, sleeping bags and equipment spread across the concrete floor, a sea of faces turned in his direction. There was suddenly a deathly hush.

He said: "Right, lads, it's on."

The frozen tableau of figures broke into feverish activity and the rush of voices rose to fill the silence as kit was hurriedly stowed.

"Sarn't Major Hunt and all Troop Commanders," he called. "In my office in ten minutes!"

Hunt joined him as he turned. "What gives, skipper?"

"The kidnappers have just had instructions from overseas. To kill both the hostages and the house owners tonight. Picked it up on the phone tap. So COBRA have finally decided to jump."

"About time."

"Trouble is we don't know *exactly* when the executions will take place – just in 'the early hours'. So the bastards are likely to be up all night getting ready to leave tomorrow morning, when our plan was for most of them to be tucked up in bed."

"Why the hell didn't they let us go in last night like we wanted?"

"The embuggerance factor," Seagrave said helpfully. "Even if we forget it, the politicians don't."

While update briefings, final preparations and more assault rehearsals took place as the day progressed, the Dirty Tricks Department of SO7 moved into top gear.

In the afternoon Lionel Witcher telephoned Ali Christie at his gallery and kept him talking in soothing and reassuring terms. As he was doing this, two plain-clothes SO7 officers approached Christie's Mercedes, which was in its usual place in a nearby multistorey car park. They opened it with a set of duplicate keys.

It took less than ten minutes to drive it to Savile Row police station. There behind closed doors, ventilation holes were drilled in the lower sides of the rear panels, through to the large boot space. At the same time a replacement lock was fitted which allowed the boot lid to be opened only from the inside.

As the work finished Rix and Villiers stepped forward. They were awesomely dressed in black Panotex antiflash suits with black ceramic body armour and black hoods. Rix carried a compact 9 mm Heckler & Koch MP5 sub-machine gun; Villiers, as 'doorman', a sawn-off Remington repeater, loaded with solid shot. Without a word they climbed in, tested the lock, and gave the thumbs up.

When Lionel Witcher ended his conversation with Ali Christie, the Mercedes was back at the multistorey car park.

In the early evening the terrorist Matchsticks was watching *Neighbours* on television as he ate a snack. He was surprised when the Newsflash interrupted his favourite programme.

He recognised the pretty features and twinkling eyes of newscaster Moira Stuart instantly and watched with fascination as she spoke: "In the past few minutes it has been reported that police have arrested four men in Birmingham in connection with the abduction of Mrs Ashi Nadirpur and her daughter Sousan.

"The kidnap of the wife and daughter of the wealthy Iranian shipowner was first reported a few weeks ago.

"A police spokesman said he was confident that today's arrests would bring the investigation to a conclusion. There is no word yet of the whereabouts or the safety of the hostages."

Matchsticks's squeal of delight was picked up on the sound probe as he called the others to tell them the good news. The stupid British police had mistakenly arrested the wrong people!

He was unaware that his was the only television set in the whole of the United Kingdom to receive this particular Newsflash.

Captain Seagrave wasn't happy. Neither was Sergeant Major Brian Hunt. The assault was compromised and they both knew it. It was now five minutes to midnight and the house was a hive of activity as the terrorists prepared for a dawn departure.

There was one saving grace, in that SO7 had skilfully interjected another false Newsflash on the television half-an-hour earlier, promising a news bulletin update on the Nadirpur family kidnap within the next hour. The sound-scans suggested that, following on the earlier broadcast, this had not unnerved the terrorists. Indeed it had the desired effect of reassuring them. They remained talkative and in high spirits.

All, that was, except the leader Shamlou. He had become withdrawn and monosyllabic. The professor from the London School of Psychiatry believed that this might be because he was unhappy at the thought of killing unarmed women and a child. It was unlikely, he added, that this reluctance to kill would extend to the black-clad seige busters.

Major Fraser's voice came over Captain Seagrave's personal radio. "*Zulu Control to X-ray. Confirm area cleared. Repeat. Confirm area cleared. Over.*"

"Roger Zulu Control. Over."

"*Advance to preliminary assault positions. I will update on final enemy dispositions within hostage house. Over.*"

"Roger. Out."

That was it then. Earlier that day a search warrant had been granted in private under the Firearms Act by the chief magistrate at Bow Street. After darkness fell surprised neighbours in the immediate vicinity had been visited by plain-clothes Anti-Terrorist Branch detectives and given a time at which quietly to leave the area. One by one, husbands, wives, grandparents and children had shut their front doors and walked inconspicuously through the invisible cordon, to be held politely incommunicado for the next few hours. A chance call to the tabloid press was the last thing that was wanted.

That cordon now became physical reality, the private road sealed off by uniformed police from the local station.

In their shadowy eyries on the rooftops of the adjoining houses, police marksmen of the 'Blue Berets' waited patiently with their sniper rifles. Below them the controllers of the sound and visual probes relayed their scans direct to Zulu Control.

Within the yellow British Telecom van Bob Tanner of Anti-Terrorist Branch officially handed over the operation to Major Johnny Fraser, CRW of 22 Special Air Service Regiment, in writing.

In the nearby spur road where two olive green Bedford trucks waited, Hunt turned from Captain Seagrave to 'Brummie' Turner, 10 Troop's Commander, unrecognisable now behind the black rubber respirator mask. An alien being from another planet. "GO!"

Sixteen men disgorged from the truck, melting silently into the darkness on lightweight rubber-soled boots. They slipped through the cordon and into the inky black roadside shadows, heading towards the hostage house. Had they still been in their homes, residents might have telephoned the local council to complain that tonight the streetlamps weren't working.

Hedge leaves rustled although there was no wind. It was the only sound as two fire-groups of eight men set up in the two corners of the Christies' garden, facing the front of the house.

*"Zulu Control to X-ray. Sitrep update on target house as follows: Two hostages remain in cellar. Sound only. Hostile 1 Kamal is with them. He is silent. Woman is conversing with child. No detail. Ground floor: Hostiles 2 and 3 Matchsticks and Jalal Shamlou are having supper by the television. Bickering. Discussing when and how executions should take place. Matchsticks is goading.*

*"Remote-control detonator on coffee table. Have visual. Repeat detonator on coffee table. Very portable.*

*"First Floor: Householders in front bedroom. Handcuffed. Talking quietly together. Hostile 4 Hamid is seated on a chair outside the door. Maybe dozing."*

Seagrave and Hunt exchanged glances. "Roger. Out."

Hunt watched the digits flicker up on his wristwatch – 0005.

Time for the Assault Team to move in.

Seagrave pulled a tight, reassuring grin. Hunt knew the man must be hating the necessity to command which kept officers out of the front line on duties like this.

Hunt adjusted his respirator, beckoned his team and led off without a backward glance.

He knew that immediately behind him was 8 Troop's Commander, WO2 Bill Mather. They had served together in a particularly tough show in Sweden; they'd become blood brothers – assuming that there was blood and not icewater in Bill's veins.

Monk and Pope had been in on that one, too. They were close on Bill Mather's heels.

Behind them was Sergeant Belcher – medic, 'bush doctor' and fully qualified gynaecologist, and Jim 'Nature Boy' Perkis from London's East End.

With Rix and Villiers, already in the garage, they made up the first team.

The second eight would clean up any mess. And if there was any mess left, it would take some bloody clearing, Hunt thought savagely.

They were there now, the adjacent house. Into the front gate, down the tarmac drive, round the side, rubber soles pounding silently on crazy paving. Side gate, in. Along the fence, the fragrance of the dense honeysuckle unnoticed within the respirators. On, on, under the rose arch. There. Through the hole where a segment of fence had been removed, into the shrubbery of azaleas and the herbaceous border next door.

Two blacked-up faces, grinning. The two CRW sergeants who had been manning the OP since Friday night.

In the hostage house grounds. The killing grounds.

Hunt's throat mike was on whisper-mode. "One to X-ray. In position. Sitrep update from Zulu, please."

"*Zulu Control here. You are now on continuous update.*" Uncertainty had crept into Major Fraser's voice. "*Things are starting to happen. Wait. Out.*"

Shit! Hunt looked at his watch – 0015 hours. Precisely five minutes to go for phase one.

"I don't care, I'll kill the whore," Matchsticks offered, a fat grin on his face. He added: "If you're not man enough to do it."

Shamlou glared at him. "Your mind is a sewer, Ahmad. And your mouth is a drain."

Matchsticks sneered. "It's midnight, oh Chosen One. How late are you going to leave it? All the neighbours will be in bed."

"I will tell you when I'm good and ready!"

Bastard! Shamlou rose from the sofa and left the room. He paused for a moment in the hallway, thinking. Then, on impulse, he rushed up the stairs to his room. There he took the AK47 with the folding butt from his suitcase. He screwed on the silencer and thumbed in a fresh magazine. Then he tiptoed back down the stairs and through the hall, taking care not to let Matchsticks see him. Then he descended into the cellar.

Kamal looked up from his crossword. "What is it?"

"Go upstairs."

"What's happening?"

"Nothing, just go."

Shrugging, Kamal left. He was ready for his supper anyway.

Shamlou took a deep breath. He wasn't prepared to give Matchsticks the pleasure of seeing what he was going to do. Shoot the child first, that bastard had suggested. Let the mother watch the daughter bleed to death. Then shoot the mother and watch them choke to death together in a pool of each other's blood and vomit. *Taghouti* scum!

Angrily Shamlou ripped aside the blanket. Ashi looked up, surprised, and smiled at him. The daughter blinked and smiled too. She was eating from the packet of sweets he had given her that morning.

The boy-man had come.

Shamlou froze, the AK47 hanging loosely in his grip.

And he heard the words of his veteran comrade at the camp. "Whatever you do, do it for Allah and for Islam. Not for anyone who uses His holy name for their own ends." He saw again the tattoo above Hamman's wrist. *To God and Yourself be True.*

"We were reciting poetry," Ashi said. She turned to Sousan. "Say that poem for our friend."

Shamlou's eyes narrowed.

The girl frowned, remembered, and began speaking: "Sit near my tomb, and bring wine and music – Feeling thy presence, I shall come out of my sepulchre – Rise, softly moving creature, and let me contemplate thy beauty . . ."

"Do you know it?" Ashi asked.

Shamlou's eyes widened in silent horror. His hand was

452

trembling as he pulled back the cocking-handle of the AK47.

0020. Phase One. Diversion.

"HEY! JALAL! QUICK!" Matchstick's near-hysterical voice echoed down to the cellar.

Shamlou dropped the blanket, shocked and short of breath. He turned and ran up the steps, the last-minute reprieve not unwelcome.

As he burst into the room, he found Matchsticks and Kamal standing as they watched the television. Hamid came down from upstairs, curious to find out the reason for the commotion.

"It's about the kidnap, look!" Matchsticks cried with glee as he again watched the familiar features of Moira Stuart. "Look, pictures of the men they have arrested."

Kamal laughed. "They look nothing like us."

In the adjoining garage Rix released the catch and allowed the boot lid of the Mercedes to swing up and open. He climbed stiffly out, his Hockler sub-machine gun sweeping the darkness. Clear. He helped Villiers out. They stretched their legs, easing away the cramp.

H-minus four.

A chink of light came from the door that opened onto the kitchen. Please God, let no one be in here.

Standby.

In the garden Hunt checked his watch. "Let's go."

Six shadows flashed under the overhanging foliage. Six blackened, silent wraiths with padded footsteps. Four pressed hard up against the exterior kitchen wall at the side of the house. Hunt was first, Hockler at the port, cocked, safety off.

The last two of the eight were crouched over the eighteen-inch circular coal-chute cover. Medic Sergeant Belcher was prising it open with the delicate and tender care of a surgeon. Cockney 'Nature Boy' Perkis was poised, stun-grenade in hand.

The chute led straight into the cellar. It was partitioned from the rest of the basement where the hostages were held by a wall of heavy railway sleepers. That was why they had soundscans only, deprived of visual data.

Hunt felt the sweat in the small of his back. Watch. H-hour minus two. His heart was starting to thud. Thought of Ashi and Sousan. Wondered how he would feel if that were his wife down there, and his step-daughter Jessica.

Major Fraser's voice was intoning in his ear. *"Hostile Shamlou has realised hostages and the Christies are unguarded. He tells hostile Hamid to return upstairs. Hostiles Shamlou and Matchsticks moving towards cellar steps, talking . . ."*

Shit! Two minutes earlier would have been better. Too late now. All synchronised. Ready. Standby, standby.

Minutes were hours. His body armour weighed a ton, his respirator mask was starting to fog.

"I am not afraid to kill them!" Matchsticks shouted. "I know your orders!"

"Keep out of this," Shamlou retorted. "I'll do it myself."

"Let us do it together, comrade – now! Let them feel the cutting edge of the sword of Islam!"

Shamlou broke. In the name of Allah why not? Why not let Matchsticks do what he himself could not? Was it not the will of Allah?

The voice was scratchy in Hunt's ear, its flat monotone beginning to crack. *"Hostiles Shamlou and Matchsticks moving out of sight. Going down steps to cellar . . . ?"*

Sod! No more visual coverage down there. Blind.

*"Explosive control remains on coffee table."* Good news. *"Hostile Kamal is watching end of false broadcast . . ."*

Now, Hunt willed, get the bastard away. Five.

The telephone rang. Four. Its sound shattered the tension in the house. Three. Kamal stood. Would he answer it? It was the coded ring. Was it the 'controller'? Would he fall for it? Two. He moved towards the telephone in the hallway.

0025.

GO!

Everything happens at once.

The stun-grenade bounces down the coal-chute, and detonates. Its effect is awe-inspiring: a flash as brilliant as forked lightning, and a paralysing, high-pitched noise that hurts the ears. In the cellar Shamlou and Matchsticks are rooted to the spot, staring at the blinding light glowing behind the timber partition. The second coming. They buck and twist to escape the pain in their ears. Coal dust swirls in a choking black fog.

Ten seconds. Ten seconds of disorientation.

Villiers twists the handle of the picked garage door lock. He is in the kitchen and turning. Cellar door facing. Stand back, up and fire. With two blasts of solid shot from the Remington repeater the 'doorman' takes it out at the hinges. And Rix is in, bursting through the splintered timber with his shoulder. It falls apart, resistance gone.

Outside Doorman Two opens up, blowing aside the kitchen door, and Hunt is in. The place is swathed in blue cordite smoke as the blackened figures rush through.

Mather is at Hunt's back, both men joining Villiers and Rix to form A Group as they plunge into the black hellmouth that leads to the cellar.

The second four of B Group are hiving off for the hallway and the reception rooms. 'Big Joe' Monk is the first through, a giant mutant being in respirator mask. The air is full of the sound of cracking windowpanes and the urgent hiss of CS gas rounds as they are fired through the shattered glass by 10 Troup's support-teams.

Terrorist caught wrong-footed, halfway between the hall telephone and the living room door. His mouth agape, his eyes streaming from the CS fumes. Thick black beard. Monk puts the name to the face. Kamal.

His eyes cross to the remote-control device on the coffee table through the open door. Monk sees it too, and his finger squeezes on the trigger.

Half a magazine of stammering fire. No time for double-tapping this. Rounds tear through the front door as though it's made of rice paper. Then fist-sized bites rip into the plaster as Monk's aim arcs to hit the running figure.

Bullets chew at the doorjamb, splinters flying. Sod! Missed!

Kamal is at the coffee table, skidding on the carpet. Fingers outstretched.

The burst from Monk's backup takes him out, blowing him halfway across the room. Crimson liquid drips from the sofa and from the shredded wallpaper awaiting redecoration.

Within the respirator masks the eyes of Monk and Pope meet momentarily. Nothing said, no sign. No need. The unholy alliance. Par for the course.

Medic Belcher and Cockney Perkis, last of B Group, have already overtaken. Already pounding up the staircase to the first floor.

Monk had heard the rounds that Belcher put through the ceiling. Now sees the torn and yawning gap where the upstairs guard is usually located.

They had got lucky. A round had passed up and through the seat of the chair where terrorist Hamid had been sitting. Now he lies twitching on the landing floor, screaming, his trousers sodden from the bubbling red spring flowing from his ruptured anus.

Belcher unholsters his 9 mm Browning and jams it in the base of the dying man's skull.

But in the cellar luck is a bitch.

Seven.

Hunt is still counting A Group's ten-second reprieve. Ten seconds granted by the stun-grenade and by God's blessing. Ten precious, life-giving seconds of disorientation.

Eight.

He's right behind Rix now on the stairs. Villiers is already down. Somewhere. Lobbing in the CS canisters. There's coal dust everywhere. Choking black clouds, swirling. Visibility zero.

Nine. And Hunt bangs up against Rix's back.

Christ, what a mess! Why didn't anyone think of the fucking coal dust?

The crack of gunfire shatters the eardrums in the confined space. Muzzle flashes dead ahead in the murk. Sparks, vivid as the ricochets hit brickwork all around. Spent shells sing in venomous glee. Wild, untamed and deadly.

Duck, sod it, keep down.

Terrorist between us and the hostages. Shooting at us. Want to shoot back, can't shoot. Must get a visual. Must, must, must.

Hunt is at the side wall. Blinded by his own sweat, eyes stinging. Smelling the slimy wet rubber of the respirator against his skin. Feels the damp bricks under his fingers. Orientates himself. Now crawling, low and fast towards the muzzle flashes.

Through the vortex of filthy dust a figure appears. It is like the slow motion of an action replay. The face turns. Pretty, young. Boy-man. Pale face and dark eyes with long lashes. A gleam of horror and madness. Wide despite the gas fumes. Shamlou. ID. ID. Positive visual.

Die, you bastard, die.

The Hockler jumps in Hunt's hands, spitting out its killing seed.

"No, no, not HIM!"

The woman's chest is punctured as she throws herself protectively in front of Shamlou. A human shield. Together they fall to the floor, clutching each other like lovers as they die.

Where did she come from? She wasn't in the cage! Oh, sweet Jesus Christ, they'd let her *out*!

Hunt crouched over the corpses, looking up as the coal dust began to settle.

Saw the child, cowering in a corner. Saw the tall gangling figure with the AK47. Saw Rix and Mather swing their Hocklers as one, the twin-headed harbinger of death. Saw the petrol can in the terrorist's other hand.

"N-O-O-O!"

His cry was cut off by the noise of exploding rounds as hammers ate hungrily through two half-magazines. The noise was followed by the almighty rush and roar of igniting petrol. A sudden fireball erupted with the searing heat of a blacksmith's furnace, driving them back.

Flame dripped from the bricks of the vaulted roof and walls, and rose from the flickering pyre of the body of the one called Matchsticks.

Hunt was up and running. Ignoring the intense heat, through the tangle of burning bodies and blankets, kicked aside twisted coils of chicken wire, pulling at obstructing lumps of glowing timber with his gloved hands.

He scooped the unconscious child in his arms, smothering her flaming clothes. Then on his feet again, carrying her through the shattered ruins of the cellar partition, offering her up to the gods.

A willing pair of hands reached down through the coal-chute manhole, and she was spirited away he knew not where.

Four ragged, black-hooded figures stood limply, exhausted, in the smouldering carnage. At their feet the melted flesh of the woman and the boy-man had become one.

# 19

Sleep defied him on the flight to Muscat.

D'Arcy could not erase the mental image of the house in Harrow from his mind. During the journey he had lived through every second of the SAS assault. After all, had he not resigned from the Army two years earlier, it might well have been he who had been commanding the operation.

He hoped to God that the lads would make it in one piece. Most of the old 'characters' who would be going in, he knew personally: Hunt; Mather; Pope; Villiers and Rix. In many ways they were more like brothers than friends.

Images of the imprisoned woman and her daughter, too, flashed through his mind. Always the same unwelcome picture of their pale naked flesh against the black background. As though the scene had been etched indelibly on his retinas.

He knew why the terrorists had chosen this night to slaughter Ashi and Sousan. Because he would be on the flight to Oman, unaware of events at the hostage house in Harrow.

But he did not understand why the hold over Nadirpur was suddenly no longer important?

Perhaps he would never know. Would anyone from the terrorists' organisation still contact him when he arrived in the sultanate? Certainly he could do nothing for the hostages in London now. But would the *Pessarane Behesht* still want the two million sterling in uncut diamonds?

Philippe Chaumont was still in Beirut, so was that what they had in mind?

Again he asked himself why the Nadirpurs were no longer relevant to the terrorists? He could think of only one possible answer. And he didn't like it.

It was dark when the aircraft touched down to be immediately cocooned in the humid night air. To D'Arcy's surprise Shaykh Zufar himself waited by the 'No Objections Certificate' kiosk with his driver.

The watery eyes lit with delight and a smile transformed his gnarled features. His scampering walk was very unministerial as he came forward.

"Excellency –" D'Arcy began, the breath crushed from him as the old man hugged him like a lost son.

"Mr Robert!" he exclaimed. "*Ahlan wa sahlan! Ahlan wa sahlan*! It is so good to see you! It has been too long."

"It has indeed, Excellency," D'Arcy replied as he recovered from the embrace.

"Excellency bah!" the old man said with a dismissive wave of his hand. "We are as we've always been. Friends first and enemies second!" He chortled at his own joke. "Will I not always be as you first saw me – sitting on a carpet in the sand? No grand car and cool offices will ever change that. To you I am always Aziz."

"You do me the greatest honour, Aziz, to meet me here."

His good eye twinkled. "I do not want you to have the trouble that your friends have, the Frenchman with the girl's hair and the woman who thinks she is a man."

"Saint-Julien and Chantal."

"The one who has a fiancé in Beirut?"

"An ex-fiancé, yes."

"Ah." A hesitation. "And you wish her to be *your* wife?"

"I hope that might be so."

The old face wrinkled.

"You do not approve?"

"She is very skinny. Like a young mountain goat. But I confess I like her eyes. She persuaded me to help against my best judgement." He laughed. "When she gets fat she will be a good woman – for a Westerner like you!"

"I hope you won't be in trouble for coming here."

He waved the thought aside as though it were a pestering fly. "Bah! It is like old times. As I say, you will always be the same. Always the smart young soldier who came to my village, who calls me a scoundrel and then drinks my coffee." He glanced around conspiratorially at the Immigration desks. "It is like the old days with the 'Whisper Service' – it still works, you know. That is how we find your ship."

D'Arcy raised a finger. "We must not talk about it here."

"Of course," Zufar agreed, and beckoned his driver. "Pick up the case and follow us."

The shaykh pushed his way to the head of the queue and demanded the immediate stamping of D'Arcy's passport. Seconds later he was walking imperiously through the Customs hall.

"Your Excellency, we must check this man's luggage."

"I will vouch for him," Zufar said dismissively.

The officer was cowed, but stood his ground. "Your Excellency, please."

A voice came from behind them; it was as clipped and British as a privet hedge. "I am afraid, Excellency, the officer is right. This man's bag must be searched."

D'Arcy came face to face with his old adversary. Major Harry was instantly recognisable. He had become an institution in Oman, never changing, just a little worn by the years. Perhaps the girth was thicker, the ramrod bearing slightly stooped, the sandy toothbrush moustache just flecked with white hairs.

"Still trying to bend rules, D'Arcy?" The tone hadn't mellowed, nor had the gimlet eyes.

D'Arcy smiled. "Still trying to straighten them, Harry?"

"Never were a respecter of authority, were you?"

The smile remained. "Many people have *earned* my respect, Harry. People like Shaykh Zufar here."

It was Major Harry's turn to smile, but it wasn't very

pleasant. "You'll need more friends than a junior minister, if you're not to be on the morning's first flight out of Muscat." He nodded in the direction of a partitioned office. "We'll talk in there."

D'Arcy followed whilst Zufar ran beside the major, gesticulating and protesting that this was an outrage.

"I will remind you, Excellency, that I act with the personal authority of His Majesty Qaboos," was the brusque reply.

Zufar looked dubious.

D'Arcy said nothing and remained standing.

Major Harry sat. "I have had a signal from a mutual friend. Roy Bliss. He said to tell you that the operation in London was a partial success. The child was badly burned, but is alive. Her mother was foolish enough to try and protect one of the kidnappers and was killed. Bliss said something about the Stockholm syndrome, if that means anything to you. The two owners of the house are safe."

D'Arcy absorbed the news numbly. "And the kidnappers?"

Major Harry blinked as though it were a very stupid question. Perhaps it was. "They are all dead. Both the father and his daughter will be returning to Paris."

D'Arcy felt a great weight lifted from his shoulders. It was done. There was no room for recriminations, for sentiment. Nadirpur would have to bear his own grief. He now had a daughter on which to lavish the love he was unable to give his wife.

Zufar listened intently. "So the child lives. Allah wills it."

That surprised Major Harry. "You know about this?"

"It was the reason that I lend my support. What kind of man holds a woman and child to ransom? A barbarian! Even Arabia has abandoned such brutalities with the wisdom of time." He glanced at D'Arcy. "And this woman friend of yours who dresses as a man, you say she still has a fiancé in Beirut?"

462

"I'm afraid so. For the moment, but we will try to get him released."

Zufar sucked on his lower lip, searching for the words. "If I were you, my friend, I would not try too hard."

D'Arcy looked at him curiously.

Then Major Harry interrupted. "That's why I am afraid that your case must be searched. I understand that you have agreed with your client to pay a two million pound ransom."

"Goodness, Harry, your intelligence network here is as strong as English mustard. Is that something else that Roy Bliss told you?"

"Open the case."

"What is this to do with you?"

Major Harry's eyes hardened. "Don't be an idiot, D'Arcy. His Majesty does not deal with terrorists, nor allow others to do so on his sovereign territory. Especially if that hostage is a French diplomat – and even if the French Government is breaking rank with the rest of the Western world."

"I wonder which country is in step with which?" D'Arcy provoked.

"The case, if you please."

"Of course."

D'Arcy lifted it from the floor and dumped it on the empty desk. For several minutes the major rummaged through the few items of clothing, mostly lightweight windproof cottons, silk socks and underwear – all the hallmarks of an experienced tropical traveller who didn't need luxuries.

Zufar began to chuckle quietly.

The blood vessels reddened in the major's cheeks.

"No money, George?" D'Arcy asked quietly.

For a moment the major appeared not to hear, then suddenly he looked up. "What did you call me?"

"George."

Major Harry frowned, the expression of anger giving way to one of concern. "What are you talking about,

D'Arcy? Are you trying to be amusing?"

"Isn't that a name you use in other circles, George? George Cupplewaite?"

"You're talking gibberish, man," Major Harry blustered.

"George Cupplewaite, director of Spidex International. Unofficial representative of the Omani Government. Co-conspirator in a plot to bring about the downfall of the Khomeini régime."

Zufar's mouth dropped. Village and internal politics were his bag, but clearly international affairs were not entirely beyond his grasp.

D'Arcy reached for his inside jacket pocket and dropped a buff envelope onto the desk.

Major Harry resisted the temptation to snatch at it. He picked it up slowly, put on his tortoiseshell spectacles and glanced through the contents of papers with an air of disinterest.

By the time he'd read the third page his façade crumbled. "Where the hell did you get this garbage, D'Arcy?"

"That's privileged information."

"It's bloody libel. A total fabrication. Damn forgeries." With contempt he screwed the papers into a ball and tossed them into his wastepaper bin.

D'Arcy's smile was genuine. "You'll have noticed they are copies."

"You're on the first plane out tomorrow," Major Harry snarled.

"The originals are filed with our solicitors," D'Arcy added blandly.

The other man looked suddenly winded. "What game are you playing, D'Arcy?"

"No game, Harry. I'm here to find my client's ship and deliver the paid-for cargo to its rightful owner. But I'll settle for full restitution to my client so that he can put affairs in order."

Major Harry gave up his pretence. "You'd deal with terrorists? God, you've changed your tune."

"It's just giving Iran back the money your cartel stole."

"And the two million sterling?"

"What two million?"

"Don't piss me about, D'Arcy. The two million the French have donated to get their hostage back."

"I would say that's the business of the French Government, wouldn't you?"

Major Harry glared.

"So what about it?" D'Arcy pressed. "Can you persuade the cartel to make restitution? In, say, forty-eight hours?"

"Impossible!"

"Nothing is impossible."

"Sheikh Hayira is dead, if you hadn't heard."

"Then as vice-chairman of Spidex, it's time you called an extraordinary meeting of the board."

"You've got a bloody cheek."

D'Arcy turned to Zufar. "Are you aware of the Sultan's policy with Iran, Aziz?"

The old man said: "His Majesty is clear. On Persian matters we should remain strictly neutral. As friendly as good protocol allows, but no more. Diplomatically we are working to end the Gulf War." He smiled the smile of someone who knew something that others didn't. "I think that may be very soon."

D'Arcy turned to Major Harry. "I think hijacking *Clarion Call* isn't very consistent with that policy, do you?"

The other man smirked. "Secret Service matters do not always reach the big ears of even the Shaykh Zufars of this country."

"Then let's telephone His Majesty and confirm it," D'Arcy said. "It's a long time since he and I had tea together."

Major Harry made no attempt to take up the suggestion.

D'Arcy added: "Perhaps the truth is that His Majesty hasn't been kept entirely in the picture?" Colour drained from the other man's face. "What was it, Harry? Greed? Wasn't the pension His Majesty offered you big enough for your ego? Or have your business ventures in the Caribbean come unstuck?"

"Go to hell!"

D'Arcy took his case from the table. "I'll be in Oman for as long as it takes. You've got two days to persuade your Spidex chums to deliver. Otherwise the truth of your involvement hits the world headlines, with a special personal report to His Majesty. It's all in hand already, should anything happen to me. And Shaykh Zufar here is now another witness."

"Sit down," Major Harry said.

"There's nothing more to say."

"Have you found the ship?"

"That would be telling."

"Leave it alone." The voice was as near to pleading as it was ever likely to be. "I'll do as you ask, but leave the ship alone. If you try to seize it, or if the Omanis do, someone will get hurt. There are Jordanian commandos on board; I'll see they're discreetly returned to their mother ship off the coast. Besides, the crew know too much. They'll have to be paid off for their silence and dispersed to different ports where they can't corroborate each other's stories."

"We are efficient at retreating, aren't we, Major?" D'Arcy observed sourly. "I've a man held on board, I believe. Rick Clay. I want him released here, unharmed."

Major Harry nodded. "And the ship can turn up with a new salvage crew at any port of your choosing. Some yarn about piracy, abandoned ship, *Marie Celeste* job."

D'Arcy watched the man squirm to protect his own skin. "Enough conflicting rumours to confuse everyone, eh?"

"Yes." The major's eyes narrowed. "*If* the cartel agrees."

"They'll agree, Harry. You'll see to that."

D'Arcy telephoned *Gulf Bullpup* from the Holiday Inn hotel and spoke to Chantal. She sounded overjoyed to hear from him, and even more delighted that they were

466

free to return to Mina Qaboos harbour without fear of retaliation by Major Harry.

She confirmed that *Clarion Call* was still where it had always been. Nothing had changed. He breathed a sigh of relief.

"But, *chéri*, Saint-Julien will be furious. He has been practising his diving and using Rick's submersible and the Jet Raider. He is convinced you will want us to make an assault." She laughed lightly. "He has made a whole attack plan with Tokyo."

"Thank God we won't have to find out if it would have worked."

Chantal was right in her prediction. When the salvage tug nosed into harbour at noon the next day, Saint-Julien was morose. He kept glaring resentfully at D'Arcy as though he had received a personal snub.

Her welcome, however, more than compensated. After days at sea her body was the colour of burnished mahogany, set off against the scant yellow bikini. Her hair was windswept and bleached platinum by the sun. Against her tanned skin, her eyes were as white as milk, accentuating the stunning jade irises with their tiny yellow flecks.

Her kiss was moist and sweet, with just a trace of sea salt. It was lingering and passionate, and he felt her nails dig into the skin at the nape of his neck. The effect was electric, and he knew immediately what she wanted. How she wanted it.

"It is so good to see you, Rober'." Her voice was harsh in his ear. "It has been so long."

But it was to be a few hours more before they could be alone together. They spent the afternoon in the shade of the deck awning. Saint-Julien and Tokyo recounted the events of the past weeks and outlined, with great enthusiasm, their plan to retake *Clarion Call*.

In turn D'Arcy explained what had happened in London, and the outcome. The news of the death of Nadirpur's wife had a sobering effect, reminding them that they were not out of trouble yet. And Rick Clay would remain in danger until Major Harry persuaded the cartel that their scheme was well and truly torpedoed.

"Please, I do not understand," Tokyo said. "How is it that Major Harry does not find the ransom diamonds in your bag?"

D'Arcy grinned. "Well, if he hadn't been so personally vindictive towards me, he might have realised that a French diplomat was travelling out on the same flight. He passed through with immunity just minutes before I did. The diamonds are currently under lock and key at the French Embassy in Muscat."

As twilight fell D'Arcy took Chantal back to his hotel where they dined alone in the restaurant overlooking the floodlit pool.

They were halfway through the main course when the effusive *maître d'hôtel*, impeccably dressed in black tie, approached apologetically.

"There is a gentleman to see you, sir. He will not give a name but says you are expecting him."

D'Arcy experienced a shiver of apprehension. The air-conditioning suddenly felt like an Arctic breeze. His appetite was lost.

"Who is it?" Chantal asked as the stranger was shown towards their table.

"The only person I'm *expecting*, is someone from the *Pessarane Behesht*."

"*Mon Dieu!*" she breathed. The eyes widened in her tanned face. "*Salauds!*"

"Bastards or not, keep cool. Philippe's life depends on it."

He had been half-expecting a berobed mullah with a fanatical gleam in his eye. Not the slim, urbane man who approached wearing a well-cut suit without a tie. He did not smile, and the eyes were dull and lacklustre, reminding D'Arcy of a dead mullet on a marble slab.

"Drink?" D'Arcy offered.

"Just a mineral water," the man said, without moving his eyes from D'Arcy."

"Sit down."

The *maître d'hôtel* scurried away with the order.

"I am a representative of the Islamic Republic of Iran."

D'Arcy nodded acknowledgement.

"We are very displeased with events in London. Four of our nationals are dead."

"That was nothing to do with me. Your boys got careless."

"You are full of trickery."

D'Arcy shook his head. "My client's wife was killed when the rescue assault went in. Do you think any of us wanted that? My client instructs me that the deal is still on. We have gained nothing from it."

The man eyed D'Arcy suspiciously, then glanced up irritably as his mineral water was served with unnecessary panache and ceremony. "You have the two million's worth of diamonds with you?"

"It is available. To be paid on the release of Philippe Chaumont."

The man was hesitant. "I see."

"When can he be released?"

"Shall we say sunset tomorrow?"

D'Arcy's face remained deadpan, but he was completely stunned at the rapid agreement.

"Where?" he managed to ask without his voice cracking.

"Have the diamonds with you by tomorrow morning. You will receive a telephone call with the full arrangements. As soon as the French Embassy in Beirut confirms the release, you will hand over the diamonds. You understand?"

D'Arcy nodded. "But listen, first I want evidence that he is still alive by first thing tomorrow morning. It must be delivered to the French Embassy in Beirut before I even withdraw the diamonds from safekeeping. I want none of *your* tricks."

"It is agreed." The man stood up, bowed slightly from the waist, and left the restaurant.

As D'Arcy turned back to her he saw the tears trickling down Chantal's cheek, her tortured smile a grimace of joyous disbelief.

"Rober', I – I do not think this is 'appening –" She threw her arms around him and sobbed uncontrollably on his shoulder.

It was a full five minutes before she regained her composure and dabbed at the smudges of mascara beneath her eyes.

D'Arcy beckoned the *maître d'hôtel*. "A magnum of your finest champagne."

Chantal laughed. "But you hate champagne."

He winked. "At a time like this, there can't really be anything else."

"I love you, Rober'. And I cannot thank you enough for trying to get my Philippe released."

But that night she thanked him more than enough, making love with a passion and inventiveness that left them satiated and exhausted. It was almost as though it were their last chance before the end of the world, and they both knew it.

He awoke with a start.

His watch told him it was just two a.m. It was warm, as Chantal always kept the air-conditioning off at night, and he walked naked to the open window.

As he lit a cigar and watched the smoke waft away towards the dark outline of the *jebel* beyond the town, the nagging fear returned.

The stranger in the restaurant earlier had not asked about the ship, he realised. Suddenly it had been dropped from the equation. As though it no longer mattered. It made no sense. At the time D'Arcy had counted his blessings; it had seemed hardly wise for him to raise the issue himself.

Now he wondered.

And as he stood, deep in thought, he had no way of knowing that three hundred kilometres up the coast a rusty Iranian tramp steamer had passed through the Strait of

Hormuz. It was on its way to the southern fjords of the Musandam Peninsula, and it showed no lights.

They came in from the command ship. Four Boghammars, throttled right back.

Four men crouched in each. Head to toe in black boiler-suits and balaclavas, faces sweating with anticipation beneath the cam cream. Blue headbands for identification, with white Farsi script. *Pessarane Behesht – Allah akbar.*

Sons of Heaven – God is great.

Darvish Hamman squatted in the first boat, glancing anxiously left and right as his bosun slowed to allow the snake of vessels to spread out line abreast.

He glanced at the rubberised watch on his wrist. On-line. To the second. Superb timing.

A glimmer of a smile showed on his face. These men might have been commandeered by the bearded one to serve under the bloody flag of the *Pessarane Behesht*, but they were still his men. He allowed no religious bullshit. No weeping and wailing. Just professionals as he had taught them, as he had been taught years before by the British Special Boat Service.

Water sprayed in his face, obscuring his view of the steep *jebel* wall of rock ahead, its high sharp ridge etched in silver by the moon. Up the jagged cliff, over the ridge and down the other side. That was where the prize lay. *Clarion Call.* Moored tight against the rock shelf in the next inlet. Camouflaged to perfection by experts, its guardians becoming complacent that it would never be found.

As the sentries were no doubt struggling to keep awake, the last place they would think to look would be behind them, at the towering, near vertical drop of ancient rock.

That was the sort of tactic that worked. That was what Darvish Hamman had learned from the SBS.

H-hour minus one.

Even as they neared the bouldered water's edge, the second wave of Boghammars would be leaving the safety of the rusted Iranian tramp. Travelling slow and steady on

471

a compass bearing to arrive in the next inlet for the frontal assault in exactly sixty minutes.

"Standby!" called the bosun, cutting the throttle.

The men braced themselves, and the nose of the Boghammar scraped onto the first rock. Boats two, three and four nudged home.

The leaders were already out, kit beginning to be passed ashore, ropes, lines and weapons. Each man wore a Manhawk abseil harness of butyl nylon, complete with built-in ammunition pouches and a descent lever that could be used one-handed, leaving the other free to fire.

Hamman waited until he received the okay from each group; he nodded. The climbing leaders began to scale, following the route they had chosen from photographs taken by divers two days before. They moved swiftly and effortlessly, like human flies, often using just fingertip pressure grips on meagre handholds and hairline fractures in the rock. Steady rhythm, one limb at a time, always upright, never overstretching.

It was a joy for Hamman to watch as they went up and up without faltering until they reached the ridge. Four black snakes coiled down from the heights and the main party began to follow up the guide ropes.

Twenty minutes later the entire sixteen-man team was perched precariously on the ridge, 62-metre abseil ropes anchored, everyone ready. Anxious, waiting. Adrenalin pumping, sweating freely. Masters of the heavens, a clear view down to the camouflaged drapes that disguised *Clarion Call*.

Hamman studied the ship through an image-intensifier, noting the sentry-points in the aft superstructure, amidships and in the bows. Two men at each, and heavy machine guns, the barrels pointing out over the inlet.

H-hour minus ten.

Any moment.

He scanned the mouth of the inlet. Nothing. He scanned again. Still nothing. Then he caught sight of the first Boghammar, low and sleek in the water. It was throttled back to minimise the telltale wake. Dark blotches on a dark, choppy surface.

Two hundred feet below no one stirred. The sixty seconds dragged by. Hamman's heart began to pound.

H-hour minus five.

Surely the sentries must see. Were they blind? Asleep? Any second now someone would pick up the approaching craft. They had to.

Minus three. Minus two.

Hamman raised his hand. The four leaders stood up from the ledges and crags that had served as seats. They checked their descent-levers, checked the tidy rope coils. Safeties off, handles cocked.

Minus one.

His hand dropped. They were away. Sixteen specks on a curtain of jagged rock, drop-bouncing down towards the shelf below.

It happened. A shout from the midship observation-post.

Hamman's heart was in his mouth. But no, it wasn't the abseil team that had been seen. At last someone had spotted the stealthy approach of the Boghammars.

The stammering blast of a heavy machine gun cut through the sound of his own breathing, an arc of tracer glowing towards the advancing craft. To Hamman's left, one of the group leaders stopped on fail-safe and took a two-handed aim with his sub-machine gun. Death rained down from heaven, stunning the midships observation-post as the occupants turned and looked up in astonishment. A second burst cut them down, whipping ferociously through the bodies, tossing them aside like rag dolls.

Giving up all pretence of cover, the Boghammars now accelerated with a roar of unleashed power. Their machine guns hammered away, eating up the ammunition belts as *Clarion Call* was hosed with fire.

A searchlight on the bridge suddenly pierced the darkness. Almost instantly it was shattered by gunfire from the leading Boghammar as it sliced through the monofilament net with its specially fitted bow-saw. The bosun cut power, allowing the craft to drift into the comparative safety of the lee of the ship. On the freighter's deck, commandos leaned out in an effort to find a target, only to be subjected to a withering return of fire from the second Boghammar.

Now the compressed-air launcher was lifted to the shoulder of a crewman in the first craft. With a hiss the carbon fibre grapnel spiralled skyward and over the ship's side. A quick tug and the claws hooked round the ship's rail. Another grapnel soared up, followed by another and another as the three lead Boghammars bucked alongside, while the last stood off and blasted at the top deck with its guns.

Suddenly a flare went up, bursting its brilliant incandescence over the scene like a film set.

Hamman lost sight of the seaward side as he dropped behind *Clarion Call*'s superstructure and his feet touched the rock shelf. Immediately he snapped the harness free and began running towards the ship's side, other abseilers already closing in behind him.

A man appeared on the small afterdeck. Hamman saw the muzzle-flash and heard the crack of gunfire. The round sang off the chipped stone by his feet. He kept running, firing from the hip. The man spun back against the rail, struggled to keep his balance, and toppled over the side.

Hamman's men were appearing on the far side of the deck, hauling themselves over the rails where the grapnels held fast. Out on the foredeck a firefight was taking place, but the action was obscured by drifting blue clouds of cordite. A sound like firecrackers filled the air.

Hamman did not stop to watch. He was aboard, leading the way up the steep steps of the stairwell towards the bridge. Behind him, two of his men hived off on each deck landing and burst through the doors in turn, raking the quarters with fire.

By the time he reached the wheelhouse only Hamman's backup man was still with him. Hamman paused, chest heaving from exertion as he reloaded. He looked at the grease-smeared face beside him. Both men nodded.

Hamman waited as his partner pressed his boot against the hatch, and shoved. It yawned open on its heavy hinges. Hamman had a direct view down the short passage to the wheelhouse. He could see only one man, tall and darkly dressed. He was talking frantically into the radio transceiver held against his cheek, his back to the hatchway.

He turned and Hamman glimpsed the drooping moustache and the eyes, black and glowering. No sign of surprise, just anger and perhaps grim acceptance of the inevitable.

Hamman squeezed the trigger and the burst blew out the man's stomach, splashing vivid red intestines over the bright chromium controls. The body twitched once, twice and fell still.

It was over.

Reports came over Hamman's personal radio: all enemy positions taken, all resistance ceased. Two of the Boghammar assault group had died. An early casualty hung on his abseil rope, suspended like a dead spider, halfway down the *jebel* wall. All other injuries were minor.

They met on the deck with the surviving crew members. There were only two. A giant of a man with a wild beard and unkempt hair, and the Gambian chef.

The big man spoke: "Are you Omani soldiers?"

Hamman looked at him. "Who are you?"

"I am Dimitrios Mános. Master of this ship."

"No longer," Hamman said. "Kneel down."

"What?"

"Just kneel down," Hamman repeated, impatient.

"You cannot do this! I am retiring. This is my last voyage."

Two *Pessarane Behesht* fighters kicked the men behind their knees, so that they fell obediently to the deck, heads bowed.

Hamman looked away from them. If Sabbah wanted no survivors, there would be no survivors. He turned to his men and said: "Do your duty."

As he walked away along the foredeck he heard the muffled *crack-thud* of the pistol shots and the spontaneous cries of jubilation "*Allah akbar!*" "*Allah akbar!*"

He wondered if they were still his men. And suddenly he felt very lonely, and not very proud.

On the foredeck his men were clearing away the corpses from the observation-post.

"Chief!" We've got someone here!" called a voice.

Hamman descended the ladder to where more of his men stood by the open bulkhead hatch of the chain locker.

A tanned naked man with fair hair looked bewildered, shielding his eyes against the torch beams shining on his face.

Hamman saw the tattoo on the man's bicep, a parachuting frog and crossed paddles. He had seen that tattoo before, years ago. The unofficial insignia of the SBS.

He looked hard at the gaunt face. "Who are you?"

"Clay. Rick Clay."

Hamman shook his head in slow disbelief. "China Clay?"

"Yeah."

"Why are you locked up here?"

"What? What the hell's going on? Are you with the Jordanians?"

"Answer my question."

"I came to find this ship for the owners. Only I got caught."

Hamman frowned. "You work for Nadirpur and the man they call D'Arcy?"

"Sort of, by default."

One of the *Pessarane Behesht* drew his pistol impatiently.

Hamman unholstered his own weapon and said: "Leave this to me. Get on with clearing up."

Reluctantly his men drifted away.

Clay was curious. "Do I know you?"

Hamman pulled a bitter smile. Evidently he was unrec-

476

ognisable beneath the cam cream. He thought of the tattoo on his own arm. *To God and Yourself be True*. "You do now, China Clay. And you've got thirty seconds to jump over the side and forget you've ever seen me."

"What?"

"Before I change my mind." Hamman cocked the hammer.

Clay didn't wait to ask more questions. He launched himself at the ladder and scrambled up to the foredeck.

Cries of alarm went up from surprised members of the *Pessarane Behesht* assault group as he leapt the rail and dived for freedom beneath the waves.

"I am so sorry," Ahn said.

Nader Nadirpur stood in the hallway of his avenue Foch apartment. The familiar smell of polish filled his nostrils as he looked around the sombre panelled room. It was as though nothing had ever happened. The tropical fish tank had been replaced and restocked. The rugs had been cleaned. Some of the furniture had been restored; other items were missing, irreparable.

He said softly: "It was the will of Allah."

"And your daughter?"

"She is badly burned and in intensive care. I have been with her while they fly her back here by air ambulance. There is a surgeon at the clinic, a fellow Iranian – a very good man." There were tears in his eyes. "At least she is still alive."

"I thank God for that."

"She will never have her mother's beauty."

Ahn said quietly: "Maybe she will have the beauty of her spirit."

Nadirpur nodded stiffly, breathed deeply and forced a smile: "And you, dear Ahn, how are you? I see you have been so busy."

"I am fine now, just a little sore. And I have only done what is my duty."

Nadirpur drew the other man to him and hugged him

477

close. As the skin of their cheeks touched, each felt the other's tears.

Then Nadirpur swallowed hard and stepped back.

"Champagne?" Ahn asked, unsure.

"I have lost the taste. Some coffee perhaps; there is no decent coffee in England."

Ten minutes later they sat together by the open balcony window, Czarina the cat content on Nadirpur's lap.

For a while no words were spoken, until Ahn asked: "Your wife, Ashi. Did you love her very much?"

"Dear Ahn, she was a most wonderful, understanding creature. I loved her, but, I suppose, it was like loving someone in a glass case. Mine or hers. However much I might want to hold her, I could never really touch her. Nor her me."

Ahn's hand touched his. "You must not blame yourself. Time will heal."

"Only my daughter will heal me. At least she is not in a glass case; I am free to love her and to be loved."

"Soon things will be normal again."

Nadirpur looked weary. "No, dear Ahn, things will never be normal again. My business is on the brink of collapse – I am at the mercy of insurance companies. Even if I am lucky, most of my staff will have to go. The office in Monaco will be closed. If Allah smiles on me I may have one ship left; more likely I will have to hire transport. It will be building again from the beginning."

"You can count on me."

"If I can afford you."

"You can count on me," Ahn repeated. "I do not need money."

"You are a sweet man."

"You deserve loyalty. To give you strength to rebuild."

Nadirpur sipped thoughtfully at his coffee. "Sousan will be my strength. I will rebuild for her – and in honour of her mother."

"And this place?"

He glanced around at the heavy furnishings, the melancholic gloom. "This apartment depresses me now. Besides, I doubt I càn afford it. I will move out as soon as possible. Maybe somewhere cheaper in the 13th *arrondissement*. And I will have the new place decorated light and airily. The girlfriend of Monsieur D'Arcy is a designer, very good. I am sure she will do something suitable for a little girl like Sousan."

"And your ship. What has become of that?"

"It is in the hands of Allah. Monsieur D'Arcy is now confident he can get it returned, or persuade the hijackers to pay some compensation."

Ahn remembered the tall dark stranger who had saved his life. "He is a remarkable man."

"Remarkable."

The brassy ring of the old telephone broke into the sepulchral hush of the room. Ahn stood and went to the hallway to take the call. It was the clinic, Nadirpur knew it. Sousan had relapsed. The neatly manicured nails of his hands dug into the fabric of the chair in which he sat. His knuckles were hard white marbles.

Ahn returned. "It is the hospital. Your daughter, Sousan, she is out of intensive care."

*My name is Philippe Chaumont, and I am forgotten.*

*I had come alive in those moments when, suddenly, I was to have been released. Then, just as quickly, I was plunged back into the deepest nadir of despair it is ever possible to know.*

*No one has spoken my name for weeks. This pitiful existence is back to how it always has been. Three years. Or is it five?*

*But somehow it is even worse now. I can feel myself ageing as I sit. I am watching my own flesh decay. I can sense my brain cells going rotten, no longer able to think.*

Even my soul is beginning to fester. I can feel those maggots of despair gnawing away somewhere deep within my being.

My mistake was believing in my release. Before then the Holy Mother had protected me, cocooned me. But I betrayed God and myself by believing my captors, and I have not been forgiven for that.

I can no longer conjure pictures of Chantal in my mind. Nor my parents, nor friends. None come to visit me. All is blackness. A bottomless pit so deep I cannot see the sky. No one can see me and no one can hear me.

I am going mad.

Then I am dreaming. Or was it reality? Yesterday, the day before – or was it last year?

The guards came, lifted me to my feet, told me to bow my head in respect as the man entered.

He was plump-faced and middle-aged, with a bushy greying beard and a harsh gleam in his dark liquid eyes. He wore the robes and turban of a cleric.

And as he stomped about the room, gesticulating and shouting, I knew I recognised the face from somewhere deep within the recesses of my memory.

Sheikh Fadlallah, a fanatical local leader of Hezbollah. I remembered the photograph from the briefings at the French Embassy, light years ago. Remembered Chantal's father, Pierre Roquelaure revealing that Fadlallah was responsible for many hostages in Beirut, along with Sheikh Obeid and Sheikh Musawi.

How they used many names like Islamic Jihad, Revolutionary Commando Cells, Revolutionary Justice Organisation, Armed Struggle Cells, and the Oppressed of the World – to confuse and confound. But were in fact all from the Iranian-controlled Hezbollah and its inner caucus, the Pessarane Behesht.

I remembered then Roquelaure explaining his plan to put out the telephones, to send in his agents as repair engineers and to approach through the sewer network – a surprise *attack to rescue French and other Western hostages.*

*It was an audacious plan. But on the day I was kidnapped, that plan was still gathering dust somewhere on a shelf in the Ministère de la Défense in Paris. As no doubt other plans by other soldiers of other nations gathered dust in other ministries because politicians feared electoral defeat if they failed.*

*And before me now was the very subject of Roquelaure's plan, the intended target. A living nightmare from my past.*

*He was still pacing, still ranting, I hardly listened. "Allah is merciful! By rights you should be dead. Punished as the Great Satan should be punished! You deserve no better! But Allah is merciful."*

*I was reeling, uncomprehending. Was I hallucinating?*

*More guards. A hand-held video camera, its bright light blinding me.*

*A copy of a newspaper was thrust in my hand and I was bid hold it across my chest. On the back of it a piece of paper had been glued. There were ill-written words in French. My script.*

*"Talk! Read it!" a guard said. "If you value your freedom."*

*I stared at him. I could not believe him, would not.*

*It was just a dream.*

*Sheikh Fadlallah smiled at me, reminding me of a grey-bearded St Nicholas offering a child a gift at Christmas. "They want evidence, infidel. Evidence that you are still alive. Then you will go home."*

*What cruel tricks the tortured mind can play.*

*I began to read: "My name is Philippe Chaumont."*

## 20

D'Arcy awoke to the chant of the *muezzin* calling from the nearby mosque.

The courier from the French Embassy in Muscat arrived with the diamonds in a steel grip minutes after breakfast had been brought to his room. It was confirmed that a video tape of Philippe Chaumont had been delivered to their embassy in Beirut. Quality had been poor, but there was no doubt about the identity of the hostage.

Chantal was elated and they both laughed and joked, the simple fare of croissants and coffee suddenly becoming one of the most memorable meals of their lives.

However, indigestion followed rapidly with the unexpected arrival of Major Harry.

His face was red with fury as the door was opened. "Christ, D'Arcy, what sort of bloody game do you think you're playing?" he thundered.

"Sorry, Harry, I'm lost."

The dark brown eyes blazed with distrust. He took a deep breath. "The bloody Iranians have seized *Clarion Call*. You must have led them to it. Was this all part of your crazy deal to get that French diplomat out of Beirut?"

"For God's sake, Harry, this is the first I've heard of it."

"I don't bloody well believe you."

D'Arcy's eyes narrowed. "I'd hardly put the Iranians on to it when a friend of mine is on board. Use your brains, man."

"Then how did they find out?"

"I've no idea. Anyway, when did this happen?"

"Some time during the early hours."

"So how did you find out?"

Major Harry had calmed himself slightly. "The ship was being held by Jordanian special forces. They had a mother ship standing by off the coast. They say radio contact was lost around two thirty this morning after they had picked up local transmissions in Farsi. There was also an Iranian tramp steamer in the vicinity – probably not unconnected. Half-an-hour ago they picked up *Clarion Call* on radar leaving Musandam."

"They didn't attempt to intercept?"

"Of course not! It isn't armed and all their commandos were on *Clarion Call*. Besides, they ran off – there's no way the Jordanian Government wants to be linked with this business."

"What about one of the Sultan's fast patrol boats? Couldn't you get one to – ?" His voice trailed off. The answer might as well have been stamped across the major's forehead. "Of course, Harry, I'm forgetting that you haven't exactly been keeping His Majesty in the picture, have you?"

Major Harry ignored the remark. "We've got to do something."

Chantal looked horrified. "If he survived, I suppose Rick Clay will still be on board?"

D'Arcy grimaced. "And if the Iranians haven't killed him. Under different circumstances, Harry, I wouldn't lift a finger to help you. But if Rick is held by them – Do we know how many Iranians are on board, or what's become of the original crew?"

"No idea."

"Then if you won't do it, it had better be me who tells His Majesty what's happened. Perhaps he'll agree to send out a patrol boat."

"You can't do that!"

"And drop you in it? Sorry, Harry."

"There's no way Qaboos would agree – and if he did, it would be too late by the time he arrived at a decision."

"What's the alternative?"

Major Harry was a drowning man. He grabbed at the only straw he could find. "Yesterday you suggested a deal. Help me stop them, and it's on."

"How the hell can I stop them?"

"You had plans to seize the ship if you could, didn't you? You're a bloody mercenary and you've got a gang of thugs out here with you –"

"I'm not a mercenary, Harry, and I don't have a proper team here."

Major Harry ignored the protest. "But you did plan to seize the ship."

Chantal said: "Saint-Julien and Tokyo were working on something, using the submersible."

D'Arcy shook his head. "It was just a contingency. And to say it was foolhardy would be putting it kindly."

Major Harry sprang on the admission. "Then you *could* still do it – if I can get the ship stopped."

"And how would you do that?"

"I've friends in the Sultan's air force. If I can persuade a pilot to fly out and strafe the ship."

"You're crazy."

"It could be done, I'm sure. You could do the rest."

"No way."

"Do you want your friend back or not?"

"You might kill him in the strafing."

Major Harry smiled sourly. "And what would happen if they got him back to Iran?"

D'Arcy studied his fingernails. "I'd need backup, Harry. Maybe some guys from the Sultan's Special Forces. Someone who would take the risk for old times' sake."

Chantal frowned. "There's that strange man who dresses like an Arab."

"Hawksby?" the major guessed with distaste.

D'Arcy said: "I can try him, but he's a difficult cuss at the best of times."

Major Harry smiled enthusiastically. "Then I'll get on to my pilot friend."

As he picked up the bedside phone, Chantal turned to D'Arcy: "Rober', if you recapture the ship, what will this mean for our deal to release Philippe?"

"I don't know, I'm afraid."

"But we cannot go now, not if those people are to telephone about the exchange for the diamonds . . ."

D'Arcy saw the confusion and hurt in her eyes. "Rick may be aboard that ship. I have to do something. As friends we go back a long way."

"And Philippe?"

"I'll try and pick up the deal after we've sorted out *Clarion Call*. My bet is the Iranians will still be around to get their hands on the two million pounds worth of stones if they possibly can. I'll leave a message saying there's been a forty-eight hour delay, and to get back to me then."

It was as though a cloud had passed over the sun in her eyes.


Twenty minutes later a Jaguar attack jet in the dun and brown desert camouflage of the Sultan of Oman's Air Force took off from 8 Squadron's base on the island of Masirah.

The British pilot set a sweeping northwesterly course to take the aircraft over the deserted, baking empty quarter, far behind the populated coastal area and the busy roads.

After crossing high above the solitary Nizwa–Salalah road – the only link between the north and south of the country – he swung over the remote interior oilfields. Below him a succession of corrugated wadis scarred the scorched earth as his twin Adour engines powered him on.

After getting clearance from Dubai, he entered United Arab Emirates airspace which separated the main Omani territory from the isolated Musandam region. There he dropped height until he was skimming the crusty tops of the Ruus *jebel* range.

The Jaguar thundered through the inlet where *Clarion Call* had been hidden, dropping to just above the waves until the afterburners tore a wake through the placid surface water.

As the coastline of Oman disappeared behind him, a shape emerged from the heat haze on the horizon.

The attack jet came in fast from the stern on its first pass, catching the crew by surprise as it screamed out of nowhere, shot alongside and carried on past, gaining height until it became a distant speck.

Satisfied with the words *CLARION CALL – Monaco* stencilled on the vessel's stern, he radioed Masirah base to report on the progress of his test flight. He reported the presence of a dhow behaving suspiciously. He suspected smugglers or infiltrators attempting to land, and requested permission to fire a warning salvo as a deterrent.

As a respected and senior officer – and given the state of current tension in the Gulf area – the permission was swiftly granted after the briefest consideration.

The Jaguar completed its circle and headed back towards *Clarion Call*.

This time he came in from the side, low and fast. The pilot waited until the area immediately below the superstructure was in his sights. His thumb found the button.

The two 30 mm Aden cannons burst into action simultaneously, arcing across the water, tearing apart the steel plates of the hull to wreak havoc in the engine room.

Peeling away, the Jaguar swept behind the short afterdeck, and began to gain height.

The pilot checked and double-checked his available loiter time, then made one final high pass before taking the most direct route back to Masirah.

Far below, like a black-and-white toy plastic ship on a village pond, *Clarion Call* was stopped dead in the water. A plume of oily smoke stained the cobalt sky. He couldn't be certain, but she appeared to be listing.

Satisfied, the pilot steered his trusty warbird towards home.


Alan Hawksby glared at D'Arcy across the chart table as *Gulf Bullpup* steamed north. His usual native garb had been replaced by khaki fatigues, but the features remained

486

as dark and Arabic as any Omani. Only the fierce blue eyes gave a hint of his British bloodstock.

"It's lunacy," he pronounced adamantly. "If I'd had any idea what you were up to, I'd never have come."

D'Arcy said: "I'm afraid I could hardly discuss it on an open line. I'm only thankful you were back in Muscat."

"Well now I know, I'm afraid it's just not on. The best solution is to call His Majesty and mobilise a specialist unit. Maybe Special Forces or some navy divers."

Major Harry had been standing, arms folded, as he leaned against a bunk. He had adopted an air of detachment as though the events that were happening had nothing to do with him.

"We've been through all that. There's no time," D'Arcy said. "And no guarantee the Sultan would co-operate. We were on the spot – even now we may be too late. And Rick Clay's life has got to be the priority."

"A patrol boat could still have reached *Clarion Call* before us," Hawksby pointed out.

"And invite the *Pessarane Behesht* to use Rick Clay or the crew as hostage?"

Hawksby thoughtfully conceded that point. "I'd still like HM's clearance. It is their damn country after all."

Major Harry spoke for the first time in a long while. "I'll do the necessary with HM – afterwards. So you can consider yourself under orders if you like. Besides the ship's now in international waters, just."

Hawksby glowered. "Sometimes, Harry, I think HM places just a little too much trust in you." It was a perceptive comment, considering that D'Arcy had not told him of the major's involvement in the conspiracy.

Major Harry adopted a practised expression of affronted dignity.

D'Arcy said: "Now let's look at the plausibility of what we are trying to achieve. The ship's dead in the water. There's probably only a skeleton crew on board. When Major Harry's pilot overflew he could count no more than four. That doesn't mean there aren't more people below decks, but it certainly wasn't swarming with gunmen.

"On the other hand we've got a motley team of two Omani crew and just four competent combat swimmers: you Alan, Saint-Julien, Tokyo and myself. Tokyo will have to command the submersible. That will leave Chantal in charge of *Bullpup* with Major Harry."

Hawksby raised a sceptical eyebrow.

D'Arcy smiled. "Chantal is an experienced sailor, Alan. Handled many a floating gin palace off St Tropez."

Hawksby said: "That gives us a combat team of three – against we've no idea how many odds."

"But using Tokyo's plan, we have surprise on our side. We can take all day to gain control of the ship from the bottom up. Quietly, stealthily. One terrorist at a time. One level at a time. I don't intend they should even know we're there."

Hawksby nodded slowly. He'd left the SAS shortly after the Falklands War – long enough ago to have lost some of the old way of thinking. Now he could see how it would work.

"In the way of weapons, we have two Service revolvers from the *Bullpup*'s strongbox. Plus four Sterling 'smudges' with silencers supplied by Major Harry. Not a lot, but sufficient to do the job."

Their conversation was interrupted by Tokyo clattering down the steps to the fo'c'sle. His face was gleaming with excitement. "Hey, skipper, we have your ship on radar. No other vessel in area. So far so good, no?"

"What range?" D'Arcy asked. "Twenty-five miles?"

"Just under now, skipper. Say twenty-three?"

"And what does that submersible of yours make?"

"*Moby*, she makes three knot full whack. I think maybe I pull round and approach broadside on to *Clarion*. Say, three mile stand-off. While Major Harry here communicate, we lower *Moby* on our blind side." He looked at his watch. "In one hour half sun is setting. We position so it is in their eyes. Then, within one hour *Moby* makes the distance. Does that sound good?"

"It sounds good."

The next ninety minutes were filled with frantic activity as Tokyo prepared *Moby* for diving and checked that everyone's equipment was in good order.

As the moment approached D'Arcy was nagged by apprehension. It was a good seven years since he'd done a combat-swimmers' course with the Regiment; in all that time he had dived only once – with Chantal off the coast of Provence the previous year – hardly the best preparation for the riskiest dive of his life. Just managing to board *Clarion Call* would be a bonus.

He joined Tokyo in the wheelhouse where Chantal was at the helm, squinting into the tangerine brilliance of the sunset.

Tokyo tore a strip from the chattering radio monitor: "See, she has been making much conversation with Bandar Abbas. Very interesting. Unfortunately all in code."

"She's seen us approaching," D'Arcy guessed, "and she's probably taking advice."

"Probably an Iranian salvage ship is on the way," Tokyo said. It wasn't a very consoling thought.

Chantal began to turn the helm. *Bullpup* nudged stolidly into a broadside trough, salt spray whipping the glistening white paintwork of her port side. Then she settled in, running with the current burbling around her short stem.

Major Harry entered the wheelhouse.

"Just the man," D'Arcy said. He pointed to the radio. "It's all yours. And, for God's sake, break the habit of a lifetime and don't get up their noses. We need a good hour and a half."

The major scowled. "I'm not a fool, D'Arcy." He picked up the mike and checked the frequency. "This is *Gulf Bullpup* calling *Clarion Call*. *Gulf Bullpup* calling *Clarion Call*. We are a salvage tug come to render assistance."

For some minutes *Clarion Call* attempted to ignore the

message. At last Major Harry's persistence achieved a response. "*Thank you, but assistance is not required.*" The English was good and very polite.

"You are not making headway and you are listing," the major continued. "You are a hazard to shipping."

"*We are making our own repairs.*"

"I shall come alongside and pass the tow."

"*NO! That is not necessary.*"

"You need assistance."

"*We have already called for assistance.*"

Major Harry grinned to himself. "If you are without power, then I claim salvage rights. I shall come alongside."

The voice became angry. "*You are warned not to come alongside.*"

"Then we will stand off in case we are required." He turned to Chantal. "Take this tub into three miles, m'dear. Just so they can see us."

They ran out the sea anchor while the sunset poured liquid gold over *Bullpup*'s superstructure, blinding any attempt at close observation by those aboard the stricken freighter.

*Moby* was swung out on the starboard davits, her gleaming yellow hull then lowered into the water. The PC1202 submersible was an American-built vessel with a thirty-one foot fuselage, the for'ard observation window forming its snub nose. The circular conning tower hatch was situated to the fore and its acrylic plastic viewports were used by the pilot who sat immediately beneath it like a tank commander. Hanging on struts below the fuselage were two parallel battery pods which gave the vessel the appearance of a particularly ugly and ungainly waterbug. Its looks were not enhanced by the vertical and horizontal thruster motors that looked as though they had been added as an afterthought.

Hawksby and Saint-Julien took their places in the cramped Divers Lock Out (DLO) in the aft section of the fuselage. They sat with legs drawn up to their chests to avoid the low arch of steel above their heads. D'Arcy, with his theoretical experience of diving physiology when serving with Boat Troop, took the observer's position in the nose cone in front of the pilot.

Satisfied that everyone was ready, Tokyo stood up in the conning tower and signalled Chantal to cast them off. He then sat down, closing the hatch locks above him. Placing the small console—like a radio-model control set—on his lap, he switched on the power. As the hum began the strange-looking yellow vessel trembled with a life of its own.

Water splashed across the conning tower viewports as Tokyo reversed away. He opened the ballast tanks; the last thing he saw was Chantal leaning anxiously against *Bullpup*'s gunwale. Sea water bubbled up around the viewports and they descended into the green depths.

"One fathom," D'Arcy intoned as instructed as he watched the needle swing round the large depth gauge. "Two fathoms, three."

Slowly the inelegant beast sank deeper into the Arabian Sea, fish shoals scooting away from the strange intruder.

"Fifty fathoms," D'Arcy informed.

"That will do us," Tokyo decided with satisfaction. *Gulf Bullpup* was now some three hundred and fifty feet away on the surface. He trimmed the ballast and selected forward thrust. The pitch of the engine changed, the only sensation of movement was the plankton streaming past the observation ports.

Tokyo suddenly chuckled. "You are very quiet in the back there."

The rubber-clad divers looked at each other, and in unison realised they had hardly breathed since the hatch had been sealed.

Saint-Julien wiped the sweat from his brow. "I have never been so terrified in all my life!"

D'Arcy laughed and even Hawksby managed a grim smile.

It was the longest hour that any of them had ever spent in such claustrophobic and uncomfortable conditions. D'Arcy found it especially nerve-racking as he coped with the sonar and depth gauges as well as juggling with the air mix, a mistake in which could have had fatal consequences.

He was particularly thankful when Tokyo announced he was taking the submersible up. The pinging of the Wessmar sonar acoustic-locator, that had begun as an irritating background beat, was growing louder and increasing in tempo as the bulk of *Clarion Call* filled its scan. Now D'Arcy could see the luminous trace of the hull outlined on the cathode-ray tube.

Tokyo smoothly changed course to bring the submersible round to approach line astern beneath the freighter's keel. At twenty metres he cut back the horizontal thruster. "This is your stop, gentlemen. I wish I am going with you."

D'Arcy picked up his Sterling in its waterproof pack. He left his seat in the front to squeeze past Tokyo, who was maintaining the trim before making the submersible positively buoyant to hold her in position.

There was another tight squeeze as D'Arcy worked his way through the hatch to the DLO compartment where Hawksby and Saint-Julien helped him into his weighty scuba set.

Finally they were ready and Tokyo sealed the connecting hatch. That was the cue for D'Arcy to unclip the lower hatch which remained firmly shut under the external water pressure. The noise and steam began as Tokyo started pressurising the compartment, and the three divers were obliged to keep clearing their ears.

D'Arcy kept his feet pushed firmly against the lower hatch so that it would swing open before any telltale air bubbles could escape to the surface.

After making final equipment adjustments in the air pocket of the compartment, D'Arcy allowed himself to drop gently out of the submersible and into the fathomless deep like a man in space.

Above him the gigantic hull of *Clarion Call* sat like a dark and menacing storm cloud. He hauled himself back along his tether.

When Saint-Julien and Hawksby joined him he resealed the hatch so that Tokyo could dive deep in the shadow of the freighter's hull before setting course back to *Gulf Bullpup*.

It was Saint-Julien who carried the additional oxygen cylinder-and-Kerie pack strapped alongside his scuba tank. He manoeuvred awkwardly until he established the right balance of neutral buoyancy with his inflatable stab jacket. At last he gave the thumb-and-forefinger 'O' sign that all was okay.

All set. D'Arcy kicked his fins and moved up under the barnacle-encrusted hull, feeling his way slowly towards the stern as he tried to determine the entry point he had decided on after studying the construction plans of *Clarion Call*.

After two passes he was certain. It was a point twenty feet below the waterline, directly beneath the bridge superstructure. He nodded to Saint-Julien who struggled in close while Hawksby kept watch with harpoon gun at the ready. The Corsican unravelled a length of the Kerie thermic-lance cable from his backpack and lit the end with a Chemical Discharge Ignition primer. The lance comprised a plastic-coated cable with a hollow wire core through which oxygen was pumped from the 3000 psi cylinder via a reducer to provide a pressure of 150 psi greater than that of the surrounding water. The hissing flame gave the lance an incredible cutting performance that instantly began to bite into the heavy-gauge hull plates.

It took the full six minutes' supply of lance cable before Saint-Julien was able to prise away the rough circle of steel he had cut and work his way inside. It was the 'dead area' between bulkheads which housed wiring and other utility pipes. Its flooding would make no noticeable difference to a large ship already listing.

The three divers made their way up between the twin skins of steel until they reached the ventilation shaft. Inside, the engine room was in chaos. Smoke-charred machinery and heavy pockmarks were evidence of the fighter pilot's adept use of his Aden cannons. Not surprisingly the area had been abandoned.

D'Arcy used both feet to kick in the grille before climbing out onto an engine gantry. It took under five minutes to unharness the diving equipment, replace fins with trainers and to unpack the silenced Sterling sub-machine guns.

Three black shadows negotiated the engine plant and padded quietly up the steps of the stern stairwell which led to the superstructure. They had never worked together before, but the three men's professionalism showed. At each level they would listen at the door. Then Hawksby would throw it open and stand back to cover while D'Arcy and Saint-Julien stepped briskly in.

Nothing. There was nothing and no one in the galley or the crew's mess. A pile of dirty dishes filled the sink. Meals were left half-eaten on the tables. Flies buzzed contentedly.

Saint-Julien gestured upward. The faint sound of voices drifted down from the top of the stairwell, several levels above. A dim, flickering glow suggested that emergency lighting was in use. No other light or sound came from the intervening levels.

The three men crept silently to the next level. Again the crew's quarters were deserted. Bare-breasted girls with plastic smiles posed on the locker doors. Clothes and shoes were scattered at random.

D'Arcy knelt suddenly and ran his fingers over the cheap carpeting. The muddy red patch was virtually dry now, but he'd seen enough spilt blood in his time to be sure.

"Bastards," he breathed.

Saint-Julien picked up a spent brass cartridge – 9 mm.

The three men looked at each other. Each knew what the other was thinking. Please let this not be Rick Clay's blood. The poor sod deserved far better than this.

Tension mounted at the next level as the odds of coming face to face with the *Pessarane Behesht* increased. More caution, more adrenalin flowing, hearts thumping heavily. Doorman in, one, two covering . . . the engineers' quarters were empty.

Now the voices were more distinct, speaking in Farsi.

Static fizzed and squawked from the radio room. Next level. Officers' quarters.

D'Arcy pointed. Light under door. Quick nods all round. Hawksby braced himself against the far side of the stairwell, Sterling at port. His knee up and foot hard into the door, smashing it open. D'Arcy is first with Saint-Julien right behind.

The two startled men in black seamen's sweaters looked up from where they sat at the mess table. Hands reached for the guns lying before them.

Cries of warning died on their lips as the quiet *phut phut* from each Sterling blew them back off their benches with obscene violence for such a gentle noise. D'Arcy and Saint-Julien moved in fast, using their Gerber diving knives to finish the job quietly and efficiently.

Suddenly Hawksby was in at the door. He gesticulated madly, pointing up. Someone was coming down from the bridge. D'Arcy and Saint-Julien drew back, tight in behind the lockers. Hawksby sidestepped to the back of the door.

The newcomer had already begun talking in Farsi as he walked in: "That idiot salvage boat is still hanging around . . ."

As his eyes registered the grotesquely contorted shapes of his shipmates, Hawksby's forearm sprang like a steel vice round his throat. Saint-Julien rushed forward and, with enthusiasm verging on relish, plunged his Gerber in and under the man's ribcage, circumscribing an arc to sever the arteries to the heart.

Hawksby let the body fall. He glanced disapprovingly at the Corsican for his lack of finesse, but he said nothing.

D'Arcy led the way up the final section of the stairwell. A short passage led through to the wheelhouse where two men stood talking at the helm.

D'Arcy motioned to Hawksby, indicating that sound was coming from the radio room which led off the passage. The man nodded his understanding and eased the door ajar. The gabbling Farsi voice grew louder.

*Phut, phut*. Another perfect double-tap and the voice

fell silent as D'Arcy and Saint-Julien closed in on the wheelhouse.

The two Iranians must have sensed something, perhaps alerted by the abrupt halt of the voice from the radio room.

A round from the Corsican's gun took one as he turned. The other, facing them, had a pistol already drawn.

D'Arcy saw the drained, fearful expression on his face. The quizzical, uncomprehending look transforming to anger as realisation dawned. Then D'Arcy heard the dreaded deadfall click as his Sterling jammed.

The pistol barked as he dived for the deck. A round sang its way around the bright chromium instrument panel.

Another muffled double report from Hawksby's gun hit the Iranian squarely in the stomach, throwing him back against the helm. He slid down, legs outstretched. His head lolled forward like a sleeping peasant at siesta time.

D'Arcy stepped forward, kicked the gun aside and picked it up.

"He's gone." He stood stiffly. "We'll have to check the rest of the ship, but I reckon this could be the lot."

Saint-Julien grinned. "Congratulations, boss," he said, slipping happily into SAS jargon. "You have got your ship back."

Hawksby allowed himself a smile. "I confess I haven't enjoyed myself so much for years."

"Thanks, Alan," D'Arcy said. "I owe you one."

"Then repay me by getting out of HM's country – and staying out."

D'Arcy tugged the blue headband from the dead man's scalp and looked at the embroidered Farsi script. "What does it say?"

Hawksby looked at it. "Sons of Heaven – the Sword of Islam. God is Great."

"*Pessarane Behesht*," D'Arcy murmured. "You know, this is really the first time I've seen one of the bastards close to."

Saint-Julien grunted. "Let's hope it will be the last."

One hour later *Gulf Bullpup* had the giant freighter in tow, crewed by the two Omani seamen.

It should have been a time of great celebration. But the bottle of Japanese Scotch that Tokyo opened was to drown their sorrows on the assumption that Rick Clay had perished along with the rest of the *Clarion Call*'s crew.

Tokyo was inconsolable. "If only there was body, I would be certain. This way I never know if China is wandering *jebel* or is in belly of some fat shark!" He pounded his fist on the table.

Chantal hugged D'Arcy's arm. "I am just grateful that the rest of you did not kill yourselves. I am proud of all of you and what you have done."

D'Arcy swallowed hard on his whisky. "Let's hope our luck holds while we try to negotiate Philippe's release."

Her eyes were very wide. "You had to put Rick's life first, I know that. I did not like it, but what else could you do, *chéri*?" She shrugged. "Besides, I had grown very fond of Rick myself. So in a way, I shared your dilemma, you know?"

He kissed her forehead. "Yes, I know."

They all tried to sleep before the dawn, but D'Arcy's mind would not let his body rest.

He contented himself with lying on the cramped bunk bed with cigar and whisky to hand while Chantal curled up against his chest, sleeping like a child.

The urgent call of *Bullpup*'s klaxon eventually shook him from a shallow doze. As Chantal's eyes opened, he was already off the bunk and clambering up the steps to the deck. The brightness of the dawn light igniting the dazzling sapphire sea hurt his eyes. Behind him steel hawsers ran up to the towering black bows of the freighter as *Bullpup* strove slowly and manfully with its tow.

D'Arcy swung up to the wheelhouse as the others began appearing on deck. Tokyo, in shorts, singlet and baseball cap, was at the helm. He indicated the distant speck of a vessel off the portside.

"She is on interception course, Rob," he said grimly.

"Are you sure?"

"Plenty sure. With this load a rowboat could overtake us."

"Any idea what she is?"

Tokyo shrugged. "I've looked through the glass. I cannot see name, but she looks familiar. An old tramp steamer. Sails under the Iranian flag. Maybe she comes after *Clarion Call*. Only we get there first."

D'Arcy decided to hold a hurried council of war. There was little they could do except hand out the weapons in case events became nasty. Put down a hail of gunfire, drop the tow and run like mad for harbour.

That prospect looked decidedly unlikely. As the tramp overhauled them it became clear that what looked like a rusty tub in fact housed far more powerful diesels than usual for a ship of its type and age.

"Take the radio," Tokyo suggested. D'Arcy pushed aside the canvas screen into the radio shack and sat in the chair.

"Islamic Challenger *calling* Gulf Bullpup. Islamic Challenger *calling* Gulf Bullpup." The voice spoke excellent English, but the accent was heavy. "*Do you read me? Over.*"

"I'm receiving, *Islamic Challenger*," D'Arcy confirmed.

"*Please heave to, I am coming alongside.*"

"Negative to that. I am making for Mina Qaboos with legitimate salvage. Please keep clear, I cannot manoeuvre safely and you may place your vessel in danger."

A grunt at the other end. "*Right*, Bullpup. *I have someone to speak to you. Stay on the net.*"

"I confirm."

D'Arcy stared out of the scuttle at the Iranian tramp steaming off the portside. Rust stained her black flanks and the Gulf sun had long since faded and peeled the paint on her upper decks. And it was there that he saw the Bofors guns, finally confirming that this was no ordinary ship. An array of aerials and antennae bristled around its monkey-island.

The screen was pushed aside and Major Harry poked his head in. "What the devil do they want, D'Arcy?"

"What do you think? The same as us."

"You can tell 'em to bugger off."

D'Arcy's anger surfaced. "Don't talk through your arse, Harry. Just take a look what's on her decks." He turned away as a new voice began crackling over the net.

"*Hello, Bullpup. Do I understand you are turning down our request to heave to?*"

"You've got it, sailor."

"*I wouldn't be talking to Robert D'Arcy by any chance?*"

A shiver thrilled down D'Arcy's spine. To hear his name mentioned in the tiny radio shack on the open sea by a sinister Iranian merchantman was uncanny. He said: "I'm afraid you have an advantage over me, *Challenger*."

A low laugh without humour. "*How true that is Mr D'Arcy. After you cancelled our meeting yesterday, I thought there was a good chance you would be on your friend's boat. My name is Al-Hasan ibn-al-Sabbah – does that mean anything to you?*"

D'Arcy almost choked. It was a theatrical touch, but none the less effective for that. Unconsciously his jaw jutted in defiance. "We have another name for you, caller. But whoever you are, the answer's the same. Negative. Now please keep clear."

"*Watch our ship, Mr D'Arcy.*"

He glanced up at Major Harry who now appeared equally concerned. They looked together through the scuttle. The Bofors guns were swivelling in *Bullpup*'s direction.

Suddenly Tokyo pushed in behind Major Harry. "Hell, what goes on? This ship threatens us! What you do to make him do that?"

D'Arcy waved him to silence, as he spoke into the mike. "My finger is on the Mayday button, *Challenger*. Do you want the Armilla Patrol or the American fleet falling on you from a great height? They monitor all traffic, you realise?"

"*It will not do you or your friends any good when your ship lies at the bottom of the Gulf, and you with them.*" His voice had taken on a new, harsher tone. "*We claim what is ours. Our men will recrew* Clarion Call *and sail her to*

*Bandar Abbas. When it is unloaded, Nadirpur Shipping can come and collect.*"

An idea began to form in D'Arcy's mind. "Listen, *Challenger*, we need time. You must give us ten minutes to discuss it."

"*There is no time. Your time is up.*"

D'Arcy snapped into the mouthpiece: "I have that two million in diamonds with me – do you want to sink that as well?"

An involuntary pause told D'Arcy that he was in with a chance. "We had a deal," he reminded, "for the release of the French hostage in Beirut. That can still hold good."

"*You joke – after the tricks you have tried!*"

"Give me ten minutes," D'Arcy repeated.

Another hesitation as D'Arcy imagined the dollar signs ringing up in the terrorist's head. "*Ten minutes, Mr D'Arcy, that is all.*"

D'Arcy fell back against the seat with a profound sense of relief.

"What the hell are you doing?" Major Harry demanded.

D'Arcy ignored him. "Tokyo, can you put Saint-Julien on the helm and join the rest of us for a meeting in the fo'c'sle?"

"Sure, skipper. No problem."

Minutes later *Bullpup*'s motley crew were cramped together around the table in the fo'c'sle cabin as D'Arcy outlined developments.

At the end of his explanation there was a grim silence, broken first by Major Harry. "Are you seriously proposing we hand back the bloody ship?"

Chantal was horrified. "After all the risks you all took to get her back . . . ?"

"We've one card to play," D'Arcy said. "And that's the deal we had lined up to get Philippe Chaumont released. And the carrot of two million pounds worth of diamonds might just persuade them."

Chantal's expression transformed. "Do you think so – that would be *fantastique!*"

"It's what your father arranged the money for."

Major Harry's face was thunder. "And you intend to give a damn terrorist organisation two million pounds as well as the ship! I don't believe it! How many people would be assassinated or butchered in Beirut – or Europe for that matter – as a direct result of those funds? These bloody Shi'ites aren't too choosy about where they place their bombs."

"Are you speaking for yourself or as Britain's Secret Service representative?" D'Arcy cut in. "Now will you shut up. There might just be a way round this. The original deal was to let Chaumont go to the French Embassy in Beirut at twelve noon today. That could still give us six hours to arrange for the Sultan's air force and navy to get their act together and hit the *Challenger* as soon as we get confirmation of his release – but before we hand over the diamonds."

Chantal whistled softly. "Is that not very dangerous, Rober'?"

He agreed. "But we must try to minimise that risk. We can work on it."

"HM would never agree," Major Harry stated flatly. "He's working for a cease-fire in the Gulf War, so how would it look if he started blowing up Iranian ships?"

D'Arcy looked scathing. "Or is that your wishful thinking, Harry? Because it would mean your dirty dealings getting a public airing. My guess is you'd be on the next plane out – with no time to collect your pension."

Hawksby said: "I don't know what mischief the major's been up to, Rob. But I tell you one thing. The Sultan's a tough bastard, but he'd consider this a private matter between ourselves and the Iranians. Harry is right in that respect. At best he'd throw us all in the slammer and let the lawyers sort it out."

Chantal was finding the prospect of capitulation unacceptable. "So even if we got Philippe released, that terrorist *salaud* gets all the arms and the hostage money? And gets away with killing Rick and that poor woman in London? It all seems so wrong."

Hawksby agreed. "But without a strike by HM's forces, we are at the mercy of that Iranian ship."

Tokyo had been listening intently. For once there was no smile on his face. Then his mask of inscrutability broke. Softly he said: "I think maybe there is way –"

Everyone turned in his direction.

Their discussion was rudely interrupted by a blast on *Islamic Challenger*'s foghorn. Over twenty minutes had passed and the terrorist calling himself Sabbah was losing patience.

D'Arcy returned to the radio shack and recalled the Iranian tramp. "Listen, we've talked it over and you can take the ship – and the money. But we want Philippe Chaumont released in Beirut at midday. On receiving confirmation from the French Embassy there, you can collect the cargo and the diamonds."

"*How do I know you have the diamonds as you claim?*" Sabbah demanded. "*I will send two of my men to check it.*"

"Only two men. Unarmed. That is agreed. When they are satisfied we will cut the tow. At twelve noon – when Chaumont's release is confirmed – you collect the diamonds and take over *Clarion Call.*"

"*Do you think I'm an idiot, Mr D'Arcy? That ship was wired with explosives by the Jordanian hijackers. My men left them in place.*"

"That is *my* insurance that you keep your word."

"*Then you go on board yourself, with the diamonds. You can sit on your own bomb.*"

Tokyo was listening to the exchange. He tapped the Englishman's shoulder and nodded. For a long moment D'Arcy stared at the intense pale bronze face, the skin smooth and oiled with sweat.

In a short space of time he had come to trust and respect the Japanese diver as no doubt China Clay had learned to do. There was no time now to discuss Tokyo's idea; no time but to make an instant decision.

He had to take that chance. Again Tokyo nodded, urging acceptance of the deal.

D'Arcy's mouth was dry as he spoke into the mike. "Then we agree."

The voice at the other end sounded self-satisfied; he had everything he wanted. "*You are a very lucky man, Mr D'Arcy.*"

From his position in the wheelhouse of the *Islamic Challenger*, the bearded one lowered his binoculars.

He beckoned the man called Darvish Hamman to his side.

"I want you to go across to the big ship. Take the expert from Teheran with you; let him inspect the diamonds. Ensure they are not fakes, then personally have the case they are in hauled up on the mast where we can all see it."

"Yes, sir."

"And watch out for trickery. As you know the ship is wired with explosives and I do not trust this man."

Hamman hid his surprise. "You will release their hostage as they wish?"

The bearded one smiled. "There will be a price to pay, my trusted friend. My brother wants D'Arcy dead and I agree with him. But he is as slippery as a snake. You, Hamman, will be the instrument, the sword of Islam that will sever the snake's head."

"As you wish."

D'Arcy took the inflatable back to *Clarion Call* with Saint-Julien. Making it fast to the lowered companionway, they waited for the launch that crossed the intervening stretch of water from the tramp. The bosun steered the craft in neatly and two passengers jumped the small gap onto the mooring platform.

One was a shy-looking man in his thirties, dressed in an inappropriate suit and open-necked shirt; he appeared distinctly uncomfortable in his maritime surroundings. The other was a stockily built middle-aged man with grizzled hair and the hard, solid features of a veteran soldier. The eyes were dark, alert and cynical.

"There is no need for those," he said, indicating the sub-machine guns D'Arcy and Saint-Julien carried. "We came unarmed as requested."

Saint-Julien lowered his Sterling. "We will make sure."

"Of course."

The newcomer raised his hands while the Corsican carefully frisked him. "Clean, Rober'."

"You go first," D'Arcy said. The steel briefcase was handcuffed to his wrist.

Darvish Hamman and the diamond expert trudged up the companionway to the deck, then took the stairwell to the bridge.

D'Arcy held out a small black plastic box. "This is the control device. You can tell your master that if he makes one false move, the ship will be scuttled. You can see for yourself that the explosives are still in place."

"I understand. Let me see the diamonds."

Saint-Julien stood back, his Sterling at the ready, while D'Arcy placed the case on the chart table and opened the combination lock. He lifted the lid. Four neat polythene packs of precious stones were fitted in recesses. The diamond expert opened each one in turn and examined the contents with an eyeglass. After thirty minutes he appeared satisfied.

Hamman said: "I ask you to raise the case to a mast where everyone can see it."

D'Arcy was impressed; it was a smart move and he could hardly refuse to co-operate. He summoned the Omani helmsman, gave him the case and they all waited while he ran it up a flag mast beside the monkey-island.

"I will order *Bullpup* to drop the tow," D'Arcy said, "and to stand clear. We will then wait for the deadline."

Hamman said: "Afterwards you must remain aboard until we have dismantled the explosives." His eyes were hard and steady.

D'Arcy had anticipated that, but it was no less an uncomfortable thought. At that point he would be at his most vulnerable.

The Iranians were then escorted back down to the waiting launch.

As its engine coughed into life and the craft drew away, D'Arcy said: "You can take the Omanis back to *Bullpup* in the inflatable now, and tell the others to stand off, out of range of those Bofors."

Saint-Julien glanced across the glittering blue sea; the heat haze was gathering strength. "I have not seen Tokyo since our meeting . . ."

D'Arcy said: "Don't even think about it."

It was going to be a long wait for high noon.


D'Arcy shared the last can of beer with Tokyo as they sat on the open bridge wing, alone on *Clarion Call*.

In the baking oven heat sweat dripped from their foreheads and soaked their shirts. It was even worse in the wheelhouse since, without a generator, there was no air-conditioning.

All round them the white hot sun refracted blindingly off the sea, appearing to set it on fire with a trillion pinpoints of specular light. Hardly a breath stirred the burning air. The metal of the bridge wing parapet was impossible to touch.

"It ten past midday," Tokyo observed, sitting in what little shade was offered by the lee of the wheelhouse. He began checking over his Sterling sub-machine gun for the umpteenth time.

D'Arcy looked down at the short-wave radio transceiver, willing it to start into life with news from Beirut. It remained obstinately silent.

Beirut. Torn land of rival fiefdoms. Warlords of revolution. Total anarchy. Unpredictable and treacherous. A beautiful land that had once been the Riviera of Arabia. Now reduced to rubble and squalor. The nearest place to hell on earth. He must have been crazy to have thought he could arrange a deal with the madmen who thrived there along with the rats and cockroaches. That he even stood an outside chance of pulling off what numerous governments had failed to achieve.

Philippe Chaumont. A man he did not even know. Did not even want to know. A man incarcerated ever since he had first known Chantal, and who had haunted him like a ghost.

And Sabbah. Man or legend. An evil terrorist whose real name no one knew. Yet wielding an obscene power, selling his skill to assassinate and maim to any state or organisation willing to pay. A network of evil that could touch even the most innocent and unsuspecting. Nader Nadirpur in Paris, his wife and child in London, and Chaumont in Lebanon. Even he himself back in Northern Ireland.

How many healthy young limbs had been blown apart by the Semtex his organisation had delivered through Libya? How many would never walk again? Never see again?

How many mothers and fathers would weep at unexpected moments, knowing that they had outlived their own sons and daughters? How many women's wombs would ache for the children they would never have, because their husbands had been cruelly taken from them?

How many more would have to die under the black flag of revolutionary Iran before the madness ended?

Suddenly he felt a pang of sympathy for Major Harry and his fellow conspirators. For Roy Bliss at Century House and his cousins in the CIA. In their own way, doing their treacherous best to destroy a régime that had managed to hold the free world to ransom.

He stood up, Sterling hanging loosely in his grip. *Islamic Challenger* still bucked off the portside. *Bullpup* was a hazy white mirage two miles off the bow.

The transceiver squawked. Both men started in surprise.

D'Arcy reached out. It was Chantal. Her voice was almost hysterical with joy. "He's out! He's out! *Mon Dieu*! My Philippe is out. We just have confirmation from Beirut! He is safe! He is alive! Oh, Rober', you are wonderful!"

He could visualise the tears of happiness running down her cheeks.

He could hardly believe the words he was hearing. "That's terrific news, kitten." He felt the thick knot of emotion catching in his own throat. "I'm very happy for you."

Tokyo was grinning very widely.

D'Arcy said: "Ask Saint-Julien to signal *Islamic Challenger* to come alongside for the takeover. Then get the hell out of here. There is nothing an unarmed ship can do. Tokyo and I will make for the nearest fishing village."

The jubilation had drained from her voice as she spoke. "You will take care, Rober'? I do not want Philippe back only to lose you."

"We'll be okay," he said. He switched off the set deep in thought. However well-intentioned, her words had hurt. Both he and Philippe Chaumont in the same sentence. The same breath. As though there was nothing to choose between the two of them.

He stared out at the Iranian tramp as she began manoeuvring closer to *Clarion Call*'s towering side.

So that was it, he thought grimly. For Chantal there was no choice. And the ghost had returned from the dead.

"Here they come, boss," Tokyo warned.

Below them the decks of the tramp were filled with dark-clad seamen, armed, some with *Pessarane Behesht* headbands of blue silk. The first men were already clambering up the ladder, ready to take the lines about to be cast across.

D'Arcy thumbed the safety off his Sterling. Somehow he doubted that Sabbah would stick to their agreement. That Hamman would come alone and unarmed to the bridge. If that pledge was broken he and Tokyo had decided that they would press the button and blow the charges. They would take their chances as the water rushed into the big ship.

Now they backed away in the direction of the outer ladder which ran down to the lower deck. D'Arcy's mouth was parched. Footsteps clattered up the stairwell behind the bridge. Excitable voices came from inside. Someone was on the bridge, passing down the short corridor by the radio room.

D'Arcy's finger tightened round the trigger. His heart was thudding heavily. The sun throbbed down on his head. Sweat from his hair was trickling onto his face, stinging his eyes.

An outline figure was in the wheelhouse.

Alone.

Darvish Hamman stepped out into the searing daylight of the bridge wing.

D'Arcy said: "You have kept your word?"

Hamman glanced up at the case swinging on the mast beside the monkey-island. It had been in full view ever since he had supervised its raising. "And so have you, Englishman. Unless you are a magician."

D'Arcy said: "The control device is here." The black plastic box with its switch and coiling trail of flex was by his feet. He slid it carefully across with his foot.

Hamman reached down and disconnected the lead. He stood up again. "I am to be the instrument of your destruction. No – don't say anything. I have grenades – but I am not going to use them. Go now, fast. You do not have long. Nor do your friends in the *Bullpup*. You have been told."

D'Arcy stared blankly. Not at the treachery, but at the Iranian's warning.

Hamman smiled grimly. "Just go, Englishman, while you are able. You have only a few minutes before Sabbah realises that something has gone wrong."

"Tokyo, get going!" D'Arcy snapped.

He kept his Sterling level as his companion started down the outside ladder. His eyes questioned the strange Iranian, but he had no time to wait for answers.

Besides, he had no real trust in words.

D'Arcy stepped back, one hand gripping the ladder rail, the other the sub-machine gun. Then he was lost from view behind the bridge parapet. It was a long way down to the main deck on the blind side to *Islamic Challenger*. It took a full sixty seconds, but it felt like as many minutes.

Tokyo hit the deck, with D'Arcy close on his heels. He began running alongside the ship's rail where the companionway dropped down to the mooring platform. On the far side of the hold covers black-clad *Pessarane Behesht* were milling, talking, awaiting their orders.

As Tokyo reached the head of the companionway, a cry of alarm was raised. By the time D'Arcy arrived the first shot had been fired. It was a snatched aim, the bullet whining angrily as it struck a metal stanchion next to him. He leapt for the companionway, dropping down the steps several at a time until he was out of sight.

Already Tokyo was astride the rear control pillion of the Jet Raider, revving its inboard engine impatiently as salt spray burst over the fuselage.

"LET'S GO!" D'Arcy yelled as he jumped from the mooring platform onto the front seat. Gripping with his knees, he used his free hands to aim the Sterling back up at the companionway. Tokyo opened the throttle wide.

The first shots were unleashed from *Clarion Call*'s deck and telltale splashes peppered around the tiny craft as it creamed away.

D'Arcy returned a sweeping arc of fire at the heads appearing by the ship's rail. They ducked hurriedly.

"HOLD ON, BOSS!" Tokyo shouted, leaning forward.

As D'Arcy lowered the Sterling and grabbed the general purpose machine gun, Tokyo threw the skimmer into a series of tight turns to throw the enemy's aim, keeling over like a racing cyclist. First one edge of the ski-foot bit deep into the water, and then the other.

Any shots were inaudible now above the scream of the Selva engine as it rendered its full thirty-five horsepower. Glancing back at the receding bulk of the freighter, D'Arcy still saw the blink of muzzle flashes. But they were well out of range as Tokyo ceased the exhilarating corkscrew course. On the Iranian tramp, dwarfed beside *Clarion Call*, figures raced towards the Bofors.

Then, thankfully, the sea haze and the distance conspired to draw a gossamer silver shroud across the seascape.

D'Arcy breathed a sigh of relief. Over the fore-mounted GPMG he searched for signs of *Bullpup* emerging from the mist.

A finger prodded him rudely in the back. Again he turned his head. This time Tokyo was jabbing a finger excitedly towards their portside.

D'Arcy's heart sank. Instantly he recognised the grey outlines, low and fast in the water. The dreaded Boghammars of the Iranian Revolutionary Guards.

At forty knots they were more than a match for the tiny Jet Raider which was wave-skimming at twenty-eight. But the *Bullpup* would be entirely at the Boghammars' mercy within minutes.

Now D'Arcy understood the strange Iranian's warning, even if he did not know why it was given. He and Tokyo were to have been killed with a hand grenade as they attempted to leave *Clarion Call*. And Sabbah had launched the Boghammars to intercept *Bullpup* and send her to the bottom. And with her any evidence of the events that had taken place.

"DECOY!" D'Arcy screamed above the engine noise and sound of breaking wavecrests. "CAN WE DECOY?!"

Tokyo nodded fiercely, his face a grim mask of concentration. He tipped the handlebar controls hard over, circling tightly to bring them on a head-on collision course with the fast approaching Boghammars. "USE MACHINE GUN!" he shouted back.

The GPMG was loaded with just one belt of ammunition for demonstration purposes. D'Arcy would have to make every precious round count.

Ahead the Boghammars were fast growing in size. He counted one, two – no, three of the bastards, coming in line abreast.

He leaned forward, checked the machine gun feed, released the safety and gripped the weapon like the gunner of a World War One biplane.

Tokyo veered a course between two of the oncoming Boghammars. D'Arcy held his breath and his fire, squinted

510

through the veil of spray. The Iranians opened up, the harsh stammer of their guns unmistakable but muted by noise and distance. Then D'Arcy realised where the skimmer had the edge. The Swedish-built speedboats might be fast and agile, but even their agility did not compare with the darting manoeuvres of the Jet Raider.

As the chattering half-inch rounds arced above D'Arcy's head, he saw their own advantage – presenting a small, elusive target that was quick and very close to the surface. For once the Boghammars were facing the same disadvantage as their usual victims. They could not dip the tripod-mounted guns low enough to get an accurate aim as the Jet Raider came in close.

He saw the flat bows through the spume, slamming contemptuously into each wave. Saw the white faces, blurred with speed as the Jet Raider careered alongside. Squeezed the trigger for one long, raking burst down its full length – and it was gone as both craft passed each other at a combined speed of almost seventy miles an hour.

Then Tokyo was slewing round, hard behind the stern of the three Boghammars. D'Arcy's target had peeled away, smoke billowing from its engine compartment. Limp bodies were being tended by other crew members as the vessel slowed to a halt.

"READY?" Tokyo shouted.

D'Arcy gave the thumbs up, and was jolted back as the skimmer surged forward again.

The second Boghammar was closing on its stricken brother to give assistance. The third had slowed and now circled warily some distance off.

A torrent of heavy machine gun fire now broke from all three craft as Tokyo bucked and weaved his skimmer, using the trough between each shrugging wave to hide his approach on the assisting Boghammar.

A second sweep back the other way, this time from stern to bow. The GPMG vibrated in D'Arcy's hands, spitting out its lethal load, unmercifully tearing into steel and human flesh with equal contempt. And then they were clear. Tokyo zig-zagged again to throw the enemy's aim, now heading flat out in the direction of the coast.

D'Arcy signalled to Tokyo that he was out of ammunition.

The standby Boghammar revved up its engine, power growling, moving off with a boiling wake bursting from its stern. Now it had the advantage, gobbling up the distance with ease. A thoroughbred gaining on a lively colt.

The ragged shoreline was maddeningly distant, a mere faded chocolate smudge on the horizon.

Christ, D'Arcy thought, we aren't going to make it. There's no way! He turned back to Tokyo. The Japanese diver was concentrating hard. He shook his head at D'Arcy, irritated at the distraction.

Behind, the Boghammar was shortening the lead inexorably. Its machine guns began taking advantage at optimum distance, slowing noticeably to keep the skimmer in range. Some of the rounds were coming unnervingly close.

D'Arcy looked again towards the coast. He frowned. He noticed the disturbance on the water's surface as the waves broke and bubbled.

"CHRIST! TOKYO! WATCH IT!"

Tokyo shook his head furiously. "HOLD ON, SKIPPER!"

He took the submerged reef at a full twenty-eight knots, the Jet Raider's ski-shoe creaming a mere four inches off the surface.

D'Arcy braced himself, heard the sudden crack and scrape, felt a minor jolt, then the skimmer was clear of the coral, arcing in a wide loop on the open blue waters beyond.

The Boghammar bosun saw what was happening, but at thirty knots there was little evasive action he could take. He spun the helm to port. The speedboat's gunwale dipped to the water as it curled around – only to plough straight onto another lump of hidden coral.

At that speed what followed was inevitable. The craft

512

launched itself up the side of the underwater mound. Momentarily it cleared the water, a spectacular leaping fish. Then, almost in slow motion, it began to somersault. Bodies flew out like rag dolls as sunlight glittered on the airborne spray. Twisting like a wounded beast, it spiralled down into the waiting coral fangs.

As the petrol tanks ignited, the wreck became a second sun. With a sudden pulse of blinding light it evaporated in an exploding ball of flame. Fragments of boat and crew were tossed on the eddying wind.

Burning debris hissed in a rain of fire as it hit the water. There was no sign of survivors.

Tokyo did not smile. Solemnly he turned the Jet Raider around, throttled back, and set course for *Bullpup*.

Willing hands helped them back aboard the bucking salvage tug and the Jet Raider was hoisted on the davits.

D'Arcy had never seen Chantal so happy. She looked radiant as she threw her arms around his neck and planted salty kisses on his cheek. But, as he went to hold her, she had already slipped away, showering a bemused Tokyo in the same way.

"You are all so wonderful!" Next it was Saint-Julien's turn.

Only Major Harry escaped the flamboyant exhibition of sheer joy. He homed in on D'Arcy. "It would be churlish not to congratulate you, I suppose. I didn't think you'd ever get off that ship alive, and when I saw those blessed Boghammars I was sure our number was up too."

"It was down to Tokyo. He had faith in that contraption he and Rick Clay built – we'd never have managed it in a conventional boat. Certainly not when those Boghammars turned up."

"Well, the French are going to be happy about the way things turned out," Major Harry said pointedly.

"But not your friends in the cartel?"

"Nor the people at Century House. They won't find it easy to forgive what you've done."

513

A faint smile crossed D'Arcy's lips. He didn't answer, but left Major Harry waiting for his reply while, cupping his hands to shield against the sea breeze, he lit a small cigar. Then he leaned with his forearms against the rail and stared out across the glimmering cerulean waters of the strait.

Major Harry suddenly frowned. He glanced quickly at the landfall, then astern at *Bullpup*'s turning wake. The Omani flag snapped violently with the change of direction. "Christ, what's Tokyo playing at? Is he taking us back –?" His voice trailed away in disbelief.

The slipstream whipped at the black comma of hair on D'Arcy's forehead as he spoke. "We're not going too close."

"This is madness. They've still got those bloody Bofors guns . . ."

In the glare of the distance two indistinct dark shapes were emerging, so closely made fast together that they appeared to be one ship.

*Bullpup*'s foghorn blasted three deep notes of defiance.

Chantal appeared at D'Arcy's side. "What is happening, Rober'? Why are we going back?"

He put a comforting arm around her waist. "I want witnesses to this. I want us all to see it."

"I do not understand – ?"

He glanced at his watch. "This is for you, and Philippe. Call it a wedding present."

"What?"

He smiled at her then, knowing that he was enjoying the closeness of her for the last time, knowing that he would never stand near enough again to feel the soft flesh of her body beneath his fingers. Nor be close enough to see the gold flecks in her pale green eyes.

And as he saw the shadow pass over them he knew he had been right. He had fought against a ghost, and the ghost had won. It was all there in the hurt, confused expression on her face.

Major Harry was becoming impatient. "Are you going to tell me, D'Arcy – ?"

514

"I'll tell you, Harry. When all this started, Roy Bliss told me Century House wanted to know everything I could learn about Sabbah. They wanted to establish his whereabouts. In short, they wanted him destroyed."

"Of course, but we never knew where he was . . ."

"As Tokyo pointed out to me. We know now. He was doing it for Rick." He inhaled heavily on the cigar. "Me. I'm just settling an old score. I left the Regiment for something I hadn't done. Well, this time there are no rules. I'm doing it for me. Tell Roy Bliss that when you see him."

"What in God's name have you done?"

D'Arcy glanced again at his watch, then across the intervening stretch of water. *Bullpup*'s engine stopped abruptly and the deck vibration ceased. Like a yacht becalmed they felt the silence close in, the only noise the creak of timber and the gurgle of water breaking around the bow. A light breeze murmured in the shrouds.

D'Arcy said in a quiet voice: "While we were waiting for the noon deadline, Tokyo took the demonstration limpet-mine from the Jet Raider. It was inert, of course, but he still had the original fuse . . . he's a very good diver. It took him just an hour to do the job – "

His words were cut off by the sudden bursting flux of brilliant light around the dark shape of *Islamic Challenger*. The vessel appeared to be lifted physically in the water. A split second later the seismic boom followed, causing the very ocean to tremble with the force of displaced water.

"Jesus!" Major Harry's mouth fell open.

A second explosion followed, then another and another as the scuttling-charges around *Clarion Call* began to detonate in sympathy.

Now everyone was at *Bullpup*'s side as the cacophony grew. The mighty orchestral percussion reached a deafening crescendo, scarcely muted by the distance or the breeze. Flames lapped from the *Islamic Challenger* and an oily twist of thickening smoke belched skyward, blotting out the sun.

And as the shadow was cast over *Bullpup*'s decks, the

raging fires on board *Clarion Call*'s listing hulk reached the cargo holds. It was a volcanic eruption, spewing flame and debris with an almighty roar that sucked the surrounding air into the vacuum of its own creation.

"*Mon Dieu!*" Chantal gasped in awe and shock, ducking instinctively as a burning hail of debris cascaded down and the pyrotechnic display rose in pitch and momentum. A rolling barrage of thunder drowned out all other sounds, each of the following explosions louder than the last.

Then, as suddenly as it had begun, it was all over.

Behind the sheets of flame burning on the oil-slicked waters, no one saw the Iranian tramp go down. But no one could miss the towering leviathan of *Clarion Call* as she half-sank and half-toppled like a falling wall of steel onto the place where the adjacent ship had been.

A gigantic whale, she suddenly plunged and, with escaping air hissing from her hull and geysers of sea water spurting all around, *Clarion Call* gave herself up to the deep.

*My name is Philippe Chaumont.*

*And now my one name has become two. I am enjoined by Madame Chantal Chaumont.*

*It has a certain ring to it, I think. And it has made me the happiest man in all of France.*

*The wedding was in the early autumn. It was truly beautiful and like something frozen in my mind from my wild imaginings in my prison in Beirut.*

*Of course the blessing was at the family chapel on the Roquelaure château estate with many a famous face amongst the guests. For me it was an opportunity to thank the Virgin Mary for saving my sanity during my purgatory on earth. No man has ever cried so much at his own wedding. My new in-laws must have thought me quite mad.*

However, it was at the wedding breakfast that I finally accepted my dreams had come true. To see my bride in purest white silk against a background of red and gold autumn leaves, illuminated by a cool October sun. Her father Générale de Brigade Pierre Roquelaure was clearly every bit as proud of his daughter as was I.

And the bridesmaids, including little Sousan Nadirpur. What a sweet child she is. One cheek is hideously scarred, and yet she has the loveliest smile. I noticed sometimes, when she thinks no one watches, the look in her eyes of someone way beyond her years. Poor dear child. But the delight in those same eyes when Chantal tossed her bouquet and she caught it . . .

Her father is very proud of her, too, you can see that. What a quiet, sad man he is. But they tell me that his fortunes are slowly being restored. Between you and me I think there is great persuasion put by the secret services of France and Britain on the insurance companies to make a fair settlement for the loss of Clarion Call.

It is said he hopes to commission the building of a new ship which he will call the Spirit of Ashi.

'China' Clay was at the wedding also, with his stout-hearted little friend Tokyo. Chantal has told me all about their exploits and the shock they received, after the sinking of Clarion Call, when China turned up at Muscat in the company of an engineer called Keith Evans, who had found him exhausted on the shore having swum throughout the night after jumping ship. They all thought the man was a ghost.

I know that feeling. This seems to be the year of ghosts returning from the dead.

There is a rumour now that 'China' and Tokyo have been diving to retrieve two million pounds worth of diamonds. But I don't know.

And Shaykh Zufar. Chantal insisted he be invited from Oman, but he protested he was much too busy. He had been promoted to head a very important ministry by the

517

Sultan after he revealed the misconduct of the trusted Major Harry.

Of him little has been heard since. He was banished in disgrace. One story said he was doing business in Singapore. Another said the Cayman Islands.

But the man to whom I owed all this was not there. The day before the wedding he sent a telegram explaining that he would be unable to attend. Apparently an industrialist had been kidnapped in some lawless South American state and held to ransom. Robert D'Arcy was on the next flight.

My heart goes out to him and the poor victim. And I wonder if this cruel lunacy will ever come to an end.

I wonder, too, in private moments if Chantal's heart isn't with him sometimes. She lingered a long time over the spray of red roses he sent to the wedding.

And yesterday I awoke to find her sitting by the window of our new apartment in Paris, staring out into space. There was a photograph of him – the only one she says she has ever seen – beside her. It is very battered and must have been taken a long time ago. She was very subdued and I could tell that she had been crying.

Once she told me that D'Arcy felt that he was haunted by my ghost at the time when no one knew for sure if I was still alive or dead in Beirut.

I wonder now if it is not my turn to be the haunted one.

# EPILOGUE

Dusk was falling over the palm-grove beside the Palestinian village of mud-brick huts where the three brothers had been born.

Cooking smells lingered in the still warm air; a goat's bell clanked discordantly on the rocky hillside. It was the only sound apart from the grate and rasp of the spade as it shovelled the last of the stony soil on the unmarked grave.

At last the bearded one was laid to rest.

It had taken two months to arrange for his remains to be smuggled from Iran into Israeli-occupied Palestine. Back to the barren soil for which he had always fought.

Yet even as the last pat of the spade levelled the ground, the twin brothers knew that they were living out a lie. The remains of the bearded one were just that. Remains. All that was left from the terrible fireball that had consumed the *Islamic Challenger* and the big freighter. The arm and the leg did not belong to the same body. Charred as they were, clearly neither had ever been part of the bearded one. His wrist had never borne the tattooed Islamic script: *To God and Yourself be True*.

Nevertheless they had claimed these fragments of humanity as those of their older brother who had dreamed the dream of Sabbah and recreated it in his own image. In a way the deception seemed fitting.

Sabbah was dead, yet Sabbah lived. Because Sabbah had never existed; not, at least, in the way that his enemies believed. Sabbah had always been a triumvirate of the

519

bearded one and his younger twin brothers.

That had been the secret of their success, the secret of the legend that had awed and perplexed antiterrorist experts throughout the world, from Arab and Israeli enemies to those of France, Britain and the Great Satan of America. It was why rumours of his identity were always contradictory and never confirmed. Why he was reliably reported as being in two different countries a continent apart on the same day.

Sabbah was never one man, but three. A three-headed serpent.

The twin brothers turned now in the failing light, and walked in silence back through the palm-grove towards the battered estate car parked at the village edge.

An old man approached, bent and white-bearded, supported by a wooden crook. The goatherd's eyes were as dim as the surrounding twilight.

"Do I know you boys?"

"We lived here once. Our father was a cobbler here in the village."

His hearing was as good as his eyesight was poor. "Yes, I remember we had a cobbler once. You must be the two youngest of the three brothers . . . Then you left." He smiled a toothless smile. "Tell me, has fortune smiled upon you?"

"We have made our living as best we can."

"And your brother?"

"He is returned. He is at peace."

The goatherd didn't understand, but it was impolite to say so. "Is there anything I can do for you?"

One brother said thoughtfully: "One thing, old man. Tomorrow, when we have gone, tell the village just two words. Sabbah lives."

As the car bumped its way into the dimming landscape the old man turned the words over in his mind. He must not forget.

Sabbah lives, Sabbah lives, Sabbah lives . . .

**TERENCE STRONG**

STALKING HORSE

He was a man on the edge. Six years in deep cover to penetrate the IRA. Now he was starting to crack and wanted out.

London and Washington had other ideas. Iraq had invaded Kuwait and Saddam Hussein threatened a terror strike to win him the Gulf War before it began.

They needed a stalking horse to get close to the enemy – and he was their man. Whether he liked it or not.

So he was plunged into the nightmare mission with the SAS and the American Delta Force.

A mission that put his wife, his future and his very life on the line.

'Frighteningly plausible – a powerful plot and sharply-drawn characters result in an action-packed page-turner which defies the reader to put it down'
*Yorkshire Evening Post*

**HODDER AND STOUGHTON PAPERBACKS**

**TERENCE STRONG**

**THIS ANGRY LAND**

For fourteen years he has kept the demons at bay.

The former SAS sergeant from Ulster has renounced the gun. With help from the bottle and a village girl, he devotes his life to others in war-torn Mozambique.

But as the terror spreads, he must fight again. Plunged into the savage cauldron of Africa's killing fields, he confronts two enemies . . .

'When the bullets begin to fly, the non-stop action takes off with a vengeance.'

*Western Morning News*

'Superbly written, this is an enthralling and poignant read.'

*Oracle*

**HODDER AND STOUGHTON PAPERBACKS**

**TERENCE STRONG**

THAT LAST MOUNTAIN

He was a sergeant-major in the SAS. His task was to snatch a defecting Russian 'Star Wars' scientist from Stockholm.

She was the she-wolf. Leader of the crack Soviet Spetsnaz pack. Her job was to get the scientist back. Dead or alive.

Their paths had crossed before. Now the score had to be settled.

In between was the scientist, ruthlessly manipulated by both sides. Torn between loyalty to his country and the love of a woman.

A story of sweeping passion and betrayal. Of endurance and breathtaking action in the Scandinavian mountains – the most inhospitable place on God's earth.

'Breathless entertainment'

*The Guardian*

HODDER AND STOUGHTON PAPERBACKS

**TERENCE STRONG**

## CONFLICT OF LIONS

The pulsating inside account of an SAS peace mission that finds itself pitted against the insidious forces of Colonel Gadaffi.

DATELINE: WEST AFRICA '82

A vicious assassination attempt is made on the President of a fragile African democracy by Libyan terrorists. The call for an advisory training team goes out to 22 Special Air Service Regiment:

WHATEVER THE COST – KEEP THE PEACE

But is it already too late? Beneath the sleepy surface of the 'friendliest nation in Africa' the dark forces of a secret enemy advance inexorably. Hampered by diplomatic ineptitude the crack SAS team struggle against the odds. Emotions and passions run high as they battle to stop the sweep of revolutionary fervour and bloodshed . . .

**HODDER AND STOUGHTON PAPERBACKS**